Amanda Stevens is an award-winning author of over fifty novels, including the modern gothic series The Graveyard Queen. Her books have been described as eerie and atmospheric and 'a new take on the classic ghost story.' Born and raised in the rural South, she now resides in Houston, Texas, where she enjoys binge-watching, bike riding and the occasional margarita.

Addison Fox is a lifelong romance reader, addicted to happily-ever-afters. After discovering she found as much joy writing about romance as she did reading it, she's never looked back. Addison lives in New York with an apartment full of books, a laptop that's rarely out of sight and a wily beagle who keeps her running. You can find her at her home on the web at addisonfox.com or on Facebook at Facebook.com/addisonfoxauthor and Twitter @addisonfox

DIGGING DEEPER

AMANDA STEVENS

DANGER IN THE DEPTHS

ADDISON FOX

MILLS & BOON

First Published in Great Britain 2023
by Mills & Boon, an imprint of HarperCollins*Publishers* Ltd
1 London Bridge Street, London, SE1 9GF

www.harpercollins.co.uk

HarperCollins*Publishers*
Macken House, 39/40 Mayor Street Upper,
Dublin 1, D01 C9W8, Ireland

Digging Deeper © 2023 Marilyn Medlock Amann
Danger in the Depths © 2023 Frances Karkosak

ISBN: 978-0-263-30734-4

0723

MIX
Paper | Supporting
responsible forestry
FSC™ C007454

DIGGING DEEPER

AMANDA STEVENS

Chapter One

The wooden box was a tight fit, a perfect fit. If she stretched her toes and tipped back her head, she could just touch both ends. Her shoulders brushed against the sides, and she could only lift her hands a few inches above her chest. It was dark inside that box. Not the blackness of night, but a complete absence of light.

Thora Graham turned her head to the side and tried not to vomit. Slowly, she counted to ten as she struggled to control the nausea and the hysterical wail that was lodged in her throat. When she'd awakened earlier—minutes ago? Hours ago?—she'd lost control, screaming in terror as she tried to push open the lid of the container. In her frenzy, she'd expended too much oxygen too quickly and blacked out. Now she knew to be more careful.

Contorting her neck and body, she managed to place her mouth over a PVC pipe through which fresh air flowed. Another count of ten as she beat back a stronger wave of panic. *Think!* What did she know of her current predicament? Not much. At some point during a rare evening out, she'd been drugged and placed in a wooden box the size of a coffin.

Was she underground?

Hysteria once again bubbled. She gulped more oxygen.

The air tube was a clue. She was being kept alive for a reason. That meant she had time to find a way out or, at the very least, figure out who had put her in here and why. FBI analysts were trained to search for obscure threads and anomalies, to fit all the pieces of a puzzle together. But she no longer worked for the feds. The Bureau's vast resources couldn't help her out of this jam. She had to rely on her wits and on the skill and resourcefulness of a man whose heart she'd once broken.

He'll come.

Will Dresden was a good man and, more important to her at that moment, a tenacious detective. He'd spent years running investigations before a promotion had tied him to a desk. Deputy Chief Dresden. She'd been back in Belfort, Texas—a small city near the Louisiana border—for nearly six months and his title still took her by surprise. She couldn't imagine him in an office. The paperwork alone would aggravate him. Fieldwork had always been his passion, but what did she really know about him these days, anyway?

She wondered if he had the same problem accepting *her* new moniker. Professor Thora Graham. Adjunct professor, to be precise, since she considered her position at the University of Southeast Texas—U-SET—to be temporary. From Quantico to a small regional school in one fell swoop. *How the mighty have fallen.* Never mind that it had been her choice to leave the Bureau. She'd seen the writing on the wall. The notation in her record would stymie future advancements. Maybe it was for the best. Maybe a change was all she needed to get her life back on track. But was that really something she needed to be worried about when she might only have hours to live?

Inhaling more air, she closed her eyes and pretended

to feel a breeze across her face. It was hot inside the box. Nighttime temperatures were bad enough, but in the heat of the day, the container would become unbearable. Even with a supply of fresh air, she wouldn't last long. Dizziness and confusion would set in, accompanied by rapid heartbeat and shallow breathing. Her skin would turn red-hot and her muscles would weaken. She might experience seizures before she lost consciousness and fell into a coma. Then, death.

She shuddered and tried to turn her thoughts away from the inevitable. What time was it, anyway? How long had she been trapped? Her best guess was several hours, but it was hard to measure the passage of time since she'd been unconscious for much of her confinement. Still, she had clues. The effects of whatever drug she'd been given—Rohypnol most likely or possibly ketamine—were starting to wane and thirst wasn't yet a problem.

Closing her eyes, she tried to relax her cramped muscles as she directed her mind to the last thing she could remember. It was Friday night, and she'd been invited for drinks at a popular pub near the university to celebrate a colleague's birthday and the end of the summer session. Any number of excuses had flitted through her head when she'd been asked. She was tired. She had finals to grade. She needed to check in on her mother. Over the years, she'd become adept at bowing out gracefully, which was why her social life had been nonexistent since returning to her hometown. Despite having been born and raised in Belfort, she felt like a fish out of water. Most of her old friends were long gone or busy raising families and she'd never been that great at forging new relationships, even with the people she saw every day. Since the death of her husband five years ago, she'd sunk deeper into the seclusion of her work, obsessing over cases and becoming all too comfortable behind her computer screen. The social aspect of the classroom was a whole new world for her.

"Of course, you'll go," her sister had insisted as she'd fussed with Thora's hair. "A night out is just what the doctor ordered. You say you don't fit in here anymore. Well, what do you expect when you act as if you're just biding time? Don't bother denying it. We all see it. Even Mother. This is your chance to prove that you're not waiting for something better to come along. You're one of them. And like it or not, you're one of us, too. The prodigal daughter, as it were."

Prodigal daughter? Did Claire really think of Thora as wayward and repentant? She had regrets like everyone else, but her time in the FBI had hardly been misspent. She'd found success and purpose in her work, and before Michael's death, she'd been happy. Still, her sister's point was well taken. For however long she planned to stay in Belfort, she needed to make an effort.

The pub had been crowded and noisy. The cheery chaos had been off-putting at first, but Thora had forced a smile as she joined her group. Just her luck that her first social outing had to include her nemesis. She winced at the term. *Nemesis* was an overstatement, but she had little patience or regard for Logan Neville and his ego.

Ten years ago, the tenured professor had penned a true crime opus that had sat at the top of the best-seller list for over a year. His talk show appearances, along with his charm and charisma, had garnered an almost cult-like following, but without a successful sequel, his literary presence on the national stage had eventually faded. Locally, however, he was still something of a rock star, particularly in the Department of Criminal Justice and Criminology at U-SET. A classic big fish in a small pond, though his weekly podcasts had recently created ripples when he and a few of his star pupils had solved a cold case that had eluded local law enforcement for years.

Professor Neville's classes were always the first to fill up—or had been until Thora arrived on the scene. Her own credentials included the seven-year manhunt of a notorious serial killer named James Ellis Ridgeway. Dubbed the Weatherman because of his penchant for killing during inclement conditions, Ridgeway's hunting ground had spanned the I-10, from Alabama to New Mexico. The long gaps of dormancy and his cross-country killing sprees had kept him at large for nearly a decade, but Thora was nothing if not persistent. Once she'd been assigned to the case, her dogged research and in-depth analysis had eventually helped guide the FBI and local law enforcement to Ridgeway's modest brick home on the outskirts of Mobile, Alabama.

Her real-world experience with the National Center for the Analysis of Violent Crime, and in particular, her time with the Behavioral Analysis Unit, made her an irresistible draw to the more serious and ambitious students in her department. For whatever reason, Professor Neville seemed to take her popularity as a personal affront. But was he threatened enough by her expertise to drug, kidnap and bury her alive?

Methodically, Thora worked her way back from their brief interaction at the pub to every other meeting with Logan Neville that she could recall. Conducting a mental investigation clue by clue, thread by thread, kept her from clawing at the lid of the coffin until her fingers bled. It kept her sane.

Take another breath and concentrate.

Using every ounce of her willpower, she forced her mind's eye to linger on each person seated around the two tables that had been shoved together to accommodate their large party. People had come and gone from the group all night. Some left temporarily to play darts or shoot pool, while others like Professor Neville mingled with a few students that had gathered at the bar. Thora couldn't help but notice how blatantly he flirted with one of the young women. She'd heard rumors of his notorious affairs. Every year, he picked a favorite grad student to mentor, and more often than not, the relationship turned sexual. His most recent acolyte was his TA. Addison March was smart, beautiful and sophisticated for her age, the type of ambitious young woman who would be drawn to an older, urbane academic like Logan Neville.

There'd been some kind of ruckus at the bar earlier that night. Thora strained to recall the details. Angry words between Addison and another student named Baylee Fisher had erupted into an ugly shoving match that Professor Neville managed to break up. Thora had been surprised to see Baylee at the pub, let alone involved in a physical confrontation. From what she'd observed in the classroom and around campus, Baylee was a shy introvert who mostly kept to herself. She was smart and driven, but in every other way the complete opposite of Addison. How the former had ended up in the latter's orbit was anyone's guess. That Neville was somehow in the middle was hardly a shock.

Thora wondered if her wine had been spiked during those awkward moments when everyone's attention had been riveted on the clashing students. Unlikely. She would have felt the effects long before her departure a few hours later. Besides, she was always on guard in public places. She knew better than to leave a drink unattended, even among friends. She hadn't left the table until she'd finished her first glass of wine, and if the second glass had been laced with a knockout drug, it may have occurred at the bar.

Which brought her to the stranger. He'd been seated on a stool with his back to the room, but she'd noticed his reflection in the mirror behind the shelves of bottles and glasses. He was tall, attractive, well-dressed. And he'd been staring at her. As their gazes met in the mirror, he slowly rotated the barstool so that they were facing one another across the crowded pub. The back of Thora's neck had prickled in excitement. Or was it a warning? There'd been something unnervingly familiar about his half smile, about the hard, knowing glint in his eyes as he lifted his drink in salute.

Her pulse accelerated at the memory. Hysteria choked her again. She sought the air tube and counted to ten.

Stay calm. Don't let fear trip you up. What else do you remember?

A little while after the confrontation between the students, Will Dresden had come in with an attractive blonde. Thora didn't want to dwell on that particular aspect of the evening because the smile he'd flashed at the woman and the protective way he'd taken her hand as they navigated the crowd had jolted Thora in a way she would never have imagined. *Did you really think he'd wait for you forever? You left him, remember? You went off to Virginia and got married.*

Thirteen years was a long time to carry a torch. Of course he'd moved on. These days, he was nothing more than an old acquaintance. A stranger, really. They had nothing in common except ancient history.

He'll come.

No matter their past or any lingering bad blood, Will was a professional. He'd leave no stone unturned once he knew she was missing, but how long before anyone realized she'd been taken? Claire and her husband were driving to Houston for a wedding the following day and wouldn't return until late. Thora had a brunch date with her mother on Sunday, but could she hang on for that long? What did her abductor have in store for her? How long would she be allowed access to the air tube?

She pounded on the lid. "Can anyone hear me? What do you want? Just tell me what you want!"

Placing her ear to the pipe, she listened intently for a sound that would give away her location. Nothing came to her. No traffic, no barking dogs, nothing but the echo of her heartbeat inside the box. For all she knew, she was miles from town, miles from anywhere. How would anyone ever find her?

He'll come. Please, God, let him come.

Chapter Two

On the rare Saturday morning when Will Dresden didn't have to go to the station for a meeting or to catch up on paperwork, he liked to sleep in. Today, however, one of the neighbors had decided to cut his grass at what seemed like the crack of dawn and Will had awakened with a groan and a string of oaths. It was only a matter of time before some jerk fired up a leaf blower.

You're just cranky because you know you should be out there doing the same thing. Why he'd ever thought home ownership a good idea was beyond him at this ungodly hour. Maintenance, repairs, yard work. The chores never ended, and on a morning like this, he longed for his old apartment.

He plopped a pillow over his head and tried to drift off again, but then—typically—the phone rang. There'd been a time when he might have been able to ignore the annoying ringtone, but his promotion had come with added responsibilities. As one of two deputy chiefs with the Belfort Police Department, he supervised the Criminal Investigations Division, which included Major, Special and Property Crimes units, Vice, Narcotics, Domestic Violence, Missing Persons and CSU. Which meant he was basically always on call. He grabbed his cell without checking the screen and hit the accept button.

"This better be good," he barked, expecting to hear a muttered apology from one of his rookie detectives. Too late, he realized the caller might well be *his* superior, a former Marine who brooked no disrespect or insubordination from his underlings. The Belfort Police Department was small compared to that of the neighboring city of Houston, but in the last ten years, drug and human trafficking in the area had exploded. Despite the challenges of a limited budget, Chief Burnett remained committed to running a tight ship.

"Hello?" The tentative voice was female and sounded faintly familiar. "I'm calling for Will Dresden."

He expelled a breath of relief and adjusted his tone. "This is Dresden," he said politely.

There was a nervous hesitation before she said, "I'm sorry to call so early on a Saturday morning, Will. I hope I'm not disturbing you. Your brother said I could probably reach you at home—"

"Who is this?"

Another pause. "It's Maddie Graham. We used to be next-door neighbors. Your mother and I were best friends before she remarried and moved away."

And your daughter and I used to be lovers.

A thousand images swirled in Will's head as he swung his legs over the side of the bed and ran a hand through his clipped hair. "She still speaks of you fondly," he said. "What can I do for you, Mrs. Graham?"

"I'm not sure. You'll probably think I'm overreacting…" She trailed away and started again. "I'm calling about Thora."

His pulse quickened despite his best efforts. "What about her?"

"You've heard she moved home a few months ago? She's an adjunct professor at U-SET. She taught the spring semester and now she's just finishing up the summer session."

"Yes, I heard she was back." He rose and walked to the window to glance out. "You must be happy about that. She's been gone a long time." Thirteen years to be exact. He rubbed the scruff on his face as he idly tracked the offensive mower and thought, *what an odd conversation for so early in the morning.* It seemed a lifetime ago that his family had lived next door to the Grahams. A lifetime ago since he and Thora—

"—didn't know who else to call."

The tension in Maddie Graham's voice snapped Will back to the present. He scowled out the window as a beam of early morning sunlight caught him in the face. "What's going on?"

"She went out last night. I haven't been able to reach her since."

He refrained from pointing out the obvious, that Thora was a grown woman who had been trained in self-defense at the FBI Academy. A night out was hardly cause for alarm. "I'm sure there's nothing to worry about," he said. "I saw her at a pub on Second Street last night. She was with a group of friends."

He heard her draw a sharp breath. "You saw her? Did you talk to her?"

"As I said, she was with friends. I didn't want to intrude."

"But…she seemed okay?"

"I only caught a glimpse of her, but she seemed fine." He let his mind drift back for a moment. Despite a growing population, Belfort was still a small enough community that he'd recognized several of the people seated around the table. But his attention had lingered only on Thora. She wore those thirteen years well. Maturity suited her, as did the soft waves of dark hair that framed her face. Strange to think that she was a widow at thirty-five. He could feel sympathy even as a more troubling emotion stirred beneath the surface. Jealousy? Resentment for a dead man after all this time?

Probably a good thing he'd been on a date. Otherwise, he might have done something he would have later regretted. Like striking up a conversation or offering to buy her a drink. That ship had sailed a long time ago and he'd learned the hard way that when it came to old relationships, the past was best left buried.

"Did you see her leave the pub?" Maddie asked anxiously.

"No, I left first. It was still early. Probably around nine thirty or so. You want to tell me why you're so upset? She probably got home late and turned off her phone so she could sleep in."

"She wouldn't do that," Maddie insisted. "I've been having some health issues lately. She'd want to make sure that I could reach her."

"I'm sorry to hear that," he murmured.

"It's been an ongoing problem for a while now. Thora moved back to Belfort to help out. She wanted to take some of the pressure off her sister now that Claire's pregnant. And I think there may have been some personal reasons for the move as well. She'd never say anything, of course, because she wouldn't want to worry me. But a mother can tell when something is wrong—" She broke off as if realizing she might have strayed too far from the original intent of her phone call. And maybe her daughter's old boyfriend wasn't the person in whom she should confide. "I don't mean to ramble on like this."

"No, I get it," Will said. "You're worried."

"Yes." Her voice caught and she fell silent for a moment while she gathered her poise. "I'm sorry. It's just such a relief to say it out loud. I didn't want to upset Claire this morning when we talked so I tried not to let on how scared I was. But I can't shake the feeling that something bad has happened. I was a cop's wife for a long time. I learned early on to trust my intuition. Your mother would know what I mean by that. The two of us used to commiserate when one of our husbands was late checking in."

"I remember."

"Rationally, I know it's too early to be so upset, let alone to file an official report. Thora is a grown woman and I saw her less than twenty-four hours ago. The police would think I'm a foolish old woman with too much time on her hands. That's why I'm calling you, Will. I realize I'm putting you in an awkward position, but you were once like family to us and I can't help thinking that if something truly is wrong, then time may be of the essence."

"I'll be happy to help in any way I can," he said, keeping his voice low-key. "When was the last time you spoke to her?"

"Yesterday around six. She stopped by the house on her way to meet friends. She didn't want to go out last night, but her sister and I encouraged her. Browbeat might be a better word. You have no idea how deeply I regret that now." Her voice trembled with emotion.

"Take your time," he said.

Another few seconds went by before she said softly, "Claire and I thought it would do her good to get out more. Make some new friends. She's become so reclusive since she lost Michael."

"That was the last time you heard from her?" he asked, ignoring the reference to Thora's dead husband.

"Yes. She said she'd call when she got home last night if it wasn't too late. When I didn't hear from her, I took it as a sign that she'd had a good time. But when I couldn't reach her this morning, I started to worry so I called Claire. She and her husband drove by Thora's place on their way out of town and then they went by the pub. They found her car in the parking lot, but no sign of Thora anywhere. That's when I called your brother to get your number. I heard about your promotion. I was hoping you could pull some strings. The longer we go without hearing from her…"

"I'll do what I can," Will assured her. "My advice at the moment is to try and stay calm. It's too early to jump to any conclusions. Is it possible she had too much to drink and called a cab or ride-sharing service? That could explain why her vehicle is still at the pub."

"Absolutely not. She never has more than a glass or two of wine, but even if she did, she'd still answer the door and her phone."

Maybe she went home with someone.

Will thought of the man at the bar eyeing Thora in the mirror. He'd seemed so fixated that Will had sidled up to the bar and bumped against him, pretending to be jostled by the crowd in order to check him out more closely. The man had shrugged at Will's apology and turned away, but not before Will had caught the quick flare of annoyance in the stranger's eyes.

Aloud he said, "Did Claire say whether or not the vehicle was locked? Did she notice anything out of place? Any dents or scratches in the paint?" *Any blood stains on the door handle?*

Maddie gasped. "Do you think Thora could have been in an accident?"

"Right now, I'm just asking questions. As I said, there's

no reason to assume the worst. Thora is a trained professional. She knows how to take care of herself. Let's assume for a moment that she did have too much to drink. If she's nursing a hangover, she might not have heard her phone or the doorbell. It's even possible she spent the night with a friend." When Maddie tried to protest, he said quickly, "If it'll put your mind at ease, I'll take a run over to her place and check things out for myself. In the meantime, sit tight and try not to worry. I'll call you when I know something."

"Don't you need her address?" Maddie asked.

"Uh, yeah. Let me put it in my phone." No need to, though. News traveled fast in Belfort, Texas. He knew where Thora lived. Her complex was only a few miles from his neighborhood. He'd taken the long way home once just so he could drive by the gated entrance. He wasn't sure why. He told himself it was just idle curiosity.

"You'll need the gate code."

"Thanks."

Fifteen minutes later, he was showered, dressed and ringing Thora's doorbell. It was still early and the complex was quiet except for the swish of sprinklers that watered the tropical landscaping. Thora's front stoop was recessed into the brick facade, affording privacy from three angles. When no one answered, he tramped through one of the flower beds to glance inside her front window. The blinds were open, but the glass was tinted to keep out the blistering rays of the Texas sun. He could see little more than shadows inside. He rang the bell one last time before returning to his car.

His next stop was the pub. He wheeled into the parking lot and pulled up next to Thora's dark blue Volvo. He got out and checked the locked doors, then circled the car. No dents, no scratches, no sign of foul play, but the abandoned vehicle lifted the hair at the back of his neck. He trailed his gaze over the building, noting the location of the security cameras. Maybe something had been caught on video.

Maybe there was nothing to catch. A former FBI analyst had had a few drinks with colleagues and then left her car in the parking lot because she'd had the good sense not to get behind the wheel. She wasn't answering her door because she'd spent the night with a friend. No reason as of yet to think anything untoward had happened except for that unsettling irritation at his nape.

He circled the car a second time, then lowered himself to the pavement and checked underneath the vehicle. Nothing...no, wait. What was that? He thought at first the dull gleam of metal was a pull tab from a soft drink can, but he flattened himself against the ground and reached for it anyway.

Then he rose, clutching a key ring with a single latchkey attached. The key could have been there for months or even years, dragged from someone's purse or pocket and forgotten. But the brass wasn't weathered or tarnished and the fact that he'd found the key beneath Thora's abandoned car triggered yet another alarm.

He pocketed his discovery, then rounded Thora's vehicle a third time, peering through the windows and examining the door handles for blood stains. Satisfied that he hadn't missed anything, he drove back to her townhouse and tried the key. The lock *clicked* open and the door swung inward with an ominous squeak.

Hovering on the threshold, he trailed his gaze through the narrow foyer as he called out her name. "Thora? You home? It's Will Dresden." He entered slowly. "Thora Graham?"

A sensor had chirped when he opened the door, but the system had been deactivated. The question was, by Thora or someone else?

Don't jump to conclusions.

She'd only been missing for one night and part of a morning. For all he knew, she wasn't missing at all, but had simply failed to check in with her mother. She might walk through the front door at any moment and catch him standing in the middle of her foyer. He could only imagine the look on her face. Best case scenario, they'd have a good chuckle over the awkwardness of their first meeting. But Will wasn't laughing now. Like it or not, he was also starting to have a bad feeling about her absence.

He walked from the foyer into the living room and then on through to the kitchen, taking care not to touch anything. The townhouse was well-appointed and spotless, yet an ominous feeling of abandonment had already descended.

Every room was as clean and tidy as the last. In the kitchen, the dishwasher had been emptied. Upstairs, the bed was neatly made. No discarded clothes on the closet floor, no damp towels in the bathroom. How disciplined one must be to keep a place so meticulous, he mused. And where were her personal mementoes, the keepsakes from her travels and the awards and accolades accumulated from a successful career? Where were the photos of her late husband?

The only trace of Thora that lingered was the faint scent of lavender in the bathroom. The subtle fragrance brought back another round of memories. He'd always loved the smell of her hair. He turned abruptly and went back downstairs, stepping into the small rear courtyard for a breath of fresh air as he called Maddie.

She answered on the first ring. "Thora?"

"It's Will Dresden."

"Will." Her worry and disappointment were palpable. "Please tell me you've found her. Is she okay?"

"I'm sorry. I don't know anything yet, but I'm at her place

now. Either she didn't come home last night or she left the house early this morning. Her bed's made and the coffee maker washed. Might she have caught a ride to her office to grade papers or something?"

"Why wouldn't she have gone back to the pub for her car? And anyway, she'd still have her phone with her," Maddie reasoned.

"True."

She paused. "How did you get into her townhouse? Claire said both the front and back doors were locked."

"I found a key underneath the Volvo." No use keeping the truth from her. The poor woman was already imagining the worst. He remembered that Thora's mother had always been a worrier, but in this instance, he was beginning to think she had every right.

"Underneath her car?" she repeated in horror. "How did it get there, do you suppose?"

"She must have dropped it as she was leaving the pub."

"Then she never made it home last night," Maddie whispered.

Unfortunately, that was also Will's conclusion.

"I was right to be worried, wasn't I? Something's happened to her."

Will gentled his tone. "We don't know anything yet, but I do need to ask you a few questions. I'd like to come by your house if that's okay. Maybe it would be a good idea to ask Claire to come over and wait with you."

"She and her husband canceled their plans as soon as they found Thora's car. They're on their way here now. We'll do whatever we can to help. Answer as many questions as you need to ask. But Will...tell me the truth. You're worried, too, aren't you? I can hear it in your voice."

"Not worried. Concerned, is all. I'm on my way over. Hopefully, you'll have heard from her by the time I get there."

"Will?"

"Yes?"

"Thank you."

"I haven't done anything yet."

"You're taking me seriously. That means everything to me."

Her gratitude humbled him. "You don't need to thank me for doing my job. Just try to stay calm, okay? I'll see you in a few minutes."

He walked back to his car and got in, scowling through the windshield as he swept his gaze over the buildings and grounds. The meandering pathways and shadowy court-yards seemed portentous somehow, as if evil had slipped through the gated entrance while no one had been looking. Maddie Graham's dread was contagious. Will felt tense, restless, like he needed to be out combing the streets for Thora. He had to remind himself that there wasn't yet sufficient cause for alarm, but the circumstances were concerning. Her pattern of behavior had been broken. And why wasn't she answering her damn phone?

He thought again of the man at the bar and his unwavering focus on Thora. That wasn't so unusual in and of itself and certainly no crime. Thora was a beautiful woman. She drew attention even in a crowd. Still, the intensity of the man's gaze had bothered Will. He wished now that he'd struck up a conversation with the stranger. Maybe a few pointed queries from a cop would have been enough to send the guy on his way. Instead, Will had gone back to his table, finished his drink and left the pub with his date. Maybe if they'd stayed even ten minutes longer, he could have pre-vented…what? *What do you think happened to her?*

A car pulled into the adjoining space. A woman in white trousers and a yellow top climbed out and headed up the walkway toward Thora's building. Will got out of his vehicle and called to her. "Excuse me, ma'am! May I have a word?"

She turned with a start, ducking her head to peer at him over the frames of her stylish sunglasses. "Are you talking to me?"

"Yes. Do you live in this building?" He held up his badge and ID as he approached.

Her expression turned anxious as she glanced at his credentials. "I live in 4B," she said. "Has something happened?"

"Do you know the woman in 4A?" He nodded toward Thora's door.

"The teacher? We've met. I wouldn't say I know her exactly." The neighbor shoved her sunglasses to the top of her head as she gave him a nervous scrutiny. "What's this about, anyway? What did she do?"

"She didn't do anything. I just need to speak with her. When was the last time you saw her?"

She shrugged. "I really couldn't say. I don't keep track of my neighbors' comings and goings."

"Try to remember," he pressed. "It could be important."

She adjusted the strap of her shoulder bag as she glanced past Will to the covered commons area just inside the entrance. "If I had to guess, I'd say it was probably at the mailboxes."

"Can you be more specific?"

"Not really. Like I said, I don't keep track." She gave him another assessment. "I do find all these questions a bit strange, though. For someone who hasn't done anything wrong, she sure has a lot of people looking for her."

Will's voice sharpened. "What do you mean?"

"I didn't think much of it until you showed up just now, but another guy came by a couple days ago. That was on Thursday, I think." She seemed to consider the time frame and nodded. "Must have been around six or so. I remember because I was getting home from my yoga class. He stopped me on the walkway just like you did. Claimed to be an old friend. He said Thora had asked him to come by, but she wasn't answering the door or her phone. He wanted to know what time she usually got home from work."

"What did you tell him?"

"Nothing." Her gazed hardened. "Unlike you, he didn't have a badge, and I wasn't born yesterday. I figured there was a reason she didn't want to talk to him."

"Did he give you a name?"

"I didn't ask for one."

"Can you describe him?"

"Tall, slim, late thirties or early forties. His hair was long-ish and kind of unkempt, like he couldn't be bothered to run a comb through it. Other than that, he was nicely dressed and attractive if you didn't look too closely. But there was something about him that didn't add up."

"How so?"

She smiled. "I work for a lawyer. I know a thing or two about suspicious behavior."

"Go on."

"I couldn't shake the feeling that he'd been looking for a key under the doormat when I walked up. He tried to make it seem as though he dropped his phone, but I didn't buy it. He was up to no good. Smooth and handsome on the surface, but the eyes will always give a guy like him away." She cocked her head as she searched Will's face.

"You didn't think about calling the police?"

"And tell them what exactly? I couldn't prove he was

looking for her key, could I? Besides, he would have been long gone before you guys got here."

She had a point. "Did you happen to see his vehicle when he left?"

"No. But I did wonder how he got through the gate."

"Maybe he followed another car through," Will suggested.

"Maybe. Or maybe he was telling the truth and she gave him the code. I doubt it, though."

Will didn't think so, either. He wished he'd snapped a shot of the guy at the bar last night to see if the neighbor recognized him. He handed her a card. "If you see him again, I'd appreciate a call."

He thanked her for her time and went back to his vehicle. A text message pinged as he backed out of the parking space. After braking, he checked the display. A video from an unknown number appeared on the screen. He pulled his car back in and pressed play.

The black-and-white footage had been shot in a confined space using a fiber-optic camera, not unlike the kind plumbers used to determine the source of a clogged pipe. Will couldn't make sense of the scene at first, but realization dawned as a familiar voice called out, "Can anyone hear me? What do you want? Just tell me what you want!"

She appeared to be lying on her back in a rectangular container. The lens had been situated above her so that he could only see her profile and upper torso as she pounded frantically on the lid of the box. Then she dropped her hands to her sides as she placed her mouth against what he could only guess was an air tube. After a few moments, she fell back against the bottom of the container and closed her eyes.

The video ended and a moment later, a second one appeared on his phone. The new footage had been shot during the day, probably early that morning given the angle of the shadows and the softness of the light. The camera zoomed out to reveal a wide-angle view of a densely wooded area that seemed to extend for miles. Then the lens focused back on a single pipe protruding about a foot out of the ground.

Just then, another text pinged.

They say you're a clever investigator, Will Dresden. A smart lawman whose talents and intellect are wasted in a Podunk town like Belfort, Texas. I say they're wrong. Dead wrong.

How much skill is required to round up a few tweakers and gangbangers every week?

Will texted back:

Who is this?

The replay came instantly.

Think of me as your Moriarty (look him up!).

The mockery wasn't lost on Will. He scowled at the screen as he thumbed his message.

Is she alive?

Yes, but for how long depends on you.

What do you want?

Several seconds went by until Will began to worry that the conversation had ended. And then:

I want to see how you measure up against a worthy opponent. You've probably deduced from the video that your precious Thora is at this very moment buried six feet under. You've got twenty-four hours to find her before the air tube is removed. Good luck, Deputy Chief Dresden, and may the best detective win.

Chapter Three

Thora awakened with a start. For a moment she thought she must still be dreaming. Darkness pressed in from all sides and the heavy weight of claustrophobia threatened to crush her. She lifted her hands expecting—hoping—to find nothing but air above her. Instead, her palms pressed up against a wooden barrier. The box. The nightmare came rushing back. She was trapped inside a coffin-sized container with only a PVC tube to supply air. No food, no water, no means of escape. For all she knew, she was deep underground, buried in the middle of nowhere.

Hysteria welled in her chest as panic clawed at her throat. Her impulse was to scream for as long and as loud as she could until someone heard her cries and came to her rescue. Instead, she counted to ten, then twenty, then fifty as she tried to slow her racing heart. Her head pounded and her throat burned. She needed water. She needed air.

She sought the tube and drew in measured breaths. How long had she been asleep? *How* had she been able to sleep? Was she still under the influence of whatever drug had been slipped into her drink? Or was she drawing poison into her lungs at that very moment, causing lethargy and then unconsciousness?

So many questions swirled in her throbbing head, none of which could be answered in her agitated state. She concentrated on clearing the cobwebs from her brain. As the fog began to lift, her breathing slowed and the pain in her head subsided. She flexed her cramped muscles for relief. It was hot inside the box. Perspiration drenched her hair and clothing and her skin felt feverish. She would grow weaker with every second of captivity, but if she preserved her energy, if she refrained from trying to fight her way out of the container, she might get through this. Or she might only prolong the inevitable.

What if no one had even missed her yet? Her mother and sister would try to reach her at some point, but by the time they panicked enough to call the police, it might be too late. If no one reported her missing, how would Will know to look for her? She still wanted desperately to believe that he would come, but wishful thinking could only keep her sane for so long. Already she could feel the tentacles of despair coiling around her fragile resolve.

Shake it off. Shake it off! You'll get through this. One minute at a time, one hour at a time, one day at a time...

He'll come.

She had to cling to that fleeting hope because it was all she had left. Will was an excellent detective, as good as they came. She'd kept up with his career over the years. She knew of the offers from big-city police departments, even from the FBI. He could have gone anywhere, pursued any specialty, but he'd stayed in Belfort because he felt it was the right thing to do, initially for his family and then later for his community. He'd stayed while Thora had fled.

Strange how much he'd been on her mind lately, even before the abduction. She'd found herself hoping to catch glimpses of him on the rare occasions when she happened to be downtown near police headquarters. She'd been dreaming about him before she awakened just now. Visions from their past mingled with the stolen glances from yesterday evening. She'd tried not to be obvious when he came into the pub, but it was hard not stare after so many years. He looked good. Older. More confident and maybe a tad jaded. More guarded, too, she'd noticed, though that might only have been projection. But the dark hair was the same, thick with a slight wave. And from what she'd been able to tell from across a crowded and dimly lit bar, the same intensity still smoldered in his blue eyes. What those eyes had once done to her.

Guilt prickled at her even after all this time, even under extraordinary circumstances. Michael had been gone for half a decade. There were days when their short marriage seemed surreal, like a hazy, half-forgotten dream, but her memories of Will Dresden were sometimes so vivid that their time together might only have been yesterday. Maybe that wasn't so surprising. She'd known Michael Fleming for less than two years in total, but she and Will Dresden had grown up next door to one another, had attended prom together, graduated high school and gone to college together. They'd been inseparable for so long that back then Thora couldn't have imagined her life without him—until she could.

Seeing him in the pub had brought back so many of those old memories. So many of those old feelings, too, if she dared to be honest with herself. But dwelling on what might have been never did anyone any good. Especially not her. Not now. Not here in the box when her next moment was an uncertainty.

Shuddering in the stifling heat, she closed her eyes and tried to center herself. Panic was only a hair's breadth away, but if she succumbed to the terror, she might never find a way out. If she started to scream, she might never stop. So she did the only thing she could think to do in her current situation: she resumed her investigation.

With the passage of time, bits and pieces of her night out had started to come back to her. She forced herself back into the noisy chaos of the pub as she mentally explored the room. A little while after Will and his companion left, she'd decided to call it a night. The timing was a coincidence... or so she told herself. Their exit had nothing to do with her leaving. She'd simply had enough. The loud music and constant chatter had started to wear on her nerves.

Plus, the eye contact with the stranger at the bar had left her unsettled, though if pressed for a reason, she couldn't explain why. Maybe she'd been out of the game for too long, but his attention seemed more derisive than flirtatious. She couldn't imagine why. She was certain they'd never met, yet his slow smile had triggered her defenses. She didn't know him, but his sardonic salute seemed to suggest that he knew her. Had their paths crossed since she'd moved back to Belfort or had he followed her here from Virginia?

An unnerving thought, but a long shot. Her job with the FBI had required almost no contact with the general public and even less face-time with the criminals she'd studied and tracked. She never ran investigations or made arrests. The bulk of her workday had been spent staring at a computer screen, so chances were slim that she'd attracted the attention of a stalker or someone who harbored enough of a grudge to shadow her all the way down to Texas. Still, she couldn't discount the possibility. She'd been a target two years ago. Maybe her tormentor had resurfaced, but kidnapping would be a dramatic escalation from anonymous phone calls and text messages. Even the break-in at her apartment seemed innocuous compared to being trapped inside a box.

She'd been certain at the time that the harassment was somehow connected to the Weatherman case. The incidents had occurred within weeks of James Ellis Ridgeway's conviction and incarceration. Thora's role in his takedown had been leaked to a reporter. After her name had appeared online, she'd begun receiving dropped calls in the middle of the night, followed by a series of taunting and vaguely threatening text messages. On several occasions, she'd spotted someone in the park across the street watching her building. The stalking had culminated with the break-in at her apartment and then, just like that, it was over. The police detective assigned to her case concluded that she'd been the target of a malicious prankster. Nothing had been taken from her home and no overt threats had been made. His suggestion was to put the episode behind her.

Thora had managed to do exactly that. Compartmentalizing various aspects of her life had become second nature to her. She'd retreated back into her low-profile existence, burying herself once again in her work. Eventually, the seven years she'd devoted to the capture of James Ellis Ridgeway grew less significant to her career as more monsters came along for her to track. The Weatherman, like all the others, became nothing more than a case study, a subject to be dissected and analyzed and then filed away.

Two years had gone by without further incident, but the job had started to take a toll. Thora's decision to move back home had had nothing to do with a stalker. The phone calls and text messages were long behind her, and she had no reason to think her current predicament was in any way connected to that brief episode. Yet she couldn't get the stranger at the bar out of her head. She couldn't stop picturing his taunting smile and knowing stare.

Taking another gulp of air, she kept her focus in the pub, letting her mind's eye wander through the room. At some point after Will and his date exited, she'd left her second glass of wine unfinished and said good-night to her colleagues. She knew there had been significant conversations and observations between her arrival and departure that she could later examine, but right now, she wanted to concentrate on the moments leading up to the abduction.

She remembered feeling a little light-headed when she rose from the table. She wasn't by any means intoxicated, but she couldn't deny a strange unsteadiness as she made her way through the crowd. By the time she left the building, nausea bubbled in her stomach as the parking lot started to spin. Stumbling toward her car, she fumbled for her phone to call Claire. Something was wrong, but if she could just make it to her vehicle and lock the doors until help came…

The bright lights had come out of nowhere, catching her directly in the face. Blinded and disoriented, she threw up a hand to shield her eyes. The sudden motion initiated the vertigo. She staggered back as the asphalt tilted beneath her feet. A car door slammed and then someone grabbed her arm, holding her upright.

"Don't fight it."

The voice in her ear sounded strange, distorted, electronic. A million miles away.

"Who are…? What do you…?" Her own speech came out slurred, almost unrecognizable. "What did…?"

"It'll be a lot easier if you just let go."

Thora had a vague recollection of being shoved inside a vehicle. She remembered the sound of the engine, the flicker of passing car lights and then nothing. The next thing she recalled was waking up in the box.

Thankfully, the nausea and dizziness were finally subsiding, which meant several hours must have passed since she'd been drugged. Maybe it was morning. Maybe her mother had already tried to call her. She would want to hear about Thora's night out. When she couldn't reach her, what then? Would she call Claire? The police? How much time would she let go by before she sounded the alarm?

Putting her ear to the PVC pipe, she strained to detect a noise from the outside world. Anything would have been welcome.

Nothing like that came to her, but there was a sound on the other end of the air tube. Faint taps. She listened for a moment, her pulse leaping in excitement before she put her mouth to the opening.

She called up into the pipe, "Hello? Is someone out there? Can you hear me? Can you please help me?"

The drumming grew louder. She wondered if she'd imagined the sound. A strange pattern emerged, rhythmic and hypnotic. Tap, tap...pause...tap, tap. Tap, tap...pause...tap, tap.

"I don't understand. What do you want from me?"

Tap, tap...pause...tap, tap. Tap, tap...pause...tap, tap.

She put her fist to the lid of the box and repeated the sequence.

A few drops of water landed against her face. Was it raining?

Almost euphoric by the feel of moisture against her dry lips, she let the water trickle into her mouth and down her parched throat. *Careful. Don't get strangled.* When she'd had enough, she tapped out the sequence on the air tube. The dribble stopped.

"Hello? Are you still there? Please, what do you want? Just tell me what you want."

Her pleas seemingly fell on deaf ears.

She banged her fists against the lid of the container. "Let me out of here! Please! I haven't seen your face! I don't know who you are! Nothing will happen if you just let me go!"

When no response came back to her, she pounded even harder. "Let me out of here! Do you hear me! *Let me out of here!* You can't keep me here. You can't do this!"

She was seriously in danger of losing control, but she didn't care at that moment. She kept right on screaming and pounding until she grew hoarse and her bruised hands fell helplessly to her sides. "Please," she sobbed. "Please let me out."

After a moment, the rhythmic drumming came again. She placed her lips to the tube. When no water trickled out, she repeated the sequence and rasped into the tube, "Water. Please."

A few drops dribbled down the pipe. She lapped them up and then let her head fall back against the bottom of the container. "Thank you."

More drumming. She realized now the sound was a command. She wouldn't be given what she wanted until she answered in kind. She tapped out the sequence and waited. Instead of water, something cool and metallic slid down the tube and fell against her cheek. She groped in the dark until she had the object in her hand. Running her fingers along a chain, she found a circular charm. Even in the pitch blackness of the box, she knew the medallion was the one Michael had worn for good luck, a gift from the grandfather who had raised him. The keepsake had been tucked away in a jewelry box since the day her husband's personal effects had been returned to her.

Whoever put her in the box had been in her house, gone through her things and taken Michael's good luck charm for a reason. That chain had been around his neck the day he died. The medallion had lain against his chest the moment his heart had stopped beating. No other possession, including her wedding ring, would have had the same emotional impact. Somehow the kidnapper had known that. Delivering a gut punch when she was at her most vulnerable was a deliberately diabolical act.

She clutched the medallion to her breast. It would have been so easy in that moment to give up and let fear and despair take control. But she wouldn't. She couldn't. Not until she knew who was on the other end of the air tube. Not until she knew *why*.

She pounded fiercely on the lid and called up once again, "Who are you? What do you want?"

Nothing came back to her. No drumming, no trickling water, nothing. The silence in the box became unbearably heavy.

Whoever had been on the other end of the pipe was gone, leaving Thora alone to brood in the dark confines of her prison.

Chapter Four

After leaving Thora's townhouse, Will drove straight to police headquarters to activate the necessary protocols for a kidnapping victim in imminent danger. He called Maddie en route to alert her of a new development, but he didn't go into specifics, and he kept the conversation short because he didn't want to break the news of Thora's abduction over the phone. Back at the station, he briefed his team before sending someone to the Graham home to meet with the family. He stayed behind to orchestrate the dozens of details that went into a citywide search. The situation wasn't ideal, but his title greased wheels and every second counted when a twenty-four-hour-deadline loomed over their heads.

By the time he finally pulled to the curb in front of Maddie's house, the Tech Unit had already scoured his phone and begun the painstaking task of analyzing the video. In the meantime, the Crime Scene Unit had processed Thora's townhouse and car and delivered sealed bags of trace evidence to the lab. More than a dozen officers had been dispatched to search the immediate area around the pub while every other available personnel tracked down the people that had been with Thora the previous evening. Law enforcement agencies within a hundred-mile radius had been alerted and a call had gone out to the FBI field office in Houston.

Will glanced at the clock on his phone as he got out of the vehicle. He'd received the videos and text messages just before nine that morning. The time was now closing in on noon. Twenty-one hours before Thora's air tube would be removed. How long could she last after that? So much would depend on her frame of mind and whether she could hold it together enough to conserve her strength and oxygen. That was asking a lot, even of a trained professional. He tried to put himself in her place…trapped in a box with barely enough room to raise her hands above her chest. Buried underground with no idea if anyone even knew she was missing.

He felt sick to his stomach when he thought of what she must be going through, but he couldn't afford to get sidetracked. Each and every unit in his division had an integral part to play in the search and he was the one who had to make sure the operation ran like a well-tuned engine. It was imperative that he stay focused and unemotional. Thora's life might well depend on a split-second decision.

Maddie's son-in-law answered the door. Will knew the man only slightly by reputation. Jared Hartley was a partner in a big downtown law firm. Highly successful if the late-model X6 in the driveway was any indication. The two men shook hands and then Will followed the attorney across the narrow foyer and down into a sunken living room.

He took in the area with a single glance. Nothing much had changed since he'd last been there. The white slip-covered furniture looked the same, as did the framed photographs of Thora and Claire on the walls and the overkill of porcelain knickknacks in the built-ins. Maddie and Claire sat side by side on the sofa. Detective Angel Reyes balanced his notebook on his knee as he faced them across the coffee table. Mother and daughter jumped to their feet when Will entered.

Maddie took an imploring step toward him. "Will—"

He headed her off before she could get her hopes up. "We don't know anything yet, but it's early. We're not even three hours into the search. We've mobilized the entire police force and have requested support from the FBI. I know it's hard not to worry, but we're doing everything we can to find her."

Maddie's shoulders drooped despondently. "I don't even know how to process what's happened. Detective Reyes told us about the videos. Claire wouldn't let me watch them…" She clutched her daughter's arm. "What kind of person could do something so cruel to another human being?" She gazed up at Will, eyes pleading for answers.

He'd been asking himself the same question all morning. In the course of his career, he'd witnessed a lot of disturbing things, but video footage of a woman buried alive had to be one of the most twisted. The impact was even more devastating because he knew the victim. "The thing to remember is that she's alive, she's strong and she has an air supply. She'll be able to hang on until we find her."

"How are you going to do that?" Maddie wrung her hands in distress. "I know you'll do what you can, but she could be anywhere. It would take weeks if not months to search all the wooded areas around Belfort. Not to mention the swamps." She closed her eyes and swayed on her feet. "When I think about what she must be going through… I just don't know if I can stand it."

"We have a lot of smart and dedicated people going through those videos frame by frame, pixel by pixel," Will said. "We're searching her car, her home, the area around the pub. We'll find something. We always do."

Claire wrapped an arm around Maddie's frail shoulders and held on tight. "Come sit down, Mom. And please, please try to stay calm. You know what the doctor said about your heart."

Maddie let her daughter lead her back to the sofa. "Nothing matters but Thora. I don't care what happens to me. I just want my daughter back."

"Well, I care," Claire insisted. "I'm worried about Thora, too, but it won't do her any good if you make yourself sick."

Will exchanged a glance with Reyes and nodded, signaling that the older detective should continue the interview. Meanwhile, Will stepped back so that he could observe the entirety of the room. Instead of being at his wife's side, Jared Hartley had retreated into the dining room. Will could see him through the wide casement opening that separated the two spaces. He was on his phone, but every now and then he'd glance up, as if one of the detective's questions had caught his attention.

Ignoring the attorney, Will looked through the dining room into the kitchen where he could see a portion of the backyard through the large window over the sink. He could even glimpse the roof of the old tree house that their dads had built when the families were neighbors. It was sad to think that the tree house had outlasted both of those tough men. Will's dad had gone first—killed in the line of duty—and then Thora's several years later from pancreatic cancer.

When Will had first learned about his dad, all he could think was that he needed to get home as fast as he could to take care of his mother and younger brother. But later on, when the arrangements had been made and all the neighbors and fellow officers had departed, he'd gone outside and climbed up into that tree house to be alone with his grief. After a while, Thora had slipped through the hedge and followed him up. She'd known exactly where to find him that night. Somehow she'd always known.

Now it was his turn to find her. She was trapped in a box, buried only God and her kidnapper knew where. The task seemed overwhelming if not impossible. Maddie was right. Belfort was surrounded by hundreds of acres of dense forest and swampland. It would take a miracle to pinpoint Thora's location with nothing marking the site but a PVC pipe protruding a foot from the ground. *Like looking for a needle in a haystack.* Will had to trust that clues would be found in the video or that the lab would discover a print, a hair, a fiber—*something* from her car or townhouse that would help identify her abductor.

Rationally, he knew everything that could be done was being done, yet it took every ounce of his willpower to fight off a terrible feeling of inevitability, especially when he observed Maddie's haggard face. No matter how old the child, a mother's need to protect never waned.

He went back over the video in his head. Had he missed something? Had he overlooked a subtle but vital piece of information that only he could decipher? The one clue that would lead him to Thora?

They say you're a clever investigator, Will Dresden. A smart lawman whose talents and intellect are wasted in a Podunk town like Belfort, Texas. I say they're wrong. Dead wrong.

A wave of anger washed over him, but he quickly stifled the emotion because he knew those taunting messages were meant to rile him up and throw him off balance. Make him second-guess his decisions. He forced a cool head as he went back over in his mind every line of the text. The sender had referred to Thora by name. *Your precious Thora.* Whoever had taken her knew their history—or wanted him to think so—but that hardly narrowed the field. Could be anybody. Someone Will had arrested. A former classmate or neighbor. Someone who carried an old grudge. Someone who likely regarded themselves as the smartest person in the room.

He caught Claire's eye. She gave him an enigmatic look before she stood and collected empty cups from the coffee table. A few minutes later, she returned with a tray of clean cups and a fresh pot of coffee. She served her mother and Detective Reyes first, offered a cup to her husband, which he declined, and then brought one over to Will. The outside temperature had already soared to the nineties and humidity hovered around sixty percent. It was way too hot in the middle of the day for a steaming drink, but he accepted the cup and murmured a thank-you.

"Can I talk to you for a minute?" She nodded toward the foyer. "Out there. In private."

"Sure." He followed her into the narrow entrance, glancing through the sidelights on either side of the front door to check the peaceful street.

The light streaming in through the narrow windows caught the diamond on Claire's finger as she tucked back her hair. The stone was square cut and just slightly smaller than ostentatious.

For a moment, she seemed unsure what to do with herself. She splayed her hands protectively across her still flat belly as she glanced over her shoulder into the living room. When she turned back to Will, her expression seemed almost blank except for a glint of anger—or was it fear?—in her brown eyes.

In that moment, she looked very much like her sister. So much so that Will was taken aback. Same dark, glossy hair.

Same soulful eyes. Personality-wise, the sisters had always been polar opposites. The Thora he'd known could remain calm and collected in almost any situation while Claire, he suspected, still had a temper and a flair for the dramatic.

Her uncharacteristic silence seemed somehow portentous. He tilted his head as he gazed at her across the narrow expanse of the foyer. "You okay?"

The innocuous question snapped her out of her stupor. Her mouth thinned as she glared up at him. "I just learned that my sister has been kidnapped and buried alive so, no, Will. I'm not okay. I'm far from okay."

"I know."

"God, it's like a nightmare. I keep telling myself it can't be real, but it is. I saw the videos." She closed her eyes on a shudder. "You know what keeps running through my mind? All those years Thora spent with the FBI working cases that involved the worst kind of criminals. Finally, she gave all that up to come back to the one place where she should have been safe, and she ends up in the clutches of a human monster." Her voice shook with emotion as her gaze pinned Will with relentless intensity. "How could something like this happen in Belfort? How could you let it happen in our town on your watch?"

He did nothing to try to counter her rage. People reacted differently to fear and grief. Sometimes a person under stress or in crisis needed someone to blame. If Claire had chosen him to be the scapegoat, so be it. He could take it.

"We'll find her," he said.

Her chin shot up. "Is that a promise?"

He sighed and set his cup on a nearby table. "There are never any guarantees in a situation like this, but we're doing everything in our power to find her and bring her home safely. I can promise you that."

"Well, I'm sorry. That's just not good enough." Despite her anger, she managed to keep her voice low so that no one in the other room could overhear her tirade. "You've already let my mother down once today. You'll forgive me if I'm reluctant to take your promises to heart."

He kept his tone gentle. "What are you talking about, Claire? How did I let her down?"

"She called you for help this morning. She called *you*. You should have been the one to tell her about Thora instead of sending a stranger to her door to deliver the worst kind of news a mother can hear. She's always held you in the highest regard. You were once like a son to her. I would have thought after everything our families have been through together, you would have shown her that kindness."

So that was the root of her wrath. Or at least a convenient excuse. In truth, her anger probably had very little to do with him and everything to do with her own feelings of guilt and helplessness. He understood those emotions only too well.

"When your mom called this morning, she told me she had a feeling that time was of the essence." He glanced through the opening into the living room where Maddie sat with clasped hands and bowed head. "Turns out, she was right. Once I received those videos, a lot of wheels had to be set in motion as quickly as possible. I couldn't spare even a second. I didn't want to tell her over the phone or risk having her hear the news from someone else, so I sent Detective Reyes. He may be a stranger to you, but I've known him for years. He and I were partners for a time. He's one of the best investigators I've ever worked with, and I'd trust him with my life. That's why he's here."

"Is he better than you?" The way Claire challenged him made him think of the taunting tone of the text messages.

He answered without hesitation. "In this situation, he is

unquestionably the better detective. He spent ten years in El Paso investigating cartel kidnappings. He has more experience working abductions than anyone in the department."

Claire seemed only slightly mollified. "Well, I hope and pray you're right. But for Mom's sake, I still need some assurances from you."

He suppressed an impatient sigh. "What kind of assurances?"

"I need to know that you'll remain invested in my sister's rescue. You, personally." When he would have interrupted, she put up a hand to stop him. "You're well-respected in the police department and your name and title carry weight. I know this because my husband is connected, and he tells me things. Detective Reyes may be the better detective, but you're the one who can keep the search going for as long as it takes." She stared him straight in the eyes. "I need to know you won't stop looking for my sister…no matter what."

No matter what. The meaning of her request wasn't lost on Will. "We're a long way from that, Claire."

"Are we? In less than twenty-four hours, Thora's air tube will be removed."

"The threat could be a bluff," Will said. "We're treating it as though it isn't."

"Then say it. Tell me what I need to hear."

"I won't stop looking for her." *Ever.*

Something in his voice seemed to convince Claire of his honesty. She nodded. "Thank you. I know I'm being difficult, but I couldn't bear the thought—" Tears filled her eyes and spilled over as if the gravity of her own request seemed to hit her. Will reached in his pocket for a handkerchief. He'd learned early on in his career that a clean linen handkerchief was sometimes more effective than a loaded weapon.

"Don't give up on her," he said.

She accepted the handkerchief and dabbed her eyes. "I'm not. But you know better than I the reality of the situation. I have to be mentally prepared so that if and when the time comes, I can be strong for my mother. She'll need me as she's never needed me before. It would be a comfort to know that you'll be there for her, too, Will."

"Of course, I will."

She handed the handkerchief back to him. "That's that, then." She straightened her shoulders and her chin came up once more, a stance he knew only too well from all those years with Thora. "I want to focus on the search now."

"What is it you want to know?"

"You mentioned earlier that you have people studying the videos and going through my sister's car and home, but is anyone actually out there looking for her? Has a search party been formed? I have nothing against Detective Reyes, but if he's as good as you say he is, shouldn't he be out there instead of in here wasting time with an endless stream of questions?"

"He's doing his job. The more questions he asks, the greater the chance that something will come back to you," Will explained. "Even the smallest detail could be important. Until we have a concrete lead on Thora's location, the best way to find her is to find the person who took her."

"Seems to me the best way to find the person who took her is to look for someone with a grudge against you." Her stare was stone-cold. "I read those text messages, Will. The tone was derisive and superior and the kidnapper referred to my sister as, your precious Thora. Whoever took her has to be someone who knows you and is familiar with your history."

"We haven't overlooked that possibility, but the list of possible suspects is long considering my years in law enforcement. We're in the process of scouring arrest records, flagging threats, tracking down inmates recently released from jail or prison. All that takes time."

"What about someone with a more personal grudge?"

He searched her features. "Why do I get the feeling you already have someone in mind?"

"Elise Barrett," she blurted.

He absorbed the shock, then said, "You're serious."

She scowled up at him. "Why do you find it so hard to believe? Because she's a cop or because she's a woman? Or because you were once engaged to her?"

He returned her scowl. "I don't know where you got that idea. Elise and I went out for a while. We were never engaged."

"Oh, really? Because she tells a different story. She called it an unofficial understanding. She said at the last minute you couldn't commit because you still had feelings for my sister."

There might have been more truth to that claim than Will wanted to admit. However, in all the months that he and Elise Barrett had been together, the subject of marriage never once came up. Where she'd gotten the notion of an understanding, official or otherwise, he couldn't imagine. He'd always been open about where he stood in the relationship, which was why when the time came to end things, he'd gone for a clean break. He'd always thought Elise felt the same way.

Maybe she had. Maybe Claire's interpretation was skewed by her current frame of mind.

"I didn't realize you and Elise were such good friends," he said.

Claire shrugged. "We aren't. Which is why I was so surprised when she cornered me at a party awhile back. She'd had too much to drink—way too much—and decided to unload her grievances. It was an illuminating conversation." Her gaze darkened. "That woman has a serious chip on her shoulder where you're concerned, Will. She said after you dumped her, she was forced out of the Criminal Investigations Division while you ended up with a promotion. Is that true?"

Will felt stunned by the revelation and more than a little angry. "She wasn't forced out. She asked to be transferred to Internal Affairs."

Claire gave him a tight, almost pitying smile. "Again, not how she tells it. Did you know that she and Thora had some kind of friendly rivalry back in college? Although now I have to wonder how friendly it actually was. This is going to sound truly bizarre, but I think *she* thinks Thora's career with the FBI should have been hers."

"She said that?"

"Not in so many words, but that's the impression I got. She never talked about Thora to you?"

"Not really. I never knew they were anything more than acquaintances."

"I think there are a lot of things you don't know about Elise Barrett," Claire said. "Are you going to send someone to talk to her or should I go confront her myself?"

"No, don't do that. You need to keep your distance. Let me handle this," Will said. "The best way you can help is to stay put and look after your mother. Earlier she mentioned something I've been wondering about. She said she had a feeling that Thora had reasons other than being close to family for moving back here. Do you have any idea what she meant?"

Claire shook her head. "No, but I wouldn't read too much into it. Mom is a worrier. She's always getting bad feelings about something. Sometimes her intuition pans out and sometimes it doesn't."

"You don't know of any problems or confrontations that Thora may have had at work or in her personal life?"

"She keeps things pretty close to her chest. I would never have known about all that business with the Weatherman if she hadn't let something slip. Then I badgered her into telling me the rest."

Will was instantly on alert. "What business?"

"It turned out to be nothing, but a few weeks after James Ellis Ridgeway was sent to prison, Thora started getting anonymous phone calls and text messages…" She trailed off. "You do know who Ridgeway is, don't you?"

"Every law enforcement agency along I-10 knows who James Ellis Ridgeway is."

"Okay, well, Thora worked that case for seven years. She's the one who connected his kills to weather patterns. She's the one who first suggested that something traumatic occurred in his childhood to make him equally repelled and fascinated by storms. Turns out, his mother used to lock him in a storm cellar for days at a time. No food, no water, no bathroom. Anyway, after his conviction, Thora's name appeared in an online article that went viral. The write-up wasn't very flattering. The reporter made her sound like an obsessed loner. Soon after the article was published, she started getting threatening phone calls and text messages."

"Threatening in what way?"

"Things like, *You're lucky the sun is shining today.* Or, *Be careful. There's a storm brewing tonight.* Nothing overt, but the underlying intimidation was clear. She came home one day to find that her apartment had been broken into, but nothing was taken. Nothing that she missed, anyway. After the break-in, the phone calls and texts stopped. She changed her number and the locks on her door and went about her business as if nothing had happened."

"She never heard from this person again?"

"Not that I know of. The cops chalked it up to a 'malicious prankster.'" She air-quoted the term before glancing over her shoulder. "We never told Mom. I would appreciate it if you didn't say anything. She doesn't need another thing to worry about right now."

"I won't mention it if I don't have to." Will removed a piece of paper from his pocket and unfolded it. "Take a look at this." He handed the computer-generated rendering of the stranger he'd seen at the bar the night before to Claire. "Do you recognize this man?"

She studied the image for a long moment. "I don't think so. Who is he?"

"He was seen in the pub last night at the same time Thora was there. Her neighbor said a man matching his general description came by her townhouse last Thursday looking for her. He claimed to be an old friend. He said they were supposed to meet but he hadn't been able to reach her by phone and she wasn't answering the door. Did Thora mention anything about a friend coming to town?"

"No. She never said a word. She's extremely private but I think she would have told me about a visitor." Claire glanced up from the rendering. "Do you think this man had something to do with her abduction?"

Before Will could answer, Jared Hartley came up behind his wife. He studied the image over her shoulder, then reached around and took the paper from her hand. "Who's this supposed to be?"

"Right now, he's a person we'd like to have a conversation with," Will said.

"He was seen in the pub last night the same time Thora

was there," Claire explained as she turned to her husband. "You don't recognize him, do you?"

"No, but it's hard to say definitively from this drawing. He could be any one of a dozen guys you'd see in a bar on any given night."

"We're circulating the image in Thora's neighborhood and around campus. Maybe we'll get lucky and someone can give us a description of his vehicle. Or better yet, a license plate number." When Hartley tried to return the image, Will said, "Keep it. Study it. You never know when something may come back to you."

Hartley folded the paper and tossed it on the entrance table beside Will's abandoned coffee cup. "I'm sure I don't need to remind you of the ticking clock that's hanging over your head. A crime of this magnitude can make or break a reputation." He slipped his arm around Claire's shoulders. "I hope for my wife's sake, and for her sister's, that you're as good as they say you are, Dresden. The whole town will be watching."

Chapter Five

Will elected not to call Elise Barrett to request an interview but instead drove straight to her place after he left Maddie Graham's house. His decision was twofold. He wanted to keep the meeting casual while also catching her off guard. A spontaneous reaction could often be telling.

He still considered the possibility of her involvement in Thora's kidnapping slim at best. He'd known the woman for years. They'd gone through the police academy together and had worked side by side in the Criminal Investigations Division before her transfer to Internal Affairs. During their time as a couple, he'd never had anything but respect for the way she conducted herself personally and professionally. She had a wild streak. He wouldn't deny that, but she had her limits. His trip across town to see her was probably a huge waste of time, but he couldn't take the chance that Claire's instincts might prove right. What if he didn't know Elise as well as he thought?

She lived on the far east side in a little two-bedroom bungalow she'd inherited from her grandmother. The neighborhood had been working class until college students and starving artists discovered the affordable housing. With their arrival, the streets had taken on a distinctly bohemian air.

The changing vibe hadn't bothered Elise as it had some of her neighbors. She'd wholeheartedly embraced the colorful murals and overabundance of yard art.

The scent from the roses that spilled over the neighbor's fence bombarded him as he climbed the porch steps and knocked on Elise's door. When she didn't answer, he rapped harder. Hearing signs of life inside, he tried a third time and waited.

She answered the door belting a silk robe around her waist. Judging by her damp hair and glistening skin, he'd gotten her out of the shower. She looked momentarily startled to see him and none too happy.

"What are you doing here?" Her gaze flicked past him to the street. "You're about the last person I expected to find at my door on a Saturday morning."

"It's the afternoon," he felt compelled to point out.

"Barely." She coiled her hair around her fingers and fashioned a bun at her nape. "What do you want?"

"I need to talk to you. It won't take long. Can I come in?"

She observed him through the screen. "This isn't a good time. Can you come back in an hour? Or better yet, call me later and we can meet somewhere for a drink."

"This isn't a social visit and it can't wait. I wouldn't be here if it wasn't important."

She glanced over her shoulder, then unlatched the screen door and stepped on to the porch. Will could have sworn he saw a shadow move inside before she pulled the wooden door closed.

"Well?" She leaned back against the door frame. "You wanted to talk, so talk."

Something about her attitude caught *him* off guard. He wasn't quite sure why he felt so on edge all of a sudden. Elise's expression remained one of mild annoyance, but her eyes seemed to guard a darker emotion. He couldn't help noticing that she'd checked the street a second time when she stepped outside. Was she expecting someone? Or was she worried he might recognize a car parked at the curb? And why would she care if he did?

He tried to gauge her reaction without overtly scrutinizing her features. "I need to ask you a question and I'm hoping you won't take it personally."

She folded her arms. "Which pretty much guarantees that I will but do go on. What's the question?"

No easy way to ask so he went for the direct approach. "Where were you last evening between the hours of eight and eleven?"

"I shouldn't take that personally?" Despite the note of sarcasm, she didn't look particularly surprised or offended, just curious. "What's this about, Will?"

"Answer my question first and then we'll talk."

"Tell me what this is about and then I'll answer your question."

He started to counter but his attention was momentarily diverted by a twitching curtain at an open window. Maybe the breeze had stirred the panel, but he had a feeling someone stood on the other side listening in on their conversation. He shifted his focus back to Elise. "Did I interrupt something?"

"Yes, you got me out of the shower." She tucked back a strand of damp hair as she moved away from the entrance, forcing him to turn away from the open window and that twitching curtain. She plopped down on the low concrete wall that encased the shady porch and leaned back on her hands as she gazed up at him.

Outwardly, she seemed relaxed if still a bit peeved, but instinct told him she wasn't as calm as she'd have him believe. There was a reason for his uneasiness. He'd picked up on a worrisome vibe.

"I think I know why you're here," she said. "Is this about Thora Graham?"

He scowled down at her. "How do you know about that?"

"Last I checked, I'm still a member of the Belfort PD. You mobilize the entire police force on a Saturday morning, word gets out." Her expression turned serious. "Is she alive?"

An image of Thora lying flat on her back in that buried box flashed through Will's head, sending a cold chill down his spine. *Can anyone hear me?*

I heard you and I'm trying to find you. Just hold on.

He struggled to keep his tone and demeanor impassive. "We've every reason to believe she's alive." But for how much longer? He resisted the temptation to check his watch.

Elise shivered. "I can't imagine what she must be going through. It's surreal when you think about it. Here we are on my porch enjoying a nice breeze while at this very moment, she's out there somewhere, buried in a box in the middle of nowhere. Nothing but her own thoughts to keep her centered. And her poor family. They must already be worried sick."

"I was just with them," he said, still in a careful tone. "They're holding up as well as can be expected."

"And you?"

That was a loaded question. He refused to glance away from her probing stare. "I'm worried."

She gave him a pitying look. "The things one human being is willing to do to another just keep getting sicker. Remember little Danny Hagan? The nine-year-old boy who disappeared in broad daylight while walking home from school? We were first-year detectives when he went missing. It killed me that we couldn't find him."

"That was a tough case," Will agreed.

"A decade later, still no trace. The world is a very dark place."

"Sometimes it can be."

"Cops see the worst of it. The first responders. I don't miss that part of the job. It's a particularly heavy burden when the victim is a child, or in this case, someone you know. I'd like to ask about leads, but I'm sure you're unable to share details of the investigation at the moment."

"No, I can't, but your intel seems pretty sound so far."

"Even an IA investigator has friends." She swung her legs up to the wall and hugged her knees. For a moment, she seemed mesmerized by a potted fern stirring in the breeze. Will glanced around. She'd always been into gardening. Terra-cotta planters crowded the small porch, and her front yard was like a jungle. He could still smell the neighbor's roses. The sticky scent reminded him of a funeral.

"I'm going to need an answer to my question," he said.

She glanced up at him, her expression still solemn save for a spark of defiance in her blue eyes. "Isn't it rhetorical?"

"Why would you think that?"

"I assume the reason you're here is because you already know that I was at Molly's Pub last night. You were there, too. And Thora. I also assume you're tracking down anyone you can think of who might have seen or heard anything out of the ordinary. Sorry to say, I didn't."

He said nothing for a moment. Then, in a quiet voice, "You were at Molly's last night?"

She looked surprised. "You didn't see me come in?"

He shook his head slowly.

"I guess that makes sense. The place was packed and you were otherwise occupied. New girlfriend?"

"A friend."

Something hard gleamed in her eyes. "Let's just back up for a minute. If you didn't see me, then why—" She broke off as realization seemed to dawn. "You really did come here to find out my whereabouts last night."

"That's what I said."

"Are you trying to tell me I'm a *suspect*?"

"I never said—"

Before he could finish his thought, she jumped to her feet. "That's the most ridiculous thing I've ever heard! What possible motive could I have for kidnapping the poor woman and burying her alive? For God's sake, Will. You know me. Do you really think I'm capable of something that evil?"

"I never said anything of the sort."

"This is *unbelievable*." In her agitation, the belt of her robe loosened and the silk lapels gaped, revealing an angry red scratch across her collarbone.

"Elise, what happened to your neck?"

Her hand flew to her throat as if she'd forgotten about the wound. "The hazard of trimming rose bushes. But you know that. You've seen scratches on me before. You used to berate me for not wearing gloves." She shoved up the sleeves of the robe so that he could see several grazes on her arms. "Now that I'm a suspect, maybe you'd like to subject me to an imprint analysis, just to make sure it was thorns and not fingernails that got me."

He ran a hand through his hair as he said wearily, "I never said you were a suspect because you're not."

"That's the implication. Why else would you be here?"

"You said it yourself. We're tracking down a lot of people and asking a lot of questions. Time is not on our side.

We can't afford to overlook any possibility no matter how remote. When there's a ticking clock, we have to cast a wide net."

She wasn't buying it. "Why me, specifically? Your explanation made sense before I realized you had no idea that I was at the pub last night. You knew I wasn't a witness so why single me out? Why waste precious time driving all the way over here when you could be out there looking for Thora?" Her mouth tightened. "Someone pointed a finger at me, didn't they? I still have friends in the department, but I've also made enemies. Who sent you here, Will?"

She was starting to work up a good head of steam. Will couldn't say that he blamed her, but the last thing he needed was to lose control of the situation. He kept his voice purposely calm, almost dismissive as he explained his predicament. "It's not like that. I'm only here because certain information was brought to my attention and either I came knocking on your door or someone else would. This seemed the best option. Just a casual chat between old friends."

Her eyebrows soared at that. "What's the information? If someone is making accusations, overt or otherwise, I have a right to know the identity of my accuser. You tell me *exactly* why you're here or this conversation is about to get very loud and extremely unpleasant."

Will glanced across the street where a neighbor watering her yard with a garden hose stood watching them. He lowered his voice as he turned away from her prying eyes. "Thora's sister told me about a discussion the two of you had a while back."

"Claire Hartley is the reason you're here?" She looked utterly bewildered. "Wait. Are you talking about what happened at that party last winter?"

"Claire said you two had an illuminating conversation."

Elise winced. "More like the equivalent of a drunk dial." She seemed genuinely embarrassed about the incident. He could see a faint blush beneath her freckles. "Talk about making a mountain out of a molehill. Everything said that night was meaningless. I got hammered and shot my mouth off. End of story."

"We've all been there," he muttered.

Her chin came up. "And yet you were perfectly willing to come over here and interrogate me based on a one-sided account of a drunken conversation."

"This is hardly an interrogation," he said. "I agree, the information Claire provided is thin, but there's another component you may not be aware of. We've reason to believe the person who took Thora has a grudge against me. Claire seems to think you've still got a chip on your shoulder from our breakup. Do you?"

She looked as if she wanted to deny the contention, then shrugged. "You know how it is. You get strung along for months then dumped. Tends to leave a bad taste."

Will canted his head. "And here I thought we had a mutual parting of the ways."

"You would think that."

"What's that supposed to mean?"

"Nothing." She moved back to the edge of the porch and leaned a shoulder against a post. "You never answered *my* question. Do you think I'm capable of something so heinous as kidnapping a woman and burying her alive?"

"Of course I don't. I'm just trying to do my job, Elise."

"Then I'll make it easy for you. Since you've already pissed me off, you may as well ask any other questions you have that I shouldn't take personally."

The sarcasm was thick with that one. The whole conversation was starting to leave a bad taste for Will. "What time did you arrive at the pub last night?"

"Eight thirty, nine. I ordered a beer at the bar and went to the backroom to shoot some pool. The tables were full and there was a line. You know me. I've never been one to watch and wait my turn, so I left early and went straight home. Alone."

He resisted the urge to glance over his shoulder at that open window. "What time was this?"

"Ten-ish."

"You said you saw Thora at the pub?"

"I caught a glimpse of someone I thought was her. She was seated at a table with a large group of people I didn't know."

"You didn't talk to her?"

She sighed and crossed her arms. "Why would I talk to her? I haven't seen her since college, and we were little more than acquaintances back then. We had a couple of classes together and that's it. I doubt she even remembers me."

Will studied her expression, intrigued by the flicker of conflicting emotions she couldn't quite conceal. "Claire seems to think you and Thora were rivals."

"Rivals for what? You? Don't flatter yourself." She sounded even more irritated. "Besides, everyone on that campus knew the two of you were joined at the hip. No one in their right mind would have tried to come between that."

"Let's go back to last night."

She smirked. "Why? Is the conversation making you uncomfortable? Par for the course. You've always been good at dodging and deflecting. Not to mention, cutting and running."

He ignored her taunt. "Did you happen to notice if Thora was still seated with her group when you left?"

"No, but I wasn't keeping tabs."

"Did anyone see you leave?"

"I didn't make an announcement, but I'm a regular at Molly's. If you recall, I'm the one who introduced you to the place. I'm sure if you ask around someone will remember my departure."

Will removed another copy of the computer rendering from his pocket. "Did you see this man last night? He would have been seated at the bar."

She scanned the image and glanced up. "Who is he?"

"A person of interest," Will said. "We don't yet know his name."

Her anger faded and she once again became a cop. "You think he had something to do with Thora's kidnapping?"

"That's what we're trying to find out."

"I don't remember seeing him, but the rendering is pretty generic." She studied the likeness for another long moment. "Mildly attractive. Hair not too long, not too short. No facial hair, no noticeable scars, piercings or tattoos. He's almost too nondescript. Nothing about him would have stood out in a crowd except for his eyes." She glanced up. "He has that deranged, Charles Manson kind of stare."

Will remembered only too well the concentrated focus of the stranger's gaze as he'd watched Thora in the bar mirror. If only he'd said something, done something. If only he'd stuck around to follow the guy outside.

Elise handed him the rendering and straightened. "I didn't see him. Not that I remember. Are we done now?"

"We're done." He folded the image and stuffed it in his pocket. "Sorry for the interruption." He glanced toward the open window. "I don't blame you for being upset, but—"

"Yes, I know. It's not personal. You're just doing your job." She moved past him to pull back the screen door. "You keep telling yourself that and you might actually start to believe it."

"Elise?"

She paused.

"Why did you tell Claire Hartley you were forced out of Criminal Investigations? I was told you asked to be transferred."

She turned slowly to face him. "Told by whom? You were my commanding officer. You had the last word."

He shrugged. "I thought you'd gone over my head. I didn't make a fuss because it seemed to be what you wanted."

"Then you should have asked *me* what I wanted. But you didn't, did you, Will? It was easier to believe what you wanted to believe."

"It wasn't like that."

Her composure cracked. "It was exactly like that. From the moment you decided to become a cop, the powers-that-be had big plans for you. You were fast-tracked right out of the academy. One advancement after another. The youngest officer to ever make lieutenant and now you're a deputy chief at thirty-five. Unheard of. But not for you. You're their golden boy. A legacy. The handsome son of a fallen hero. You couldn't ask for a more perfect face for the Belfort Police Department. Me? I was just in your way."

Will frowned. "I never thought that."

"Maybe not, but you have to admit my departure smoothed things over for you. No loudmouthed ex-girlfriend in CID trash-talking your sterling reputation." She pushed open the wooden door and stepped inside, letting the screen door snap shut between them.

"Regardless of what happened between us, I never wanted you to leave Criminal Investigations," Will said. "You were a good detective."

She glared at him through the screen. "I'm still a good detective. Far better than anyone ever gave me credit for."

WILL CIRCLED THE NEIGHBORHOOD, giving Elise enough time to go back inside before he turned down her street and parked behind a utility van at the curb. The neighbor with the water hose took note of his return, but he hoped the large vehicle would give him sufficient cover from the other side of the street in case Elise happened to glance out her front window.

While he waited, he mulled over their conversation. Her bitterness had taken him by surprise, even though Claire had warned him about the chip on Elise's shoulder. Their breakup last year had seemed amicable at the time. She'd pretty much shrugged off his apology and agreed the relationship had run its course. Maybe he'd misread her. Maybe that was another case of him taking the easy way out. Believing what he wanted to believe. Had he really been that much of a clueless jerk? No wonder Elise resented his career advancements. The promotion after their split must have seemed like a slap in the face. But nursing a grudge over a breakup was a far cry from kidnapping his old girlfriend and burying her alive.

If Elise's time line checked out, she'd left the pub before Thora. On the surface, his trip to see her seemed like a monumental waste of time. He'd learned nothing concrete to suggest she was in any way culpable. But something apart from her lingering animosity bothered Will. He'd caught flickers of rage in her eyes. A cold, righteous fury that the whole department had done her wrong on his behalf.

There was also the matter of fresh scratches on her neck and arms...

The shadow of a visitor he'd glimpsed inside her house...

What's going on with you, Elise?

He called the station to check in while he waited. The Tech Unit was still going through the videos. Thora's kidnapper had used an untraceable number to send the text messages, but triangulation had placed the phone downtown at the time they'd been sent, miles away from any wooded areas. Officers were searching dumpsters and gutters near the location in the hopes of finding the discarded burner so that the serial number could be traced back to the point of purchase. That was another long shot. Whoever had taken Thora apparently knew how to cover their tracks. Only one of the security cameras outside the pub had been operational. Whether by luck or careful planning, the kidnapper had managed to evade the working camera.

His gaze shot back to Elise's front door. A man wearing gray slacks and a white shirt stepped out on the porch. He kept his back to the street as he spoke to someone—presumably Elise—through the screen. Will fished in the console for the compact pair of binoculars he kept handy. He lifted them to his eyes and adjusted the focus ring. He still couldn't get a look at the man's face, but his rigid posture suggested the conversation was anything but casual. He stood with his feet slightly apart, hands jammed into his pockets.

After a moment, Elise stepped out on the porch to join him, letting the screen door slam shut behind her. She was fully dressed now in jeans and a white T-shirt. She appeared just as tense as her partner, jabbing her finger in the air as he backed toward the steps. Will rolled down his window but he was too far away to catch anything other than the muted drift of their angry voices on the breeze.

The argument had attracted the neighbor with the garden hose. She seemed to forget about her task as she stared unabashedly across the street. Then slowly she turned to glance in Will's direction. For an anxious moment, he thought she might head down the sidewalk and give away his position. Instead, she sat down on her porch steps and fanned her face with a straw hat as she pretended to take a breather.

Elise and her companion seemed oblivious to their audience. They argued for several seconds longer and then the man turned and ran down the steps. Elise hurried after him, briefly clutching his arm before he shook her off and strode toward the street. When he emerged from the deep shade of her front yard, Will finally got a look at his face.

He lowered the binoculars and gaped in surprise. *What the hell...?*

Then he lifted them once more and adjusted the focus as he followed the man across the street to a vintage white Mercedes parked beneath an oak tree.

Logan Neville unlocked the car door and climbed inside. He took a moment to put on his sunglasses and check the rearview mirror before he pulled away from the curb. Will slumped in the seat as Neville sped past him but the man stared straight ahead, seemingly intent on making a quick getaway.

Will tracked the car in his mirror until Neville turned at the first intersection and disappeared. Then he straightened, once again toying with the focus ring to bring Elise's front porch into view. She stood at the top of the steps staring back at him.

Chapter Six

With each second that passed, Thora grew weaker. The influx of fresh air from the surface kept her alive, but the heat inside the box had become unbearable. Her legs had started to cramp and hunger pains had long since given way to a fresh wave of nausea. Her skin and clothing were soaked with sweat. Perspiration would help keep her body cooled for now, but she was starting to experience signs of dehydration.

She ran her tongue over her dry lips and tried not to dwell on the passage of each moment. Time simultaneously slowed to a crawl and rushed headlong toward an inevitable conclusion. Without water, the heat would soon do her in. How long since her last drink? Could have been minutes, could have been hours. She had started intermittently drumming on the air tube and lid in the same specific sequence her abductor had used: tap, tap…pause…tap, tap. Nothing had come back to her yet. No answering tap. No trickling water. No stolen keepsake. Nothing but the rasp of her own breathing to keep her company.

Placing her mouth to the air tube, she drew the warm air slowly into her lungs and tried to stay focused on her self-assigned tasks. Namely, keeping fear and panic at bay while she figured out who had imprisoned her and why. Anything to help keep her sane while she waited for someone to come to her rescue. Or not.

Where are you, Will?

Was he even looking for her yet?

Thora could only guess at the time. Surely enough hours had gone by and her mother would have become concerned when she couldn't reach her. Maddie Graham had always been a worrier and Thora had never been so deeply thankful for her mother's neurosis as she was in that moment. Maddie wouldn't let too much time go by before she notified the police. And if she couldn't get anyone to listen, she'd enlist Claire's help. Her sister had a natural proclivity for drama and contrariness. She wouldn't hesitate to drive back from Houston and raise holy hell if she thought a loved one was in trouble. She wouldn't give up or back down until someone agreed to look for Thora.

As soon as the police found the Volvo at the pub, an alarm would surely be sounded. Or had someone driven her car back to the townhouse to delay discovery of the abduction? What if the kidnapper had used her phone to send reassuring text messages to Claire and her mother? What if nobody would start looking for her until she failed to turn up for brunch with her mother on Sunday? She wouldn't last that long. She might not make it through another day.

Thora still wanted to believe that Will would somehow find her. He had the power, resources and determination to make things happen. But hope had started to dwindle and despair once again needled at her. Where was he at that moment? At the station marshaling his forces, or at home relaxing with a beer and a ball game? Or sleeping in with the woman he'd brought to the pub last night?

Stop obsessing over Will Dresden. Concentrate on the investigation. Figure out who did this to you and why.

Although if she died in the box, did it really matter who had put her there?

Yes, it matters. Puzzle it out.

She ran down a list of questions.

Did you see anyone in the parking lot before you were grabbed? Did you hear anything other than the distorted voice in your ear?

Did anyone follow you out of the pub? Think!

The queasiness pushed up into her throat, making it difficult to breathe through the tube. Through sheer force of will, she forced back the nausea and rapped on the lid. Tap, tap…pause…tap, tap.

Don't waste your energy. The kidnapper isn't coming back. Now concentrate! Go back to the beginning. Go back to the pub.

She closed her eyes and drifted back in time, back into that crowded, noisy bar with the cloying smell of perfume and aftershave mingling with the malty smell of beer. It was like having an out-of-body experience. Like watching a movie. Thora could see herself seated at the table with her colleagues. Everyone was talking and laughing, having a good time. She observed herself going through the motions. Sipping her wine. Smiling politely at the person across the table from her. Happy on the outside, miserable on the inside. *Just get up and leave. Go home. Five minutes can save your life.*

But, of course, she couldn't get up and leave. She couldn't go back in time and change the past. The abduction had happened. She was living through it at that very moment. All she could do was lie on her back in that sweltering box and try to solve the mystery of her capture.

Relax. Let the memories unfold without forcing them. Stay in the pub. Focus on the people with whom you came into contact. What did you notice about the interactions?

She had remained seated at the table with her colleagues for most of the evening, trying to converse over the background noises. She'd only left the table once to visit the ladies' room after finishing her wine. *Never, ever leave a glass unattended in a bar.* She hadn't. At that point in the evening, the drug had yet to be administered, of that she was certain. She'd been steady on her feet and keenly observant as she made her way through the crowd.

Strange how everything had been hazy when she'd first awakened in the box, but now she could remember that walk to the ladies' room so vividly she wondered if she might be dreaming. Or hallucinating.

Focus!

She'd scanned the faces at the bar and taken note of someone coming out of the restroom. She'd even tracked Will and his date out of the corner of her eye. Her situational awareness had remained high at that point. Or so she'd thought. But had she missed something? A figure slipping through the crowd behind her? A lifted phone, a subtle nod to an accomplice?

Except for the unsettling stare of the stranger in the mirror, she'd had no hint of trouble at that point in the evening. Even when someone had entered the restroom behind her, she hadn't been concerned. The pub was busy and there were multiple stalls. People would come in and out all night.

But…who had come in directly behind her? That struck her as important, so she needed to remember.

She squeezed her eyes closed and tried to corral her scattered thoughts.

Breathe in, breathe out. Relax. Focus.

Yes, now she had it.

When she came out of the stall, a woman with red, curly hair and vivid blue eyes had stood at one of the sinks refreshing her lipstick. She wore large hoop earrings that tangled in her ringlets and a pair of faded jeans that fit her athletic physique like a custom-made glove. As Thora stepped up to the adjoining sink to wash her hands, their gazes met briefly in the mirror.

The hand holding the lipstick tube paused. The redhead said in surprise, "Thora? Thora Graham? Wow. I heard you were back in town, but I never expected to run into you here. How in the world are you?"

"I'm well, thank you." The woman's effusiveness made her uncomfortable. She placed her palms underneath the automatic soap dispenser while she desperately searched her memory banks. The redhead looked familiar, but she couldn't place her and Thora always hated that awkward moment before a name came back to her.

Their gazes met again in the mirror. The woman smiled, but her eyes were coolly assessing. "You don't remember me, do you?"

Thora rinsed her hands and reached for a paper towel. "I'm sorry. I'm terrible with names, but you do look familiar."

"No need to apologize. It's been a long time." The woman finished applying her lipstick and pressed her lips together. "Elise Barrett. You and I were at U-SET together about a hundred years ago. We always seemed to end up in the same criminology classes."

Thora said in relief. "Of course. Elise. It has been a while, hasn't it?" She discarded the paper towel, wondering how long she would be expected to stay and chat. She wanted nothing more than to go back outside, pay for her wine and go home. But wasn't this the kind of thing a normal person was expected to do when returning to her hometown? Reconnect with old acquaintances? For her mother's and sister's sakes—and for her own mental health—she decided to make the effort. She smiled at Elise's reflection. "You've changed your hair. The curls threw me."

Elise wound a corkscrew around one finger and released it. "You wouldn't believe how long it used to take to straighten this mess. I don't bother these days."

"It suits you," Thora said for lack of anything better to contribute.

"Thanks. I guess we've all gone through changes since college, some of them not so trivial." She paused, her attention still captured by Thora's reflection. "I was sorry to hear about your husband."

Thora frowned. How did Elise Barrett know about Michael? "It was a long time ago."

"Some things you don't get over no matter how much time goes by. It was a car accident, wasn't it?" She must have noticed Thora's closed expression because she looked instantly contrite. "Sorry. Belfort is still a small town in a lot of ways. Your sister and I have mutual friends. You know how it is. People talk."

Maybe she would need to have a word with Claire about discretion. Thora didn't like people prying into her personal life, especially when it came to her dead husband. She considered it a gross violation of his privacy, too, and shutting down idle curiosity was the last and only way she had of protecting him. So she did what she could in the moment, which was to quickly change the subject. "You stayed in Belfort after college?"

Elise sighed. "Yes. I never intended to, but you know what they say about the best laid plans. I was accepted into the police academy after graduation, and I've been with the Belfort PD ever since."

"That's great."

"Is it?" She shrugged. "I started out in Patrol and then worked my way up to detective in the Criminal Investigations Division. Now I'm Internal Affairs. You know, the cop that other cops love to hate."

"I'm sure that's not true."

"Oh, it is. The level of vitriol would surprise you." She dropped the lipstick in her bag and turned to face Thora. "What about you? What made you decide to come back to Belfort after all these years?"

How much longer before she could politely excuse herself and go back to the table? Thora resisted the urge to edge toward the door. "My family still lives here. When the university offered me a position as adjunct professor, I decided it was time for a change."

"From Quantico to Belfort. That's quite a big change," Elise observed. "I would never have expected that of you."

"Why?"

She leaned back against the sink. "You were so passionate about the FBI back in college. You had your future and career all mapped out and you weren't about to let anything or anyone stop you."

Even the love of my life. "As you said, the best laid plans."

Elise cocked her head. "You don't find it boring? Surely teaching at a small college in the armpit of Texas can't compete with the work you did at the FBI."

Thora had a feeling the woman was fishing for some kind of response. The conversation was starting to drift from uncomfortable into disquieting, but possibly she was overreacting. She'd forgotten how casually nosy people in small towns could be. Well-meaning for the most part, but invasive nonetheless.

"You seem to have the wrong idea about my work," she said. "Most of my time was spent researching and analyzing data in a basement cubicle. It was rewarding but rarely exciting."

Elise looked skeptical. "I find that hard to believe. From what I hear, you were involved in at least one intense manhunt that spanned the better part of a decade. I can't imagine what it would be like to devote that many years of your life to tracking a monster like the Weatherman. It must have seemed at times like you were trapped in a nightmare."

"You learn to cope."

"I guess." Elise gave an exaggerated shudder. "I read somewhere that you were instrumental in his capture. You were the one who alerted the local authorities to be on the lookout for an underground bunker or storm cellar on his property. Turns out, that's exactly where he was hiding."

"You seem to know quite a lot about the case," Thora noted.

Elise smiled. "I'll admit to a particular fascination for the Weatherman. Our proximity to I-10 makes it likely that he traveled through Belfort dozens if not hundreds of times during his killing sprees. There was even speculation that he might have a dumping ground around here somewhere. I've often wondered if I might have encountered him at some point, in a bar or convenience store. You never know."

"It's possible," Thora said.

"From what I've read, he's extremely charismatic and manipulative. Have you ever met him?"

"No."

She looked surprised. "I would have thought you'd want to talk to him if for no other reason than to satisfy your curiosity."

"I know all I need to know about James Ellis Ridgeway," Thora replied.

Elise gave a vague nod. "Can I ask you a question?"

Thora had tried very hard to put that case behind her, but the Weatherman was all anyone ever wanted to talk about when they found out who she was and what she did. She nodded politely.

"During the time you were hunting Ridgeway, did you ever worry that he might also be tracking you?"

"What do you mean?"

"He's intelligent and surprisingly sophisticated for his level of education. He claimed to have contacts in various law enforcement agencies all across the country, including the FBI. That's how he eluded capture for so many years. If he knew about you, about your work, what would have stopped him from coming after you? Hypothetically speaking, of course."

"A lot of people worked that case," Thora said. "Why would he target me?"

"Because you were the one who had him all figured out."

Her definitive tone sent an inexplicable chill up Thora's spine. "That's giving me too much credit. Or too little, depending on your perspective. If I had him all figured out, I would hope we'd have caught him a lot sooner than we did."

"I see your point, but still." Her smile seemed cagey, as if her outer friendliness didn't quite match her internal motivation. "I think I would have had a hard time sleeping at night knowing he was out there. Especially after your husband died. Did you ever wonder if Ridgeway might have somehow been responsible for the accident?"

The notion jarred Thora even though the thought had crossed her mind from time to time. The local police and her colleagues at the Bureau had assured her Michael's car accident was just that—an accident. The driver that hit him had fled the scene and was found days later in his garage with a self-inflicted gunshot wound to his head. The investigation had revealed a long history of alcohol and substance abuse, multiple DUIs, driving with a suspended license— case closed. But something hadn't seemed quite right to Thora. At the time, Ridgeway was still three years away from capture. It wasn't as unlikely as some of her colleagues wanted her to believe that he'd uncovered her identity.

"Food for thought." Elise straightened from the sink. "Not to change the subject, but have you talked to Will Dresden since you've been home? You two were pretty tight back in the day."

"That was back in the day," Thora said. "We didn't keep in touch after college."

"Then you don't know—"

The door swung open and one of the young women who'd been involved in the earlier altercation came in. Baylee Fisher froze, her hand still on the door as her gaze darted back and forth from Thora to Elise.

She focused in on Elise for a moment before she said, "Sorry. Am I interrupting something?"

"Not at all." Thora turned back to Elise. "It was nice catching up."

The redhead nodded. "I'm sure we'll see each other again soon."

THE MEMORIES WERE coming fast and furious now, but Thora wasn't sure she could trust her recall. She was in bad shape mentally and physically. Her mouth, lips and eyes had gone dry. Her head pounded and she had intermittent spells of dizziness and confusion. All signs of dehydration and heat stroke. For all she knew, her memories might well be hallucinations. Sometimes they were almost too raw and intense. But whether real or fantasy, the visions were the only thing keeping her calm when the instinct for survival demanded that she claw her way out of the box. She knew that even the slightest physical exertion would use up too much air and energy and yet she still had to guard against a natural inclination to fight.

She lay motionless with her hands balled at her sides and gave herself a pep talk. She could do this. Above all else, she had to remain focused. She had to be smart. She was running out of time and she still hadn't figured out the identity of her kidnapper. She'd come into contact with a number of people at the pub and as far as she was concerned, all were suspects. But the name that had popped into her head when she'd first awakened in the box was Logan Neville. That had to mean something. *Dig deeper.*

Returning to the table after her trip to the restroom, she'd had every intention of saying good-night to her colleagues. To her chagrin, Neville had seated himself next to her. If her drink had, in fact, been drugged, his proximity in hindsight seemed significant, if not downright ominous.

Thora struggled to recall the details of their brief encounter. She must have ordered a second glass of wine at some point, but why would she have done so when she'd been determined to leave? Something about a toast…

Yes, that was it. Before she could escape, Neville had insisted on making a birthday toast to the colleague for whom the celebration was in honor. He'd called for a fresh round of drinks for everyone at the table, which was how Thora had ended up with a second glass of wine. The logical place to spike a drink without notice was at the bar, but Neville's positioning himself in the chair next to her now seemed deliberately strategic. Thora had sipped gingerly. Was that why she hadn't experienced immediate side effects? Because the drug had entered her system in such minute amounts?

Had she noticed anything dubious in Neville's conduct? Had he distracted her at any point? Or had he seated himself at her side so that he could monitor her reaction to the already drugged wine? Thora tried to analyze his behavior in retrospect. Had he watched her closely as she drank, perhaps losing patience when she allowed the liquid to barely touch her lips?

"I feel we've gotten off on the wrong foot," he'd said after the toast. "I've always believed in the direct approach so I'm just going to come right out and ask. Have I said or done something to offend you?"

"Why would you think that?"

"Call it intuition." The corners of his mouth twitched. "You don't like me much, do you?"

She shrugged. "I hardly know you. I don't have feelings for you one way or another."

"That's blunt, but I appreciate your honesty. Maybe you would be better able to form an opinion if you didn't spend so much of your time alone in your office."

Was he hitting on her? The very thought made Thora cringe. He was elegant and attractive in a scholarly sort of way, but his appeal was lost on her. "When I'm on campus, I like to work," she said. "It's nothing personal."

He picked up his glass of scotch. "Let me try this again. I'm hoping we can bury the hatchet over a drink. I'll be the first to admit, I haven't been as welcoming as I should have been. My only excuse is that I'm an old dog and we tend to be a bit territorial."

His candor surprised her. "I'm not here to upset the status quo. My contract is only for a year. We don't have to be friends, but we don't need to be enemies, either."

"To keeping the peace." He clicked his glass against hers, then raised the scotch to his lips, pausing for a fraction of a second until she did the same. He returned his drink to the table and wrapped both hands around the glass as he studied her with a curious smile. "Now that we've sufficiently wiped the slate clean, I wonder if I could ask a favor."

Thora was immediately on guard. "That all depends on what the favor is."

"I have a podcast called *Exploring the Criminal Mind.* Our guests span the gamut from writers to forensic experts to psychics. I'm sure you've heard of it. It's become quite popular in recent months."

He didn't frame it as a question, but an assumption that, yes, of course she knew of his podcast and all his other impressive endeavors. "I've heard of it."

"Would you be willing to come on as a guest?"

She hadn't expected that. He'd taken her completely by surprise. "That's…really not my kind of thing."

"Oh, I think with your experience and expertise it could be exactly your sort of thing. Think of it as a lively, sometimes controversial chat among peers. You'd be surprised how quickly an hour can fly by."

"I'm sure it would be interesting, but like I said, not my thing."

He seemed reluctant to take no for an answer. "You might change your mind when you hear the topic. I'll be interviewing a freelance journalist who's writing a book about the Weatherman."

"Is that so?" Now Thora understood his persistence.

"He's followed the case for years and has formulated

some interesting theories regarding Ridgeway and his victims. Aside from you, he probably knows more about the Weatherman and his modus operandi than anyone else in the world. The two of you together would make for a dynamic discussion."

"I'm afraid my answer is still no."

"What if I told you this reporter recently visited Ridgeway at the Donaldson Correctional Facility in Alabama?" His tone sounded conspiratorial. "Would you be at all interested in *that* conversation?"

"Not really. I've heard all I need to from James Ellis Ridgeway."

Neville leaned in. "What if I told you that your name was mentioned in the course of their visit?"

Her heart thudded. "In what way?"

"Be a guest on my podcast and find out."

She couldn't tell if he was bluffing or not, but something told her she was being baited. "I don't speak publicly about any of the cases I've worked on, in particular the Weatherman. I have a rule against glamorizing monsters."

He looked as if he wanted to argue, but then he shrugged. "That's a pity. There's so much to be gleaned from predators like Ridgeway and from the hunters who track them." He lifted his drink, observing her over the rim of his glass. "Hunters like you."

Something flickered in his eyes before he could disguise the emotion behind his smile. The brief lapse unnerved Thora and she reminded herself that Logan Neville wasn't to be trusted.

"I never thought of myself as anything more than an analyst," she said.

Whatever she'd glimpsed behind his smile was gone. He said without a hint of guile, "Which is exactly why I'd like to ask another favor. My team and I are currently working on a cold case that the local police, in their typical fashion, badly bungled. A nine-year-old boy disappeared on his way home from school. The child vanished in broad daylight on a crowded street. The investigators concentrated so much of their time and effort on the boy's stepfather that they let the trail go cold. I've obtained copies of the official police file. Whether you agree to do my podcast or not, I wonder if you'd be willing to take a look at the case."

"How did you get a copy of the file?"

"Mostly by submitting a request, but the file I have is incomplete. It seems there are sealed records connected to the case. If I told you I have a confidential source in the department willing to provide access, would you take a look?"

"I'll think about it," Thora said.

"Don't take too long. I'll be going away for a few days and I'd like to have an answer before I leave. The boy's family has been in limbo for ten years. They deserve justice. And the lead detective that botched the case finally needs to be held to account. Instead, he's been elevated to the position of deputy chief."

Thora said in shock, "Are you talking about Will Dresden?"

A brow lifted. "Why, yes. Do you know him?"

"I used to."

"Then your insight could be invaluable. You know where to find me when you make a decision."

The conversation had ended abruptly. Neville had excused himself from the table and rejoined Addison March at the bar. They made very little effort to disguise the intimate nature of their relationship. Neville's hand had rested at the small of the young woman's back as she'd leaned in to whisper in his ear. While she spoke to him, her gaze had vectored in on Thora and she'd stared boldly before turning to disappear into the back room. Neville took out his phone, thumbed a text message and then followed her.

Upon reflection, it all seemed choreographed to Thora. And very suspect. The brief conversation with Logan Neville. The chance meeting in the bathroom with Elise Barrett. Even the scuffle between Addison March and Baylee Fisher earlier in the evening. Everything had meaning. Thora could look back now and recognize the undercurrents flowing in the pub throughout the evening. At the time, though, she'd been oblivious to anything but her desire to escape the noise and go home.

She'd left her wine unfinished, settled her tab and stood. The slight dizziness had been her first clue that all was not well. Why hadn't it occurred to her then that she'd been drugged? *Because no one believes it will happen to them.* Even someone with her training and experience could fall victim to a false sense of security. All she remembered feeling in that moment was relief that the evening had finally come to an end. And if she were truthful, she'd thought about Will and his companion. She'd wondered in passing if they'd gone to his place or hers and how serious they might be.

None of her business, of course. She'd had her chance with Will Dresden. *You can't go home again.*

Except she had and look where it had gotten her. She pressed her hand against the top of the container, confirming to herself that her captivity wasn't a hallucination or a dream. The box was real. Would her captor come back with more water or had she been abandoned for good? Tap, tap… pause…tap, tap. *Keep at it.* Tap, tap…pause…tap, tap. Each sequence more desperate than the last.

Even the air from the pipe couldn't keep her alive for

long. Little by little she felt herself slipping away. The only way to save herself was to mentally leave the box.

She pictured herself once more in the pub, making her way through the crowd to the entrance. Had someone followed her out? Wait...*wait*...

Someone had tailed her to the door and called her name. She'd turned so quickly the room had started to spin. A female face swam before her. Slowly the young woman's features came into focus.

"Professor Graham? Are you okay? You don't look so good." When Thora didn't answer, the woman said, "It's Baylee Fisher. I was in your Psychology of Criminal Behavior class. Tuesdays and Thursdays? I was wondering if I could have a word."

"I was just on my way out—"

"I don't mean *here*!" She quickly glanced around. "Maybe we could meet in your office."

"You can stop by on Monday morning."

"I don't think this can wait." She sounded anxious, almost frightened. "I overheard something I shouldn't have. I wouldn't bother you except..." She cast another furtive glance over her shoulder. "This might be *really* important."

"Be at my office at nine tomorrow morning. I don't usually take meetings on Saturday, but I'll make an exception."

Baylee looked relieved. "Thank you." She backed away. "Just one more thing. *Be careful.*"

With that, she was gone.

The memory flitted away.

Thora lay in the box and berated herself for not having remembered the cryptic warning earlier, but she had little control over the amnesia. Her memories came and went. She was still laboring under the influence of the drug. She felt feverish, delirious. *Will, where are you?*

*He isn't coming. Why should he? You left him, remember?
You chose your career over him. What makes you think he's
even looking for you?*

*Yes, I chose my career, and I've regretted that decision
for thirteen long years.*

She couldn't allow herself to think that way. It seemed
disloyal to Michael's memory. He'd been a good husband
and she'd loved him. She wouldn't betray what they'd had
by thinking about another man in her last hours.

Instead, she concentrated on compiling a list of suspects,
Logan Neville and the stranger at the bar being the two most
obvious. She added anyone else she could remember from
the pub, including Elise Barrett, Addison March and Baylee
Fisher. And reluctantly, she added James Ellis Ridgeway.

With the last of her waning strength, she tried to determine means, motive and opportunity for each of the suspects, but a disturbing thought suddenly occurred to her.
What if the kidnapper had never set foot in the pub? What
if her abduction had been completely random? A case of
being in the wrong place at the wrong time like so many
of James Ellis Ridgeway's victims. That would complicate
her investigation immeasurably. That would make figuring out who had abducted her in the time she had left next
to impossible.

Chapter Seven

Will was on his way back to the station when he got a call from Thora's neighbor. After she explained who she was, she said in a low, anxious tone, "You said to call if that guy showed up again. The one I saw outside the townhouse next door. He's here right now."

Will's hands tightened around the wheel as he automatically checked the rearview mirror. "What's he doing?"

"I can't see him at the moment. But when he first walked up, he rang Thora's doorbell. Then he went around the building. He hasn't come back yet."

"But you think he's still on the premises?"

"Unless he took the long way around to get back to the parking lot." She hesitated, then said. "I have a question for you, Deputy Chief. Some police officers were here earlier. I recognized the CSU patches on their uniforms. They came with all their cases and they stayed for quite some time. I'm sorry, but before we go any further, I'd really like to know what is going on. I'm right next door, and I live alone. Should I be worried?"

"There's no reason to think you're in any danger," Will said.

"That's not very reassuring. Can you at least tell me what happened to Thora? That's her name, right? Is she—"

"She's alive. That's all I can say at the moment."

The neighbor expelled a sharp breath. "I think you just told me more than you meant to. Did this guy do something to her?"

"Right now, we just want to talk to him."

"If he's harmed her and the police know it, why would he come back to her house?"

"I need you to stay focused," Will said. "Take a breath and stay on the phone. I'm going to put you on hold while I get a patrol car over to your complex." He used the radio in his vehicle to alert dispatch while he whipped off the road into a parking lot and turned in the direction of the townhouses. "Okay," he said to the neighbor. "Tell me exactly what you saw when he came to the door. It's important."

"I was at my front window when the police left. I'm not usually the nosy sort. I don't care what my neighbors do as long as they leave me alone. But a Crime Scene Unit gets your attention, particularly after our earlier visit. They loaded up their cases, got in a van and drove away. That's when I spotted him coming up the walkway. I don't think the timing was a coincidence. He must have been watching her townhouse and waiting for the police to leave."

"Did you see his vehicle this time?"

"No. I'm guessing he either parked outside the gate or in front of another building. Which, in itself, seems sketchy."

"Are you sure he was the same man you saw last Thursday?"

"I'm one hundred percent positive. I don't forget faces and I got a good look at him both times. He was dressed the same as before—nice pants and shirt, hair longish and kind of messy. If you only saw him in passing, you wouldn't think twice about him. But I noticed two things straightaway. He acted like he was in a hurry, and he kept glancing over his shoulder as if he thought someone might be following him. Or maybe he was worried about being seen in front of Thora's townhouse. My first inclination was to go outside and confront him. A gated community is supposed to keep out creeps like him. But then I remembered my previous impression and thought better of it. As I said, I live alone and guys like that are unpredictable."

"You did the right thing," Will said. "Has he come back around to the front of the complex yet?"

"Hold on, let me take a look." She was only gone for a couple of seconds. "I can't see him, but something just occurred to me. He probably rang Thora's doorbell just to make sure all the cops were gone. He already knew she wasn't home. If someone had come to the door, he would have given them the same line he tried to feed me the other day. He's an old friend, been trying to get in touch, etcetera. I bet the reason he went around the building was to try and find a way inside. Each unit has a walled courtyard in the back. He could break a window and no one would see him." She lowered her voice as if afraid of being overheard in her own place. "For all we know, he could already be inside her house."

She was starting to get a little worked up again so Will said, "Don't worry. I'm only a few minutes away and the first patrol car should be pulling up at the complex any second now. In the meantime, stay inside and lock your doors. And keep away from the windows. Whatever you do, don't confront him. He isn't after you, but you're right to worry that he could be unpredictable. We also don't want to tip him off before we have officers on the scene."

"Okay, just please make sure he doesn't come back here again. I don't like the idea of that guy skulking about the grounds. I have a hard enough time sleeping at night."

Will ended the call and tossed his phone aside as he checked his mirrors and changed lanes. His foot was heavy on the accelerator, but Saturday afternoon traffic had started to back up on the main thoroughfare. He took as many shortcuts and backstreets as he could and arrived before the first patrol car. Not surprising since almost every available unit had been reassigned to search for Thora.

Entering the gate code on the keypad, he let himself in and parked next to the neighbor's car directly in front of Thora's building. He pocketed his phone, checked his firearm and approached the building cautiously, using the lush landscaping as cover. Easing up to the front window, he glanced inside, then jerked back when he caught sight of a moving shadow.

He waited a few seconds, then chanced another glance. The man stood with his back to the window going through Thora's desk. Will retreated and tried the front door. It was locked. Which meant whoever was inside Thora's townhouse had probably broken a rear window as the neighbor suspected.

Will hurried around the building, pausing to check his surroundings as he approached the gate. No one was around. Under the circumstances, that was a good thing. Bystanders were always a worry.

Peering through the iron rods into the courtyard, he scanned the enclosed area. He didn't see any broken glass on the brick floor, but the back door stood ajar. Unless the CSU team had left it open, which was unlikely, the suspect had either jimmied the door or picked the lock.

He released the latch and the gate swung inward on creaking hinges. The sound stopped him cold, and he waited a beat before entering the courtyard. Sensing an unwelcome presence, a dog in a nearby unit started to bark. Between the excited canine and the squeaky gate, Will had little hope of a stealthy approach. He flattened himself against the outside wall and listened as he unholstered his weapon. The smart play here was to stay put and wait for backup. He had no idea what he might walk into. But if the intruder had heard the dog and the gate, he might get spooked, go out the front door and get to his vehicle before Will could catch him. He wouldn't take that risk. Not when every second was so vitally important to Thora's survival.

Pushing the door open with his toe, Will entered silently and eased through the small laundry room into the kitchen. The townhouse was an open concept design. From the kitchen, he could see straight through the dining room into the living room, but he'd yet to catch another glimpse of the intruder. If he rushed the room, he might still have the element of surprise, but he had no way of knowing whether or not the man was armed. Or whether or not he'd heard Will's approach. He had to assume the affirmative on both counts.

Bracing his weapon with his left hand, he moved quickly through the dining room and into the living room, drawing a bead on the spot where he'd last seen the intruder. No one was at the desk. Will spun, taking in every nook and cranny of the room before moving into the foyer. He checked the front door. Locked. His gaze lifted to the top of the staircase. The suspect must have gone up to the second floor. Did he know Will was in the house or had he gone upstairs looking for something?

Will glanced out the front window. Still no sign of backup, but patrol cars would surely arrive on the scene any minute now. He could plant himself in the living room and wait for the intruder to come back downstairs or he could go up after him. He went up, his footsteps silenced by a thick runner on the hardwood steps. He checked the guest bathroom at the top of the stairs, the first bedroom and then moved down the hallway to Thora's room. He could hear sounds from inside as the man rummaged through her things.

Weapon still drawn, Will planted himself in the doorway. "Police! Don't move. Stay right where you are."

The man was halfway out the open window. He paused and glanced back. Will recognized him instantly as the stranger from the pub. The dark eyes and probing stare were unmistakable.

Will checked the corners of the room from his periphery as he entered. Satisfied that he was dealing with only one suspect, he said, "Move away from the window and keep your hands where I can see them."

The man's gaze remained riveted on Will. He didn't look so much concerned as extremely focused, waiting for an opportunity. "If you want to talk, we can talk, but please put away the weapon first. I don't like guns and we both know you're not going to shoot me, anyway."

His response only served to tick Will off. Anger and adrenaline in a tense situation were never a good mix so he made sure his emotions were firmly under control as he advanced. "You sound awfully certain for a guy staring down the barrel of one of those guns you don't like."

The man's gaze never wavered. "You won't shoot because I have something you want."

"And what is that?"

"Put away the weapon, and I'll tell you."

His smugness wasn't altogether unwarranted. Even if he were to attack, Will would do everything in his power to subdue him without firing a shot. He wasn't about to take out the one person who might be able to lead him to Thora. But the guy's confidence needed to be shaken. "Tell me where she is first and then I'll put away the gun." When the suspect remained unresponsive, Will took aim. "You tell me where she is right now!"

Dead silence.

Will said in a calmer voice, "I don't have to kill you. I can shoot you in a place that will just make you wish you were dead."

"I don't think you'll risk it."

"Try me."

The stranger hesitated for a split second, then pushed away from the window and jumped. Will lunged across the room and glanced down. It was a long way to the ground. He was hoping the fall would temporarily disable or at least slow the man's escape, but he was already scrambling to his feet, apparently unharmed. Another few seconds and he'd be gone. Will did the only thing he could do. He holstered his weapon, swung his body through the window and leaped two stories to the ground behind the suspect. The banana trees broke his fall, but the impact still hurt. Time enough later to worry about injuries. Springing to his feet, he checked his surroundings. The suspect had headed across the landscaped grounds toward the common area and the parking lot beyond. Will took off in a dead run after him.

Hurdling over a metal bench and sprinting around the bank of mailboxes, he tackled the man at the edge of the parking lot. They hit the pavement hard with a barrage of expletives. The second bone-jarring jolt seemed to take the fight out of the suspect. Will rolled him to this stomach and cuffed him. Then he jerked him to his feet, patted him down and spun him around. There was still no doubt in his mind that he was the stranger from the pub.

The adrenaline still spiraled through Will's veins. He took a moment to grapple with his baser instincts as he fished a wallet from the suspect's pocket and checked his ID. If this guy had taken Thora and buried her alive, Will needed to keep his cool in order to get as much information from him as quickly as possible.

"You're Noah Asher?"

"I am."

He held up a current Alabama driver's license. "You still live at this address?"

"I do."

Will closed the wallet but didn't return it. "You're a long way from home, Mr. Asher."

"Farther than you think," he said.

"Meaning?"

He smiled. "Distance isn't always measured in miles, Detective."

"It's Deputy Chief and that's cryptic."

"For some, maybe."

They stood face-to-face for a moment, staring one another down in silence. Then suddenly, it was as if a switch had been flipped. The stranger's demeanor subtly altered, like a chameleon changing colors right before Will's eyes. His expression softened and his posture relaxed. In the space of a heartbeat, the arrogant miscreant in the window seemed to have transformed into a slightly awkward, more compliant everyman. The unlikely metamorphosis fascinated Will. It was almost as if he stood facing an entirely different person. Almost. But even the most sophisticated con man had a tell, and Will knew enough to look for the signs. The glimmer of cold calculation at the back of the eyes. The uncontrollable twitch at the corners of the mouth.

He also knew better than to let down his guard. If anything, he grew more cautious. The guy was up to something.

Will could almost see the wheels turning inside his head as he tried to figure a way out of an arrest.

Will gave him a prompt. "This will all go a lot easier if you just tell me where she is."

Asher dropped his gaze. "I don't know what you're talking about."

"Really? Because you seemed to know before you jumped out that window."

"You surprised me. I said the first thing that popped in my head."

"Just to refresh your memory, you said I wouldn't risk shooting you because you have something I want." Will's voice hardened. "Did you take her?"

"Take who?"

"Enough with the games," Will said in frustration. "You're wasting my time. You know damn well who I'm talking about. Why were you in her townhouse just now?"

Asher looked as if he wanted to keep dodging Will's questions, then decided a little cooperation might be better for his immediate well-being. "It's not what you think."

"Then start talking. You were caught red-handed breaking into a private residence. From my view, things don't look too good for you at the moment."

"I didn't break in. The back door was already open when I got here. The police had just searched the premises, so I didn't see the harm in having a look around. It wasn't like I was going to contaminate evidence or anything."

"If you knew the police were here, then you must have been watching her place."

"No, I—"

"I wouldn't lie to me again if I were you."

He closed his eyes briefly and nodded. "Okay, yes. I

waited for the police to leave and then I found a way in. But I wasn't going to take anything."

"Then why go in?"

"I'm a freelance journalist. I was looking for a story. I *swear* I didn't break in."

"Does the term unlawful entry mean anything to you?"

"I may have trespassed, but that's hardly the crime of the century." He turned slightly to the side to display his cuffed hands. "I hurt my arm when you tackled me. Are these really necessary? You have my word I won't try to run."

"You ran before so the cuffs stay on," Will said. "Let's try this again. What did you mean when you said you have something I want?"

Those wheels started to grind again. He took a moment to consider his answer. "I have information that might prove useful to your investigation."

"What kind of information?"

He was still fidgeting with the cuffs. "Are you sure you won't reconsider?"

"You're lucky I don't put you in leg irons," Will said. "You're fine. Just relax your arms. What kind of information?"

A lock of hair fell across his forehead and he tossed back his head. "I wasn't entirely truthful before."

Shocker, Will thought. "Go on."

"I know about Thora Graham's abduction, but I didn't take her. I would never hurt anyone. I have a police scanner app on my phone. There's been a lot of chatter about her abduction all morning. It's not illegal to monitor police broadcasts in the state of Texas," he hastened to point out. "It's also not hard to follow along if you know the standard codes, which I do. I've been covering the crime beat for years as a reporter. I don't know where Ms. Graham is, but I may know who took her."

Will didn't know whether to believe him or not. He could sense he was being played, but to what end, he had no idea. "Tell me everything you know starting with a name."

Asher ignored the instructions and began with a shrug. "It's more of a hunch than anything else, but I have reason to believe her disappearance has something to do with a case she worked on at the FBI."

"Which case?"

"Are you familiar with the serial killer they call the Weatherman?"

Cold dread prickled at Will's nape. "I'm familiar enough. Last I heard, he was sitting on death row in Alabama. Which happens to be where you're from. I'm guessing that's not a coincidence. What's he—and you—got to do with Thora Graham's abduction?"

"She was the FBI analyst who helped the local PD in Mobile take him down."

Will scrutinized Asher's features. He didn't trust the man. Nor did he accept at face value anything coming out of his mouth. The guy found himself in a tough spot. He'd likely say or do anything to take the heat off. But there was a reason he'd been in Thora's house and Will needed to keep chipping away until he uncovered the truth. "You're saying Ridgeway is behind Thora's abduction?"

"I'm saying he could be. I'd put the probability as extremely high. I've followed his case for years, even before his capture. I've written about him extensively. Two weeks ago, I drove to the Donaldson Correctional Facility in Jefferson County to interview him. He talked a lot about the manhunt that eventually led to his arrest and conviction and how he was able to elude the authorities for years by making friends with people in all walks of life, including law enforcement personnel. He was surprisingly candid. And quite credible for a serial killer. I can see why he's so dangerous. He's intelligent and compelling."

"He's also a pathological liar," Will pointed out.

"That, too. Thora Graham's name came up in the course of the conversation. He knows about her role in his capture, and he's aware of her departure from the Bureau. I suspect he knows a lot more than he let on. He seems to have something of a fascination for Ms. Graham. He insinuated the two of them have unfinished business."

The thought of Ridgeway in his cell obsessing over Thora made Will's skin crawl. "He said that to you?"

"Essentially, yes."

"And I suppose you want me to believe you came all this way to warn her. It's just another coincidence she disappeared when you hit town."

"I don't expect you to believe anything, but I'm telling you Thora Graham is only part of the reason I'm here. I came because I was invited to be a guest on a popular podcast to promote my upcoming book."

Will lifted a brow. "So you're a novelist now?"

"True crime. *Storm Warning* chronicles nearly a decade of my personal coverage of the Weatherman."

"Clever title," Will said dryly.

"I know it's cliché, but you have to give the public what they want."

"You think the public is eager for a book about James Ellis Ridgeway?"

"I know they are. The fascination for serial killers hasn't waned. You just have to reach the right audience."

"And you came all this way to do a podcast?"

"It's a popular broadcast and the host thought it would be

more effective if we conducted the interview face-to-face rather than remotely. Now I'm starting to wonder if *he* had an ulterior motive for luring me down here."

An answer for everything. "Who's the host?"

"A man named Neville."

That stopped Will for a moment. "Logan Neville?"

"Yes, why? Do you know him?"

"We've crossed paths," Will said.

"Then you must also know he's a professor at the same local university that recently hired Thora Graham. I'm starting to believe there are a lot of interconnected and overlapping threads to this story. And a lot of players moving around in the shadows. Nothing is as it seems, Deputy Chief."

"Including you," Will said. "If you came to Thora's townhouse looking for a story *after* you heard about her abduction, explain to me why you were spotted outside her townhouse two days before she was taken and again last night at the pub where she was last seen. You seem to have more than a passing interest in Thora Graham yourself."

"I wasn't stalking her if that's what you're implying. I freely admit I've been trying to reach her. That's not the same thing."

"Why were you trying to reach her?"

"Partly to tell her about Ridgeway, but also to ask for an interview for my book. She's elusive. To my knowledge, she's never spoken publicly about the Weatherman case."

"Maybe she just wants to be left alone," Will said. "Did that thought ever cross your mind?"

"She's got a story to tell, and I'd like to help her tell it. Taking down James Ellis Ridgeway wasn't without cost. She lost her husband during the course of the manhunt. She also suffered what used to be referred to as a nervous breakdown."

Will's gaze narrowed. "What are you talking about?"

"I don't know the details. I just heard the rumors. The reason she left the Bureau is because she had some kind of episode. That's all I know."

The direction of the conversation made Will uncomfortable. He hated the invasion of Thora's privacy. For all he knew, Asher had made the whole thing up, but something was starting to niggle. "You're telling me you have sources that close to Thora Graham?"

"I keep my ear to the ground like any good reporter learns to do," Asher said. "I ask questions and people tell me things."

"You hear things all the way from Quantico, Virginia?"

"From all over. This is the information age. Word travels fast when you know where to look and how to listen."

He's right about that. In just the thirteen years Will had been in law enforcement, technology had revolutionized data collection and surveillance. The sheer volume of information that could be acquired and exchanged in a narrow time frame was sometimes mind-boggling. He didn't put a lot of credence in the rest of Noah Asher's claim, but he couldn't afford to dismiss it out of hand, either. Something Maddie Graham had told him that morning came back to him. She'd indicated a concern that Thora had returned to Belfort for reasons other than to be close to her family.

The information only mattered to the case because Thora's current mental state was critical to her survival. Will had to believe she was strong enough to get through this. She'd always been tough and determined and she'd been trained by the best in the world. Beyond those known facts, he wouldn't allow himself to speculate.

He returned his attention to Asher. "So regardless of her

wishes, you set your sights on an interview. And you weren't going to take no for an answer."

Asher frowned, sensing a trap. "I wouldn't put it that way."

"When you couldn't reach her at her home or on the phone, you decided to follow her to the pub. You were seen watching her from the bar. And now you've unlawfully entered her premises." Will paused. "That sounds a lot like stalking to me."

"You're mischaracterizing everything I just said," Asher protested. "You're presenting my actions in the worst possible light."

"Then tell me the truth. Why were you in her house just now? It wasn't curiosity. You were looking for something besides a story."

He tossed back that pesky lock of hair while he seemed to consider his answer. "I thought I might find evidence."

"Of her disappearance?"

"Of the Weatherman's involvement." He glanced around nervously as if worried the incarcerated killer might have someone close by listening in. "I've talked to Ridgeway. I've seen firsthand how he's able to control and manipulate the prison guards. He could have enlisted any one of them to abduct Thora Graham. Or if not a guard, then someone else on the outside. Someone from his former life, perhaps. I thought whoever took her might have left a calling card, something so subtle the police would have overlooked it."

"Ridgeway never left a calling card," Will said.

"That we know of. If he's behind the abduction, he'd want to find a way to take credit." He turned to stare at Thora's townhouse and Will could have sworn he saw a shudder go through him.

"You're quick on your feet. I'll give you that," Will said. "No shortage of ready answers."

Asher tried to look sincere. "I realize how far-fetched all this must sound, and you've no reason to take my word for any of it. But you can check my credentials for yourself. I'll give you the names and phone numbers of my agent, my publisher, my neighbors—anyone you want to talk to. Even my sister if that would make you feel better. Just please try to keep an open mind. For all we know, Ridgeway could have planned this whole thing to make me look suspicious."

"Well, you do look suspicious," Will agreed. "How do I know you're not the one working with Ridgeway? You've spent time with him. You're writing a book about him. Maybe you're the one who's fallen under his spell."

"A reasonable conclusion, but would I have told you as much as I have if I were working with him?"

"Yes. I think that's exactly what you would do. Which is why I'm taking you in," Will said. "You can cool your heels at the station while I check out your story. You better hope I don't find inconsistencies."

"You won't. I'm telling you the truth."

"Then you've got nothing to worry about." He held up Asher's wallet. "I'll hold onto this in the meantime."

A black-and-white pulled through the gate and wheeled into the parking lot. Will watched as two uniforms got out and headed their way. He turned back to Asher. "Before I turn you over to these fine officers, there's still one thing you haven't explained. If you're innocent, why did you run?"

He answered without hesitation, "It seemed the prudent thing to do. You were holding a gun on me. I had no idea who you were."

"I identified myself as police."

"Yes, but for all I knew, you or someone in your department could have been working with Ridgeway. Take a moment to consider my situation. What if I'm right about him? If you take me in, I'll be a sitting duck."

"You'll be protected. We won't let anything happen to you."

"The way law enforcement protected his other victims? You'll understand if I'm not reassured. Why not let me go and put a tail on me? If I'm innocent, no harm done. If I'm guilty, I could lead you to Thora Graham."

"Tempting, but I'm not done with you yet. You'll be easier to keep track of at the station. We'll put you in a cell where no one can get to you. You broke the law. You're not walking away from this."

"Then my blood will be on your hands."

Will nodded to the officers coming up behind Asher. "Take him straight downtown. No stops along the way, and don't let him talk to anyone. No one goes in or out of his cell until I get there."

One of the officers took his arm. Asher tried to shake him off. "You're making a big mistake."

The officer tightened his grip. "That's what they all say, buddy."

Asher kept glancing over his shoulder as if he expected Will to change his mind and intervene. He didn't. Instead, he turned and surveyed Thora's building from the parking lot. The images running through his head left him in a cold sweat. He had a terrible feeling that no matter what he did, he'd always be one step behind the kidnapper.

And time was running out. A voice in his head still whispered the same warning: *Hurry, Will. She's dying.*

Chapter Eight

Wake up, Thora. WAKE UP!

The voice was so loud and distinct, she thought for a moment someone had opened the lid of the box and crawled inside with her.

"Will? Is that you?"

No answer.

She tapped the sequence on the air tube. "Will, are you up there? Please, can you hear me?"

Silence.

"Will!"

He didn't answer because he wasn't there. No one was there. The voice hadn't been real. But for one split second, Thora had been certain he'd found her.

Hope drained quickly and she wanted to sob in despair. Instead, she hardened herself to the anguish, refusing to give in to the debilitating gloom even for a moment. She might only be clinging to sanity by a thread. If she started to cry, she might never stop. If she started to scream, she wouldn't be able to stop. She felt helpless and so far away from the people she loved. A million miles from Claire and her mother. And from Will. She had no doubt that all of them were looking for her by now, but she'd been put in a box and buried underground for a reason. She wasn't meant to be found. Ever.

She'd conjured Will's voice because the imagined sound was her only comfort. Or maybe she really was starting to lose it. Dehydration could cause confusion, anxiety and, in extreme cases, hallucinations. Even now, with her eyes wide open and her lungs full of oxygen, she felt as if she could easily become untethered from reality and float off into an even darker place from which there would be no rescue or return.

What could be darker than the box?

"Death," she whispered.

But she wasn't dead yet and she needed to delay that finality for as long as she could. She still had work to do. Motives to ponder. Means and opportunities to explore. She flattened her hands against the lid as if she could physically push herself back down to reality.

"I'm okay," she said aloud. "I'm fine. I can keep going for as long as I need to. Do you hear me? For as long as I need to!"

Good! Then let's get back to work.

"I don't know where to start."

Yes, you do. You just don't want to go there.

"Go where?"

You need to think about James Ellis Ridgeway. It's time to deal with the Weatherman once and for all.

He was the last person Thora wanted to spend time with, especially inside the close confines of the box. Wasn't the seven years he'd lived inside her head long enough?

Don't look away, Thora. Keep digging.

There had to be a reason he'd come back into her life at this precise moment in time. In the course of one night out, Elise Barrett and Logan Neville had each mentioned his name in two separate conversations. True, people often wanted to talk about the Weatherman case if they knew of Thora's role in his capture, but two different people on the same night she'd been abducted? She wasn't a big believer in coincidences. If one looked hard and deep enough, a common thread could usually be unraveled. But if a thread existed that connected the Weatherman to Logan Neville and Elise Barrett, she'd yet to find it.

Doesn't mean it's not there. You said it yourself. Look harder and deeper.

She drew another long breath and once again committed herself to the investigation. She needed the distraction as much as she needed the truth, probably more so. But she was finding it difficult to concentrate. Water had become an obsession. She was no longer sweating and that was a very bad sign. What she wouldn't give at that moment for a single drop of moisture on her tongue. She tried to imagine herself in a rainstorm, tipping her head to the cool droplets as they splattered against her face. It didn't work. She was still trapped in the box and the walls were closing in on her.

Focus, Thora. You can do this.

She went back over the conversation with Elise Barrett, even speaking some of the remembered dialogue aloud. Far from grounding her in the familiarity of research and analysis, the sound of her own voice made reality seem far, far away.

Keep it together.

What floated to the surface from that conversation was Elise's speculation that she might have crossed paths with Ridgeway during one of his killing sprees. Rather than shuddering in dread at the prospect, she'd spoken of it in the same tone as if she were contemplating a chance meeting with a celebrity in an unexpected place. Maybe that wasn't so surprising. Elise Barrett wasn't the only one who had a fascination for the Weatherman. For a few months after his incarceration, devotees had gathered outside the prison walls hoping to catch a glimpse of him. The fixation was inexplicable to Thora, but then she'd not only studied Ridgeway for seven years, she'd also studied his victims. She could name all of them by heart. Two years after the case had been closed, the crime scene photos and videos still haunted her sleep.

She steadied her resolve and tried to remain alert. She needed to stay sharp in order to continue the investigation, but also to listen for outside noises, for even the faintest hint that rescue could be nearby. She might need to beat on the lid of the box and call up through the air pipe to get someone's attention. *Stay strong, stay vigilant. It's the only way you'll get through this.*

Funny how she now accepted the voice in her head as Will Dresden's. Or at least the Will Dresden she'd known thirteen years ago. His tone would have deepened with age and hardened with experience, but she would still know it anywhere. Even six feet under.

You can do this, Thora.

What if I can't? What if I'm not as strong as you think I am? I've got a breaking point.

You're not there yet.

How can you be so sure?

Because I know you. I know what you're capable of. Now brace yourself. We're not done yet with Ridgeway.

She had avoided concentrating on the brief conversation with Logan Neville because the revelation that her name had been mentioned in an interview with Ridgeway was far more unnerving than she wanted to admit. The thought of the killer obsessing over her role in his apprehension was downright scary. She knew what he was capable of, how he could manipulate, charm and coerce before revealing the monster inside. If the Weatherman was responsible for her incarceration, then God help her. There would be no getting out of this box. And the worst might be yet to come.

But she wasn't convinced of his involvement. Maybe she didn't want to believe it. Belfort, Texas, was a long way from his prison cell in Alabama. There was comfort in that distance. A false sense of security, perhaps. Coordinating a complicated abduction from behind bars wouldn't be easy when his every phone call, letter and visit had been monitored for the past two years. Maybe not every call. Cell phones were currency in prisons. Literally tons of the devices were found in sanitation systems every year. It seemed too coincidental that his name had been brought up to her just minutes before she'd been taken.

I don't want to do this, Will. I don't like letting a killer back into my life. It's dangerous.

I know. But you can't ignore him, and you can't assume anything at this point. You have to sift through every piece of evidence to get to the truth.

I'm tired. I just want to close my eyes and go to sleep.

You can't do that. Listen to me, Thora. You have to stay awake. You have to keep breathing. Do you hear me?

Yes, but your voice is starting to fade. You're too far away. I don't think you can make it in time.

I'll make it.

"Where are you, Will?"

Closer than you think. Just hold on.

Chapter Nine

As soon as Will got back to the station, he headed into the holding room to grill Noah Asher. As before, the reporter maintained his innocence and denied that he'd ever been inside Thora's townhouse until Will had caught him there earlier. He reiterated his conviction that James Ellis Ridgeway was somehow involved. The Weatherman was certainly clever enough to engineer a crime nearly four hundred miles away from his prison cell. He had the resources and he had an obsession with Thora. Will's every instinct warned him that Asher was playing him. He wasn't just the intrepid reporter he professed to be. The man was hiding something.

After the interview, he asked Detective Reyes to meet with him in his office. He'd assigned the seasoned investigator the task of tracking down Asher's contacts for two reasons. He trusted his former partner more than anyone else under his command and no one could dig up as much information in as short amount of time as Angel Reyes.

"The phone numbers he gave us checked out." He settled himself in the chair across from Will's desk and thumbed through his ever-present notebook. "His contacts weren't exactly thrilled to have a police detective from Belfort, Texas, interrupt their Saturday afternoon, and I can't say I blame them. We're hardly the big leagues. But after a little finessing, both his publisher and his literary agent corroborated Asher's credentials."

"That surprises me," Will admitted. "I half expected you to come in here and tell me he made the whole thing up."

"He's legit, but he's not exactly in the big leagues, either. He has a book contract with a small press out of Mobile. They work with local authors and publish fewer than half a dozen titles a year. He also writes for a free weekly newspaper, but the bulk of his work seems to be digital. He's prolific online, but I have no idea how the guy makes a living. We're talking pieces for obscure blogs and fringe sites. His writing seems more of a hobby than a career. I haven't been able to dig up a single byline for a major publication and believe me, I've looked. Over the past decade, he's written extensively about James Ellis Ridgeway, going all the way back to the first known kill outside of Baton Rouge. He lives in a house owned by his mother, drives a ten-year old Camry and has a sister in Birmingham. Like Ridgeway, Asher seems to come up with enough funds from somewhere to live a modest but obsessive lifestyle." He glanced up from his notes. "My conclusion? He's one strange dude."

"That tracks with my impression of him," Will said.

"We can't hold him for much longer on a misdemeanor. If we cut him loose, we could put a tail on him."

"He suggested the same thing himself." Will thought about it for a moment, then nodded. "He's walking one way or another, so we may as well control his release."

"I'm on it."

"What about his podcast appearance? Were you able to corroborate the invitation from Logan Neville?"

"I've left a message but Neville hasn't returned my call. I've got his address. He lives in the Paseo District. If I don't hear back from him in the next half hour, I'll drive over to his place and have a chat with him in person."

Will fiddled with a pen. "That just leaves Ridgeway. We still need to verify Asher's trip to Donaldson Correctional Facility."

Reyes allowed himself a brief smile. "Saving the best for last, boss."

Will sat forward. "You found something?"

Reyes nodded. "In my experience, prisons are notoriously uncooperative and sometimes possessive of their inmates to a creepy degree. It can be unsettling. You have to present your request with the right amount of patience, deference and intimidation."

"Which you've mastered, I'm assuming."

"I had a lot of practice in El Paso. Some of my best confidential informants were on the inside." His phone dinged. He checked the text message, answered back and then stuffed the phone in his pocket. "Sorry about that. Okay, where was I? So after getting passed around a few times, I was finally connected to someone willing to check the visitors' log. Noah Asher saw Ridgeway two weeks ago just as he claimed. He signed in at nine o'clock on Tuesday, the fourteenth, for a noncontact visit. Signed out an hour later. But this is where it gets interesting." He paused for effect. "Asher neglected to mention that he's been making regular trips to the prison since Ridgeway's incarceration two years ago. He shows up like clockwork every second Tuesday of every month. Talk among the guards is that the two of them appear quite chummy."

"That's interesting, particularly since Asher seems intent on throwing Ridgeway under the bus. He keeps trying to convince me that Ridgeway is somehow behind Thora's abduction. I don't discount the possibility, but I also don't consider it a high probability."

"Well, this may change your mind," Reyes said. "Except for Ridgeway's attorney, Noah Asher has been his only visitor until the week before last when another name turned up on the visitors' log. This person signed in at ten and signed out at eleven. She would have just missed Asher."

"She? You've got a name?"

"I've got better than a name. I have a photograph of her signature." He handed Will his phone.

Will studied the shot of the log entry, then glanced up. "Thora went to see Ridgeway two weeks ago?"

"That's what someone wants us to think, but I checked her schedule. She had an eleven o'clock class that Tuesday. Plenty of witnesses saw her on campus. Whoever signed that log wasn't Thora Graham."

Will handed back the phone. "I'll need a copy of that signature." He fell silent as his mind raced. "Let's think about this for a minute. Anyone signing in at a maximum-security facility would have to show photo ID. Prisons have a lot of leeway on who they allow to visit and how often, but I'm guessing even a noncontact visit to a death row inmate would require a visitor request in advance."

"Which means Thora's kidnapping could have been in the works for weeks if not months," Reyes said. "And I seriously doubt it was planned and implemented by only one person."

"Agreed. I think we're looking for at least two suspects." Will leaned back in his chair, deep in thought. "As for the ID, it's not hard to get a passable fake. The tricky part would be getting a photo without Thora's knowledge."

"Why not just steal the original and return it before it's missed? Question is, why would someone go to so much trouble?"

"Maybe Thora was the only person Ridgeway would agree to see."

"Again, to what end?"

"I don't know," Will said in frustration. "Maybe whoever took Thora wants to use Ridgeway as a patsy. It's possible this whole thing is one big distraction. While we're wasting our time on Ridgeway, Thora's time is running out." He told himself to stay focused, but his mind kept straying back to that box. He pictured her inside, growing weaker and more desperate with each passing minute. By now, dehydration and heat exhaustion would be a problem. And that was assuming she didn't have any other injuries. That was in addition to her mental anguish. The notion that she had been put in that box because of a grudge against him was a devil on his shoulder he couldn't ignore.

Reyes pulled him back to the task at hand. "Maybe one of us needs to go talk to Ridgeway in person. I doubt he'll cooperate unless there's something in it for him, but you never know. He might let something slip."

"Guys like Ridgeway don't let things slip," Will said. "He won't reveal anything he doesn't want us to know, but there are other ways of finding out the identity of his visitor. Call your contact at the prison and see if you can get surveillance footage from the visitors' area."

"I already checked. It's a no-go without a warrant."

"And warrants don't generally cross state lines," Will said. "I'll get the chief to make some calls. If he can get the feds on board, they can facilitate cooperation. Right now, I have something else I need you to do for me. What I'm about to request can't leave this room."

Reyes nodded. "No problem."

"Find out if Elise Barrett was on duty the day someone signed in as Thora at the prison."

Reyes stared at him silently for a moment, then nodded. "Anything else?"

"Report back to me and only to me as soon as you find out. I don't like asking you to do this. Digging into another cop's business is never pleasant. But if I start poking around, people will notice, and I don't want any gossip about this. I don't want anyone jumping to conclusions."

"Gotcha."

Will rose, drawing the meeting to a close just as his civilian assistant, Penny Yates, stuck her head in the door. "Sorry for the interruption."

"It's fine," Will said. "What's up?"

"There's a young lady at the front desk who says she needs to talk to someone about Thora Graham. Says she's a student at the university. Under the circumstances, I didn't think we should keep her waiting."

Reyes pocketed his notebook and stood. "You want me to talk to her on my way out?"

"No, you've got other things to take care of." The two exchanged a glance. "I'll handle this."

"I'll bring her on back, then." Penny held the door for Reyes and the pair disappeared into the hallway. She returned a few minutes later with the student in tow.

"Deputy Chief Dresden, this is Baylee Fisher." She waited for the young woman to step inside the office and then pulled the door closed behind her.

Will motioned for the young woman to take a chair across from his desk. "I understand you're a student at the university."

"I'm a criminology major. If all goes as planned, I'll graduate next semester." She glanced around curiously, taking in the city map on the wall behind his desk and the framed citations scattered about the room. "You've received a lot of awards," she said in awe.

"Not all of them are mine. Most belong to the department." He waited until she was comfortably settled before giving her a prompt. "You have information about Thora Graham?"

She blinked at his brusqueness, then nodded. "Yes, of course. We should get right to it. You're a busy man." She tore her gaze from the awards and gave him a tense smile. "Which is why I hope I'm not wasting your time. This may turn out to be nothing, but my instincts are usually pretty good. And I just knew I wouldn't be able to rest until I told someone what I heard."

Will sat back in his chair, outwardly relaxed as he tried to put her at ease. "Tell me what you know, and we'll decide where to go from there."

She nodded. "Professor Graham and I were supposed to meet in her office today. I showed up at nine on the dot, but her door was locked and she hadn't left a note. I thought she might be running late so I hung out in the library for a while and went back thirty minutes later. She still wasn't there. I checked the faculty parking garage and her space was empty. It's possible she forgot or something else came up, but I don't think so. I'm afraid something may have happened to her."

Will kept his tone neutral. "Why would you automatically assume something had happened to her?"

Her gaze was suddenly very direct. "Like I said, it's a feeling. An instinct. Plus, she looked kind of strange when I saw her at Molly's last night."

That got his attention. "You saw her at the pub? What time?"

"It was still early. Probably around ten or ten thirty. She was just leaving when I caught her at the door."

"Was she alone?"

"Yes."

"You didn't see anyone walk out with her? Or behind her?"

She frowned in bewilderment. "No, and I'm sure I would have noticed."

"You said you caught her as she was leaving. I take it the two of you spoke?"

"For just a moment. I asked for a meeting and she said I could come by her office today." She wiped her hands down her jeans. "When I decided to come here, I didn't expect anyone to take my concerns seriously. Now all of a sudden, I find myself in the office of a deputy chief. All these questions about my interaction with Professor Graham last night can only mean one thing. Something *has* happened to her."

"Let's just stick to my questions for now," Will said. "How did she seem to you?"

Baylee gave him a knowing look. "I understand. You're keeping information close to the vest so that certain details can be used to trip up a suspect. I would do the same thing in your shoes."

"Then you won't mind answering my questions," Will said.

"Not at all. That's why I'm here. As to Professor Graham's behavior, she seemed a little…off, but not to the point where I thought she was inebriated or anything. I didn't think too much about it at the time, but I started to worry when she didn't show up today for our meeting. It's totally out of character for her."

"Did she say where she was headed last night?"

"No, but I assumed she was going home."

"Why did you want to meet with her today?" Will asked.

She leaned forward. "Can this stay between us?"

"That depends on what you have to say."

"It's just…" She clasped her hands in her lap. "You have

to understand how it is on college campuses these days. If the wrong people were to get wind of my coming here, things could get very difficult for me. It only takes one post or video on social media to ruin your whole life."

"You came here because you wanted to do the right thing," Will reminded her.

She sighed. "I know."

"So tell me why you wanted to see Professor Graham. If I can keep the reason quiet, I will."

That seemed to satisfy her. "I'm taking a couple of summer classes so that I can graduate early. One under Professor Graham and the other under Professor Neville. I don't know if you're aware of Professor Neville's reputation, but it's very difficult to get into any of his classes. They fill up quickly, which makes it something of a Catch-22. If you want to be taken seriously as a criminology major, you not only have to take his classes, you also have to excel. He has favorites. The rest of us have to work twice as hard just to get a fair shake. One low test score or one wrong word from him and you're finished."

"I get it," Will said. "You don't want to get on his bad side."

"Yesterday, I left my notebook in his classroom. When I went back later to get it, I heard him arguing with someone. He mentioned Professor Graham. I didn't hear what he said, but the *way* he said her name stopped me dead in my tracks. I think he secretly resents her popularity. He's always been a big deal in the Criminology Department and then she comes in with her years of FBI experience and it makes his work seem trivial by comparison. Maybe that negative impression was already in my head when I heard him and I projected, but his tone didn't sound angry or bitter to me. I would describe it as ice-cold and diabolic."

"You didn't catch any of the conversation?"

"Just a bit when his voice rose. He said something like, *Don't you dare let me down*."

Will lifted a brow at that. "That's pretty specific. Are you sure you heard correctly?"

"I may be paraphrasing but that's the gist of it."

"You didn't recognize the other voice?"

"Only that it was female. They were almost whispering, and I didn't want to get caught eavesdropping outside his door. Any one of his students would rat me out in a heartbeat just to get his nod of approval. I'd probably do the same if I were in their shoes. I ended up leaving without my notebook. But the tone of his voice stayed with me all day. It gave me a chill every time I thought about it. When I saw him talking to Professor Graham at the pub last night, I decided to warn her. Maybe what I overheard was something, maybe it was nothing, but I felt she needed to know."

"Why didn't you tell her last night if you thought it was that important?"

"I didn't want to be seen in a deep conversation with her or take the chance we'd be overheard. As I just explained, there's a lot at stake for me."

"How long did you stay at the pub after Professor Graham left?"

"Not that long. I think I left around eleven. It's really not my kind of place. I don't even drink. But Professor Neville invites his team to Molly's every Friday night and if I don't show up, I get left out of the planning. I'm already treated like a misfit. Sometimes I think the other members are just waiting for an excuse to kick me out."

"What kind of team are we talking about?" Will asked.

She sat a little straighter. "We investigate cold cases."

"You're amateur sleuths, in other words."

She didn't seem to care for his characterization. "You underestimate us. We don't get paid for our work, but I would hardly call us amateurs. We're all criminology majors. Most of us are just a semester or two away from doing what you do. One of us may even occupy this very office someday."

"More power to you," he said sincerely. "How many members are in this club?"

"We're a *team*," she stressed. "There are four of us, including Addison March. She's Professor Neville's TA."

Her expression altered almost infinitesimally when she mentioned the TA's name. Will watched her closely, noting the tension in her posture and the flicker of disapproval in her eyes.

"Could she have been the one you overheard in the classroom arguing with Professor Neville?" he asked.

She shrugged but her body language was hardly casual. "I wouldn't be surprised. She's certainly wormed her way into his good graces. And by good graces, I mean his bed. Everyone knows they're sleeping together."

"Not against the law," Will said.

"Though highly inappropriate. Needless to say, she receives preferential treatment. It's annoying that she gets the most interesting investigative assignments when there are smarter and more deserving members on Professor Neville's team."

"Like you?"

A frown flickered. "That's not for me to say."

"Let's go back to the conversation you overheard in his classroom. You said they spoke in a near whisper. How can you be so sure his companion was a woman?"

"I heard enough to recognize a female voice. Whether it was Addison or not, I don't know. There's an older woman who hangs out at the pub where we meet. I've seen her on campus a few times. I did wonder if it might have been her. Apparently, she and Professor Neville were involved for a time and I think she's still into him. She seems a little desperate for his attention."

Will was starting to get the bigger picture. Addison March and the desperate older woman weren't the only ones vying for Professor Neville's attention. "Was this woman at the pub last night?" he asked.

"Yes. I saw her talking to Professor Graham in the restroom. I think she's a cop. That's probably how she and Professor Neville met. I've heard him call her Elaine or Elise. Something that starts with an E."

Will said sharply, "Can you describe her?"

His curt tone seemed to catch her off guard. She stared at him wide-eyed for a moment before she answered. "Five seven, I would guess. Slender but fit. Blue eyes, curly red hair."

He strove to regain control of his outward reaction. Elise Barrett had deliberately misled him earlier about her interaction with Thora at the pub. Why lie about something so innocuous? "Are you sure you saw her with Thora Graham?"

"Yes, I'm positive. Is it important?"

"It might be. Did you see Professor Graham with anyone else last night?"

"Mostly she stayed with her group. As I said earlier, she spoke to Professor Neville for a few minutes at the table. Their conversation seemed friendly. I wouldn't have given it any thought if I hadn't overheard him mention her name earlier that day." She tucked her short hair behind her ears. "I understand you can't talk about an ongoing investigation, but can you at least tell me if Professor Graham is okay?

She's not only my favorite instructor—she's been an inspiration ever since she came to U-SET."

"I'm sure she'll be gratified to hear that."

"I hope so. My dream is to work for the FBI. I want to hunt serial killers just like she did. Professor Neville doesn't think I have what it takes, but he's wrong."

Dead wrong? "I'm sure you'll do fine."

Will was about to rise and show her to the door when Penny popped her head back in. "Sorry for another interruption, but I thought you'd want to know." She held up her phone. "Tech just called. They've found something."

Will stood so quickly, his chair bumped back against the credenza. "Tell them I'm on my way."

Baylee rose more slowly. "She means the Technology Unit, right? Could I come with you? Whatever they're working on, I'm sure I could be of some help."

"Thanks for the offer, but I think we can manage. Penny?"

She nodded in understanding as she cut her gaze to Baylee. "I'll show you out."

Reluctantly, Baylee turned to follow her into the hallway. She paused at the doorway to glance back. "Good luck, Deputy Chief."

A FEW MINUTES LATER, Will stood staring at a series of stills from the second video the kidnapper had sent as one of the officers in the Tech Unit explained their discovery.

"When the camera pulled back from the air tube to reveal the forest…" The officer used the eraser end of a pencil to draw a pretend circle around the expanse on which he wanted Will to focus. "A tall, thin structure was captured in the distance rising above the treetops. The angle of the sun made it invisible until we isolated and enlarged the frame.

Even then, we didn't know what we'd found. A cell tower seemed unlikely in such a densely wooded area."

Will studied the image. "Could it be the old fire tower? From what I remember of local history, it was built by the Forestry Service after World War II and abandoned sometime in the seventies. We used to hike out there when we were kids and climb to the top of that thing. You could see for miles."

The officer nodded appreciatively. "Good eye. That's exactly what it is. Once we made the identification, we could pinpoint the location using the recorded longitude and latitude. It's roughly ten miles north of the freeway, in the southernmost tip of a heavily wooded area that borders the Preserve. Using the tower as a landmark helped to narrow our search field, but we were still looking at acres and acres of deep forestland." He drew larger circles over the image.

Will noted the quiet excitement in his voice and glanced up from the frame. "I assume from your tone that you've found something else in the footage?"

"We did. Another marker here…" He pointed to a spot at the lower edge of a second still. "And here." He moved the pencil to the right. "When you put the two enlarged images together, you can see how the tower in the distance lines up dead center between the two artifacts."

"What are the artifacts?" Will asked.

"We think they're old gate columns. They may once have marked the entrance to a private road. The rows of thick vegetation on either side indicate a fence line. Now look at the location of the columns in conjunction to the air tube." The third image was an enlarged still of the PVC pipe jutting from the ground, which the officer fitted between the other two frames like a puzzle piece. "When you watch the video, you don't notice the columns. The footage goes by too quickly and they're all but hidden by the congested growth. We only found them when we blew up the individual frames. But once spotted, we could tell the video was shot looking through those columns toward the air tube with the fire tower in the distance. See how everything is in alignment?" He traced a straight line from the center of the columns to the other two markers.

Will gave him a skeptical glance. "I'm still not convinced those are columns and even if they are, you don't think the positioning is a coincidence?"

"Virtually impossible. The orientation is too perfect. We think it's a map." He traced an X over the air tube.

Will tried not to jump ahead, but his adrenaline was already pulsing. "Just to be clear, you're saying the kidnapper planted a map of Thora's location in the video?"

"I'm saying the evidence is right here in front of us," the officer said. "What we don't know is why they'd leave such an obvious clue."

"I may have some idea. The map is only obvious if you're observant. In other words, someone without a keen eye and enough patience to go through the individual frames of the video could have easily overlooked one or all of the markers. The person or persons we're dealing with think they're smarter than the rest of us—or at least smarter than me. The text messages were provocative and condescending. They probably think they're still several steps ahead of us, but they underestimated you guys. They never expected you to find and identify the reference points so quickly."

The tech smirked and turned to fist-bump a colleague at the desk behind him.

"This is like a game to them," Will mused. "A deranged and dangerous contest."

The text messages had belittled his abilities and intellect in order to draw him into the investigation. For whatever reason, they wanted to pit their skills against his. If he couldn't find Thora in time, the hidden map in the video would be used to further disparage his competence. The guilt and second-guessing would eat him alive, which was almost certainly the intent. But why? He had a hard time imagining that someone from his past could be so dark and vindictive, but even the people you knew and trusted could be unpredictable.

Whatever the intent, he wouldn't allow himself to be caught in the trap of making it personal. He cleared his mind of self-doubt and any thoughts of retaliation as he studied the markers. He'd been born and raised in Belfort. He and his friends had roamed all through those woods as kids. If there'd been an old road with stone columns, they would surely have known about it.

Memories started to prod as he studied the frame.

"It's not a road," he said. "Not a road per se."

The officer glanced up from the screen. "What is it, then?"

Will tapped the image with his fingertip. "The columns mark the entrance to an old cemetery."

The officer looked startled by the revelation, then nodded excitedly. "That makes sense when you think about it. Easy to hide a new grave among the old ones."

"You wouldn't even have to disguise fresh digging," Will said. "The cemetery hasn't been active for decades. Most people probably don't even remember it's out there. I only know because my buddies and I came across it one day after we'd been to the fire tower. We were looking for an old house some kid told us about. Someone had supposedly been murdered inside and we wanted to see the bloodstains."

"Did you find it?"

"Yeah, finally, but we discovered the cemetery first. If memory serves, it's about three miles north of the tower. The area was so overgrown we didn't even realize we were walking over graves until we stumbled over pieces of broken headstones in the weeds. But I do remember a pair of columns and portions of a fence or wall. Back then, there was a wrought iron arch attached to the columns. I don't remember the name, but it may have been a private burial ground for the family who originally owned the property. This has to be the same cemetery."

The officer seemed intrigued by Will's recollection. "That's wild. I've lived here for nearly eight years, including college, and I've never even heard of the place. The county should have records, but that'll take time to comb through the deeds. Do you think you can find it from memory?"

Will thumped the screen. "We'll find it. We've got a map." He took out his phone and called Reyes. Once he'd briefed the detective on the discovery, he said, "Grab every available officer ASAP. The more boots on the ground the better. Even with a map, we've still got a lot of ground to cover."

"What about a warrant? Do we know who owns the property?"

"Exigent circumstances," Will replied.

"I'm more concerned about getting shot," Reyes countered.

"The place has been abandoned for years. We'll worry about finding the owner after we find her. We'll need shovels, ground-penetrating radar, a fiber-optic camera and anything else you can think of. Have an EMT team on standby. Let's go!"

Chapter Ten

Twenty minutes later, Will led the caravan with lights and sirens blasting down I-10 before exiting onto a two-lane county highway that took them deeper into the countryside. They made another right turn onto a dirt road that wound back east. A mile or so in, the road split. Will had to rely on memory to make the call. To the best of his recollection, the house was to the left and the cemetery to the right. The narrow trail that had once cut through the woods to the burial ground was long gone; the remnants of furrows now covered over with stands of evergreens and a thick carpet of brambles and underbrush.

Once the search party was in place, Will provided stills from the video that showed the alignment of the air tube with the columns and the distant fire tower. The image was fresh on everyone's mind as they fanned out in teams of two and began the slow trek through the woods. Eyes on the ground, they searched through dead leaves and tangled undergrowth looking for evidence of sunken graves and broken masonry.

All the while, Will had to beat back those stubborn doubts. What if he was wrong about the location? It had been years since he'd been out this way. What if the images from the video were deceiving? They could waste too much precious time searching in the wrong place.

Minutes passed and then an hour. And another hour. Sweat trickled down his back and soaked his shirt. Mosquitoes buzzed in his ears. It was nearing on five o'clock. Once the sun went down, the light would fade fast in the woods. They wouldn't have a prayer of finding the air tube after dark and by morning, it would be too late. *Thora, where are you? Where are you?*

"I found something!" an officer yelled.

Will's heart thudded as he turned. "What is it?"

"Looks like part of an old headstone."

Which meant they were at least in the right place. Or near the right place. Will let out a long breath of relief before he followed the sound of the officer's voice. As he approached, he spotted a second officer positioned between two crumbling stone pillars looking off toward the woods. The officer lifted an arm and used his finger to sight the fire tower in the distance. "The air tube should be straight ahead."

"Watch where you step," Will cautioned. They had no idea how shallow she might be buried or how flimsy the container. To an officer, they were eager for a rescue, but care had to be taken to avoid injury to the victim.

"Over here!"

By the time Will made his way through the columns, a loose circle had formed around a fresh burial site. The searchers parted, giving him a glimpse of the PVC pipe.

"We haven't heard any sounds coming from below," one of the officers said worriedly.

Will dropped to his knees and put his ear to the pipe. A sound echoed up through the tube. A rhythmic tapping...

"Shush. *Shush!*" He listened for a moment then said directly into the tube, "Thora? It's Will Dresden. Can you hear me?"

No answer.

A cold chill ran up his spine. What if they were too late? Or what if the kidnappers had already moved her? "Thora, please answer me!"

It seemed an eternity before a muffled voice came back to him. "Will?"

A smattering of cheers broke out at the sound of her voice. Then everyone fell into an awed silence. The gravity of the situation gripped them all. A woman had been buried alive just beneath their feet. It was only human nature to imagine themselves in her situation.

Will closed his eyes in relief. "I'm here, Thora."

"It's…really you this time?"

This time?

"Yes, it's me. Are you hurt?"

"I don't think so. I'm in some kind of box. Can you get me out?"

"Yes. Hang tight, okay? We'll have you out in no time."

Some of the officers had already started to dig. Will moved out of the way, watching, waiting and then taking his turn with a shovel. It was hard work, but no one minded. No one said anything, just quietly focused on the task at hand. When the first blade hit wood a few feet down, everyone scrambled to finish uncovering the container. The lid had been fastened in place. A crowbar was used to pry up the nails and then finally, *finally*, the top was carefully removed and Will got his first glimpse of Thora.

She lay on her back in the narrow container with her hands pressed to her sides. Her skin looked clammy; her eyes dazed by the light streaming down through the leaf canopy. Even though he'd heard her voice moments earlier, the terrible notion ran through his head that they really were too late.

His breath deserted him. He'd seen the video. He'd known what to expect. The image of her inside that box had run on repeat inside his head since early that morning. And yet the impact hit him as hard as any physical blow.

Applause and cheers erupted again as arms reached down to help her. Will's was the first. She grasped his hand and he hauled her out of the box and up over the side of the hole they'd just dug. And then he held onto her while she regained her equilibrium. He held onto her far longer than she probably needed him to.

"Are you sure you're not hurt?" He looked her over. She still had on the clothes she'd worn to the pub last night. The soft blue top was wrinkled and dirty, her dark hair tangled with twigs. No blood that he could see. No obvious wounds, thank God.

"I'm okay." Her voice sounded croaky. "Dehydrated, I think. Overheated. A little dizzy." She sat down abruptly on the mound of dirt at the edge of the hole. "Can I have some water?"

An officer handed Will a bottle. He twisted off the cap and knelt in front of Thora, observing the ashen tint to her skin as he gave her the water.

"Thank you." She lifted the bottle and drank deeply.

"Take it easy," he said. "Not too much too soon."

She nodded and took a smaller sip before handing back the bottle.

"The EMTs are on the way," he told her. "Just rest until we can get a stretcher out here."

She glanced at the now empty box and shivered. "I don't need a stretcher. I can walk."

"I don't think that's a good idea. It's at least a quarter mile back to the road and you seem a little unsteady on your feet."

"I'll be all right in a minute." Instead of turning her back on the box, she sat facing it. "How long was I down there?"

The shock of what she'd been through hit Will anew with that question, but he managed to cover his reaction. "We think you were taken sometime around ten last evening. It's five o'clock in the afternoon of the following day. Saturday. Roughly nineteen hours."

She let out a breath. "I couldn't tell. It was dark in the box. I lost track of time. Nineteen hours isn't so long."

"It must have seemed like an eternity."

She nodded. "The heat was pretty intense. I was given a little water through the tube but that was hours ago."

He latched onto her revelation. "One of the kidnappers was out here today?"

"Someone was. Early morning if I had to guess because the box got a lot hotter as time wore on."

Will tore his gaze from Thora and focused his attention on the container. It looked to be made of pine plywood, a material light enough to be carried through the woods without much trouble by two fit adults. The lid had been constructed to rest snuggly over the top and had been hammered in place at the corners. A hole had been drilled at one end to accommodate the air tube, which had been fixed in place with a ring of silicon. The box was incredibly narrow. Thora wouldn't have been able to stretch her arms and legs, much less roll to a new position. She'd had to lie flat on her back in pitch blackness for nineteen hours, not knowing where she was or if anyone would find her in time. Will could only imagine the things that had gone through her head, the struggle she must have fought to keep her sanity. Under the circumstances, she seemed miraculously calm and steady.

As to the grave, he judged the depth at around four feet. Probably dug well in advance and outfitted with the container before Thora had been kidnapped.

"It was built for me, wasn't it?" She was still staring at the open box. "The size is custom."

"All we know for sure is that it was built for someone your size or smaller."

Her gaze met his. "Do you know who put me in there?"

"Not yet. We believe we're looking for multiple suspects. We were hoping you could help us identify at least one of them."

She shook her head. "I never saw the person who grabbed me. I'm certain I was drugged. I think someone spiked my drink in the pub. I felt light-headed before I left. Then I remember bright lights in my eyes and someone telling me not to fight. I was shoved in the back of a vehicle and then the next thing I knew, I woke up in the box."

The terror she must have felt in that moment... Will swallowed and kept his tone even. "You didn't recognize the person's voice?"

"They used a voice changer. Or maybe that's just the way I remember it. The parking lot was spinning by that time. I'd taken out my phone to call Claire when the lights blinded me..." She wrinkled her brow in concentration. "That's it, I think. That's all I remember."

"Don't try to force it," Will said. "Something else may come back to you later."

She nodded before turning to scour their surroundings. After the sound of clanging shovels and human effort, the forest had grown quiet again. All activity had ceased as soon as Thora had been freed from the box. Now the officers stood back respectfully to allow her some privacy, but Will had a feeling they were hanging on her every word.

The tableau seemed surreal. More than a decade had passed since he'd last spoken to Thora Graham and there they sat at the edge of her would-be grave.

It was still hot out and hundreds of mosquitoes were swarming. He swatted one from her hair, but she hardly noticed. She seemed a little dazed and slightly in awe of the landscape. She ran a hand up her arm and shuddered. "Where are we? It looks like we're in the middle of no-where."

"We're about twelve or thirteen miles north of I-10. The old fire tower is just south of here." He paused. "If you look over your shoulder..." He pointed toward the thick row of vegetation behind them. "You can make out a pair of stone columns rising up through the vines and shrubs. Believe it or not, that's how we were able to find you. It won't make a lot of sense without the video for context, but from a certain angle, the air tube they put in the box lines up perfectly with the columns and the fire tower."

She drew her knees up and wrapped her arms around her legs. The position seemed poignantly protective to Will. "What video?"

"I was texted two videos early this morning. One of you inside the box and an external shot of the air tube sticking up from the ground. The camera panned wide from the tube to show the density of the surrounding woods. It was meant to make us feel that searching for where they buried you would be like looking for a needle in a haystack. And it did seem that way until Tech discovered landmarks in the footage."

She stared at him in confusion. "That all sounds...elaborate."

"It's definitely one for the books," he agreed.

A light breeze blew down through the trees and she

tipped her face, eyes closed as the wind ruffled her hair. Will studied her profile. She was dirty, pale and haggard, but she'd never looked more beautiful to him.

She caught him staring at her. "You said the fire tower is just south of here?"

"Yes, that's right. We're at the edge of the Preserve."

"Then I think I know where we are." Her voice turned slight accusing. "You didn't want to tell me, did you?"

Now Will was confused. "Tell you what?"

"They buried me in an old cemetery."

He stared at her in surprise. "How could you possibly know that? You can't see the graves or the headstones without tramping through the weeds looking for them. Did you regain consciousness at any point after you were taken? Did you hear someone mention the location?"

She shook her head. "I woke up in the box."

"Then how did you know about the cemetery?"

She glanced over her shoulder toward the columns. "You told me about it once." When he continued to stare at her blankly, she said, "Don't you remember? You and some of the other boys in the neighborhood discovered it one day when you were hiking in the woods. There's an old house around here somewhere. You said it was haunted. You took pictures because you thought I wouldn't believe you."

"I told you about this place?" He shook his head. "I guess it made more of an impression than I remembered. I must have filed it away in my subconscious. Do you still have those photographs?"

"Maybe at my mom's house. I could look through my old photo albums if it's important."

"It might be. I'm curious how the kidnappers knew the cemetery was here."

"Maybe one of them grew up in the area. Or maybe you told someone else, and they also filed it away in their subconscious."

Which only bolstered the theory that at least one of the kidnappers was someone he knew, someone with a deep-seated grudge against him.

Thora took the water bottle from his hand and sipped slowly.

Reyes walked over, and Will rose. "Did you find anything?"

"Not yet. If there's any trace evidence that hasn't been contaminated by the digging, we need to protect it until CSU can sweep the area for DNA and fiber samples. It'll be a miracle if anything can be recovered, but you never know. Sometimes all it takes is a partial print." He glanced down at Thora. "I'm Detective Reyes. You have no idea how happy we are to see you."

"Almost as happy as I am to see you," she said.

He smiled. "I bet."

"ETA on the paramedics?" Will asked.

Reyes reluctantly tore his gaze from Thora. "Ten minutes. They made a wrong turn."

"You're kidding me."

"GPS can only help so much when you're this far off the beaten track." He glanced around. "How do you think the kidnappers even found this place?"

"We were just wondering the same thing. I knew about the cemetery as a kid. Maybe one of them did, too."

"I've been thinking about that map," Reyes said. "If they wanted us to find her, what was the point of all this?" He motioned to the box.

Will moved a few steps away from Thora and lowered

his voice. "I'm guessing they didn't expect us to find her so quickly. Not until after her time ran out."

Reyes muttered an expletive, which mirrored Will's sentiments.

"Someone was here this morning," he said. "They brought her water. We need to comb these woods. Look for plastic bottles, drink cans, food wrappers. Anything we can lift a print from. They must have made a few trips out here getting everything ready before they took her. If something got left behind, we need to find it."

Reyes nodded. "Already on it, Boss."

Will moved back to Thora. "How are you holding up?"

"How far did you say the road is from here?"

"Quarter of a mile, maybe less." He hunkered beside her once more. "Why?"

"I don't want to wait for the paramedics. I'm starting to feel—" She tucked back her hair with a trembling hand as her voice lowered to a pleading whisper. "I need to get out of these woods. Will—"

He took one look at her panicked expression and nodded. "Come on. We'll head back toward the road together." He took her hand and drew her to her feet.

For a moment, she looked on the verge of losing it. *And who could blame her?* Then she took a steadying breath and nodded. "I'm okay."

He kept a hand on her arm as he nodded to Reyes. "We'll meet the EMTs at the road."

Reyes gave him a questioning look before he returned the nod.

"No one except CSU gets back here," Will said. "We need to station a couple of officers out on the road in case any reporters or onlookers get wind of this."

"No worries, I'm on it."

They were well away from the scene before Thora stopped and turned to him. The scent of pine permeated the warm air, and he could hear an owl in the distance. The dreamlike feeling persisted. "What's wrong?"

"I just wanted to thank you for not making me wait back there. I was okay when I first got out of the box." She glanced away. "I thought, 'I did it. I actually made it through to the other side and I'm perfectly fine.' And then…"

"Shock set in. It happens."

She hugged her middle. "Maybe I'm not as strong as I've always wanted to believe."

"Do you think any one of us could have handled it better? Back there, when you talked about waking up in the box…" Words failed him. He swallowed past a sudden tightness in his throat. "I can't begin to imagine what that must have been like."

Her eyes took on a faraway look as if she were reliving the moment. "What happens now?"

He didn't know if her question was literal or metaphorical. He answered in a matter-of-fact way. "Once we get to the road, I'll call ahead so your mom and sister can meet you at the hospital."

When he would have moved forward, she took hold of his arm and held him back. "Thank you, Will. Thank you for finding me."

"You don't need to keep thanking me. I'm just sorry it took us as long as it did."

Her eyes looked dark and luminescent in the light that spangled down through the trees. Now it was Will who shivered.

"It doesn't matter," she said. "I knew you'd come."

WILL WATCHED THE ambulance as it turned and headed back toward the highway with Thora safely tucked inside. A cloud of dust followed in the vehicle's wake. He'd resisted the temptation to crawl in the back and see her safely to the ER, but there was still work to be done out here. Besides, it wasn't his place to go with her. Hadn't he vowed earlier not to make this personal? A difficult task when the kidnappers seemed to be goading him at every turn.

He could hear shouts from the woods as officers combed through the underbrush and the CSU team processed the box and immediate burial area. Once they'd swept for fibers and DNA, the grave would be covered with a tarp and the box would be transported to the station where it would be logged into evidence.

Despite the activity, he didn't immediately return to the site. The men under his command needed to know that he trusted them to get the job done without looking over their shoulders or second-guessing their decisions. Instead, he decided to scout a wider area. If the house still stood, he decided it might be worth his time to take a look around the property. Probably a long shot, but if the kidnappers knew about the graveyard, they may also have known about the old homestead.

He searched along the ditches for a few hundred feet and then doubled back to the split in the road. Turning left this time, he followed what remained of a narrow lane until he caught a glimpse of the house through the trees. He approached cautiously on the slim chance that someone might be hiding inside.

Weeds and brambles had taken over the once spacious front yard. The thorny tendrils clutched at his ankles, making him thankful for his leather boots and denim jeans. The vegetation was flattened in places as if a vehicle had recently been driven back that way. Probably hunters looking for javelinas or hikers searching for a shortcut into the Preserve. Or someone scouting a meth lab location. Whatever the case, the proximity to the cemetery triggered Will's curiosity. Taking out his phone, he called Reyes to alert him of the find.

Once Will had reported his position and described his surroundings, Reyes said, "Want me to meet you there?"

"Not yet. Let me poke around first. No need to waste your time and mine on a wild-goose chase. I'll call if I need you."

Will slid the phone back in his pocket and set out across the property. Honeysuckle grew in tangled thickets and as the sun sank beneath the treetops, the sticky scent thickened. Mosquitos swarmed, drawn by his body heat and the carbon dioxide he emitted. Once he was past a sentry of live oaks, he got his first unimpeded look at the house.

The structure was in a lot worse shape than he remembered. The wraparound porch sagged badly in places and portions of the peaked roof had collapsed beneath the weight of the kudzu creeping over the shingles. Most of the windows were broken from what he could see, and the overgrown yard was littered with tires, rusty appliances and an old box spring. The place had obviously been used as a dumping ground over the years, which could explain the flattened weeds he'd noticed earlier at the edge of the yard.

As he stood gazing up at the two-story facade, memories of that first visit came back to him. His friends had run across the yard and up the wobbly steps to the porch while Will had hung back, both fascinated and repelled by the house. Even now he felt the tug of those warring emotions—a strange sense of melancholy that mingled with the innate creepiness of the place. He hadn't gone inside that day with his friends and he could never explain why, even

to himself. They'd come out a little while later with gruesome tales of blood splattered walls and piles of old bones,
none of which Will had believed. Or so he'd told himself.
Maybe his inexplicable skittishness was why he'd put the
house and the neighboring cemetery out of his mind for so
many years. Maybe he just didn't like abandoned places.

He stood at the bottom of the porch steps and texted
Reyes once again:

Going inside. Floorboards and roof look iffy. If you don't
hear back, send help. He was only half kidding.

Reyes texted back: Watch out for copperheads.

Snakes were the least of his worries, Will decided as he
put away his phone. He wasn't embarrassed to admit the
place still spooked him. Which was foolish. He didn't believe in the dead coming back and he wasn't afraid of the
living. He was armed, trained and experienced. If anyone
had driven back here to conduct nefarious business, he could
deal with the situation. Besides, the sirens would have already scared them away. His trepidation wasn't rational and
so he shook off the disquiet and tramped through the waist-
high weeds to the house.

Before climbing the porch steps, he decided to do a perimeter check, taking note of the space beneath the house
where any number of critters might hide and an old shed
in the back where something larger might skulk. Then he
returned to the front and tested those rickety steps, taking
care not to put a foot through the rotting porch. A screen
door hung on one hinge. He pulled it back and peered inside. He had no reason to believe anyone was around, but
he still felt the need to call out. "Hello?"

The greeting echoed through the empty rooms and
bounced back out to him. He stepped inside and moved gingerly across the creaking floorboards to stand in the center

of the room. Vines growing through the broken windows filtered the late afternoon sunlight, casting gloom throughout the interior. Cobwebs hung in thick drapes from shadowy corners. The only furniture left behind was a wooden table and a couple of broken chairs. The bare floor was littered with moldy books, old clothing and clumps of what looked to be animal fur. The musky odor of vermin permeated the air, the foul scent punctuated by the rustle of claws across the floor and in the walls.

It was not a pleasant place, though there were no blood splatters on the walls or piles of human bones as previously claimed by a pair of mischievous twelve-year-old boys.

As Will became accustomed to the gloom, he slid his gaze slowly over the walls and ceiling and finally back across the floor where a recent visitor had left footprints in the dust. Adrenaline started to pump as he tracked the prints from the front room, through the kitchen and out to the back porch. The trail ended at the top of the steps.

His scalp prickled a warning as he stood there listening to the countryside. *You should have waited for Reyes.*

Too late now.

He ran fingers through his hair, dislodging cobwebs as he told himself he was letting his imagination get the better of him. Was it any wonder? He and his team had just dug up a woman who had been buried alive in an old cemetery. Someone who had once meant everything to him. He had a right to be a little jumpy, particularly with all the recent talk about the Weatherman. The serial killer had spent a decade traveling back and forth across the country, leaving a trail of victims in his wake. This place was only a few miles from the interstate. The perfect dumping ground for the bodies that had yet to be found.

At that very moment, James Ellis Ridgeway was sitting

on death row in an Alabama prison. Irrational to think he'd somehow had a hand in Thora's abduction, much less that he'd stumbled across this property during one of his killing sprees. Foolish to think that his evil lingered. Yet there was something about this place...

Will wanted to laugh at himself—a seasoned law enforcement officer letting his imagination and an abandoned house creep him out—but he'd learned a long time ago that listening to his instincts usually paid off. He stood on the porch, watching and waiting as the sun slipped lower and the air finally started to cool. He could already hear the eerie yip of a coyote in the distance. A flock of blackbirds rose suddenly from the treetops, the flapping wings physically startling him. He rested his hand on the handle of his holstered weapon as he continued to observe his surroundings. A shadow moved at the side of the outbuilding. For a moment, Will could have sworn someone stood in deep shade watching him. Common sense told him it was nothing more than a bush or tree limb stirred by a faint breeze.

Still, he unfastened the catch on his holster as he went down the steps and walked through the weeds to the building. Scouring his surroundings, he slid back the barrel lock and propped the door open with a block of wood. The interior was dark, save for the light streaming in through the open door. On the opposite wall, a single window had been covered with a cloth or tarp, blocking the natural light from the west.

Will hovered in the doorway until his eyes once again grew accustomed to the gloom. The shed must once have been used as a workshop. Long tables built of plywood and two-by-fours lined rough-hewn walls where rusty tools still hung from pegs.

Like the house, the shed smelled of nesting rodents and

damp earth, but beneath those fusty odors, he caught a whiff of something that might have been fresh sawdust. Unlikely. There was no power to the house or shed and judging by the condition of the hand tools, no one had touched them in decades.

As he stepped inside, he realized what he had mistaken as another worktable or bench was, in fact, a coffin-sized box. A thrill skirted up his spine. The container looked very much like the one in which Thora had been trapped. He estimated the size to be a few inches longer and wider than hers, just large enough to accommodate a lean adult male roughly his size.

A hole had been cut at one end and fitted with a piece of PVC pipe. The lid rested on the box but wasn't yet secured. He presumed that meant the box was empty, but even as he reached for the top, he heard something that might have been fingernails scrape against the wood. Bracing himself for what he'd find, he shoved the lid aside.

The light from the doorway didn't reach far enough to penetrate the interior of the box. He couldn't immediately see what had been trapped inside until the rat scurried to the opposite end and cowered in a corner.

Will had no idea whether the rodent had been purposefully imprisoned or had slithered down the PVC pipe and couldn't find a way out. The former would suggest someone had been inside the shed recently. Perhaps only hours ago. Perhaps only minutes ago. While he watched, the rat found enough courage to scurry up the wall of the box and disappear over the side.

He removed a pair of latex gloves from his pocket and began a methodical search of the space. Whoever had built that box and transported it all the way out to the shed must surely have left something behind in the process.

Circling the room slowly, he took in the details he'd overlooked in his initial search. The cobwebs had been knocked down from the corners and the wooden floorboards looked to have been recently swept. The worktables had also been cleared of debris. He wondered when and why the box had been left in the shed.

He took out his phone, using the flashlight beam to play over the rough walls and ceiling and then he crouched to shine the light up under the worktables. Something metallic gleamed on the floor. Remembering the latchkey beneath Thora's car, he reached under the table with his gloved hand. Nothing but a nail. The floorboards were rotting through in places. Probably dozens of loose nails scattered about the place. But the one in his hand wasn't as worn as he would have expected in a place this old and leaky.

Pushing the table aside, he took a closer look at the floor. The nail heads on several of the boards looked new. He found a claw hammer to pry up the planks and then angled his beam down into the opening. A human skull grinned up at him.

Chapter Eleven

"Judging by the size of skull, we're looking at the remains of a child or a very small adult," Reyes said a little while later as he and Will hunkered beside the opening he'd created in the floor. "Hopefully, the DNA database can give us a match."

"That could take a while." Will was still shaken by the discovery. Even with the shed door propped open and several officers milling about outside, he felt a chill up and down his spine. There were things even the most experienced law enforcement officers never got used to, crimes against children being at the top of the list.

Reyes shifted his weight to his other foot. "Medical examiner is on the way. Maybe she can give us some idea of how long the bones have been down there."

"Dr. Larkin is good, but we may need to consult with a forensic anthropologist. Skeletal remains are tricky."

Reyes nodded. "I'll call Dr. Grover at Texas State, but I doubt he can fit us into his schedule before late next week. And that's being optimistic."

"The exhumation can't wait that long. Look at the size of the skull, Angel." Will's voice turned grim. "That's not a small adult. The victim was a child. I don't want to leave the remains unprotected any longer than necessary."

"I hear you."

They were both silent for a moment.

"You grew up in the area," Reyes said. "You've been on the force for a long time. Any idea who the victim might be?"

"I keep thinking about a kid that went missing ten years ago while walking home from school. Despite an intensive search, his body was never found. He was nine years old. The size of the skull looks about right."

"A decade is a long time for a family to remain in limbo," Reyes said. "What was the boy's name?"

"Danny Hagan. Only child, troubled home. Stepfather heavily into drugs. The guy looked guilty as hell. An eyewitness claimed they saw Danny get into his truck, but we never found enough evidence to charge him."

"You worked the case?"

"Elise Barrett and I did some legwork as first-year detectives. We beat the bushes for months. Never found so much as a trace. A child goes missing in broad daylight…that's the kind of case you don't forget. The kind that keeps you up at night a decade later."

"We've all got those," Reyes muttered.

"The lead investigator was a guy named Pennington. He retired a few years back."

Reyes glanced up. "Barrett's name sure seems to be popping up a lot lately."

Too often for comfort in Will's book. "Did you have time to get the information we talked about earlier?"

"Yeah, and you're not going to like it. She took two vacation days at the beginning of the week in question. Doesn't mean she hopped a plane to Alabama. Could be she just wanted a long weekend."

"But we now know it's a possibility." Will rested his

forearm across the top of his thigh. Reyes was right. The new information didn't sit well. He didn't like questioning a fellow officer's integrity, much less someone with whom he'd once been involved. But ever since he'd spoken to Elise earlier that day, doubt had continued to niggle.

Reyes narrowed his gaze. "What's going on with Barrett? I'm sure you have your reasons for digging into her whereabouts, but if any of this is personal—"

"It's not," Will assured him. "She was at the pub last night. I asked her if she'd spoken to Thora and she lied to my face. They were seen having a conversation. I don't know why she tried to deceive me about something that could be easily verified, but now I can't help wondering what else she may have lied about. Or what she might be hiding."

Reyes glanced at him. "I couldn't help noticing earlier your interaction with Thora. Feel free to tell me it's none of my business and we'll move on."

"Everything about the investigation is your business. Thora and I grew up together. We were best friends as kids and we dated all through high school. Things got a lot more serious in college. I wanted to marry her."

"What happened?"

"It's a long story and this isn't the time or place," Will said.

"I only ask because of the reference to her in the text messages. The sender called her your precious Thora. Sounds like something a jealous ex might write."

"That's one of the reasons I went to see Elise. I kept telling myself no way she could ever be involved in a kidnapping, much less burying someone alive. She's a cop, for God's sake. But then she lied to me. For whatever reason, she didn't want me to know she'd spoken to Thora last night."

"Maybe you should ask Thora what they talked about."

"Oh, I intend to. Just as soon as we're finished here."

They both returned their attention to the bones.

"You know what I think?" Reyes asked.

"I'm almost afraid to ask."

"We know the Weatherman was active as far back as ten years. The body of the first known victim was found a few miles off I-10 near Baton Rouge in an abandoned property not unlike this place."

"You think Ridgeway did this?" Will glanced around at their surroundings as his uneasiness deepened. "You're letting Noah Asher get in your head. Most of Ridgeway's victims were adult females."

"Most but not all. He started with children."

"It's a long shot," Will insisted.

"Maybe, maybe not. The FBI always believed Ridgeway held back the names and burial locations of some of his victims as bargaining chips. Let's think about this for a minute. We know Asher has been visiting Ridgeway every month for the past two years, but what we don't know is whether or not they had a relationship before Ridgeway was incarcerated. Asher claims he came to town to do a podcast as PR for an upcoming book about the Weatherman. You caught him red-handed in Thora Graham's home and we know he kept tabs on her right before she was taken. He also claims Ridgeway has a fascination for Thora, but it seems to me they both do. What if Ridgeway told him where the body was buried?"

"You think he came out here, pried up the planks to view the remains and then nailed the floor back down? Why?"

"Timing." Reyes swatted a mosquito from his face. "What better way to get your book noticed than to discover the skeletal remains of one of the Weatherman's first victims? A child, no less. You have to admit the PR from those headlines would beat the hell out of a podcast."

"He said he came to town because Logan Neville would only do the interview in person."

"Asher said a lot of things. Conveniently, we haven't been able to corroborate that part of his story with Professor Neville."

Will pondered the possibility for a moment. "Let's assume everything you say is true. How would he explain his discovery? You don't just drive across three states and happen upon human remains buried beneath the floorboards of an abandoned shed out in the middle of nowhere."

"He could basically tell the truth. Ridgeway told him where he'd hidden the boy's body and Asher wanted to make certain the claim was true before he got the family's hopes up."

"Then why kidnap Thora?"

"They struck a bargain. Asher gets the story of a lifetime and Ridgeway gets payback for Thora's part in his capture."

"It's an interesting theory," Will said. "But how do you explain the second box?"

"I haven't worked that part out yet," Reyes admitted. "Whoever left it here must have a connection to the skeletal remains...unless we're dealing with one hell of a coincidence." He paused for a moment. "But let's go with that angle for a minute. Say the kidnappers stumbled across the bones by accident. The discovery was made while they were planning or initiating the abduction. They'd have no choice but to nail the floor back in place and remain silent about the remains."

Will nodded toward the wooden container. "So who do you think the second box was meant for?"

Reyes shrugged. "That's the big question. Maybe you

were right earlier. Maybe all this business with the Weatherman is nothing more than a false lead. A red herring."

"I don't know what to think at this point," Will admitted. "All I know right now is that nothing makes sense and everything seems connected."

"Early days," Reyes said. "We'll figure it out."

He rose and went outside to meet the medical examiner, leaving Will alone once more in the shed. He rubbed the back of his neck as he stared down at the skull. The empty eye sockets stared back at him accusingly. *What took you so long?*

THE EMTs HAD hooked Thora up to an intravenous drip and checked her vitals on the way to the hospital. Upon arrival, she was whisked into an emergency room cubicle where a forensic nurse drew blood, bagged her clothing and personal effects and collected trace evidence from her skin, hair and beneath her fingernails. Afterward, she was allowed to shower and wash the dirt and twigs from her hair before a doctor came in to conduct a more thorough examination. The dehydration was severe enough to warrant an overnight IV so a few hours after her arrival, she was moved to a private room on an upper level of the hospital.

The adrenaline rush from the rescue had kept her going throughout the necessary procedures. She'd coped well enough until she was left alone while her mother and sister underwent the required screening process for visitors. The quiet was nice at first. Gave her a moment to catch her breath. She was on the fifth floor, too high to see anything more than the glow of streetlights below, but she had a perfect view of the rising moon. At any other time, she might have taken no notice, but after being trapped in a buried box, she found the night sky surreal and impossibly beautiful. In those hushed moments with nothing to distract her, she felt almost at peace. Then without warning, terror descended. Her heart started pounding and she found herself shaking so hard she had to grip the edges of the mattress.

By the time her mother and sister walked through the door, she'd managed to talk herself down enough to greet them with a smile. Her mother immediately began to fret about her color and fuss with the bed covers.

"Mom, I'm fine. I've been examined and given a clean bill of health except for dehydration, which is what this is for." She lifted her hand with the IV needle. "By tomorrow morning, I'll be as good as new. I already feel a lot better."

"You just look so frail lying in that bed."

"I'm the opposite of frail," Thora said. "I was raised by you, wasn't I?"

Maddie bit her lip. "You're strong despite me, I think."

"Please, both of you just stop." Claire moved around to the window side of the bed. She'd taken the time to style her hair and apply makeup before leaving the house, but in the harsh hospital lighting, Thora could detect worry lines across her forehead and a faint darkness beneath her eyes.

"Stop what?" she asked with a frown.

"This whole back-and-forth you have going on. Mom acting as though you're still ten and you pretending you're fine like you always do. But you're not fine. You were kidnapped and buried alive, for God's sake. I don't care how much experience and training you've had—you don't come through something like that unscathed."

"I never said I was unscathed," Thora said. "Physically, I'm unharmed."

Claire barreled on without the slightest hesitation or hint of self-awareness. "It's almost an insult to shut us down like that. We're allowed to worry. Do you have any idea what we went through? We didn't know if we'd ever see you again. Or if we'd even be able to find your body. You can't imagine the things that went through my head."

"Oh, I think I can," Thora murmured.

"Mom, stop hovering. You'll drive us both up the wall. And you—" Claire trained her gaze on Thora. "Stop trying to sweep your emotions under the rug. You need to let us in this time."

"Claire," Maddie said from the other side of Thora's bed. "Shut up."

She looked dumbfounded. "What?"

"You heard me, dear. You know I love you and I would do anything for you, but this isn't about you. We've got our Thora back. We need a moment to appreciate how lucky we are. Yes, I'm guilty of hovering and I sometimes let the negative emotions get the better of me, but your bullying doesn't help any of us right now. Just let Thora be. We'll have plenty of time as a family to process what happened. She's safe and nothing else matters."

Claire opened her mouth to retort, then clamped her lips shut when someone knocked on the door. Or maybe when she glimpsed the stubborn set of Maddie's jaw. Thora couldn't help but be amused by the unexpected dynamic. Her sister was accustomed to steamrolling over everyone and everything in her path. She didn't know how to react when someone pushed back, especially their normally docile and sometimes absentminded mother.

They all turned toward the door as Will came into the room. Thora was glad they'd had a few moments alone together in the woods. She was better prepared to conceal her emotions in his presence.

He looked a little taken aback by the trio of curious gazes. Despite the awkwardness, his focus went straight to

Thora. She stared back until embarrassment and uncertainty prompted her to glance away. She wondered if anyone else had noticed the shift in energy. The almost palpable tension that suddenly pulsed through the room. Thirteen years and a dead husband, and Will Dresden still had the power to make her heart flutter.

"Sorry for the interruption." He waited inside the door. "I just came by to see how you're doing tonight."

She forced a smile. "Much better. They let me shower and brush my teeth. I feel like a new person."

Claire muttered something under her breath as she filled a water cup.

Thora tried to ignore her sister's touchiness. "One of the orderlies said the police had requested I be moved to a private room near the nurse's station. Was that your doing?"

"It's protocol when we have cause to worry about a continued threat. The ER has too many people coming in and out at all hours, especially on a Saturday night. It'll be easier to spot someone up here who doesn't belong."

Maddie said in alarm, "What do you mean a continued threat? You don't think the person who took Thora will come back, do you?"

Thora met Will's gaze and shook her head slightly.

He said, "It's a precaution. I'm putting a guard outside the room for the rest of the evening and night. You don't need to worry. She'll be in good hands."

"A guard?" Maddie looked stricken. "That's more than a precaution. It sounds like you're expecting trouble." She wrung her hands. "I thought the nightmare was over when you found Thora unharmed."

"How can it be over when the kidnapper hasn't been caught?" Claire pinned Will with a glare. "You must have a lead by now."

Thora silently counted to ten, then said, "Will you both please relax? Nothing is going to happen to me while I'm in the hospital. And I'm certain Will and his team are doing everything in their power to identify and locate the unsub. The best thing we can do is stay out of their way."

The conversation had deflated Maddie's moment of positivity. She looked tense and unhappy, which, perversely, seemed to buoy Claire's spirits. She came around the bed and patted Maddie's arm. "I don't know about you, but now that my nerves have finally settled, I could do with a bite to eat." She motioned to Will as she moved toward the door. "Can I have a word before we go?"

Thora wondered what that was all about. For her mother's sake, she tried not to look concerned as the pair stepped into the hallway and closed the door.

They returned a few minutes later and Claire beckoned to their mother from the doorway. Maddie leaned down and kissed Thora's forehead before she reluctantly joined her other daughter in the hallway. To Will, she said, "You'll keep her safe?"

"You have my word."

And then they were gone, and Thora found herself alone in the room with the man she'd said goodbye to thirteen years ago. She thought about the imaginary conversations she'd had with him before her rescue and wondered what he would say if she told him that he'd saved her life and her sanity before he'd physically found her. The box had been a nightmarish prison and his voice in her head had been her lifeline.

She couldn't take her gaze off him as he moved to the foot of the bed. He somehow seemed different and exactly the same. "What was that about?"

"You mean Claire? She wanted to follow up on a matter we spoke about this morning."

"Anything I should know about?"

"We'll get into it later." His expression remained inscrutable, but he shifted uncomfortably.

Thora recognized the body language. He wasn't as sure of himself as he wanted her to believe. Funny how after all these years she could still read him. At least, she liked to think so.

She strove for a conversational tone. "Claire means well, but she can sometimes be a pill."

"If by pill, you mean stubborn and opinionated, yeah. She isn't afraid to tell you how to get the job done if she thinks you're slacking."

"That's Claire. Some things don't change."

"Don't underestimate her," Will said. "She's a good one to have on your side."

"I know."

He ran a hand through his hair as he watched her from the foot of the bed. He looked tired. According to Claire, his day had started early that morning with her mother's frantic phone call. Despite exhaustion, he flashed one of those devastating smiles Thora remembered so well. "So, how are you really feeling?"

"I'm fine."

He cocked his head as he gazed down at her. "It's just us now. You can tell me the truth."

"You're starting to sound like Claire."

"I've been accused of worse. Let's try this again. How are you really feeling?"

She sighed. "If you must know, I seem to have a problem being alone but it's not something I want to talk about."

"Why not?"

She turned her head to the window. "No one wants to know how you're really doing. They say they do. They probably even think they do, but most people actually prefer platitudes. The truth makes them uncomfortable."

"You don't really believe that."

Her gaze cut back to him. "It's been my experience."

"Maybe you've been hanging out with the wrong people. Or maybe you're reading the room wrong."

She thought about her sister's insistence that Thora share her experience with the family rather than sweeping her emotions under the rug. She knew Claire loved her and wanted only the best for her, but the moment she revealed even a fraction of what she'd gone through these past few years, Claire would be the first to shut down. Despite her constant needling about openness and sharing, deep down she wanted to believe that her sister was still the tough, resilient warrior from their childhood. For the longest time now, Thora had felt she was anything but.

Will was still staring down at her. "You okay? I seemed to have hit a nerve."

She sighed. "Do you *really* want the truth?"

"No platitudes. Give it to me straight."

"A little while ago, I was lying here looking out the window and I started to shake. I couldn't stop. My chest tightened so painfully I thought for a moment I might be having a heart attack. Or that I'd wake up and find myself back in the box and my rescue was just a dream. That you were just a dream." She paused on a shiver. "How's that for candor?"

"Refreshing. And look. I'm still here."

Strange how easily it had all tumbled out when she'd spent years bottling everything up inside. Maybe those moments alone in the woods had broken the ice and lowered her natural reticence. Maybe deep down she still considered Will Dresden the best friend she'd never been able to replace. Whatever the reason, the past thirteen years suddenly seemed like the blink of an eye.

She lifted her hand to observe the tremors. "I'm still shaking."

"Of course you are. The combination of adrenaline, shock and fear can make for a powerful cocktail. Mix that with the residuals from whatever drug you were given, and I'd be amazed if you didn't have the shakes."

His pragmatic tone somehow made her feel better. "How long before it wears off?"

"The drug or the adrenaline? Everyone's different. Could take hours, days or even weeks before you feel back to normal. You need to give yourself time to heal no matter how long it takes."

She mustered a smile. "I'll take that under advisement, Dr. Dresden."

His gaze was steady and observant. She'd forgotten how intensely blue his eyes could be even in the most casual moments.

"What?"

He shrugged. "I was just thinking that in spite of the circumstances, it's good to see you."

Her heart jumped unexpectedly. "You, too."

"Wild reunion, huh?"

"As you said, one for the books."

He shook his head in awe. "Of all the ways I imagined we'd run into one another when I heard you were back, I never could have predicted this."

She fiddled with her ID bracelet. "How did you imagine we'd meet?"

"I don't know. One of the usual ways, I guess. The grocery store, the gas pumps. Maybe a restaurant. You've been back…what? Six months? Belfort hasn't grown that much. I was surprised when we never bumped into one another."

Was that disappointment she heard in his voice or wishful thinking in hers? "You could have just called me."

He propped his forearms on the footboard. "I thought about it. A lot, actually. But I didn't want to put you on the spot. You've been gone for a long time. We're not the same people we were when you left."

"You wouldn't have put me on the spot. I would have enjoyed hearing from you."

"Then why didn't you call me?"

An edge of something she couldn't define crept into his voice. "I wasn't sure you'd want to hear from me. I'm the one who left town." *Left you.*

"It wasn't all on you. I drove you to the airport. I could have asked you to stay before you got on that plane. I didn't."

"I used to wonder why."

"You knew why." He came around the side of the bed and perched on the edge as if the last thirteen years was like the blink of an eye for him, too. "Getting accepted into the FBI Academy was the chance of a lifetime. It was your dream."

"The dream was that we'd go to Quantico together."

"My circumstances changed so my dream had to change. But I wasn't about to hold you back. If I'd ask you to stay, you would have ended up resenting me for the rest of our lives."

"You don't know that."

"Yes, I do. We both do. And anyway, I like to think things have a way of working out the way they're supposed to."

She clasped her hands on top of the covers. "I wish I believed that. In my experience, things sometimes go to hell no matter what you do."

His smile seemed sad and tender at the same time. "You've gotten cynical."

"I was just buried alive. I'd say I'm entitled."

"When you put it that way…"

He placed his hand against her cheek and for a split second they both froze, gazes locked. And then he leaned down and brushed his lips against her. It was barely a kiss. More comforting than sexual. She knew better than to read too much into it, and yet her pulse thudded in a way she hadn't experienced in a very long time.

Chapter Twelve

He drew away almost at once. "Sorry. I didn't mean—"

"No, don't be sorry." She looked pale and flawless in the hospital lighting. "It was nice. Comforting."

Might as well be talking about an old pair of shoes. Will felt sufficiently humbled as he stood and moved back to the end of the bed. "It's been...nice catching up, but we've got a lot to go over, so we should probably get started."

Her gaze followed him. Had her eyes always been that dark and soulful? That knowing?

She nodded. "Okay."

"We've had some new developments in the investigation. Things have happened that you should know about it."

She propped herself up against the pillows. "Things regarding my abduction?"

"Could be connected. We just aren't sure how."

"Well, that sounds intriguing. And infuriatingly vague. What's going on, Will?"

He took a moment to get his thoughts in order. Her eyes were a powerful distraction. They brought back a few too many explicit memories. "After you left in the ambulance, I did some exploring on my own. I located the old house we spoke about earlier. The one I photographed when we were kids."

She nodded. "The haunted house."

"You're teasing with that description, but you may not be as far off the mark as you might think."

Her amusement faded. "What do you mean?"

"I went searching for the house because I figured if the kidnappers knew about the cemetery, they'd also know about the homestead. And if they'd been inside, they might have left evidence."

She asked anxiously, "You found something?"

"More than I bargained for. I found another wooden container in an old shed behind the house. An air tube had already been affixed to the lid."

"What?" She bolted upright. *"Who—"*

"It was empty unless you count the poor rat that somehow got trapped."

"They must have been planning a second kidnapping," she said. "Do you know the identity of the intended victim?"

"If we assume the boxes are made to size, I'd say someone approximately my height and weight."

"You don't think—"

"No. I don't see them coming after me. I think they'd rather have me running in circles looking for them."

"I hope you're right." She lay back against the pillows. "What about tire tracks, fingerprints, hair and fiber evidence?"

"We're still checking. I'll let you know if anything turns up."

She nodded, her fingers idly pleating the edge of the sheet. "Why do I get the feeling there's more to your discovery? What aren't you telling me, Will?"

"You always were perceptive." His smile was strained. "I

noticed that some of the nails in a portion of the floor looked
new. Like someone had recently hammered the planks back
down. When I pried them up, I discovered skeletal remains
beneath the shed. Human remains."

She looked so taken aback, he wondered if the news
should have waited until morning. By her own admission,
she was still suffering aftershocks from her kidnapping and
burial, and likely would for some time to come. Will's instinct was to shield her from the disturbing discovery, but
she was every bit the professional he was. Her experience
and training had given her skills and the kind of insight
that might be just what his team needed to fit the puzzle
pieces together. Still, he needed to tread carefully. Since
the moment he'd set foot in that shed, a dark premonition
had hovered over him. He had a bad feeling that both he
and Thora were being led down a path that neither had any
wish to traverse.

"Have you identified the remains?"

He marveled at how normal her voice sounded after the
shock of his disclosure. "We'll have to wait for the DNA
analysis to know for sure."

"But you have some idea who the victim was?"

"We have clues," he said. "For one thing, the skull is
small."

"A child?"

They exchanged solemn glances.

"We think the remains may be that of a missing boy
named Danny Hagan. He disappeared ten years ago while
walking home from school."

"Wait a minute," Thora said with a frown. "I know about
that case."

"I'm sure you do. A missing child from your hometown
would have gotten your attention."

She was already shaking her head. "That's not it. Last night at the pub, Logan Neville told me he and some of his students were working on a cold case that the local police had botched. He didn't mention the victim's name, only that the boy had vanished on his way home from school. Professor Neville has an incomplete police file, which he said he obtained by submitting a public information request. But he seems to think he can get access to the sealed records connected to the case through a confidential source at the police department."

"What source?"

"He didn't say."

Will's mind went back to that morning when he'd seen Neville leaving Elise Barrett's house. He wondered again what the two of them had been arguing about on her front porch. "Why did he tell you about the case?"

"He wanted to know if I'd take a look at the file. When I told him I'd think about it, he said I shouldn't wait too long. The boy's family deserves justice and the lead investigator needs to be held accountable. Will...he said you were the lead detective on that case." She took note of his expression and said, "He lied?"

"He got one thing right. The boy's family deserves justice."

"Why would he lie about something that could so easily be checked?"

"Seems to be a rash of that lately," Will muttered. "Maybe he thought attaching my name to the case would pique your interest. Or maybe accusing the new deputy chief of malfeasance and/or incompetence makes for a more sensational podcast than putting the blame on a retired police detective."

"He does seem to crave attention and adoration," Thora

said. "But I still don't understand what any of this has to do with my abduction."

"Maybe nothing. Maybe everything."

"That's not an answer." When he didn't immediately respond, she said, "You're still holding back. Don't do that."

He walked over to the window and glanced out. The moon was up, a shimmering sliver hanging just above the skyline. It reminded him of the treehouse and the countless nights they'd spent gazing up at the stars. He suddenly longed for the innocence of those hot summer evenings.

"Will?"

He shook off the memories and turned. "I need to ask a tough question. I think I know the answer, but I have to be certain. Have you been to see James Ellis Ridgeway in the past few weeks?"

She gaped at him in astonishment. "Why on earth would you ask that?"

"Can you please just answer me?"

"I've *never* been to see Ridgeway. I've never spoken to him or corresponded with him in any way. What does he have to do with my kidnapping? Or with that child's remains?"

"That's what we're trying to determine," Will said. "Correct me if I'm wrong, but some of his earliest victims were kids."

"Five that we know of before he graduated to adult females. We think he considered the children practice before he refined his MO and moved on to his real targets."

"Do you remember the locations of those bodies?"

"They were dumped or buried in rural locations a few miles outside of metropolitan areas." She recited them without the slightest hesitation. "Mobile, Alabama; Gulfport,

Mississippi; Baton Rouge, Louisiana; El Paso, Texas; and Las Cruces, New Mexico."

"All up and down I-10," he said. "Belfort isn't exactly in the middle, but it's certainly along his route."

"Will." She said nothing else for a moment. Then in a hushed voice, "Do you realize the implication? The discovery of a sixth child victim could mean there are more we haven't found yet. That we don't even know about."

"Is it so surprising? Ridgeway admitted to withholding the locations and identities of some of his victims for leverage. We have no idea how many could still be out there."

She grew pensive. Whatever emotions she might be feeling were well hidden behind her professional facade. "Last night before Professor Neville told me about the case, he asked if I would be willing to be a guest on his podcast. He wanted to interview me along with a freelance reporter who's writing a book about the Weatherman. Professor Neville said the reporter had been to see Ridgeway in prison and that my name had been mentioned."

Will nodded. "We know about the reporter. His name is Noah Asher. Earlier today, I found him inside your townhouse."

Her eyes widened. "How did he get in? And what was he doing in my home?"

"He claimed the back door was open. He said he was looking for evidence that had been overlooked when your townhouse was processed by CSU."

"What kind of evidence?"

"According to Asher, something that would prove the Weatherman was behind your abduction."

Her mask dropped for a moment, giving him a glimpse of her raw emotions. Dread, outrage. More than a touch of fear. "Did he find anything?"

"Not that we know of. But we've since learned that he's been going to see Ridgeway every month for the past two years. Their connection is apparently a lot stronger than he let on. We know he was in the pub last night before your abduction."

"The guy at the bar."

Will nodded. "We took him into custody on a misdemeanor, questioned him and then had to cut him loose. We'll keep him under surveillance for as long as our manpower and resources hold out. Or until he leaves town." Will paused. "Are you okay? I'm throwing a lot at you at once and this business with Ridgeway is bound to be unsettling."

"It's a lot to take in," she agreed. "But I'm glad you're being honest with me. I'd rather know than not know."

"That's what I figured."

"There's something you should probably know," she told him. "Professor Neville was the second person to bring up the Weatherman to me last night."

"Who was the first?"

"Elise Barrett. Do you know her?" She searched his face. "Of course you do. She said she'd been with the Belfort PD since college."

"I know her," Will said without inflection. "What did she say about Ridgeway?"

"That she'd always been fascinated by the case and wondered if their paths might have crossed during a killing spree that took him through Belfort."

"That's a strange thing to wonder about." Particularly since he'd never once heard her mention James Ellis Ridgeway when they were together.

Thora shrugged. "People are fascinated by serial killers. She also asked if I'd ever considered the possibility that Ridgeway could have been responsible for Michael's death."

"She said that to you?" His irritation at Elise took the sting out of hearing Thora mention her husband's name for the first time. Will was glad she could bring her marriage into the conversation so openly. He wouldn't want her to feel the need to hide that part of her life. He couldn't say with complete honesty that he was happy she'd found love, but he was deeply sorry she'd lost it.

"It's not like I haven't wondered the same thing," she admitted. "Michael died in a traffic accident. Someone ran a red light and broadsided his vehicle. There was no evidence linking Ridgeway to the crash, and he never claimed credit..." She trailed off. "But I still wondered."

"You were looking for answers," Will said. "It's human nature to try and make sense of a tragedy."

"Even when there are no answers."

"Even then." When his dad died, Thora had been the only one who'd been able to offer even a vestige of comfort and understanding. He wished that he could have been there for her during the worst time of her life, but that wouldn't have been appropriate or even welcome.

"Do you think it could be true?" she asked in a hushed voice.

"That Ridgeway was involved? I guess it's possible, but not very likely," Will said. "Even if it were true, it wouldn't be your fault."

"I know." But she looked haunted by the possibility.

He wondered if it was a good idea to keep going. Everything that had happened in past twenty-four hours had taken a heavy emotional toll. "Maybe I should clear out and let you get some sleep."

"But we're not finished yet, are we?"

"The rest can wait."

"No, don't go. I'm fine. We need to get through this and besides…"

She didn't want to be alone. Will could still read her, too. "Let's go back to the conversation with Elise for a moment. In the interest of full disclosure, you should know that we used to go out."

"You and Elise? That explains some things," she murmured, then glanced up. "Was it serious?"

"It was until it wasn't. I only bring it up because your sister told me this morning that Elise still has a chip on her shoulder from our breakup. At Claire's request, I went to see her."

"You think she might be involved?"

"Not really, but I needed to have a conversation with her to set my mind at ease. It didn't. She made it clear I'm not her favorite person these days. She blames me for getting her transferred from Criminal Investigations to Internal Affairs after we split up."

"Did you?"

"No. She was a good detective. I wouldn't do that."

Thora seemed to ponder the new information. "As much as I appreciate your candor, I still don't understand what any of this has to do with Ridgeway."

"I'm still getting to that." He moved back to her bedside as he scrolled through his texts. Then he sat down on the edge and handed her the phone. "This is an entry from the visitors' log at the Donaldson Correctional Facility from almost two weeks ago."

She took the phone, scanned the image and then her gaze shot back to his. "That's not my handwriting, although it does look similar. Someone obviously took the time to practice my signature, but I've never been to that prison."

"I believe you. Someone either faked your ID or stole the

real one to gain access to Ridgeway. Where do you keep your personal belongings when you're in class?"

"Locked in my office. Bottom desk drawer."

"Your driver's license never went missing?"

"If it did, it couldn't have been gone for long. I would have noticed."

"What about your passport?"

"I keep it in a drawer in my bedroom." She looked taken aback as if something had suddenly occurred to her. "Will, my ID wasn't the only thing taken."

"What do you mean?" Instead of getting up and putting distance between them like he should have, he remained perched on the edge of her bed. She didn't appear to mind or even to notice. Her brow was furrowed in deep concentration.

"I had a medallion on a silver chain in my hand earlier when I was brought into the ER. They bagged it up with my clothes and other personal effects. Someone dropped that medallion down the air tube early this morning."

"Why didn't you tell me before now?" Will asked.

"I don't know. Maybe I wasn't thinking clearly. I was in a daze when you pulled me out of that box. The next thing I knew, I was in an ambulance, then the ER...this is the first chance I've had to really talk to you. To think about what happened. I kept that medallion in a jewelry box in the same drawer as my passport. Someone must have found it when they were looking for my ID."

"If they went to the trouble of dropping it down the air tube, it must have some significance to you."

"It belonged to Michael." Her gaze met his as her fingers slid across the bed covers. For a moment, he thought she meant to take his hand, but instead she smoothed an invisible wrinkle from the blanket. "It was a gift from his grand-father. He never took it off. He had it on the day he died."

"I'm sorry."

Her hand lifted from the blanket as if to let him know she was okay. "Somehow, Ridgeway figured out it belonged to Michael, and he knew that it would have an emotional impact on me, especially while I was trapped in the box."

"Let's not get ahead of ourselves," Will cautioned. "Ridgeway's involvement is only a theory at this point."

"I lived with him in my head for so long, it's hard not to let my imagination get the better of me," she admitted. "You mentioned videos earlier. I'd like to see them."

"Do you really think that's a good idea?"

"Analyzing information is what I've been doing for the past decade. Maybe I can help."

Wordlessly, he queued up the first video and handed her his phone. Then he watched her as she watched the grainy footage. The only sound in the room was the beating of her fists against the container lid and her plaintive query, "Can anyone hear me? What do you want? Just tell me what you want!"

She glanced up once, met his gaze and then kept her eyes glued to the video. She played it again all the way through before she moved on to the second video, which she also repeated.

"It really was like looking for a needle in a haystack," she murmured.

"As I said earlier, we had some help. I could point out the markers, but they don't look like much without enlarging the individual frames. You should also take a look at the text messages below the videos."

She scrolled through the texts, then read them a second and third time aloud using different inflections.

"What do you think?" Will finally asked.

"They're interesting on a couple of levels," she said. "Other than the mention of my name, the thing that stands out is the tone. Texting is a very casual form of communication. We tend to text the same way we speak except in an abbreviated format. These messages have an unusual formality. It makes me wonder if the tone is real or if the sender is trying to disguise his or her true voice." Her eyes remained glued to the screen. "Does the literary reference mean anything to you?"

"I know the Moriarty character is a villain in some of the Sherlock Holmes stories, but the reference doesn't mean anything to me personally."

"He's more than a villain, especially in recent adaptations. He's an archenemy, a nemesis. A cold, brilliant mastermind who considers himself the detective's equal or better. He uses his intellect and cunning to devise cruel and sometimes personal ways to best Sherlock Holmes. Whoever kidnapped and buried me alive is also cruel and cunning. And they made it personal. For whatever reason, they feel the need to prove their superior skill and intellect. I'm guessing that's why you don't think the second box is meant for you."

"Like I said, you've always been perceptive."

She glanced up. "They don't want to kill you. They want to destroy you."

THORA COULD HEAR someone on the other end of the air tube. The drumming was faint. Tap, tap…pause…tap, tap. The sound kept repeating until she came awake on a gasp, instinctively lifting her hands to press against the lid of the container. Her palms met nothing but air. It was dark, but not as dark as the box.

Still, her heart pounded in terror as she glanced around, frantic to remember where she was. Slowly, shapes formed in the darkness as everything came back to her. She was in the hospital still hooked up to an IV drip. But she wasn't alone.

From her periphery, she saw a shadow rise from the darkness. *It's okay. It's just Mom or Claire.* Her mother had insisted on spending the night, but Claire had made her leave at some point, promising to stay and keep an eye on Thora even though a guard was stationed outside her room.

You're safe. No one can get to you in here.

Not her kidnappers. Not the Weatherman.

But her heart continued to hammer, and she tried to scramble away as the shadow moved toward her.

"Thora? Hey, it's Will. Can you hear me? You're okay. You're safe." He moved closer to the bed so that she could see his face in the moonlight streaming in through the window.

"Will?" His name came out as a tremulous whisper. "You came back?"

"Yes, a few hours ago. I'm sorry if I startled you."

"I wasn't expecting you. I thought—"

"What's wrong?" His voice sounded both gentle and mysterious in the dark.

"I thought I heard tapping."

"Tapping?"

"Like this." She drummed the sequence on the mattress. "They wouldn't give me water until I responded with the same repetition. At least, that's the way it seemed."

"Sounds like a control thing," he said. "They wanted to make you submit."

"And I did," she said. "For another drink of water."

"You did what you had to do to stay alive. That's a good thing."

She shivered. "Are you sure you didn't hear anything just now?"

"Just hospital noises in the hallway."

She tried to relax but her teeth chattered from nerves and the frigid AC. "I guess it was just a bad dream."

"You're bound to have them after what you've been through."

"You said it would take time." As the fog lifted, she lay back against the pillows and drew in cleansing breaths until her heart calmed and her pulse evened.

"Do you want me to turn on a light?"

"No, it's okay. I can see you." She glanced past him into the room. "Where's Claire?"

"She was exhausted. I promised I wouldn't leave your side if she'd go home and get some rest."

"I'm surprised you were able to talk her into it."

He smiled down at her. "I can be persuasive when I need to be."

"I remember. I'm glad she went home, but you don't have to stay. I'm okay." Of course, she wasn't okay and they both knew it. Her time in the box would haunt her for a very long time, possibly for the rest of her life. Even now, wide awake and in Will's company, a tiny part of her wondered if this was a dream. If she was still lying in that buried box with nothing but the mirage of Will Dresden to keep her from losing hope.

"Tell me about your dream," he said.

"There isn't much more to tell. I just remember the drumming or tapping. The sequence kept repeating in my head. Over and over and over. Like that sound has been ingrained in my subconscious."

"It'll fade in time." He was still at her bedside, peering down at her in the dark. "Are you sure you're okay? Can I get you anything?"

"Why is it so cold in here? I can't seem to stop shivering."

"Hospital rooms are always cold." He tucked the covers around her shoulders. "Better?"

"Some."

"Hold on, I'll see if I can scrounge up an extra blanket."

"No, don't go!" She hadn't meant to sound so adamant. "Sorry."

"Your teeth are chattering."

"I'll be okay in a minute."

He hesitated, then said, "Move over."

"Will—"

"You're freezing and I have body heat to spare. That's all this is."

She scooted to the side and he lay down, spooning her body against his. "How's that?"

"Better." His warmth was dangerously addictive. "Will?"

"Yeah?"

"Why are you doing this?"

"It's not a big deal. I'm just trying to warm you up."

"I don't mean this." She tugged his arm around her. "Why are you here at all? You said it yourself. We're not the same people we were thirteen years ago."

"So? I can't show you a little kindness? I can't still care about you?" His breath fanned against her hair. "You could have stayed gone for another thirteen years and a part of me would still care about you. A part of me would still miss you every single day."

She closed her eyes. "I missed you, too."

It was very quiet in the room. Even the routine hospital noises from the hallway had faded. She and Will might have had the whole floor to themselves. The darkness cocooned them, protected them. But even as she relaxed in the safety of his arms, her internal clock reminded her that twenty-four hours ago she was just waking up in the box.

As if sensing her distress, he said in a calming voice, "I saw the tree house today."

"At Mom's house? Hard to believe it's still there after so many years."

"Built to last even through hurricanes," he said. "Seeing it this morning brought back a lot of memories. Remember the neighborhood water balloon wars?"

"How could I forget? You and I made a good team."

"Deadly, some might say."

She found herself smiling in the dark. "I loved that tree house. I loved lying out there after dark and staring up at the stars." She said in the softest voice, "My first time was in that tree house."

"I know. So was mine." His baritone was a low rumble against her ear.

She rolled to her back and stared up at the ceiling. "We were both pretty naive. I seem to recall a lot of fumbling."

"And yet…"

"It was magical," she said on a dreamy sigh.

"And only got better with practice. A lot of practice, as I recall."

She turned her head to face him. "We probably shouldn't be having this conversation."

His amusement faded. "Because of Michael?"

"Because it makes the past thirteen years seem as if they never happened. But they did. We've both been through a lot since I left Belfort."

"I know. I'm sorry."

"I'm not just talking about my husband's death. I haven't told anyone the real reason I moved back home."

He rolled to his back so their heads were lying side by side on the pillows, as if they were once again gazing up at the stars. "You can tell me."

"Remember earlier when I said people don't really want to know how you're doing? I've had some experience with that kind of social awkwardness."

"What happened?"

"I had a panic attack at work. I've experienced a few over the years, but this was a bad one. A coworker found me huddled in the corner of my cubicle. I couldn't walk, I couldn't speak. I barely even knew where I was. It was as terrifying as waking up in the box. Maybe more so. I spent some time in the hospital."

"I didn't know."

"No one did. I kept it from my mom because she's always been such a worrier and she's had a few health scares of her own lately. Which is another reason I moved back. Anyway, in order to return to work, I had to be cleared by a therapist. She helped me learn how to deal with my repressed grief and guilt, and she taught me ways to cope with the darker aspects of my job. Eventually, things returned to normal, but the episode had to be noted in my file. It shouldn't have mattered, but I knew that it would."

"So you left the FBI and came home."

"Yes. I wanted to be near my family."

He said without a hint of awkwardness, "I'm glad you told me."

"I felt you should know."

He turned his head to stare at her. "Why?"

"Because it's not too late to walk away."

"I don't walk away," he said. "I learned the hard way not to give up without a fight."

Chapter Thirteen

Will left the hospital early Sunday morning and went home to shower and change clothes. Pulling on a pair of jeans, he lay down on the bed for a few minutes to think. He hadn't slept much in the past twenty-four hours and the rotation of the ceiling fan blades made him drowsy and lethargic. He only meant to close his eyes for a moment, but the next thing he knew, his phone woke him up. He glanced at the time. After nine. He'd planned to leave early enough to drop by the hospital to see Thora before her release, but now he was already running late for a meeting at the station with Reyes.

He answered his phone and put Reyes on speaker as he finished getting dressed.

"I went by Logan Neville's house again this morning," the detective told him. "No one answered the door and his car wasn't in the driveway. Maybe he left town for the weekend."

"You tried his phone?"

"Went straight to voice mail."

"Are you already at the station?"

"Just waiting on you, boss."

"Okay, give me a few minutes," Will said. "I'll swing by the U-SET campus on my way in."

"You think he'll be in the office on a Sunday morning?"

"He has to be somewhere," Will said. "Keep me posted if you hear from him."

Ten minutes later, Will found a parking place near the Criminology Department, an ugly brick-and-glass building that spoiled an otherwise attractive campus. In his final two years of college, he'd spent most of his time in that building. Back then, he could have found his way around the classrooms and hallways with his eyes closed, but that was before recent renovations had significantly changed the layout. A custodian let him in through the main entrance when he flashed his badge.

"Can you point me in the direction of Professor Neville's office?"

"Sixth floor, straight down the hallway, last door on the left. I doubt he's in, though. Classes ended on Friday. Most everyone's already cleared out."

"What about Professor Graham's office?"

"Same floor, first door off the elevator."

Will thanked him before heading for the elevators. The building seemed unnaturally quiet, as empty classrooms and lecture halls tended to be. Except for the custodian, he didn't see anyone around. The car bumped to a stop and the doors slid open. He stepped out and stood for a moment staring down the long hallway before he located Thora's office and tried the door. To his surprise, the knob turned and the door opened without a sound. Odd, because he would have thought she'd locked up before leaving on Friday.

Sunlight streamed into the small room from a long window directly across from the door. A leather chair faced the desk and behind the workspace, a credenza accommodated stacks of papers, file folders and books. Like her townhouse, the office lacked any personal touches. Even the crowded bookcases seemed impersonal with dozens of psychology and criminology volumes that could have belonged to anyone. The featureless space reminded Will that for all he knew, Thora's time in Belfort was transitory.

Snapping on a pair of gloves, he sat down behind the desk and tried the bottom drawer where she kept her personal belongings. He didn't know what he expected to find. She would have taken her purse and wallet with her when she left on Friday. The only thing that remained was an umbrella, a small makeup bag and a first aid kit.

He removed and examined each item. As he placed them back in the drawer one by one, he noticed a single hair had been caught in the zipper of the makeup bag. Not the brunette strand that he would have expected to find among Thora's belongings, but an auburn spiral that made him think instantly of Elise Barrett.

Carefully, he untangled the strand from the zipper and placed it in a small evidence bag. Then he returned everything to the drawer and was getting ready to leave when the ping of the elevator drew him out into the hallway. Someone had just stepped inside. He tried to catch a glimpse of the passenger, but the doors slid closed too quickly. For some reason, he felt a strong compulsion to find out who was on the elevator. He located the stairwell and took the steps two at a time down to the ground level. The elevator didn't stop but continued to the basement. Probably the custodian, he decided.

He got in the second elevator and went back up to the sixth floor, then followed the directions to Logan Neville's office. His door was also ajar but unlike Thora's office, the space was occupied. A young woman dressed in jeans and a navy T-shirt reclined in a swivel chair, her bare feet propped up on the desk. She had a sheath of papers in her left hand and a red marker in her right.

He checked the name on the door and knocked.

"Go away. I'm busy," she said in a bored drawl.

He pushed open the door. "Sorry for the interruption. I'm looking for Logan Neville."

"Obviously, he's not here," she said without looking up.

Will glanced down the hallway toward the elevators. "I didn't just miss him, did I?"

"Not unless you know something I don't," she muttered.

"Do you know where I can find him?"

"Who's asking?"

"Deputy Chief Will Dresden."

That got her attention. She laid the papers and marker aside and swung her legs off the desk. She looked to be in her early twenties, suntanned and fit, with thick blond hair and light blue eyes rimmed with lashes so long they had to be fake. She wore no other makeup except for a shiny glaze on her lips.

"This is quite the coincidence," she said in that same detached drawl. "By all means, come in." She waved him toward the chair across from the desk.

He hesitated for a split second before he moved into the office and took a seat. "Why is it a coincidence?"

"Professor Neville recently conducted an hour-long lecture on you."

"On me? That's a pretty dry subject," Will said.

"To the contrary, he's always been concerned about nepotism and legacy hires in mid-to large-size police departments." She gave him a long scrutiny. "I do most of his research. After digging into your background so thoroughly, I find it a little strange seeing you in person like this."

"Thoroughly, huh? And here I don't even know your name," he said.

"Addison March. I'm Professor Neville's TA." Her gaze was very direct, as if she knew the impact of her attractiveness and dared him to react to it.

He didn't. He returned her stare with nothing more than casual curiosity. "You may be just the person who can tell me how to reach him."

A frown flickered. "Have you tried him at home?"

"He's not answering his door or his phone."

"Well, then, he's probably already gone."

"Where?" Will asked.

She shrugged. "His usual summer sabbatical. He never tells anyone his destination. Even me."

"When was the last time you saw him?"

"We were together at Molly's Pub on Friday night. We meet there almost every weekend unless something more important comes up."

"By we, do you mean you and Professor Neville or you, Professor Neville and the rest of his team?"

She twisted her blond hair into a rope and draped it over one shoulder. "How do you know about our team?"

"Word gets around. It's not a secret, is it?"

"Hardly, but we try to be discreet. It's been our experience that the CID detectives can be particularly territorial if they feel threatened. They don't like to be shown up, especially by students, but I imagine you would know better than me about egos and insecurities." She cocked her head as she gazed at him across the desk. "I do have to wonder who you've been talking to, though. Let me take a wild guess. Baylee Fisher came to see you, didn't she?"

Will kept his expression and tone neutral. "Is she a friend of yours?"

Addison dismissed the notion with a roll of her eyes. "Please. Baylee is far too jealous and emotionally immature to have friends. She can be clever and occasionally useful, but she and I are most definitely not friends."

"Then how did you know she came to see me?"

"It wasn't hard to deduce. When we heard what happened to Professor Graham, Baylee claimed to have information that could help the police find her."

"What information?"

"She wouldn't say. That's a big part of her problem. She's not a team player. And she's prone to exaggeration."

"What if I told you she came to see me before she knew about the abduction?"

Addison smiled. "Then I would remind you of what I said at the beginning of this conversation. She's a very clever girl. Maybe that's what she wanted you to think. But you didn't come here to talk about Baylee Fisher, did you?"

"No, I didn't. Have you spoken to Professor Neville since Friday night?"

"Nope. When he's gone, he's gone." She folded her arms on the desk and leaned forward. "What's all this about, anyway? Why are you so interested in Logan… Dr. Neville's whereabouts?"

"I just need to ask him a few questions," Will said.

The long lashes blinked slowly. "Why don't you ask me instead? Maybe I can help you."

"Okay. For starters, I'd like to talk about the cold case that seems to have caught your team's interest."

"You meaning the missing boy? What about it?"

"Professor Neville told a colleague that a confidential source in the police department could provide access to sealed records connected to that case. I'd like to know who his source is."

She looked disappointed. "You came all the way over here to ask about case files?"

"Sealed records are exempt from public information requests. They can only be accessed by law enforcement personnel or by court order," he told her. "We take security breaches very seriously, particularly when the leak can compromise an investigation."

"What investigation? That case had languished in the archives for nearly a decade until it came to our attention." When he failed to offer a counterargument, she leaned back in the chair with a pensive frown. "Can we speak hypothetically?"

"Sure."

She got up to close the door and then came around to perch on the edge of the desk. "What if I told you there's a certain cop who has an ax to grind for the way she's been treated by your department? What if I told you that Professor Neville has a way of finding a person's weakness and using it to get what he wants? He's an expert at drawing people in who can be useful to him. When he's done…" She dusted off her hands. "He's done."

"That doesn't paint a very flattering picture of the man," Will said. "You aren't afraid he'll do the same to you?"

She smiled. "My eyes are wide open when it comes to Logan Neville. I'm a complete realist. I know how to get what I want, too."

"I don't doubt it, but we seem to be getting a little off track."

"No, we're not. It's all connected." She crossed her legs and leaned back on one arm. "Let's say the person who accessed those sealed files was the aggrieved cop. Say she's the one who brought the case to Professor Neville in the first place. She has something to prove and she thought *he* could be useful to *her*." She gave Will a curious smile. "Do you follow so far?"

"Trying to."

"The cop had begun an investigation on her own but soon became desperate for a fresh pair of eyes. She couldn't ask anyone in the police department for help, so she came to Professor Neville. All he had to do was convince her that getting access to those sealed records was paramount to cracking the case. Once he had what he wanted, he'd no longer need said cop." She straightened. "Now do you get the picture?"

"Why would he shut her out of the investigation once he had the records?"

"Because solving this case could be big. Mind-blowing big. Like book-deal big for someone with the right contacts. Why share the limelight when you can claim all the glory for yourself?"

"What makes this case so big?" Will asked.

"If I told you that, you might decide you want the glory."

"Does it have anything to do with James Ellis Ridgeway?"

Her eyes widened. "Who told you that?"

"I think you just did."

Her mask dropped back into place. "Why would you think the Weatherman had anything to do with a nine-year-old boy's disappearance? He preyed on women."

"Not in the beginning," Will said. "Is that why Professor Neville invited Noah Asher to be a guest on his podcast? Asher has a relationship with Ridgeway. He could provide the professor access to the Weatherman. But I'm not telling you anything you don't already know, am I? Does he plan to drop Asher, too, when he gets what he wants?"

All of a sudden, Addison didn't look bored or amused. "You may be smarter than she gives you credit for."

"Who?"

"Again, hypothetically, I'd recommend you take a look at a certain redhead in Internal Affairs who seems prone to obsessions and grudges. She used to hang out with us at the pub and offer unsolicited advice until she and Professor Neville had a falling out."

"Over the case?"

Her smile turned smug. "Among other things."

Will remembered Baylee's claim that Addison March and Logan Neville were sleeping together, which was why, according to Baylee, the TA got all the plum assignments. Ordinarily, he might be concerned for a young woman who had fallen under the spell of a man like Logan Neville, but he had a feeling the professor had met his match.

"Your promotion really sent her over the edge," Addison said. "She claimed when the two of you were partners, she did all the real police work while you coasted by on your looks and legacy."

"Just to be clear, are we talking about Elise Barrett?"

"I'd rather not mention names." Addison hopped off the desk and went back around to plop down in the chair. She swiveled for a moment, her gaze steady and mocking. "You know why she started working that particular case? She thought if she could prove her investigative skills were superior to yours, she'd be reinstated as a detective in CID. And she'd take you down a peg in the process. This won't come as a surprise, but the woman *really* doesn't like you, Deputy Chief."

"So it would seem." He rose and tossed his card on the desk. "If you hear from Professor Neville, ask him to give me a call."

She didn't bother picking up the card. "Before you go, can I ask you a question?"

"Go ahead."

"It's about Professor Graham. Her kidnapping and rescue have been all over the local news. I don't know her personally, and to be honest, I was never that keen to have her on staff. I don't find her credentials all that impressive. She wasn't even a field agent. But no one deserves to go through what she did. Do you have any idea who could have done something like that to her?"

"We have leads, but I really can't say much more at this time."

She went on as if he hadn't answered. "To be trapped in a box like that and then once freed, to realize that the monster who kidnapped and buried you alive could be someone you know, someone you work with, someone you see on a regular basis. Someone still plotting your demise. How would you ever get over something like that?"

"By finding and locking up the person or persons responsible," Will said.

"Do you think that will happen, though? What's the clearance rate for the Belfort Police Department? Thirty percent?"

"A little higher than the national average."

She gave him a disparaging look. "In other words, nothing to brag about. Which is why you have so many cold cases on your hands. Which is also why Professor Neville put our team together. We can help if you'll let us."

Will moved to the door. "Thanks for the offer. I'll keep it in mind."

"You won't because your ego will get in the way, but you should. We're very good at what we do." She rose, too.

"With the right resources and contacts, we could probably find Professor Graham's kidnapper within the week."

"I admire your confidence."

"Why shouldn't we be confident? We have the skills and know-how to back it up. Not to mention youth and energy." She came around the desk to see him out. "I wonder if you'd be interested in a wager, Deputy Chief. A challenge, if you will. Our team against yours."

That stopped Will cold and he turned. "This isn't a game. You're talking about a woman's life."

"I'm well aware of the stakes."

"Are you?" Will's voice dropped. "Let's get one thing straight. If you or any of your teammates interfere in our investigation in any way, you'll be slapped with a sizeable fine and thrown in jail for at least ninety days. You won't like the accommodations, I promise you."

"We'll take that under advisement." She leaned a shoulder against the door and folded her arms. She was still watching him when he got to the end of the hallway.

AFTER WILL CONCLUDED his meeting at the station with Reyes, he drove over to Elise Barrett's place and parked at the curb. The scent of the neighbor's roses bombarded him as he got out of the car and started toward the house. Before he reached the porch steps, another vehicle pulled to the curb. Instinctively, he stepped off the walkway, using the dense foliage for cover as he watched and waited. He expected to see Elise or even Logan Neville coming his way. The sight of Thora took him completely by surprise.

She didn't see him until she was almost to the steps. Then she visibly started as her hand flew to her heart on a gasp.

"Will! You scared me half to death. What are you doing

hiding in Elise Barrett's front yard?" She glanced toward the porch. "This is her house, isn't it?"

"I wasn't exactly hiding and the better question is why are you here?"

"For the same reason as you, I imagine. I have questions." She cast another glance toward the house and lowered her voice. "Is she home?"

"I haven't knocked yet." He motioned for her to follow him back to the street where they would be out of earshot. "When did you get out of the hospital?"

"A little while ago. Claire drove me home and agreed to stay at the townhouse and wait for the locksmith." She tucked her hair behind her ears, highlighting the darkness of her eyes and the paleness of her skin. How was it possible, Will wondered, that she could come through such a nightmare and still look as appealing as the day he'd driven her to the airport thirteen years ago?

"I'm surprised she let you out of her sight," he said.

"I know. Much less borrow her car, but I can be stubborn, too, when I need to be." She glanced past Will up the walkway and her expression subtly altered. The haunted look he'd noticed the night before flitted across her features. "I keep thinking about my conversation with Elise at the pub. Why would the notion even occur to her that Ridgeway might be responsible for Michael's accident?"

"You said you'd wondered the same thing," Will reminded her.

"That's different. At the time of the accident, I'd been on the Weatherman case for more than two years. He and his victims had become a part of my daily work life. But Elise has no apparent connection to the case. Why would she care enough to even speculate? Unless she's the one who stole my ID and went to see Ridgeway in person. Maybe he said something to her about Michael's accident. Did he claim credit, plant a seed?" She let out a breath. "I have so many questions running through my head, Will. You can't imagine what I've been thinking or the rabbit holes I've fallen into. If Elise really has been in touch with Ridgeway, I need to know what he said to her."

"We'll find out," Will promised. "One way or another. But you have to let me handle this. I know Elise. If we both confront her, she'll feel cornered and either lash out or button up."

"Then let me talk to her alone."

His response was visceral and not very tactful. "That's a bad idea."

"Why? You said yourself you're not her favorite person at the moment. She still has a chip on her shoulder from the breakup. Maybe she'll talk to me."

He lowered his voice as he cast a quick glance toward the house. "Let's assume for a minute that she is the one who used your ID to visit Ridgeway. Have you taken the supposition a step further and wondered if she might have somehow been involved in your abduction? Do you think she'll admit to everything and go with you quietly to the police station? The Elise I know won't go down without a fight."

She touched his arm briefly. The gesture seemed almost protective and somehow deeply intimate. "This can't be easy for you. Do you really think she's involved?"

He took a moment to answer her. "I don't know. I have a hard time believing the woman I've known for years—much less the detective I worked with—is capable of something so brutally cruel, but, like you, I have questions."

"Then let's go hear what she has to say."

"Thora—"

She'd already turned and started up the walkway. Short

of physically blocking her path, there was nothing he could do but follow her up the steps and across the porch to the entrance. The wooden door stood open, allowing the mid-day heat to invade the house through the screen.

"That's odd," she said. "I can hear the air conditioner running at the side of the house. Why would she leave the door open? Do you think she knows we're here?"

"One way to find out." Will reached around her and rapped on the door frame.

Thora cupped her hands and peered through the screen. "I can't see anything. It's too dim inside and too bright out here."

"Maybe we should give her time to get to the door before you go all Peeping Tom," he suggested.

"Will." She sounded tense. "Does this look like blood to you?"

He moved around her to examine the red smears where a bloody hand had clutched the edge of the screen door. Then he knelt and touched a finger to a droplet on the concrete floor. "It's fresh."

"Is that enough to constitute exigent circumstances?"

"I would say so. Besides, I've already conducted one warrantless search this weekend. Might as well go for two." He pounded on the door frame and called out Elise's name. "It's Will. Are you home?" He listened for a moment then stared through the screen just as Thora had done. "Elise, are you okay?"

"Can you see anything?" Thora asked.

"No sign of life."

She pulled a pair of latex gloves from her bag and snapped them on. At his look of amazement, she said, "I saw a box at the hospital and thought they might come in handy. I've got spares if you need them."

"Thanks, I've got my own."

She tried the screen door. It opened with a creak. "Shouldn't we go in and see if she's okay?"

"You wait out here," he said. "Circumstances have changed and I have a badge. Let me check things out before we both invade her privacy."

"Maybe you should glove up first in case we're dealing with a crime scene."

"Let's hope that's not the case." But blood at an open door was never a good sign.

"If I don't hear back from you in five minutes, I'm coming in," Thora warned.

Will called out Elise's name as he pulled open the screen door and stepped inside. Pausing to listen for signs of a struggle or distress, he moved cautiously from one room to the next. He found more blood drops on the bathroom floor and watery smears in the sink where someone had tried to clean up.

Backtracking into the kitchen, he went out the rear door to the shady patio where Elise spent most of her time. He checked the garage and behind the gate before going back inside to collect blood samples from the bathroom. Pocketing the evidence, he glanced inside the primary bedroom and then the room at the end of the hall that she used as a home office.

The space was just large enough to accommodate a desk and chair and a small sofa beneath the windows. On the opposite wall from the desk, she'd pinned copies of newspaper articles to a large old-school corkboard. Will went over to the desk and sorted through the stacks of folders. They contained police reports and interview transcripts from the Danny Hagan case. He remembered the hours he and Elise had logged going door to door, searching abandoned buildings, walking untold miles along creek banks, poking through underbrush and overflowing dumpsters. Eventually, they'd been assigned to other investigations and Danny Hagan had become another missing child statistic.

Newspaper clippings about the disappearance had been stuck to the corkboard, along with dozens of pieces chronicling the Weatherman's gruesome sprees. Next to the corkboard, she'd taped a map to the wall and pinned the locations of his kills along I-10. She'd obviously been trying to connect the missing boy to James Ellis Ridgeway. She used red pins to designate his known victims and a yellow pin to represent Danny's disappearance.

Will stood studying the map and the newspaper clippings until Thora called out to him from the porch.

"Will? Everything okay?"

"Hang on! I'll be right out."

He snapped a few shots of the corkboard and map before he went back over to the desk and tried the drawers. Most of them were filled with the usual office paraphernalia, but the bottom left drawer looked suspiciously shallow compared to the one on the right. He removed a stack of papers and knocked on the wood bottom. Then he slid his hand to the back of the drawer and felt for a notch. The false panel lifted up revealing an empty envelope with a Donaldson Correctional Facility return address.

"Will?"

"I'm coming." He replaced the false bottom and returned the contents to the drawer before going back out to the living room.

Thora stood in front of the built-in bookcases perusing the titles. She glanced over her shoulder when he came into the room. "You didn't find Elise?"

"No, but there's more blood in the bathroom."

"That can't be good. What should we do?"

"For one thing, you should go back outside," he said. "You're not supposed to be in here."

"I know, but when you didn't return, I got worried. I was afraid you might have run into trouble." She turned back to the bookcases. "Come take a look at this."

He moved across the room and stood beside her. "What are we looking at?"

"Middle of the top row. A collection of Sherlock Holmes stories."

"Not exactly a smoking gun," Will said. "You'd be surprised how many people give books like that as gifts to cops. They think we all like detective stories."

"Don't you?"

"I'm more of a history buff."

"Good to know."

They spun simultaneously toward the foyer as the screen door slammed closed. Elise came through the cased opening and stopped short when she saw them. Her bandaged hand went automatically to her shoulder bag, which presumably contained her firearm.

Will said, "Easy. We didn't mean to startle you."

She kept her bag close to her side as her gaze shot from Will to Thora and back again. "What are you doing in my house?"

"We saw blood on the porch." He nodded to the bandaged hand clutching her purse strap. "How bad are you hurt?"

"A few stitches, but I'll live."

"What happened?" He kept his voice low and nonthreatening. Elise could be volatile even on a good day.

She hesitated, then said, "I went after some bushes in the backyard a little too aggressively with a pair of clippers. I couldn't find my old pair and the new ones were a lot sharper than I thought. Sliced a couple of my fingers." She came into the room but didn't put down her bag. She also made sure she kept both of them in her line of sight. "So you saw blood on the porch. That explains why *you* entered my house but why is she here?"

"I'm his backup," Thora said.

Will turned in surprise but didn't contradict her.

She also kept her voice calm and neutral. "I apologize for barging in like this, but we really were concerned for your safety."

Elise looked almost amused. "You're his backup? After what happened to you?"

Despite Thora's measured tone, Will could detect a note of tension. "I'm fine. A little worse for the wear, but like you, I'll live."

The casual way she was able to discuss her ordeal amazed him, as did the ease with which she'd taken control of the conversation.

"I'm glad you're okay," Elise said. "But I still don't understand why either of you came to my house in the first place."

"I can only speak for myself," Thora said. "I came because of the conversation we had at the pub the night I was taken. Something you said has been bothering me."

Will scrutinized Elise's expression. He saw nothing but a flash of annoyance. "What did I say?"

"You asked if I thought James Ellis Ridgeway could have been responsible for the accident that killed my husband. I can't help wondering why something like that would even cross your mind. It seems so out of the blue. You didn't know Michael. You barely even know me."

Elise shrugged, but her eyes had gone ice-cold. Her gaze darted to Will as if she sensed a trap. "It was an observation based on what I'd read about the Weatherman. Why would it bother you?"

"You know why," Will said. "We can't help wondering if someone put the idea in your head. Ridgeway himself, maybe."

Her eyes flashed angrily. "That's ridiculous. But baseless accusations seem to be your stock in trade these days. Maybe you should try doing some actual police work."

He didn't take her bait, but instead nodded toward the hallway. "Seems as though you're doing enough investigating for both of us. I saw the corkboard, the case files...the envelope from the Donaldson Correctional Facility."

Thora drew a quick breath. "Will, what are you talking about?"

Elise cut in before he could answer. "You went through my office? You violated my privacy on the thinnest of excuses just so you could paw through my things? That's a new low even for you."

"You're right," he conceded. "I shouldn't have taken it that far, but I did and now you and I need to talk about what I saw."

Her chin came up. "What I do on my own time is my business. I don't owe you any explanations."

"But you do," Will said. "If you're giving Logan Neville access to sealed files, that's very much my business and warrants at least a conversation. Where we have that conversation is up to you."

She looked as if she wanted to tell him exactly what he could do with those sealed files, but instead, she shrugged. "Fine. We'll talk. But alone."

Will turned to Thora. "Can you give us a minute?"

Thora lowered her voice to a near whisper. "She still hasn't answered my question."

"I'll make sure we get back to it," he said. "Let me talk to her."

Thora seemed to ponder her options, then nodded. "Okay. But this isn't over."

"Not by a long shot," he agreed. "I'll call you later." He walked with her into the foyer and held open the screen door.

She turned to him on the porch, her voice still a whisper. "Be careful, Will. There's something about the way she looks at you. Don't let your past with her cloud your judgment."

The way my past with you clouds my judgment? "You're the one I'm worried about," he said. "Go straight home, okay? No stops. No distractions. I'm texting Claire right now to expect you."

He waited on the porch until she was safely in the car before going back inside. The room was empty.

"Elise?"

"Back here."

He found her seated at the kitchen table with a bottle of whiskey and two empty glasses. She poured a generous dollop in her glass and hovered the bottle over his.

"No, thanks. It's a little early for me."

"For me, too, but I need something to take the edge off." She held up her bandaged hand. "Hurts like hell."

"Since when did you get so careless with your gardening tools?"

"Since I realized I could take out my frustrations on the shrubbery."

"Seems like the shrubbery has decided to fight back."

Pulling out a chair, he surreptitiously glanced around for her bag before he sat. He wondered if she'd found a strategic hiding place for her weapon while he'd been on the porch.

Her eyes glittered with emotion as she stared at him across the table. "We used to banter like this all the time, remember?"

"I do."

"We'd sit right here after work and have a drink, shoot the breeze until we decided what to do about dinner." She circled the rim of the glass with her finger. "Sometimes we'd forego dinner altogether."

"Elise."

"We were good together, Will. If only you'd been able to let go of the past. And now you're bringing your past into my house."

"I didn't bring her here," he said. "I had no idea she was coming."

"You both just turned up here at the same time? Come on."

"I'm telling you the truth."

"Whatever." She poured another drink and downed it without flinching. "Let's get this over with. I've got things to do."

Will nodded and got right to the point. "Why are you investigating the Danny Hagan case off-book?"

"I'm no longer a CID detective, remember? I have to investigate off-book."

"Why Danny Hagan?"

"Because someone has to." She shoved her glass aside, but her gaze never left his. "I ran into his mother a few months ago. She remembered me. Came right up to me on the street and asked point-blank if anything was going on with her son's case. You have no idea how small I felt when I couldn't give her an answer. I told her I'd find out and get back to her. Turned out, nothing was being done. And that's on you."

"He disappeared ten years ago," Will said. "Do you know how many active cases we get in a month? Hell, in a week?"

"You sound defensive."

Yeah, maybe he was a little. "What did you think you'd find that we couldn't when the trail was fresh?"

"Who knows? Technology changes every day. Circumstances change. Ten years ago, we'd never even heard of James Ellis Ridgeway, let alone that he started his serial killer career preying on children. The lead detective was convinced the stepfather did it and we let his tunnel vision rub off on us."

"Just because we couldn't prove it doesn't mean he didn't do it," Will said. "James Ellis Ridgeway is a long shot, unless you know something I don't."

She coiled a corkscrew curl around her finger. "What if I do? Know something you don't, that is."

"Care to share?"

She dipped her head as if afraid he might read the truth in her eyes. "Not yet. Not until I'm sure."

"Is that why you're trying to access sealed records?"

"Who says I am?"

"That's not a denial."

She leaned in. "What's the matter, Will? Are you worried I'll solve a case you couldn't?"

"It wasn't my case."

"Guess what, Deputy Chief? They're all your cases now. How will it look when a cop you had transferred out of Criminal Investigations solves a disappearance that has haunted this town for a decade?"

"Is that what this is about?" Will asked. "You trying to prove you're a better detective than I am?"

"Oh, honey. I've always been the better detective."

He knew she was trying to get a rise out of him, so he

merely shrugged. "If you have it all figured out, why did you take the case to Neville?"

"Because I still have a full-time job. I needed help with research and legwork, and like it or not, he and his team have had success solving cold cases."

"The best I can tell, his team consists of a few overconfident students."

She sat back in her chair. "Look how dismissive you are, but you and I were once just like them. Remember how gung ho we were in the beginning before we got jaded? There's something to be said for that kind of naive zealotry."

"Zealotry?"

"Enthusiasm, if you prefer."

He toyed with his empty glass. "What's your current relationship with Logan Neville?"

"Why? Are you jealous?"

"I'm wondering what the two of you were arguing about on your front porch yesterday."

Her expression hardened. "That's personal and none of your business."

"Have you been in contact with James Ellis Ridgeway?"

"No comment."

"Did he tell you where to find the boy's remains?"

"No comment."

"Did he say anything about Thora Graham?"

"No. Comment."

He folded his arms on the table. "I have a theory."

Her tone turned bitter. "Oh, I'm sure you do."

"You went to the prison pretending to be Thora so that Ridgeway would agree to see you. He probably figured out the sham the moment he laid eyes on you. But he was willing to make a bargain anyway. He'd give you the location of Danny Hagan's remains if you arranged Thora's abduction. Am I getting warm?"

"Ice-cold, but I'm flattered you think I'm that devious. And capable. Kidnapping a woman with Thora's training and experience and burying her alive wouldn't be easy."

"You'd need help," Will agreed. "A partner in crime, so to speak. Maybe that's what you and Neville argued about yesterday. He's lying low and letting you take the heat."

She rose slowly and stood staring down at him. "You've always held a high opinion of your detective skills, one that I never shared. Now's the time to put up or shut up. If I'm the monster you seem to think I am, then all you have to do is prove it." She put her hands on the table and leaned toward him. *"Prove it."*

Chapter Fourteen

The neighbor's curtain twitched as Will strode up the walkway to Thora's townhouse late that afternoon. He waved at her and then went next door to ring the bell. He imagined Thora glancing out the peephole a split second before the dead bolt disengaged. She looked surprised when she drew back the door.

"Will! I wasn't expecting you in person." Her gaze narrowed. "Wait. Did Claire ask you to come over?"

"She did, but she's not the only reason I'm here. I wanted to touch base after my meeting with Elise."

"I wondered why I hadn't heard from you." She stepped back to allow him to enter. "What happened?" He followed her into the living room and she motioned to the sofa. "Can I get you something to drink before we talk? Claire made iced tea earlier. Or would you prefer something stronger?"

"If you have it."

"I don't have any beer, but I've got tequila for margaritas."

"Maybe not that strong. I need to keep a clear head."

"Wine it is, then." She left the room for a moment and came back with a bottle and two glasses. Settling on the sofa beside him, she poured the merlot and then tucked her legs beneath her. Will could smell lavender in her hair and on her clothes, but he couldn't be certain the scent was even real.

They sipped in silence until she set her glass on the coffee table and turned expectantly. "The suspense is killing me. What did Elise have to say?"

"She wouldn't admit to contacting Ridgeway, but I found an empty envelope in her desk with a Donaldson Correctional Facility return address. At some point, she must have written to him and he responded." He took another drink and then set aside his glass. "I asked if she'd gone to see him. I even went so far as to suggest she and Ridgeway had made a deal—the location of Danny Hagan's remains for your abduction."

Thora propped her elbow on the back of the sofa as she turned to face him. "What did she say to that?"

"She told me to prove it."

"But she didn't deny it."

"She didn't." He still had a difficult time accepting Elise's culpability, but worrisome things were starting to add up. "I didn't mention this earlier, but I was on campus before I saw you at Elise's house. I found something in your office."

"Why didn't you say anything?"

"We got sidetracked by the blood on the door and a few other things. I was hoping to find Logan Neville, but I decided to have a look around while I was there. Your door was unlocked. Is that usual for you?"

"No, I'm certain I locked it when I left on Friday."

"Anyone else have a key?"

She shrugged. "Any number of people including the custodial staff. It's the office reserved for temporary staff. People come and go."

"You keep a makeup bag in your bottom drawer," he said. "I found an auburn strand of hair caught in the zipper."

A frown flitted. "You think it's Elise's?"

"I don't know of any other redheads who'd have a reason for going through your belongings, do you?"

"No, but even if DNA could prove it was hers, a strand of hair is pretty flimsy evidence," she said. "Not as flimsy as a collection of Sherlock Holmes stories on her bookshelf, but as you said, not a smoking gun. What's the next step?"

"We still need to find Neville. His TA said he'd probably already left for his summer sabbatical. She claimed not to know his location. I'm wondering if he left town in a hurry so that Elise would have to take the heat for those sealed records. Or maybe he doesn't yet want to reveal why he's so anxious to get his hands on them."

"You think he's on to something?" An edge of excitement crept into her voice. "Maybe he found a connection to Ridgeway."

"That's one of several questions I'd like to ask him," Will said.

"You're the deputy chief. Can't you access sealed records? If we could take a look, maybe we could figure out what he found. Or what he suspects."

"It all depends on why the records were sealed," Will explained. "If opening the file could put someone's life in danger, for instance, we'd likely need a court order."

"How do you suppose Elise was able to gain access?"

"We don't know for certain that she did. Maybe Neville kept pressing her and she balked. Opening sealed files without proper authorization could be a career killer."

Thora leaned back against the sofa. "This is complicated."

"It is, but we're just getting started," Will reminded her. "The investigation is barely a day old and we've already uncovered quite a lot. We'll keep surveilling our suspects and investigating motives until we find our smoking gun.

Criminals always make mistakes. We'll turn up the heat until someone breaks or screws up."

"In the meantime—"

He nodded. "In the meantime, you're left wondering if the person in the elevator with you is the one who kidnapped and buried you alive."

She picked up her glass and gulped wine. "Suddenly, I'm not feeling quite as safe in my home as I did a few minutes ago. Maybe I never really felt safe. New locks and security codes can only do so much."

Will rubbed the back of his neck where tension had set in. "I didn't mean to upset you."

"You can't worry about upsetting me," she said with blunt pragmatism. "You have a job to do."

"I could have been a little more tactful."

"It doesn't matter. Until we find the person or persons responsible, I'll be looking over my shoulder no matter what you say." Her chin came up. "But I refuse to cower in my house until he or she is caught. I haven't told Claire or my mom yet, but I'm going back to work tomorrow."

Will frowned. "You really think that's a good idea? Didn't the summer session just end? College campuses tend to be ghost towns between semesters."

"It won't be completely deserted," she said. "Most of us still have exams to grade and final scores to post. I also have student consultations all week and a meeting with the dean on Wednesday. It'll be a busy week. The sooner I reestablish a routine, the sooner I'll start to feel normal."

He wondered if she was as sure of herself as she seemed. "You'll call if you see or hear anything even the slightest bit troublesome or out of the ordinary?"

She nodded. "I won't take any chances, I promise."

They each picked up their glasses and sipped. The last

thing Will wanted was to leave her alone, but he wondered if the reason she'd gone so quiet was her way of drawing their visit to a close. He set his glass down and rubbed a hand up and down his thigh.

"I should probably go—"

"I was just wondering—"

"You first," he said.

"Claire made a casserole for dinner. She happens to be a very good cook. If you don't have any plans—"

"I could eat," he said. "If it's not too much trouble."

"No trouble at all." She swung her legs off the sofa and stood. "I'll just go heat the oven."

He stood, too. "Anything I can do to help?"

They were face-to-face in close quarters between the sofa and the coffee table with no room to step aside. They dodged awkwardly for a moment until he put his hands on her shoulders.

The moment he touched her, something shifted in her body language. Her eyes grew dark and heavy as she stared up at him. Then she took a quick step toward him. "Could I just—" She took his face in her hands and kissed him.

The feel of her lips against his was such a shock, he inadvertently drew away.

She looked embarrassed as she stumbled back. "I'm sorry. I didn't mean—"

"Hang on a minute. You caught me by surprise." He took a step toward her and slid his fingers through her hair as he tipped her face to his. He kissed her slowly and for a very long time. When he finally pulled away, he smoothed back her hair as he gazed into her eyes. "So it wasn't my imagination."

"What?"

"The lavender." He ran his fingers through the glossy strands. "I used to dream about that scent."

"You did?"

"Too many nights to count," he admitted.

"I dreamed about you, too." She hesitated, her eyes going dark with emotion. "For the longest time, those dreams made me feel guilty. I felt I was betraying Michael's memory."

That stung a little. "And now?"

"All I know is that those memories gave me something to cling to when I didn't know if I would see the light of day again. The sound of your voice kept me going. I know it sounds far-fetched, but in a way, you were there in the box with me."

"If I could have been there instead of you—"

"I know." She took his hand and drew it to her face, turning her lips into his palm.

His heart was starting to pound a little too hard for comfort. "I want to kiss you again, but I keep wondering if it's too soon. I don't want to rush you. I might scare you away."

"You're the only thing in my life right now that doesn't scare me. When I think about all those years without you…" She took a breath. "Thirteen years, Will. How did we let that happen?"

He touched his fingertip to her lips. "We need to talk about those thirteen years. There's a lot I need to say to you, but right now, tonight…"

She nodded, took his hand and wordlessly led him up the stairs.

A FAINT GLOW from the setting sun filtered into the bedroom through the gauzy curtains, making the encroaching twilight seem surreal and still far away. Will was already shirtless and shoeless. He walked over to close the blinds and for a moment, the absence of light alarmed Thora. She stood shivering in the center of the room until he moved back to her.

"Should I turn on a light?" he asked.

"No. Just…" She pulled his arms around her and kissed him.

He drew her T-shirt over her head, unfastened her bra and then she lay back on the bed while he tugged off her jeans. He shed the rest of his clothes and they crawled under the covers, familiar strangers, stroking and exploring. She ran her fingers over his shoulders and down his back, becoming reacquainted with the contours of his body. His hand slid up her leg, dipped to her inner thigh and she shuddered. It had been a long time since anyone had touched her so intimately.

"Will?"

He moved up beside her in bed until they were once again lying head-to-head on the pillows. They stared up at the ceiling as if they could already see the stars.

"It's been a long time for me," she said. "Is that a weird thing for me to tell you?"

"You can tell me anything." His voice was deep and impossibly intimate in the dimness of her bedroom.

She entwined her fingers with his as they lay side by side. "I've missed talking to you. There were so many times when I needed so badly just to hear your voice. You were my best friend. Sometimes I wonder what my life would have been like if I'd never left Belfort."

He turned to stare at her profile. "You've done important work since you left. You've been married and widowed. Those aren't small things. They made you the person you are today. If you'd stayed…who knows where we would have ended up? We were kids when we fell in love. We both needed to experience a bigger world. I don't fault you for leaving. But I'm glad you've finally come home."

She turned her head to meet his lips. One kiss became two and then suddenly they were both breathing heavily as he moved over her. His eyes were soft and mysterious as he gazed down at her. And then he smiled and Thora thought, *Now I'm home. I'm finally home.*

Chapter Fifteen

Thora spent all day Monday in her office grading finals. Her abduction had made the rounds and the curious glances from students and faculty that were left on campus were a bit off-putting but understandable. Some approached but most kept their distance, not really knowing what to say or how to act. She understood. How did one commiserate with a teacher or colleague who had been buried alive?

She tried to keep her head down and concentrate on work, but late that afternoon a general feeling of uneasiness invaded. People had been coming and going from the sixth floor for most of the day, but suddenly she became all too aware of the silence as the building emptied.

"Professor Graham?"

She jumped, her hand flying to her heart.

Baylee Fisher said contritely from the doorway, "I'm so sorry. I didn't mean to startle you. I was hoping to catch you before you left for the day. Do you have a minute?"

Thora glanced at her phone on the desk, took note of the time and motioned the young woman to the chair across from her. "What's on your mind?"

Baylee sat down, her gaze roaming the office curiously as she settled her messenger bag on her lap. She was a serious young woman with a tendency to self-isolate. Thora could sympathize. She'd turned into a bit of a loner herself these past few years.

"I hope this isn't a bad time." She looked anxious. "I know we don't have an appointment or anything, but I just wanted to stop by and tell you how glad I am that you're okay. And how much I admire the way you're handling everything that's happened. If I were in your place, I'd probably hide under the bed for a month."

Thora managed a smile. "A close, dark confinement is the last place I want to be."

"Yes. I can see how that would be." She tucked her short hair behind her ears as her gaze dropped to the phone on Thora's desk. "Did Deputy Chief Dresden mention our visit on Saturday?"

"What visit?"

"I went to the station after I heard you were missing. I told him that I'd overhead Professor Neville arguing with someone the day before. A woman, I think. They seemed quite angry, which is why I was so worried when I heard your name mentioned."

The hair at the back of Thora's neck prickled in alarm. "Mentioned how?"

"That's the thing. I don't know. I really couldn't hear the conversation. But now I'm wondering if the person with him was Elise Barrett. They were in a relationship a few months ago, but they had a falling out when he began showing too much attention to Addison."

"Do you mean Addison March?"

Baylee's eyes grew wide and solemn. "You do know the two of them are sleeping together, don't you?"

"I've heard rumors, but it's really none of my business," Thora said.

A frown flitted across her brow. "Oh, I know. I'm not the type to start gossip, but I just keep wondering why your name was mentioned in that argument—" She broke off as her gaze went to the window. "What's that noise?"

"I'm sorry?"

Baylee cocked her head as her voice lowered. "Don't you hear it?" She got up and moved to the window to stare out.

"Do you mean the flapping and clanging? It's the rope on the flagpole," Thora told her. "It does that all day if there's a breeze."

Baylee clutched her bag strap. "Doesn't it bother you?"

Thora glanced at her phone again, wondering when she could politely bring the conversation to a close. She was eager to get home, eager to get out of the building. "I'm used to it by now."

"I've heard that sound before." Baylee's voice was still low and now edged with dread. "There was a flagpole outside my bedroom window in one of the foster homes I was sent to."

"I didn't know you were in foster care," Thora said.

"No reason you should. I'm not looking for sympathy," she said. "Some of the homes were quite decent. The one with the flagpole outside my window though…" Her voice sounded distant, monotonous. Almost as if she'd put herself in some kind of trance as she thought back. "If the wind was up, the sound would keep me awake at night. I hated it at first until I realized all that flapping and clanging drowned out the footsteps."

"Footsteps?" A chill of apprehension stole over Thora.

"I used to hear them coming down the hallway, a sort of stealthy shuffling sound. They would pause at the room next door to mine. The girl in that room was a couple years older than me. Blonde, pretty, mature for her age. He would knock softly on the door with his fingertip—like this—so that he wouldn't wake up his wife or the other kids." She tapped on the windowsill as her gaze remained fixed on the flagpole. "I'd lie in bed listening to the ropes twist and flap in the wind so that I wouldn't have to hear that knock. Or the sounds that came afterwards. Then one night he tapped on my door."

Baylee's voice had a mesmerizing quality as she unconsciously tapped her finger on the windowsill. Tap, tap… pause…tap, tap. Tap, tap…pause…tap, tap.

For a moment, Thora was so hypnotized by the girl's repetitive drumming that she missed the significance of the sequence. Then realization dawned as panic mushroomed in her throat. She swallowed back the fear and even managed a sympathetic smile as Baylee turned. But she must have glimpsed something in Thora's eyes or maybe she realized she'd inadvertently given herself away.

She said, "I shouldn't have done that. Maybe deep down in my subconscious, I wanted you to know."

Thora rose. "Know what?"

Baylee's hand slid inside her bag. Did she have a gun? A knife? Thora tried to calculate if she could reach her phone in time.

Baylee withdrew hedge clippers from the bag, the kind with long, pointed blades. An innocuous gardening tool that suddenly looked lethal.

"Don't try to pretend you don't know," she said. "It's beneath you. And don't bother screaming. Everyone has already left the building. I checked before I came to your office."

Thora was acutely aware of that phone just out of reach. "Why me?"

"Because of your connection to James Ellis Ridgeway.

The plan wouldn't have worked otherwise. I'm sorry. You're my favorite professor. I know that I could have learned so much from you. But as much as I like and respect you, Elise Barrett despises you."

Thora shook her head in confusion. "You buried me alive for Elise Barrett?"

"*For* Elise? No."

"Then why?"

"It's simple, really. Professor Neville always used to say, if you want a perfect murder, you need a perfect patsy."

Images flashed through Thora's head as she rose. The auburn strand of hair carefully caught in her makeup bag. The volume of Sherlock Holmes stories placed on a top shelf in Elise's home where she likely wouldn't notice. The arguments with Logan Neville. Her bitterness over the breakup with Will. Her outrage at being transferred from Criminal Investigations. The lost garden clippers that were now undoubtedly in Baylee's clutches.

"Elise brought Danny Hagan's case to our team," she explained. "She was certain the Weatherman had abducted and murdered the child, and she wanted to be the hero detective who finally proved it."

"But Professor Neville had other ideas?" Thora asked.

"Oh, he was fully on board with the theory at first. But the deeper he dug, the more convinced he became that Danny had been lured away from the street and murdered by someone he knew, someone he looked up to, someone he trusted." Her eyes glinted dangerously. "He lived next door to my foster home. I was a bit older, and he looked up to me. When I suggested we ride our bikes out to the fire tower one day, he was beside himself with excitement. He always wanted to please me."

Thora eased toward the door. One on one, she might

be able to hold her own, but Baylee had a weapon and the glassy eyes of the deranged. Better to avoid a physical confrontation if she could make a run for it instead.

"It was an accident," Baylee said as she tapped the clippers against her thigh. "He fell and bashed his head. I knew that I would be blamed and sent away from the only place that had ever seemed like a real home."

"So you hid the body."

"With a little help. And then I told the police I'd seen Danny get into his stepfather's truck that day."

"If you want the perfect murder…"

"Exactly. I knew that if Professor Neville got his hands on those sealed records, he would likely find my name on the witness list. I did everything I could to make people think the Weatherman was calling the shots from prison through Elise Barrett. I even wrote letters to him and signed her name."

"Did you steal my ID so that you could visit him in person?"

"That actually was Elise. The woman is obsessed with proving her theory. That made her easy to manipulate."

Thora kept inching toward the door. "Why are you telling me all this?"

"Because I admire and respect you. You have a right to know why you were chosen. It wasn't personal. It wasn't at all your fault. It just had to be you."

The sound of Thora's ringtone startled them both. Baylee lunged for the phone on the desk as Thora whirled and dashed for the door. She sprinted down the hallway and was almost to the elevator when she realized she didn't hear pursuing footsteps. Was this all just a dream and she'd wake up back in the box?

The elevator doors slid open. She called out, "Help me!"

Addison March stepped out. She said in surprise, "Professor Graham! What's wrong?" Then her gaze darted past Thora to Baylee Fisher coming down the hall with the clippers. "What's going on?"

Baylee said, "She knows. Stop her!"

Addison simultaneously blocked the elevator and swung her heavy bag toward Thora's head. She dodged the blow, caught the strap and slung Addison aside. She hit the floor hard with a sputtered oath, still managing to trip Thora as she dove for the elevator. She scrambled inside the elevator and reached up to smash a button. The doors slid closed before Addison could wedge her arm between them.

DOWN, DOWN, DOWN Thora descended until the elevator bumped to a stop. She sprang to her feet, ready to sprint for the entrance. When the doors slid open, she stepped out, then glanced around in confusion. She wasn't on the ground floor. She must have pushed the basement button by mistake. She started to get back into the elevator but the down button on the second car was already lit. They were coming after her. She needed a place to hide until she could find another way out. She thought about the stairwell, but no. One of them would have that covered.

She sent the empty car back to the ground level hoping to buy some time. It was dark in the basement but not pitch black. Late afternoon light filtered in through a row of windows near the ceiling. She glanced around for a weapon or a way out. An accumulation of desks, chairs and other items that had been removed during the renovation had been stored against the back wall and forgotten. Various doors opened into other parts of the basement. Supply rooms, utility closets...

Within a matter of seconds, Thora had scouted several

hiding places, but her gaze kept straying back to those windows. If she could find a ladder or drag a table over to the wall and stack a chair on top, she could unlock a window or break the glass, hoist herself through and find help.

She tried the supply closet. Lots of cleaning products, mops, buckets and buffers but no ladder that she could find. She hurried over to one of the wooden desks and dislodged it from the pile. By this time, she'd worked up a sweat. The desk was heavy and chips in the concrete floor kept snagging the legs. Finally, she had it in place and went back for a chair. Time was ticking. She glanced across the room toward the elevators. Did they know she was in the basement or would they assume she'd gotten off the elevator on the first floor? They would have to be careful how they hunted her. The Criminology Building might be deserted, but there would be students milling about the grounds, faculty hurrying toward the parking lot, custodial staff finishing up work for the day. All she had to do was buy herself some time—

She stopped struggling with the desk as a sound invaded the quiet of the basement. The vibrating buzz of a silenced phone. Not hers. She'd left hers behind when she fled. She cocked her head, listening. The sound was very faint. She followed it through the maze of furniture until she found a metal grate that covered what must have once been a utility crawl space. The vibration came from within. As she peered through the grate, she could see a faint illumination. Then the buzzing stopped, and the light went out.

Maybe the phone had dropped out of a worker's pocket while he crawled through the tunnel to make repairs. A phone meant contact with the outside world, with Will. The phone or the windows? She stood indecisively for a moment until the clang of the elevator propelled her into action. She hunkered down, opened the grate and peered into nothing but darkness. Her heart started to pound and her palms grew clammy. She could feel the steel-like trap of inertia closing in on her as she started to tremble.

Behind her the elevator pinged.

Move!

She dropped to all fours and eased into the tunnel, closing the grate behind her. The elevator doors slid open as she moved deeper into the darkness.

Directly in front of her, the phone started to vibrate once more. She thrust her hand in desperation toward the lighted screen. Her fingers met something cool and smooth. The phone was encased in heavy plastic, the kind used in construction zones to mitigate dust. In the dull glow from the screen, she could make out a face, the features contorted by death and the thick sheet of plastic that also encased the body.

Logan Neville.

By this time, her heart was pounding so hard she felt lightheaded. She couldn't pass out now. She couldn't give into terror. She had to think. She had to hide. She had to be smarter than Baylee Fisher and Addison March. They were students. She had years of experience on them.

But so had Logan Neville…

As quietly as she could, she lifted herself over the body and pressed herself against the plastic. Then she held her breath, hoping the phone wouldn't ring again to give away her hiding place. Stealthy footsteps move around the basement. Then nothing but silence.

Thora waited. In the deep quiet, she heard the descent of the elevator as it was called back to the basement, the ping as the car stopped and then the doors slid open and closed. A moment later, the elevator ascended. Still, she waited, pressed against Logan Neville's dead body. She didn't want to think about that, but how could she not? He'd been killed because he'd dug too deeply. He'd figured it all out, a case that could have garnered the kind of coverage and attention he'd craved more than anything.

She let another few minutes go by before she eased from her hiding place. Maybe if she could find something in one of the storage closets to slice open the plastic, she could use Neville's phone to contact the police...

Too late she heard a sound behind her. Baylee had also been waiting. She struck Thora a glancing blow, but it was enough to knock her off balance. She stumbled backward, crashing into chairs as she grappled for a handhold even as she went all the way to the concrete floor.

Baylee was on her in a flash, pinning Thora's arms to her sides as she lifted Elise's clippers high above her head.

Thora freed a hand and went for the clippers. Over the sounds of the struggle and the ringing in her ears, she became aware of a descending elevator. She might be able to fight off Baylee, but she couldn't take on Addison, too.

Someone got off the elevator. A light came on and then a familiar voice commanded, "Drop your weapon!" When Baylee refused, Will said, "The building is surrounded and Addison March is upstairs right now spilling her guts, hoping to cut a deal. She ratted you out in the blink of an eye."

Baylee hesitated. "She wouldn't do that. Not after everything we've been through."

"But she did. She told us everything. How you were in foster care together. How you bribed her to help hide Danny Hagan's body. How you claimed it was an accident, but she saw you push him off the fire tower. Years went by and you went your separate ways only to end up at the same college as criminology majors. The truth might never have come out if Elise Barrett hadn't brought Danny's case to Professor Neville. You had to stop him from finding out the truth so you came up with an elaborate scheme involving the Weatherman. You even encouraged him to invite Noah Asher onto his podcast to cement the theory. But Neville wasn't buying it, was he? You had to get rid of him before he could look at the sealed files. He was intended for the second coffin—a little torture for doubting your abilities before his ultimate demise—but you had to abandon that plan once we found Thora. After Elise was arrested, you could then claim the glory of solving his murder. Like I said, she told us everything. It's over, Baylee. Get up slowly and back away."

Still, she hesitated, her gaze darting about the room looking for a way out. Then she rose and dropped the clippers to the floor. "I won't serve a day in prison. Not with my background."

"I wouldn't count on that," Will said. "Regardless, you can kiss a career in law enforcement goodbye."

She shrugged. "So what? I'll probably get a book contract out of this. I'll be a bigger deal than Professor Neville ever was. Just you wait and see."

By this time, a half dozen officers were exiting the elevators and clattering down the stairwell. Baylee was cuffed and read her rights as Thora watched it all in disbelief.

Baylee stepped on the elevator and turned with a smile. "See you soon."

A chill feathered down Thora's backbone as she wrapped her arms around her middle. Will came over and placed his hand on her shoulder. "You okay?"

"I'm okay. How did you know where to find me?"

"We traced Logan Neville's phone. Sorry it took so long."

"No worries," Thora said as she leaned her head against his shoulder. "I knew you'd come."

"Always." He wrapped his arms around her and held on tight.

* * * * *

DANGER IN THE DEPTHS

ADDISON FOX

For my new neighbors, Patience and Sam.
It's wonderful to know you're around the corner!

Chapter One

"The whales have really come back for this?"

NYPD Detective Wyatt Trumball stared down into the murky waters of the East River and corrected his dive partner, Gavin Hayes. "They're back in the Atlantic. No self-respecting mammal would touch these waters."

"Except us," Gavin sighed.

"Except us," Wyatt agreed as he fitted his full face mask down into place.

"Why doesn't anyone read the signs?" Officer Amos Yearwood asked. Although he wasn't a diver, Amos was an accomplished swimmer and a valued member of the harbor team patrol. Also dressed in a full dry suit like Wyatt and Gavin, he'd navigate the Zodiac boat as well as their advanced sonar devices while they did the dive, searching for a missing kayaker they'd been called to rescue.

Or find.

"You mean those big ones?" Gavin joked. "The ones that are posted at every point someone can possibly drop into the river?"

Amos only nodded, his gaze continually scanning the waves around them.

The water was running hard today. Despite its name, the

East River wasn't actually a river, but a tidal estuary that connected the New York Bay to the Long Island Sound. This particular body of water was a delightful quirk of Mother Nature's design and, as such, changed its direction regularly. She was mean, nasty and more than willing to chew up and spit out those who didn't respect her power.

Hordes of New Yorkers chose to ignore this fact every year. Especially the ones who loved to try and kayak in her waters.

"What's wrong with these people?" Gavin shook his head, scanning the water. "Everyone thinks they're invincible."

Wyatt nodded before fitting his breathing apparatus into place. Everyone did think they were invincible.

Until they weren't.

They'd been called out on the emergency rescue twelve minutes ago and even with the other boats already on patrol in and around Hell Gate, one of the most dangerous confluence points in the river, he had little hope they'd find the kayaker alive.

Which was a hell of a way to start a search and rescue.

Settling himself at the edge of the Zodiac, Wyatt gave one final look to the New York City skyline that rose up in front of him before dropping backward into the water.

Wyatt's entire world changed immediately. The bright, early September sunlight that glazed Manhattan's skyscrapers in gold vanished, the water surrounding him dark, murky and swift. He gave himself a moment to get oriented, that environmental change something he'd not only trained for, but lived with each time he dropped into the water.

He'd learned long ago it was best to give that change its due. To allow the moment to sweep over him, those few precious seconds to reorient himself well worth it before he began his work.

Gavin had already begun to move, the kick up of silt and murky water swirling around Wyatt's face mask.

Amos would keep up steady chatter with them via their comms unit, along with the rest of the harbor team on the surrounding boats. They had a rhythm and a system for working the bottom of the waterway and it was about time they got to it.

Wyatt took the opposite direction as Gavin, his thickly gloved hands moving through the silt of the riverbed as soon as he'd completed his descent. The visibility was minimal, even with the light mounted on his head, and Wyatt kept his movements slow and steady, even as he quickly released handfuls of silt he managed mostly on shape.

Empty bottles, rotting wood, discarded pieces of metal— he'd knocked his shin on an engine once—all lay on the estuary's floor. But it was those things on the floor that he was regularly tasked to find. Evidence retrieval, sweeps for bombs, and search and rescue were all part of the job. And while the twelve-hour shifts were long, they moved at a rapid clip when he was under the water.

A strange counterpoint to actual life underwater, which was quiet and eerie on the best of days.

If life on land was chaos, the water was a strange sort of limbo. A receiving ground for that chaos, even as everything floated and settled when in the water. A murky wasteland for all that people destroyed, eliminated or flat-out wanted to forget.

Wyatt let it drift through the back of his mind, a gentle reminder of why he did what he did.

He knew who he was. And he knew he was driven by a higher purpose, one passed down from father to son.

"Wyatt. I'm getting a signature on something." Amos's voice was crisp and clear in his comms unit. "The heat signature is cooling fast, but I'm getting a read. Fifty feet to your right."

He tapped out a quick response on the wrist unit he wore affirming receipt of the message, then shifted to his right as Amos had directed. He kept up the steady movement over silt, his fingers skimming the river's floor, even though he avoided grasping any fistfuls. This time, his aim was the lingering heat signature. He had no hope of pulling someone out alive, but if they found the lost kayaker, he could retrieve the body and they could wrap this dive.

He moved, slow and steady, in the direction he'd been given, Amos's voice alerting him as he closed in on forty feet, then thirty, and so on. The water flowed around his dry suit, a swirling, raging storm at odds with the calm above.

Damn, the water was churned up today.

It was his last thought as his hand hit something firm and solid, an image filling the hazy space in front of him.

A body, eyes wide open, stared sightlessly toward the surface.

He felt a momentary shot of sadness at the loss of life. A silly, needless waste that could have been avoided if the man had simply selected another route. Had read the posted signs and recognized this wasn't the place he needed to be, no matter how confident he was in his skills.

Wyatt tapped another note to Amos, confirming he'd found the package.

"Damn, Trumball, that was fast. Good work. Let me get Gavin and we'll head your way."

Wyatt tapped his agreement, then went back to his perusal of the body. His headlamp gave off enough light in the murky darkness to make out the long, thin form of the kayaker. As he took in the length of the body, his gaze narrowed on the man's hands. Even now in death, they were wrapped tightly around what looked to be a small safe.

Wyatt reached forward, trying to pull the safe toward him when he realized the man had harnessed himself to the metal, a series of bungee cords wrapped around his midsection. It was odd—what was a kayaker doing with a safe in the middle of the East River?—when Wyatt caught sight of the real problem and the likely cause of death.

They could blame the raging waterway and its six knots of running water this sunny afternoon, but Wyatt would bet his next paycheck that wasn't what killed the guy.

Nope.

That honor likely belonged to the large, gaping hole in his chest, shot through with what looked to be a bullet from a long-range sniper's rifle.

MARLOWE MCCOY SLUNG the large leather bag that held the tools of her trade over her shoulder and headed into the police station. The sticky, pasted-on heat of August had given way to a gorgeous late summer day of early September and she was happy to be out of the shop for a while.

And this was, after all, the 86th.

She'd been in nearly every precinct in the borough of Brooklyn, but had a lingering fondness for the 86th. Whether it was her grandfather's stories of running wild throughout the neighborhood or the fact that she could feel the history of the place in its dingy walls, she wasn't sure. But she liked it here.

She liked her shop in Park Slope a lot better, but very little police work came to her. And based on the short briefing she'd received a half hour ago, this was a job she most definitely needed to do on site.

Although she had little interest in what lay inside the safes she opened for the cops, she couldn't deny that she was intrigued by the call. A kayaker gone missing in the East River had turned up, physically tied to a small safe. The bomb squad had already done their work over it and she was pretty well guaranteed no surprises on that front.

So now she was up to open the safe in hopes it would provide some understanding as to what got the guy killed.

"Marlowe!" One of the desk cops called out to her as she crossed over to the security screening required of all guests to the precinct. "You catch that Yankees game last night?"

"You know I'm a Mets girl, Sinclair."

The man—one who'd trained under her grandfather—waved a hand. "Bah. You know that's a perpetual lost cause."

"What can I say. Hope springs eternal." Marlowe grabbed her bag of tricks off the conveyor belt and resettled the bag over her arm. "But I do wish you luck in the playoffs. New York's a lot more fun in the fall when the playoffs are running in either team's favor."

"That it is." Sinclair nodded his gray head as she passed through. "See you later, darlin'."

Somewhere deep inside, Marlowe knew she should swat him for the "darlin'," but she didn't have the heart. Sinclair had known her since she was small and the expression was one of affection and warmth.

Even if it did come with a bit of license others weren't even remotely entitled to.

"Hey there, Legs." Wyatt Trumball pushed himself off the wall next to the precinct conference room and walked toward her. "Or should I call you Darlin' Safecracker?"

He was tall—about six-one to her own five-nine—and he had a lithe, athletic form that always made her look twice.

Damn him.

She had no interest in looking at Wyatt even once, let alone multiple times, but her traitorous eyes always found a reason to seek him out when she was in his presence. For that very reason, if she could ignore him altogether without being obvious and rude about it she would.

But there was no ignoring Detective Wyatt Trumball.

And attempting it would only set him off.

Even if he was insistent in calling her some sort of nickname every time he saw her. Names that should have been insulting and objectifying, but which gave her an unbridled thrill all the same.

Maybe because, odd as it was, they weren't objectifying at all. Not when his dark, sexy voice flowed over her like a warm waterfall.

She was even in carefully selected slacks for the occasion. Forget the fact that her job went easier in her standard uniform of black slacks and button down blouse, but she'd be damned if she'd deliberately wear a skirt or dress in his presence.

He was one of the NYPD's elite. A well-respected detective with the harbor team that worked in and around the waters of New York City, with a specific expertise as a scuba diver. He was good at what he did—rather amazing, actually—but he had an ego to match that never failed to scratch at the edges of her nerves. Even as she fought the frustratingly hot licks of attraction that swirled fast and furious around those edges, too.

The man was six feet plus of muscle, sinew and attitude and if she could bottle it she'd likely make a mint.

Instead, she was forced to work with him too often for comfort.

"This is the second safe you've called me in for in the past month. It would have been the third if you hadn't made the bad and, might I add, cheap, choice to call in Jasper Middleton. You mining gold on the ocean floor?"

"Shh." He leaned in and whispered against her ear as they stepped into the conference room. "That's the last thing we need getting out. My team pulls too many amateurs out of the water each year as it is. Start letting people think there's treasure to be found and we might as well live in our wet suits."

Marlowe fought the shivers racing up and down her spine at the wash of his breath over her ear and the deeply sexy tone in his voice. She fought for something light and breezy in return and ended up being grateful her words remained steady. "I thought you lived in one already."

"You don't like my uniform?" He stepped back and her eyes did that helpless thing where they followed the lines of his body.

But who could blame her?

The way his large, capable hands moved over his flat stomach, smoothing over the deep navy blue of his NYPD T-shirt. A T-shirt that did nothing to hide the solid chest underneath as well as the firm, flexing biceps visible under the sleeves.

Biceps, she suspected, he was well aware drew attention because when her gaze returned to his liquid blue one it was lit with amusement.

Since arguing would require more looking at him she turned on her heel and headed for the safe laid out on the conference room table. Various evidence bags were set out beside it and two of the officers she knew from Forensics stood sentinel at the end of the table, hands already clad in rubber gloves.

"What do you think, Marlowe?" one of the forensics leads asked, her brow knit. "You think it'll be like the first two?"

"I don't want to assume, but I won't take a bet that you're wrong. Especially since you told me the last safe I opened for you had the same outcome as Jasper's."

"Bomb squad already went over it." The second officer moved closer. "Clean like the last two."

Marlowe considered the safe on the table. Although the police department was careful with what they told her—she was a civilian after all—gossip flowed as strong and steady as hot coffee and the local currents. And this was the third safe pulled out of New York waters in the past four weeks.

If she was going to take bets, she'd take the one that said this safe had come out attached to a body like the first two.

But why?

"Standard issue office safe." She pulled out a few of her tools, leaning over the rectangular safe that had been pulled from the water. It had already been cleaned off and no doubt dusted for fingerprints. As she examined it, she saw little to indicate it had spent time in water or covered in fingerprint dust.

The safe was about a cubic foot in size, big enough to hold papers or cash or whatever else a person wanted to keep secure. The same sort found in hotel rooms the world over.

Only unlike those hotel room safes that could be reprogrammed with a master code, this one was locked up tight. She put through the standard masters she had access to as a lock and vault technician, each one coming up empty. She took out a few of her electronics tools, trying those next.

Still nothing.

While any time spent underwater likely didn't do the electronics mechanism any good, the absolute lack of response made her think of the last safe she'd opened for the cops.

No doubt about it, she thought as she stepped away

from the table. It looked like she was going to have to drill
to unlock this baby's secrets.

WYATT WATCHED MARLOWE WORK, slow and steady as a met-
ronome, and wondered why this single woman got under
his skin so easily.

She was a nuisance, with her knowing eyes and lush,
always-smirking mouth. She walked around his cop shop
like she owned it. And, of late, she'd seemed to be under-
foot more than usual.

And damn it, he wanted her so badly he was nearly blind
with it.

He'd known of her before he'd actually known her. Chief
of Detectives Anderson McCoy was a legend in the 86th.
And although he'd been before Wyatt's time in the NYPD,
he was still a larger-than-life presence in the precinct.

The stories about him were renowned to the point of
being nearly mythical. His personal life even more so. The
hardworking honest-to-a-fault cop. His only son, the rogue
black sheep that regularly spent time with his thievery es-
capades, detailed in the New York newspapers and beyond.
And the wide-eyed granddaughter who'd become Anderson's responsibility when it became evident her father's luck
had run out.

Michael McCoy was now a lifelong personal guest of a
maximum security prison upstate, a fact that had report-
edly nearly destroyed Anderson.

And his granddaughter.

Wyatt took in the tall, slim form of the woman across
the room. Slim wasn't quite right, he amended in his mind
as he took in the athletic grace that was evident in the firm
lines of her arms, the movements of her back and the descent into a tapered waist.

But it was those legs…

He'd never considered himself particularly attracted to any given part of a woman—he liked everything about women—but Marlowe McCoy had a pair of legs that could steal a man's breath. Long, gorgeous and gracefully muscular, the woman could turn heads at a thousand paces.

Although she was always dressed down when she came to the precinct, he'd seen her running often enough through the Park Slope neighborhood they both lived in. She was as fond of Prospect Park as he was and he savored any morning that provided an opportunity to see her on an early run, her legs displayed perfectly beneath her running shorts.

He'd tease her on those mornings, pacing next to her and enjoying the banter that never seemed to progress past fourth grade insults. He'd tried often enough to get her to join him for breakfast after the run but there was always an excuse. An early morning job, a planned visit with her grandfather or, when she wasn't quick enough to come up with an excuse, a flat-out no.

So why did he keep asking?

What was it about Marlowe that intrigued him? Although he loved the thrill of the chase as much as the next guy, he also knew when to leave a woman alone. A fact that had become more and more obvious of late. His last serious girlfriend had been—Wyatt stilled for a moment as the truth washed over him—eighteen months ago already?

Damn.

Nearly two years and he really hadn't been interested in anyone since then.

Anyone except Marlowe.

That truth danced under his thoughts, those mornings when he caught sight of her in the park more exciting and enticing than any night out at the bar.

The woman got to him, in a way that was equal parts breathtaking and terrifying. He didn't do relationships. He might live several hours a day a few hundred feet under the water, but he liked the relationships in his life at surface level, giving no one a chance to dive too deep.

Yeah, sure, it was at odds with his profession. But he'd lost everything once and he knew a person didn't recover. They moved on. Went back to living. But they were never the same.

The sloppy direction of his thoughts had him drifting, his gaze on Marlowe and the long, sleek ponytail taming what he knew to be lush, deep brown hair that fell just below her shoulders. A rich shade of brown that matched the deep, coffee-colored hue of her eyes.

Which also meant his mind was quite a ways away when the shouts and clapping around the table pulled him back.

Marlowe's smile was triumphant as she stepped away from the conference table, the safe now open. She'd already turned her back on it, clearly uninterested in what was inside, but the forensics team had beat her to the loot anyway.

And pulled two kilo-sized bags of heroin out of the gaping mouth of the safe.

Chapter Two

"We ID'd your East River vic," Detective Arlo Prescott said, tossing a folder on Wyatt's desk.

Wyatt looked up, Arlo's smug smile only palatable because he'd brought the news Wyatt was looking for and he was a damn fine detective.

It helped that they'd also been friends since the seventh grade, their mutual love of comic books and eighth grade dream girl Emma Wilson bonding them young.

Arlo had the added bragging rights that came from snagging a dance with Emma at their middle school spring fling, before being left heartbroken when she'd confessed her family was moving to New Jersey at the end of the school year. While Jersey was less than twenty miles away, Bergen County might as well have been San Francisco for two young men of thirteen.

And while Emma Wilson had departed their lives for some unimagined future in the Garden State, Wyatt and Arlo had managed to keep their friendship intact for twenty years.

"If you're here to tell me his name is Luke Decker, age thirty-nine, resident of a slightly questionable building in the Lower East Side, I already know."

"Son of a bitch," Arlo muttered before dropping into the guest chair beside Wyatt's desk. "How'd you get the details?"

"I dragged him off the floor of the East River. It comes with a few privileges."

Arlo slammed a hand on the desk, the old metal still echoing when he lifted the same hand to run it through crow-black hair. "I knew Stacy Brunell in forensics liked you better."

"Everyone likes me better than you." Wyatt couldn't help grinning at his friend. "It's a trial, to be sure, but I'm up to the task."

"Last I checked, everyone, that is, but Marlowe McCoy."

Wyatt caught himself before allowing that fact—one that was 100 percent true—to settle his face in dark lines. Marlowe McCoy seemed to go out of her way to ignore him and it regularly stuck in his craw like a fist.

Unaware or willing to ignore the results of his jab, Arlo pressed on. "Heard she was the one who opened the safe the other day."

"Yep. Smooth as silk, as usual. She had it open in under ninety seconds."

Arlo let out a low whistle. "That's impressive, even for her. I heard it took Middleton nearly a half hour to manage the first one."

Jasper Middleton was Marlowe's chief competitor in Sunset Bay and throughout most of Brooklyn, really. And while he got his fair share of jobs—and considerably smaller payments—the 86th had finally gotten smart and started calling Marlowe in when they knew they could get the budget for her services. She didn't come cheap, but she was quicker and she'd yet to contaminate evidence. A feat Jasper didn't share.

"That's why he wasn't called in on the second or third."

Arlo shook his head. "Three, Trumball. What the hell's going on?"

It was the same question that had haunted Wyatt for two days and he hadn't come up with anything that made sense. Three safes, all strapped to bodies that drowned in the waters around New York. Three victims with kill shots to the chest. Same cause of death and same strange manner of discovery, but not a single connection any of them could find between three dead men in less than a month.

Canvasses of the victims' respective neighborhoods—Murray Hill for the first, Hell's Kitchen for the second—hadn't produced anything viable. And with the news of the third victim's residence far away from the first two, Wyatt wasn't holding out much hope they'd find any connections now, either.

With that foremost in his thoughts, Wyatt opened the folder to see what the coroner had come up with. Although he'd enjoyed teasing Arlo, beyond the name of the victim and basic details, he'd been waiting on the full report for the past two days.

And as he scanned the report he saw the same details that had littered the files of first victim, Sammy Robards, and second victim, Jayden Phillips. Men nearing middle age who were moving through the waters around New York in kayaks, safes seemingly strapped to their chests by choice, and a lone kill shot to the chest, just above the top of the safe.

None had anything show up on their toxicology reports, nor were any of them tattooed with any particular markings. Which made three men who'd all died the same way with nothing in common except the way they'd died.

"You think we've got a serial killer?"

"We have serial behavior but these guys are making this choice." Wyatt tapped the folder. "No sign of a struggle on the bodies or underneath the bungee cords wrapping the safe to their bodies. All were seemingly enjoying a day out on the water when their kayaks turned under and bystanders called in the disappearance. And not a single bystander noticed the gunshots, which suggests silencer."

"Professionals, then."

"But professional what?" Wyatt flipped through the slim folder once more. "Even the heroin take in the safes is small potatoes. We'll take what we can get off the streets, of course, but it feels like a plant, you know?"

"You think someone's setting these guys up?"

"I don't know." Wyatt scrubbed a hand over his face before eyeing his friend. "All I do know is a lot of people are getting killed for the equivalent of a weekend worth of sales. I can't help but think we're sitting on the tip of the iceberg."

"Maybe you're right. But what are we missing?" Arlo reached for the folder and flipped through it, his attention focused and his gaze sharp as always.

If only they could find the connection, Wyatt thought. That's what they needed to move this along. And up until now, except for the cause and manner of death, they had nothing.

Nothing, of course, but three dead guys.

MARLOWE UNWRAPPED THE various items in the steaming bag of takeout and questioned the wisdom of filling her eighty-two-year-old grandfather with fried rice and pan-fried pot stickers. And then, as she caught the scent of all that luscious pork emanating from the dumplings and the enticing scents of shrimp from the rice, she decided she needed to live a little.

And stilled herself mid-wince when she heard Pops uncap the tops of two beers—light, at least—from the fridge.

This was their standing dinner each week and take-out night was sacrosanct. Even if she was perpetually concerned about his HDLs and his blood pressure.

"You live until you die, sweetie pie," had been Anderson McCoy's life philosophy for as long as Marlowe could remember. It was strangely of-the-moment yet equally unnerving when watching him stare at a plate of Chinese take-out with a mixture of avarice and happiness.

"You order from Dim Sum Emperor this time?" Her grandfather set their beers down on the small table in the corner of his kitchen before taking one of the seats with the cushion covers her grandmother had hand-embroidered.

"Yes."

"They have the best shrimp fried rice in Brooklyn."

"You always say that but Dumpling Palace is my favorite."

"Amateurs." Her grandfather blew a raspberry her way as he placed his napkin in his lap. "Dim Sum Emperor has oil in their woks that's older than Dumpling Palace."

"And we're calling that a good thing?"

He laughed as he reached for his beer. "I'm just teasing you. You know I'm not picky as long as I get dinner with my girl."

"I still think we could try a salad from time to time. They put a great place in over on Water Street. You pick all the fixins' you want, along with a protein, and then top it with one of like thirty dressings."

"I eat healthy enough the rest of the week. I'm indulging when I'm with you. Besides, we have something a lot more interesting to talk about tonight than takeout. I heard you caught another safe this week."

She couldn't hold back the smile at his interest, the excitement in his eyes far more pronounced for details on the case than they'd been for the rice.

"How'd you hear about that?"

"I know the 86th and the 86th knows me." He said the words with no small measure of pride and, again, Marlowe couldn't hold back her smile.

Her grandfather did know the 86th and he kept up a strong pulse on the happenings inside the precinct. Where his granddaughter was involved, that went double.

"They made the mistake of calling Middleton in on the first safe."

Anderson shook his head. "I taught them better."

Marlowe shrugged as she reached for her beer. "Everyone's always watching their budgets until they get crappy results."

"'Buy cheap, buy often,' your grandmother always said."

That had been one of her grandmother's favorite sayings, even if it had always made Marlowe strangely sad. While she understood the adage for what it was, it made her think of her father. His tastes had never run toward the cheap version of anything and he was now sitting inside a maximum security facility upstate because of it.

Though, she had to admit somewhat philosophically, her father preferred his luxury items for free, lifted by his own hands, so perhaps cheap or expensive wasn't the right description for her father's tastes.

"Lowe—" Her grandfather's question hovered beneath his nickname for her. "You with me?"

"Yes. Of course." She pushed a bit of brightness into her smile. "Just working on not taking the Middleton selection too personally."

She'd never gotten much past him. His naturally keen perception and the dedication of his life's work to solving crimes making him pretty much unbeatable when it came to telling him lies of any sort, even the small white ones.

Which made the fact he overlooked her small slip both a surprise and a relief.

"Everyone has a budget they can't stretch when they're dealing with the first crime. By the time they get a repeat the purse strings loosen a bit. Three safes in four weeks has everyone asking questions."

"And those purse strings are considerably looser." Marlowe thought of the invoice she sent in that very afternoon.

"Exactly. And I have no doubt my very talented granddaughter is worth every penny."

"You sure you're not biased?"

He shot her a wink as he reached for his beer. "I can be biased and right."

Since he was both, she took it in stride and settled in to hear her grandfather's theories. As the chief of detectives for the 86th for more than twenty-five years, he loved a good mystery and took great pride in the number of cases his team closed while he was in charge.

"You see what was in the safe? I know you don't always look."

"I look, I just don't care what's inside."

"You really don't?"

It wasn't the first time they'd had this conversation, but despite her grandfather's unwavering support of her, he refused to believe she wasn't interested in the safes she opened for the cops.

Or for anyone else for that matter.

Whether it was a deliberate mental block to diligently avoid her father's life choices or the bigger fact that she just didn't care what people hoarded or hid, cracking a safe for the thrill of beating it had always interested her far more than what it held inside.

It had also felt good to create a business from scratch. Something that was uniquely her own, and physical proof that she wasn't her father. That she didn't thrive on taking things from other people.

"Heard Wyatt Trumball's working the case."

Marlowe felt that distinct stiffening in her shoulders whenever Wyatt's name came up and tried to keep her tone casual. Even if her back had already gone poker-straight. "As much as the Harbor team does. I heard he's sharing the actual detective work with the team."

Although she tried hard not to focus too much on Wyatt Trumball or the damnable fascination with him that never seemed to fully go away, she was admittedly curious about his work. While he was a full member of the NYPD, his specialized skills in scuba kept him in the water more than working cases on land. As she understood it, once he'd made detective, he'd shared the load with someone firmly land-based to work the crime.

"A mystery wrapped up in a crime?" Pops asked. "Everyone wants a piece of something like that."

Since it was clear her long-retired grandfather wanted a piece of it, too, she couldn't help but key in on his words. "You think something's going on?"

"Crimes like that? They feel like a plant or a taunt." Pops set down his fork. "I never trusted crimes that felt incomplete."

"What does that mean? Incomplete?"

"Criminals running drugs or numbers or gangs, they have a rhythm. A ritual. These unconnected kayakers with small caches of heroin? It's off, you know."

She did know. Even if she didn't care about what was actually inside the safes she opened, Marlowe knew enough of her grandfather's and her father's work to know that exact rhythm he spoke of. For all that was illegal, those successful in criminal enterprises often were because they worked at it, just like any other business. It was sad those individuals didn't know how to channel their abilities toward better outcomes, but human nature never was, nor would it ever be, fully understandable.

But it was predictable.

She nearly said as much when the doorbell to her grandfather's ground-floor apartment rang. "You expecting company?"

"I invited Detective Trumball over."

"You invited Wyatt?"

Her grandfather's gaze got suspiciously busy on the small edge of his beer label as he tugged at a frayed corner. "Told him I'd like to hear about the case. Get his thoughts. Shoot a few ideas around with him."

Pops set the beer down and stood to head for the door, but she laid a hand on his arm before he could get moving.

"I'll get it." She glanced at their nearly finished dinners. "But you could have let me know to get more food."

"He didn't want to interrupt our dinner, but he did promise he'd pick up pie from Lucille's." Those distinct hints of avarice were back in her grandfather's gaze. "Boston crème."

Marlowe avoided groaning, even as she mentally tallied the impacts of fried rice and rich, sugary cream on her grandfather's digestive system. And then she stopped for a moment and really looked at him.

Although age and the trials of life had taken their toll, carving lines in his face and threading white nearly over his entire head, Anderson McCoy still cut an impressive figure. Six foot two, with shoulders that had slimmed with age but still weren't stooped, he knew who he was and he knew how to take care of himself.

And he'd invited Wyatt Trumball over for dessert.

She didn't think her grandfather knew her frustrating, yet always electric feelings for the man, but she wouldn't put anything past him.

But now it was time to answer the bell.

And avoid thinking about how she was going to get through the next hour without showing a single hint of the attraction she felt for the man standing outside her grandfather's front door.

WYATT STARED DOWN at the pastry box with the swirling, swooping neon pink letters that spelled out Lucille's and tried to tamp down on the anticipation that had grown steadily stronger as he wove his way through Sunset Bay toward the old brownstone on Chestnut Street.

He'd spent months trying to persuade Marlowe McCoy to go out with him on a date, all to no avail. Yet now here he was, ready to have dessert with her and her grandfather. A man who was both a legend at the 86th precinct and also as sharp at eighty-two as he had no doubt been at twenty-two.

Which meant Wyatt had better put his game face on because he couldn't let the former chief of detectives at the 86th see just how enamored he was of the man's granddaughter.

"Wyatt. Hello." Marlowe stood in the open doorway, the front door of Anderson's apartment just off the inside hallway of the brownstone. "And you brought pie."

"I brought Lucille's pie," he said, emphasizing the woman's name, legendary throughout the borough. "With her compliments to your grandfather, by the way."

Marlowe smiled at that, the first genuine smile he could recall seeing from her. "Those two flirt terribly every time he's in her shop."

"I thought your grandfather was a man of action. Lucille's single, as far as I know. Why are they just flirting?"

She shot him a side eye while gesturing him through the door. "Aren't you a bit too young to play matchmaker?"

"Is it matchmaking if they're already interested in each other?"

"A good matchmaker knows where to gently push," she whispered low as they crossed the living room that sat adjacent to the kitchen, "and when to walk away."

Since it sounded suspiciously like the lyrics of a country and western song—or a distinct warning to back off—Wyatt opted to take full advantage of the need to clarify her statement.

Both because he was wired that way and because hell, it was just fun.

With a few remaining seconds to get in the last word, he leaned close. "What fun is it to back off?"

"I'd say, where's the fun in being a persistent pest?"

"Just like the matchmaking, it's only being a pest if it's unwelcome."

It was a long shot, but even no more than ten feet from his precinct's most respected retired officer, Wyatt wanted to see if he could make a dent in Marlowe's very attractive—and totally locked down—visage. Especially since it was obvious they were no longer talking about Anderson and Lucille.

He took the rising heat in her pretty brown eyes as a point for him.

Before she could respond, he turned his attention to the 86th's living legend. He still felt Marlowe's heated gaze on

him as he set the box on the small kitchen table in front of
Anderson, adding, "With Lucille's compliments."

"That woman works wonders."

"That she does. And I hear she puts a little extra love in
her Boston crème."

If Anderson was aware of Wyatt's deliberate taunts, he
kept his poker face on, instead standing and crossing the
small space to the cabinets, pulling down plates. "Lowe,
let's put some coffee on."

"You don't want another beer?"

Anderson's brows rose. "With pie?"

She shrugged before turning her attention to Wyatt. "Beer
or coffee?"

"Definitely coffee. Thank you." He used the small space
of the kitchen to stand a bit closer than actually needed. "If
you let me know where the knives are, I can cut the pie."

He delighted in the slight rise of color on her cheeks
and more of that confused heat in her dark eyes before she
pointed toward a nearby drawer. "In there."

Was it possible she wasn't completely unaffected?

Sure, he was being deliberate but the kitchen was also
small. He and Anderson had already moved around one another dealing with the pie box.

Wyatt's thoughts from a few days before in the precinct
conference room came back to him. He wasn't a man who
pursued women who weren't interested. It was a useless exercise that diminished the mutual fun of a happy, healthy
relationship. But there'd always been something about Marlowe McCoy that, in spite of the distinct freeze he always
got in her presence, made it hard to walk away.

Was there a hint of something in their interactions that
his gut recognized better than his head?

It was a tempting thought but his repeated attempts to

take her to breakfast after their morning runs had suggested otherwise.

Resolving to think about it later, he found the knife in the exact place Marlowe had indicated and returned to the table where Anderson already had the decadent dessert pulled from the box. In a matter of minutes, they had a round of coffee, steaming from mismatched, chipped mugs, and plates with very generous helpings of Lucille's love-filled Boston crème.

He'd expected a drubbing from Marlowe for the slices he'd cut but she'd dug into her giant piece with gusto.

A far cry from what he was used to.

Just like the mugs and the small kitchen, he mused as he discreetly looked around. Although he hadn't been born with a silver spoon, his mother had found her way easily enough into the high life when their family circumstances changed. The estate she now lived in on Long Island had never felt like home, and not just because they'd moved there his junior year of high school, with few of his formative years left in the place.

"You've caught quite a case." Anderson's excitement was evident as he scooped up a forkful of pie. "People have been subtle in what they're saying, but it's not hard to read between the lines."

Grateful for the distraction, Wyatt set his fork down, his smile easy. "And you made it your life's work to read between those lines."

Anderson shrugged, the move surprisingly hale for a man of his age. "It's the job. And, strange but true, it's life."

The NYPD had mandatory retirement at age sixty-three. The fact that Anderson had been out of the game for nearly two decades was at odds with the clear skill and enjoyment he had for police work.

"Would you please tell him I didn't nose around the insides of the safe, either?" Marlowe let out a small huff. "Even knowing me my entire life, he refuses to believe me."

"Maybe because it's impossible to understand how a highly competent, accomplished woman like yourself isn't the tiniest bit curious about the safes you open."

"They're none of my business."

"But they hold mysteries," Wyatt argued, still unable to comprehend how she could be so casual about it all. "And come on, you have to have seen some doozies in your line of work. I know you do more than police work. Tell us, what are some of the most interesting things you've opened?"

"I don't discuss the confidential aspects of my work. And the problem is you two, anyway."

"Us?" Her grandfather looked surprised.

"You two live in a world where you're convinced there are things hidden between those lines you're both so fond of. I live in a far simpler place. Things are locked. I unlock them. It's binary."

She spoke of her job with a simplicity and while he didn't fully agree, Wyatt had to admit that he understood it on some level. Diving was a binary profession, too. You were above the water or under it. Your equipment worked or it didn't. You found something or you came up empty-handed.

The only difference, he supposed, was that each time he came up with something, it had ripple effects far beyond the water.

Like mysterious safes strapped to dead men.

Or the ever-present memories of his father, who'd died beneath the water, too.

Chapter Three

If she hadn't been looking at him, Marlowe would have missed the flash of sadness in Wyatt's gaze.

And if she were fair, sadness wasn't even a remotely accurate description. There was a deep sorrow that she'd never seen in his expression before.

But you've felt it.

The idea haunted her, even as she rolled it over in her mind. For all Wyatt's teasing and good-natured taunts, she did recognize those hidden depths in him. And if she were even more honest, she'd detected it from the start. It was part of what drew her to him, even as she rejected the idea of having anyone look too closely at the sad parts inside her that she deliberately hid from the world.

Suddenly needing something to do, Marlowe collected their plates and put them in the sink. She turned to reach for the coffeepot, intending to bring it back to the table, and ran into Wyatt's very solid chest.

He held up the pot, out of reach of spilling hot coffee onto them. "Do you want a refill?"

"Sure. That'd be great."

His gaze captured hers and held for the briefest moment, those deep blue depths calming her racing thoughts. And then he winked, the move just ridiculous enough that it had her backing away and marching back to her seat.

Damn, the man knew how to get to her.

Which meant it was time to get them firmly back on track.

"Putting aside your disdain for my thoughts on the contents of cracked safes," she asked as she took her seat, "what do you both really think is going on with these kayakers strapped to safes?"

"I wish I knew." Wyatt finished topping off everyone's mugs. "The whole thing smacks of a setup of some sort, but there's no connection between the victims."

Captivated, her grandfather stilled, his mug halfway to his lips. "Not a thing?"

"Nothing. They're from different neighborhoods with no apparent connections with their families, schools or jobs. We've found no discernable matches on their social media pages and nothing to suggest they even used the same types of kayaks or sporting equipment."

"Strangers to each other," Marlowe murmured.

"That's a clue, though." Her grandfather had remained quiet as Wyatt spoke of various aspects of the case, but it was clear that he was not only paying close attention but processing each detail carefully.

"How so, Pops?"

"Consider the fact that nothing connects these individuals yet they've died in the exact same way. Their killer connects them which means there's some method to how the killer found them. Or used them," Anderson added, almost as an afterthought.

"Used them?" Wyatt's always-sharp gaze went as cold and as lethal as an ice pick.

"What if the killer handpicked them for some purpose?"

"Which means the killer's the thread." Marlowe marveled at the simplicity of the idea. And how quickly her grandfather had taken the lack of connection and seen such a clear link between them all.

"You're a legend for a reason."

"No." Anderson smiled, clearly pleased by Wyatt's compliment. "I'm just an old dog who has seen all the tricks."

"Maybe, but it's a big idea and something for us to dig into. Thank you."

"Thanks for making this old dog feel a bit younger for an hour."

Marlowe reached across the table and laid a hand over her grandfather's. "I keep telling you, you're vintage."

"And Lucille seems awfully fond of you," Wyatt added, his voice considerably lighter than when discussing dead bodies pulled from the water.

Marlowe shot Wyatt a look, irritated at his insistence on pushing a possible romance between her grandfather and Brooklyn's most accomplished sugar pusher when something pulled her up short.

Along with that sorrow she'd detected earlier, now she saw something else in his smile.

A genuineness that suggested Wyatt Trumball might not be the good-natured cop with a quick quip she'd thought him to be. For the past few years, each time she'd been in his company she'd written him off as a cocky cop who took nothing seriously.

But tonight had suggested something else.

A man with a sharp eye and deeper feelings than she'd ever given him credit for.

It was humbling.

And, against her better judgment, deeply appealing.

ALTHOUGH HE WAS enjoying himself, Wyatt knew it was time to get going. He'd gotten what he'd come for—help from a cop who'd likely forgotten more than Wyatt would ever know—and the added benefit of some time with the man's granddaughter.

But he needed to give them their evening back.

So it was a surprise when Anderson started barking orders.

"You drive over here, Detective?"

"Yes, I did." Although he had no interest in living the same lifestyle as his mother, Wyatt had willingly taken on the expense of keeping his own SUV in the city. The expense of a car—and the needed monthly investment in a parking garage—was a bill he happily paid each month for the convenience of having his own transportation.

"Then you can drive Marlowe home."

She'd been busy collecting her things from a small chair in the living room—the large leather bag he knew she carried her tools in and what looked to be a small bag of fruit she'd purchased en route to her grandfather's—and immediately started to protest.

"I'm calling a car, Pops. Wyatt doesn't need to drive me."

"Of course I will."

"But I'm out of your way," she offered up lamely, even as resignation already lined her gaze.

"Park Slope's not that big. I'll drive you."

"You live in the same neighborhood?" Anderson asked Wyatt, seemingly delighted.

The overbright smile he added assured Wyatt the older man was well aware of where he lived.

"Not around the corner from me," Marlowe huffed.

"Come on." Wyatt reached for her bag, not surprised at

the heft needed to carry the tools of her trade. "I got lucky and got a spot just out front."

She looked ready to argue—on the ride or his possession of her tools, he didn't know which—when she turned on her heel and hugged her grandfather. "I'll call you tomorrow."

"Not if I call you first."

The tight hug between the two lodged hard in Wyatt's chest and he turned slightly to give them privacy, surprised by how that familial ease sent a quick shot of envy zinging through his veins.

And then she was brushing past him, reaching for the door. It was only when she stopped and called her goodbyes over her shoulder that Wyatt was able to move in and open the front door of the apartment for her.

"See you next week, Pops."

"Have fun."

The slightest suggestion of a head shake ruffled the ends of her hair, but that was the only other indication Wyatt got that Marlowe was going to give her grandfather a talking-to at her next opportunity.

Instead, he was treated to her back as she marched toward the front door of the brownstone, dragging the heavy wood open on one hard swing.

Whatever advantage he'd earned through the evening was at risk of evaporating if he didn't retrench. So he moved quickly down the front stoop, clicking the alarm and locks off on his SUV, narrowly beating her long-legged stride to the passenger side door.

"Please. Let me." He had the door open before shifting to the back door. "I'll just set your tools back here."

Wyatt was careful as he set the bag down, aware she carried several fine-tuned instruments as well as heavier objects like drills.

"Thanks." He heard the comment from where she buckled in, heartened by the softening in her tone.

And then he was around the car and pulling out of the parking space, a sedan with its blinker on already waiting behind them to pull right in.

"Your grandfather's quite a man. I wasn't kidding when I called him a legend."

As conversational openers went, Wyatt figured it was safe territory and it helped that he meant every word. Anderson McCoy had given him a lot to think about tonight and his laser focus on the killer was a huge step forward. He, Arlo and the rest of the team had briefly discussed the killer but all of them had continued focusing on the victims.

It was good work and had still given them the details that there wasn't a connection between the three men, but now it was time to shift their focus.

"Thank you for spending so much time with him. He was happier tonight than I've seen him in weeks." She turned to face him, the red glow of the stoplight in front of them hazing her features. "Not that he's not a happy person."

Wyatt took in that ready defense, curious she even felt the need to qualify the comment. "Once a cop, always a cop. It gets in your blood."

"If given the opportunity, I don't think he ever would have retired."

"An admirable state, but we're forced to retire for a reason. The job's a lot. And the risks are real, too."

"Which is why I'm very glad there is mandatory retirement."

She let out a light laugh, the husky overtones tightening his body. With it, he flexed his grip on the steering wheel, willing himself to ignore the attraction.

She's not interested, Trumball, no matter how much you might wish otherwise.

He took the last turn onto Fourth Avenue and in moments they were driving through Park Slope. He'd lived in Brooklyn nearly his entire life, those last two years in his mother's home when he was in high school the exception, but he considered this particular neighborhood in the borough his home.

"I love it here."

"The neighborhood?" He saw the hint of a smile at her lips before he returned his attention to navigating the considerably lighter evening traffic. "I do, too. My shop's just down there." She pointed toward a cross street, even though he already knew where she kept her business.

"While I do know that, I don't know your address. Want to direct me the rest of the way?"

"Sure." She instructed him to turn a few more lights down before surprising him with her next comment. "Packets of hair."

"What?"

"You asked me earlier what was the weirdest thing I'd ever seen in a safe. It was packets of hair." She let out an audible shiver at the memory. "I was afraid the guy was a serial killer but it turns out it was his own hair. He was an eccentric millionaire who'd saved every lock of hair from every haircut he'd had since the day he made his first million."

"Wow, you really can't underestimate how strange people can be."

"No, you can't."

"Is that why you don't like looking in safes?"

"Again, it's more that I don't care. Whatever people keep, no matter how weird or creepy or even just mundane, really isn't any of my business."

"But for that period of time, while the safe is in your possession, it very much is your business."

"I've spent too much of my life judging others for being voyeurs over my life. I have no desire to be the same."

The words were nearly out of his mouth to ask why when a biker shot out in front of him. Wyatt slammed on the brakes, his hand immediately reaching for her arm to hold her back. Her skin was soft beneath his fingertips and he let go as quickly as he'd reached out, feeling like he'd been singed.

The action was fairly pointless—the seat belts did their job and he hadn't been going that fast to begin with—but the move had been sheer instinct.

Even as the light, electrifying impression of touching her still coursed over his fingers.

"Sorry about that."

"The joys of city driving."

With his body quickly taking over his thoughts, he'd already drifted away from their conversation before the biker, so it was a surprise when she began speaking, her tone nervous and faster than he'd heard her before.

"Do you have any leads on the guy killing the kayakers?" She added a small, nervous laugh. "Or to be fair, I guess it could be a woman, too."

"We've got nothing. But with your grandfather's inputs tonight I'm definitely getting the team to shift focus ASAP."

"Do you do detective work and dive?"

"Yes and no. Because my diving is such a specialized skill, I'm paired with landlubbers for the work."

"Landlubbers?" She let out another laugh but this one wasn't deep and throaty. Instead it held more of those nervous overtones that suggested something had changed.

The ready conversation when she'd been fairly reluctant to give him the time of day up to now had his antennae quivering. And with it, he cycled back over their conversation.

I've spent too much of my life judging others for being voyeurs over my life. I have no desire to be the same.

And there it was.

How had he forgotten something so momentous about her?

He suspected her nervous and rapid shift in subject was a tactic to make him forget the comment entirely. It was likely the same reason she'd so quickly defended her grandfather's happiness, too.

Anderson and Marlowe might make a team, grandfather and granddaughter in lockstep with one another, but a generation used to exist between them. Anderson's son had been convicted in spectacular fashion, of grand larceny. A master thief, the headlines had read, operating throughout the city. Decades of Michael McCoy's crimes had come to light after he was caught about thirteen years before. His convictions a year later had been legendary and had earned him a lifetime stay at a maximum security prison upstate.

Anderson had already been retired and Wyatt hadn't been on the force all that long, but the story of Michael McCoy's conviction had been big news. Rumors had flown that the discovery of his son's crimes had nearly ruined Anderson, the betrayal cutting him in two.

For whatever reason, while it was a fact Wyatt knew, he'd never fully connected it to Marlowe as a problem that continued to linger in her life. He'd been attracted, yes, and deeply interested in her.

So how had he totally overlooked this aspect of her life?

He knew what it was to find your adult life formed by your parents.

How much harder would that be when it came through such a deep betrayal?

Stupid, stupid, stupid.

The thought had run through her mind over and over as she tried desperately to regroup.

Had Wyatt caught her slip?

She'd only brought up the dumb story about the hair in the safe to get them onto a harmless, silly topic. A dumb story that was just weird enough to draw interest.

And then she'd slipped about her father.

Or, if not exactly about him, about her reaction to him.

She directed Wyatt to the last few turns on her street. "I'm there, about three quarters of the way down the block."

He nodded just as someone's taillights flicked on. With the smooth ease of a born-and-bred New Yorker, Wyatt pulled to the side and put on his own blinker, waiting for the parking spot that would open shortly.

"You can just drop me off."

"And miss landing this prime spot?" He flashed her a grin and she tried—honestly, she really tried—to ignore how a riot of butterflies launched in her stomach at that smile.

Goodness, the man was lethal. And the solid length of his forearm that she'd admired on the entire drive, from where he had his hand propped on the steering wheel to where he reached down to the gear shift to put the SUV into Reverse to allow the car leaving a bit more room, had been distracting in the extreme.

Was that the reason for her slip? Because it was nearly impossible to keep her full wits and corresponding armor in place when her body insisted on noticing every damn thing about the man next to her.

Those forearms.

That grin.

Even the way his broad shoulders filled the button-down shirt he'd worn for the evening. A shirt, she suddenly realized, that was at odds with his normal uniform of T-shirt and jeans.

Had he dressed up to come over to have dessert with her and Pops?

Dress to impress, baby girl.

Her father's words lit up her mind, a steady reminder of his always-present focus on running some sleight of hand. From dressing to get people to see him in a certain way to building confidence with a mark to running an extensive and elaborate heist, Michael McCoy did nothing without purpose.

Add on his purpose was rarely good or altruistic and she had her father's personality in a nutshell.

One that had been filling her mind far too often these past few weeks. Was it his impending parole hearing, set for early October?

Or just the increasing realization that his hearing was coming after more than a decade in prison? A twelve-year stretch that had seen her grandmother die, her own business build and grow and her own father—one who was alive and well—missing out on every single year of her twenties.

Wyatt expertly maneuvered into the space, his parallel parking skills truly exceptional. And then he was jumping out of the SUV and walking around to let her out, a move that she would have seen coming if she didn't have her head so far up her ass with the memories that had been extra difficult of late.

Since it would have been poor form to step out when he was nearly around the car, she waited until he had the passenger side open. The spot he'd snagged was just over a drainage grate and he extended a hand to her. "Careful. It's a bit of a drop if you don't hit the sidewalk."

His grip was firm, solid, and she felt the unmistakable zing of heat trip up her arm as he helped her out. He then dropped her hand and headed for the back door to retrieve her tools.

"You don't have to carry those."

"Consider this the door-to-door treatment." His smile was wide, knowing and delectably cocky once more. "And something you won't get from a ride service."

She should be irritated. Really, she should. But how long had it been since she'd just walked somewhere with a man who was being gentlemanly and considerate? It was only a half a block walk, so it wouldn't do to make a mental fuss about it, but it was nice.

And since her bag ran about twenty-five pounds, it was extra nice not to be the one lugging her stuff for a change.

"Thanks for carrying my bag of rocks."

"That's what's in here?" He turned toward her as they walked down the sidewalk. "I was wondering."

"It's not all stethoscopes and grease pencils to open a safe."

"They still make those?"

She caught his grin a moment before she was ready to respond seriously to the question. "The grease pencils? They do if you shop at the right art stores."

"Well, then, that's why I didn't realize they still exist. I avoid shopping whenever possible."

The laughter came smooth and easy and it was a surprise to realize she felt comfortable with him. In fact, if she were honest, she'd felt comfortable all evening. On high alert because of the attraction, but those nerves had been mixed with an underlying easy feeling when with someone you innately recognized.

Chemistry, her mother had called it when she was a kid.

A state Patty McCoy spoke of dreamily before shifting gears and lamenting how it had gotten her into trouble with Marlowe's father, which inevitably turned the discussion in a sour direction.

And which ultimately stopped happening at all when her mother filed for divorce and headed off to "find herself" somewhere in the deserts of Arizona. A place, last Marlowe knew, Patty still called home.

Just like earlier with her father, those memories of her parents were way too close to the surface. They kept tripping her up and made her feel as if the past decade hadn't even happened. Like she was a perpetual teenager, struggling to understand where she fit in a world of two selfish people who had a child they had never quite known what to do with.

"So how about if I meet you here tomorrow morning? Around six? We can take a run through the park and then I'll buy you breakfast."

"I'd like that."

She would?

Wait.

What?

Marlowe struggled to reorient herself to the conversation, from thoughts of chemistry with Wyatt to all the supposed trouble it had gotten her mother into.

And then she looked up at him—really looked at him—as they came to a stop at her front stoop and realized that while she should cancel their plans, she didn't want to.

Was that the problem with chemistry? It confused the mind until bad decisions were suddenly the only ones that made sense.

Before she could consider those implications for too long, he bent his head, pressing his lips to hers. Warm, soft and surprisingly chaste, Marlowe had just closed her eyes when Wyatt lifted his head.

"I'll see you tomorrow then."

"I—" She stammered before catching herself. Like with his help out of the car, arguing would only make her look petty and small and she hated being either. "Six. Sure."

He lifted her leather bag of tools, extending his hand with her precious cargo. She knew just how heavy that bag was and imagined the way his biceps flexed underneath the long sleeve of his dress shirt. Could see how those enticing muscles of his forearm tightened with the weight. And then she took the bag, noticing the warmth of his body had transferred to the leather handle.

"Thanks for bringing me home."

"You're welcome."

She stood there another moment, half convinced he'd say something brash and arrogant to mess things up. Only he kept his gaze steady and his mouth decidedly shut.

Which only served to confuse her more.

Ducking her head, she headed up the stairs. Her sole focus became getting the front door of her brownstone open and inside to her converted second-floor apartment before she made a bigger fool of herself.

It was only when she closed the front door firmly behind herself, waiting to hear the lock catch, that she looked through the wide pane of glass that made up most of the facing on the door.

Wyatt still stood at the bottom of the stoop, a thoughtful expression on his face.

And there wasn't a cocky grin in sight.

Chapter Four

Once again, she cursed herself for the ready agreement to the early morning run and breakfast, but as she laced up her sneakers, Marlowe also recognized there was no way out of it.

Wyatt Trumball was so smooth, so casual, so…

So interesting.

And hell, she admitted as she snagged her phone off the dresser and stared herself dead in the eye in the mirror. "You want to go."

Because the truth was, for all her frustration in his presence, she wasn't blind to his good qualities. The man was an outstanding cop and diver, impressive traits in their own right, but lethal as a combination. He was exceptionally well respected at the 86th and her grandfather was a fan, which was a testament to Wyatt's character. And his incredibly attractive body was a temple, but he wasn't pristine or annoying with it if last night's pie was any indication.

She'd believed for years the benefit of getting up and running every morning—aside from the opportunity to deal with the roiling, swirling thoughts that had found a way in since childhood—was so that she could eat the things she wanted guilt free.

Wyatt's sheer enjoyment last night over coffee and pie made her suspect he might feel the same.

And that was a special quality, too.

The ability to enjoy the moment. And to acknowledge—in that moment—that what you had was enough.

She'd begun to realize the importance of that philosophy a few years before. The twin understanding that Pops wouldn't be around forever and that her father had lived his own life never believing that he had enough was a realization that had gone down quite hard. But after that initial burst of anger and sadness, the bitter flavor of that reality began to shift her perspective.

It had been the shock to her system that forced her to recognize that the only person who could make her life what she wanted it to be was her.

The only life she had to live was hers.

So why had she always been so tetchy and reticent around Wyatt Trumball?

She dated. In fact, she'd had an enjoyable summer, finding herself out and about around the city most weekends. A Saturday spent walking the grounds of Governor's Island in early June with a college professor who lived in Red Hook had led to a few more dates before things sorted of drifted away. Not bad, per se, just…fizzled.

Then there was the cute gym instructor she'd met at a picnic in late July. They'd had a few fun weeks running around doing active things, but he'd had that whole "my body is a temple" vibe and she'd willingly let that one fade away on its own. Life was too short not to enjoy a doughnut on Sunday mornings, after all.

And then there was the incredibly promising date with the financier the Friday night of Labor Day weekend that she'd have happily extended her long weekend for, but

he'd kissed her good night at her front door and proverbi-
ally disappeared.

Marlowe hadn't spent a lot of time worrying about any
of them—or any of the men she'd dated that had come before—but now, as she headed for the park and her meet up
with Wyatt, she had to wonder.

Why didn't anything ever stick?

Was there a streak of her father embedded way down
when it came to relationships? Always something better
out there, so don't get too close.

Don't get in too deep?

Or was it more the reality of growing up with a suave,
slick and all-around feckless parent that had set the stage
for her relationships?

All her relationships.

It was a convenient and handy excuse, but one she'd spent
a lot of time working with a therapist on for that exact reason.

She didn't want excuses. Or handy reasons to explain
the way she was.

She had to own who she was.

Just like knowing that living in the moment was all hers,
Marlowe also had to own the choices she made.

Which brought her right back around to Wyatt.

For whatever reason, she'd made that choice today. And
as she saw him in the distance, just where he'd said he'd be
at the edge of the great lawn, something clutched tight in
her chest before zinging out through the rest of her body
like a wave.

The professor hadn't managed that. Nor had the sexy
gym trainer. And while able to converse casually throughout a deeply enjoyable evening, Wall Street hadn't notched
up her libido beyond a passing flash of interest.

So maybe she needed to cut herself a break. After all, attractive dinner companions were a dime a dozen.

Men who caused this sort of reaction?

Shockingly rare.

"Marlowe." Wyatt smiled up at her from where he bent, one leg extended on a park bench. "Come on and warm up."

She followed his lead, using the bench for support to go through the various stretches she'd use before and after her run. As she bent her forehead toward her knee, she kept her eyes on his, more of that heat flaring up and warming her far more effectively than any stretch could.

And as her gaze caught on his blue one, as bright as the cloudless sky above them, she had to admit one more thing.

Her summer dates had been fun and interesting and easy. No one who pushed her or tested her or made her think beyond breezy conversation and low-risk time together.

Wyatt Trumball would never fit that bill.

Was that why she'd denied him for so long? Because way down deep, on a level she hadn't even admitted to herself before, she recognized that?

As she deepened the stretch, Marlowe considered it all and had to admit it played. Like the last tumbler dropping into place, she could at least spend this morning in full acknowledgment of the truth.

Wyatt Trumball wasn't easy. Or simple. Or casual.

Perhaps it was time to lean into that instead of always dancing away.

WYATT FELT THE change in the air as sure as the cool late summer breeze wafting around them hinted clearly of fall. Whatever disdain Marlowe usually brought to their encounters, he'd yet to find it this morning.

Had last night paid bigger dividends than he'd realized?

New lines to tug in his case and a more willing version of Marlowe McCoy?

Scratch willing, Wyatt thought, and amended himself to be more open. For the first time in all their interactions he could remember, he got the sense she wanted to be there and wanted to spend time with him. It had his pulse racing in a hard victory lap and he weighed impulse mere moments before deciding what the hell.

Leaning toward her, closing the small distance between their bodies, he pressed a kiss to her lips. It was chaste by any standard he could come up with, yet the mere touch of her lips against his had something racing through him faster than a lightning strike. The lone leg he still balanced on while the other was stretched against the bench trembled from the simple meeting of lips and he nearly toppled into her before catching himself and pulling his head back.

"Why'd you—" She took a deep breath before dropping her extended leg from the bench. "Why'd you do that?"

"Do you always ask a guy why he wanted to kiss you?"

"Most guys work up to it."

"I've been working up to it for a hell of a long time." The words came out practically as a growl and he pulled himself up out of his own stretch, both feet firmly back on the park path.

She looked ready to say something else before shifting gears. "Let's just get started."

He was tempted to talk more but he'd already pushed it with the kiss and, if he were honest, was already thinking about pushing his luck with another one.

Might as well shut your mouth, Trumball. Burn off a bit of this energy with exercise.

Which made her quick shout of "try and keep up!" a more-than-fair response to his unexpected kiss.

Marlowe was off like a shot, weaving her way straight down the park path and leaving quite a few other runners in her wake. He had just enough competitive spirit to take off after her, nonplussed by the "what the hell" and "watch out, man" he got as he added a second wave of cool breeze past the other joggers.

And he had to hand it to her five minutes later when they were still pacing side by side, yet basically racing each other through the running lane along Park Drive—there was something to be said for a woman who could challenge you.

Emotionally and physically.

His breath still came in even inhales and exhales, but her pace pushed him. Wyatt had never considered his morning runs lazy by any means, but this strenuous jog through the park had him working harder than usual. While he'd never taken his fitness for granted—and knew his ability to perform under the water was tightly aligned to his workouts—their run was a sign he needed to up his game in the morning.

They said little as they ran just shy of three and a half miles around the park, slowing as they closed in on the exact place they'd started on the inner loop. Sweat coated them as they retrieved the water bottles each of them had strapped to their hips, drinking deeply. Marlowe spoke first.

"I don't usually run with a partner. That was fun and it made me realize I've been slacking off lately. Just because I'm moving every morning doesn't mean I'm pushing myself."

"I thought the same. Especially when we hit mile marker two about five minutes before I usually do."

She laughed softly. "Thanks for pushing me."

"Right back at ya, Legs."

She eyed him over the water bottle where she'd lifted it to her lips for another swig. "We're back to that?"

"You do have extraordinary legs."

"So nice of you to notice."

Her tone was dry and he lowered his own bottle to look at her.

And in that moment, he was forced to admit the endless rounds of teasing—never ill-intentioned on his part—might not have been received in the same way.

"I've never meant it as an insult or an attempt to objectify you. But I am sorry if any of my teasing up to now has bothered you or hurt you. I'll do better."

"Thank you."

"Thank you for giving me a chance to apologize."

She seemed to consider something before coming to a decision. "You can make it up to me by buying me that breakfast you promised."

"Deal."

"Pancakes." She kept her gaze level. "With hash browns and bacon."

"You got it."

As they walked out of the park, side by side on their way to the Prospect Diner, he had to admit the truth.

It was far more enjoyable to spend time with her than trying to tease her to get a few seconds of her attention—simple wisps of her time—as scraps.

Far better, indeed.

MARLOWE CONSIDERED WYATT'S apology as she flipped through her menu. It was a mindless exercise since she already knew what she was ordering, but staring aimlessly at the menu gave her time to collect her thoughts.

Even as one thought whispered over and over in her mind.

Wyatt Trumball was an endless surprise.

I've never meant it as an insult or an attempt to objectify you.

I am sorry if any of my teasing up to now has bothered you or hurt you.

I'll do better.

Had anyone in her life ever apologized to her like that? With a response that was so swift, immediate and genuine?

Marlowe was damn sure that answer was a no.

I'll do better...

She set her menu down on the table and reached for the coffee their waitress had poured upon greeting them. Wyatt's menu was folded before him and his smile firmly in place, even as she saw the deeper thoughts swirling behind his blue eyes.

"You still getting the pancakes?"

"Absolutely." He patted his flat stomach. "What's the point of a workout if there's no reward after?"

"I will admit, that aspect is a surprise."

"What aspect?"

"You're an elite diver. I'll admit I expected a bit more of the 'my body is a temple' routine out of you." She took a sip of her coffee. "So I'm sorry for judging you."

"Thank you."

Although she was usually quite good at checking her impulses, something in her ironclad will to keep her thoughts to herself had seemingly vanished. "Why do we do that? As humans?"

"Do what?"

"Judge each other. Have expectations about each other? I don't know you, not really, yet I thought that about you."

"Aside from my deeply personal, lifelong love affair with pancakes and syrup, which you'd have no way of knowing,

I wouldn't be too hard on yourself. You took a set of information you know to be true and you likely added in prior experiences with other people. It's a bit like detective work."

She was prevented from responding by the return of their waitress, but continued to chew on Wyatt's easygoing explanation as they put in their orders for a veritable breakfast feast.

After the woman was gone, Marlowe pressed on. "I think you're letting me off too easy."

He shrugged. "I don't. What's wrong with using prior experiences and the world around you to make assessments?"

"Even if those assessments are wrong?"

"You were willing to amend your beliefs when you got new information. That's part of detective work, too. You can't be so married to an outcome that you can't pivot when evidence comes to light and suggests a new direction."

It was an interesting thought and she had to admit he had a point. She had never wanted to be so intent in her opinions that she couldn't be persuaded when new information caused her to look at things in a new way or when an alternative dimension revealed itself.

Like admitting your father was a criminal?

Those memories had teeth and she fought them back, more used to them rearing their heads when she ran or when she lay in bed late at night, thinking over her family's sins.

Since those thoughts never failed to ruin her mood, she shifted gears. Opting to keep the conversation light—breezy even—she desperately willed those memories back to the places where they lurked.

"What do you do when you have no clues? Like those safes?"

"Then you work the angles until you find something."

As the memory receded it was replaced with the evening

before and the excitement that had carried Pops through the discussion over pie.

"My grandfather really enjoyed talking to you last night about those angles. I could see it in his expression and the subtle excitement humming around him. Thank you for that."

"The thanks are all mine. His reputation is stellar and he has a lifetime of experience to draw on. I appreciate his time more than I can say."

Their waitress dropped off their breakfast plates and Marlowe and Wyatt busied themselves with doctoring their pancakes with butter and syrup. After the first few, delicious bites Wyatt picked up the thread.

"I was also interested by how quickly he connected the dead bodies. Or said another way, how their lack of a connection was a connection after all. And he just saw it, like it was no big deal."

"He was quick with that."

"It's like breathing to him," Wyatt said, a subtle sense of awe in his words. "I know it's experience, but even ten years in I can't imagine making connections so quickly and cleanly."

"Oh, I don't know. You've got quite a reputation, yourself, Detective Trumball."

"I've closed my fair share of cases but I'm not sure it's the same thing. That innate, instinctive knowing? It's something special."

"Do you come from a line of cops?"

"Nope, not a one. My father was a diver, too."

Although she'd not intended anything beyond making conversation, Marlowe recognized the subtle shift in tone. A casual carefulness that pushed beneath his words. One that was immediately visible in the way his eyes darkened, any sense of openness fading away.

"So you grew up in the water?"

"Something like that."

She'd spent her life avoiding conversation about her own father so Marlowe was adept at reading the signs from another person. The keen desire to keep her own family out of her conversations had her backing off.

"It's quite a unique skill."

"It's a living."

She wasn't quite sure that was true but gave him the conversational out. And despite their earlier apologies over their mutual misjudgments, Marlowe realized how easy it had been to talk to him, even then.

A state that was only clear now once it had vanished like smoke.

Instead, they shifted to the stilted small talk of people who didn't know each other that well. Summer blockbuster movies they'd both seen and a new show that dropped recently on one of the streaming services. Their inane conversation was absent of the same land mines they'd each stepped into that morning but, somehow, Marlowe couldn't find much interesting in their surface topics.

Which meant it wasn't exactly a surprise when Wyatt pulled money out of his wallet to lay on top of the check, abruptly standing to signal the end of their breakfast.

She followed him out the diner into the late summer sunshine, the heat already notched up about ten degrees since they walked in. "It's going to be hot today. Summer's not done with us yet."

"Should make for a pretty dive. My team's on bridge duty this week."

"Bridge duty?"

He walked beside her back down Prospect Park West, away from Grand Army Plaza and toward their mutual meeting place at the entrance to the park.

"It's not an aspect of the job we talk about broadly, but you have a fair amount of insider knowledge. The team regularly dives the bridges and tunnels to make sure nothing's been tampered with." He shrugged. "It's not classified, per se, but it's not widely advertised either."

"I'll keep it to myself."

He stopped and turned toward her. "I imagine you will."

I'll do better...

Marlowe wasn't entirely sure what she'd said earlier, but she recognized that she'd misstepped. It was only her odd, persistent desire to get that easier camaraderie back that had her slowing to a stop before speaking. "You were kind enough to apologize earlier and I feel I owe you one in return."

He turned toward her, his expression carefully blank. "For what?"

"I'm sorry if I overstepped about your family. I got the sense—" Marlowe broke off, Wyatt's gaze shielded by the sunglasses he'd slipped on when they'd walked out of the diner hiding whatever she believed she'd seen earlier. "I get the sense it was a bit of a third rail topic and I'm sorry."

He shrugged but he did drag the sunglasses off. That same darkness hadn't fully faded from his gaze, but she did get the slightest sense some weight had shifted off his shoulders. "You didn't overstep and I'm sorry if I clammed up. How about if we forget about it and put that one in the category of 'when I know you better'?"

"Right. Sure. Of course."

When she knew him better?

Considering the fact she'd been apprehensive of meeting

him this morning it was a shock to realize her disappointment at his abrupt shut down.

Or the sudden fear that there wouldn't be another chance to get to know him better.

"Thanks for the workout this morning, Marlowe. I've been slacking on my fitness and it was good to push myself."

"You're welcome."

"I'd better get going."

"Of course. You've got a bridge to see to."

That surprise kiss he'd pressed on her before their run came back to mind and she was suddenly sorry she'd been so prickly about it earlier. Because an urge she couldn't dismiss kept up an insistent pressure in her mind.

If given the chance, she would like to kiss Wyatt again.

She'd like that very much.

HARRY "DUTCH" KISCO lifted the soldering iron from where he held it to the back edge of the safe, burning off the serial number. They'd been careful with the purchases of each safe, buying from different dealers and paying in cash, but it wouldn't do to have some enterprising cop backtrack the serial number to the seller. He and his partner had known that going in—they'd recognized all the risks—but had proceeded anyway.

There was too much upside to getting this right.

So far things had gone smoother than he'd expected and he was regularly the cranky bastard of the two of them. He'd spent his life in New York, figuring out ways to outrun and outsmart the cops, but he'd never once considered the water as their blessing in disguise.

More, it was their ticket to moving the biggest cache of heroin into New York and on through the eastern seaboard.

If they could figure this out, they'd be invincible.

Forget the various mobs who controlled the city. They were amateur thugs who'd bow to Dutch and Mark when they figured this out.

Dutch's excitement beat in his chest as he burned out the last digit. They had it figured out. They just needed to perfect their tactics.

The marks they'd lured for the test runs in the kayaks had worked like a charm. And the news coming out of their leak at the NYPD was promising. She said that the heroin stashes in each of the safes had everyone upside down and confused.

Which was exactly what Dutch wanted.

He'd had to push hard to stash those kilos in the safes— Mark was notoriously cheap—but you had to lose some money to make it and those kilos were a small price to pay for their proof of concept actually working.

Which was why he'd already shifted tactics with the fourth safe, in place and just waiting to be found.

Because it was time to move on to stage two.

His father had been a magician all during Dutch's growing up. His old man hadn't been all that great at the magic routine—he had a simple patter and knew enough to get basic work—but Dutch had learned at an early age that the ability to distract was an illusionist's best friend.

He'd simply taken the technique and built on it until he was a pro. And hoo boy had he put that skill to good use, figuring out the best distraction of them all.

The cops had eyes all over the city. And Dutch had made it his mission to get every damn one of them looking the other way. He also had the added benefit of tying up some loose ends.

Win followed by freaking win.

He stripped off the heavy work gloves he'd used with the

soldering iron and pulled a fresh pair of plastic ones from a nearby box. Once fitted in place, he picked up the large envelope he'd meticulously prepared earlier.

Tucking it into the open mouth of the safe, he smiled to himself.

It was showtime.

Chapter Five

Wyatt followed the protocols his department had established years ago and continued to refine over time as he worked his way around the base of the Brooklyn Bridge.

The beautiful landmark was old and while he wasn't an architect in any way, he did keep an eye to any structural abnormalities they'd need to voice backup to the Department of Transportation.

But what he really kept his eye to was the possibility of a threat.

The waters around the bridges were heavily patrolled, along with his team's regular review of their safety, but the NYPD kept a steady and firm focus on the routes that kept New Yorkers on the move. A surprise attack on one of those points connecting the city would signal catastrophe.

The world we live in, his mother would chide and shake her head on the rare occasions when she talked to him about what he did.

Occasions that had gotten rarer and rarer over the past few years.

What did it say about a man who found it easier to avoid his mother than stew in the resentment her home and her life churned up?

Probably the same thing his behavior in the diner said.

For all his attempts at charm, he consistently handled the painful things of his past with a prickly response and an all-around jerky demeanor.

A situation that sat squarely on him when it came to his mother and brother and now with Marlowe, too.

It had been a steady weight since yesterday morning and it had to stop.

God, why did it always turn weird and ugly when any hint of his father's life or Wyatt's own childhood bubbled up?

Marlowe was only making conversation. Moving that getting-to-know-you ball back and forth across the conversational lines that people on a date tossed to each other.

And he'd been enjoying it. He'd been enjoying her. She was bright and fun and challenging and their morning had been going even better than he'd anticipated.

Until he fouled it up with all the emotions he never seemed to get fully under control.

"Yo, Wyatt." His comms echoed in his ear and all those roiling thoughts vanished, firmly pushed to the back of his mind as he responded to Gavin Hayes's call.

"What's up, Gavin?"

Gav's voice was garbled around his breathing apparatus, but Wyatt got the picture all the same. "Got something over here. Twenty yards from the northwestern base."

Since Wyatt was covering the southwestern base it was a matter of swimming a few dozen yards to meet up with Gavin. Recognizing his voice would be equally garbled around his own mouthpiece, he used minimal words to announce his presence. "Left flank."

The water was cloudy and murky—when wasn't it?—but Gavin's high-powered lights filled the space around them, illuminating shapes as well as the silt floor of the harbor beneath them.

"You find something?" Wyatt asked the question, even as dread formed a hard knot in his stomach.

"Not on the bridge." Gavin shook his head as he waved him closer, pointing toward a small black box nestled in the silt about six feet from the base of the bridge. "I think we've got another one of your safes."

They were hardly his safes, but Wyatt got Gav's point all the same. "You touch it?"

Another head shake. "Called you first."

Wyatt kept his breath steady and even, working his way through the shot of adrenaline from their discovery.

Despite his comments to Marlowe the day before, he hated bridge duty. He recognized the importance of the work but he loathed the constant reminder of why they had to do what they did. The never-ending external threats. The lone wolf nuts who had a god complex. The extremists determined to make a point.

It all coalesced underneath the work, a constant reminder of where he chose to make his home and the risks he and his fellow NYPD members all took every day fighting the unending, faceless threats to the city he loved.

To the country he loved.

He'd made his peace with that years ago when he signed on for the job. And he'd recognized that it was his love for his home and his belief in the importance of safety and law and order that he wasn't just called to this job, but he'd chosen it, too.

Yet despite it all, some cases still troubled him. Made him question his fellow humans.

The small black safe—so like the three others they'd pulled to the surface—was one of those cases.

He supposed he should be grateful this one wasn't attached to a body, but it was small solace as he was forced to question if this one actually did have explosives in it.

Were the bodies up to now just to lull them into a false sense of security? And was a bomb really the end game all along?

He gave some quick directions to Gavin before extending his hands for the safe. He did some quick movements over the top, feeling for anything out of the ordinary, but other than the absence of an attached body, this didn't look much different from the other safes they'd brought into the precinct for review.

"Bomb?" Gavin asked.

"Can't rule it out." He shook his head before adding a few orders.

As the more senior member of the dive, Wyatt directed the next steps on the recovery. He'd manage the safe himself, but he sent Gavin on to the surface first to alert the team to what Wyatt was bringing up and to get the bomb squad on their way. Once he had the confirmation from the Zodiac boat up above that the new team had joined them, he'd start his ascent with the safe.

While the other safes hadn't held bombs, it was entirely possible they'd been used to set this all up, distracting everyone's attention off the real endgame.

Especially with the drugs that had been stashed inside.

The only other possibility was this safe had been attached to a kayaker, too. One who'd figured out they were expendable and had ditched the safe before they could risk being taken down with it.

But Wyatt refused to assume anything.

Even if the idea of diving around incendiary devices had images of his father's face coming to mind.

Shaking it off—those ghosts had zero place in his head when he dived—he focused on the problem at hand. With the steady calm that was not only needed in his line of work but absolutely necessary in scuba, he controlled his breathing and waited for the order to ascend to the surface.

They'd deal with this, he reminded himself. Whatever was in the safe, they'd handle it and add to the detective work already in progress, whatever it was they discovered.

He knew he and Gav would be back down here searching for a possible body as soon as the bomb squad took the safe.

When the comms came down from the surface that the team had arrived, Wyatt began his ascent.

And acknowledged the mystery of these locked boxes that kept finding their way into his waters was far from over.

MARLOWE EVALUATED THE contact points on the safe she was testing and considered her approach through the small hole she'd drilled with the aid of her pin camera. She hooked three of the wires leading to the lock, clamping them before lightly tugging them through the small opening she'd drilled.

And cursed a streak of blue when she heard the pins of the locking mechanism slam into place behind the door panel.

She stepped back, tossing the grease pencil she'd used to write notes on the door of the safe, the thin snap of the wood against her office floor little solace at the fact that she'd wasted an hour of work.

And had nothing to show for it.

Where had her head gone today?

She'd expected a challenge when she'd agreed to test this round of lock improvements for one of the safe companies she regularly worked with.

But damn it, she was a professional.

One who'd allowed the thoughts rolling around in her head like loose marbles to upset her rhythm and flow.

Which only had a few more choice words erupting from her throat.

How about if we forget about it and put that one in the category of "when I know you better"?

It had been two days since her run and breakfast with Wyatt and she was no closer to puzzling through her feelings about the morning they'd spent together. For all her inward complaining up to now over the man, she certainly had enjoyed spending time with him.

Had enjoyed even more the not-so-subtle sparks of attraction that hummed between them. Their race through the park, pushing each other forward as they ran. The lingering glances over breakfast.

And that kiss.

It had been simple—likely the impulse of a moment—but it had packed a punch.

More than any kiss she could remember in a while.

A long while, she amended to herself.

Although she usually locked the front door of her shop when she was working, the signal for the bell pulled her out of her musings. Goodness she was out of it if she'd forgotten something as simple as locking up when she was going into her office to work.

She mentally chided herself as she wove her way through the various floor safes as well as her worktable in her office before moving into the outer, decorated front area where she welcomed visitors. She kept meaning to hire help but week passed into week, month into month, and she still hadn't done it.

And abstractly wondered if she'd conjured up Wyatt

Trumball as she came face-to-face with him, standing just inside the front door.

"Wyatt."

"Marlowe." He nodded, his expression grim as he stood there.

"What's wrong?"

"We found another safe."

She moved forward before realizing the action, her hand already outstretched toward his forearm. "Oh, no, another body?"

"No." He shook his head, his glance distracted as it floated around the various locks and safes she had on display around the storefront before returning to settle on her.

"Oh, good." At the clear signs of agitation, she added, "Right?"

"That's what's so strange. We're not sure."

"Was there something else inside of it?"

"We're not sure there, either. Bomb squad confirmed there aren't any explosives, but we need to get inside of this one, too."

Although she was glad to see him, she was confused at the reason for his visit. Had he come over just to request her services in opening the safe? Anything she ever handled for the police came via a call, not a personal visit.

Then she keyed into the energy that seemed to surround him like a live wire.

Marlowe had observed Wyatt's calm, logical demeanor as he'd spoken to her grandfather. She also knew his reputation around the 86th, her involvement with the NYPD as well as the connection between her family and the precinct ensuring she knew much of what went on there.

Wyatt was calm and cool and very little ruffled him.

Which was at direct odds with the man standing before her.

"Why don't you come back into my office? Let me just clean up what I was working on." She took the few extra moments to lock the front door and turn the open sign to closed before ushering Wyatt to the back.

"Can I get you something to drink?"

"No, I'm good, thanks."

She crossed to the small fridge she kept in the corner of the office, giving herself a few more moments as well as him time to settle, snagging a water for herself and, at the last minute, one for Wyatt. When she handed it over, he took it with a small smile. "Thank you."

"You're welcome. Now," she said and gestured for him to take a seat on the large stool on the opposite side of her worktable. "Why don't you tell me what's going on?" Before he could say anything, she added, "Whatever you're able to tell me is fine."

He cracked open the water and took a long sip, reinforcing her instinct to grab him one, before setting down the bottle and refocusing on her. "We found the safe on our dive."

"The bridge dive you mentioned?"

"The same. The safe was nestled near the base of the Brooklyn Bridge."

She heard her own gasp and set down her water, unopened. "How'd it get there?"

"We have no idea. And since there's no bomb the standard concerns about terrorism aren't in play. They're not gone," he added, "but they aren't top priority. Especially when you take into account the three safes already recovered."

"It's still an odd place to put a safe. And I can't imagine an easy task, either? I realize you dive that area for a sad reason, but are the waters around it ever really empty of patrol?"

"No." He shook his head, a rueful smile tilting his lips. "But it's not like that water's easy to see through, either. If you had the right motivation and came in farther away, you could navigate under the water potentially unseen."

Marlowe had thought it before but with Wyatt's confirmation she had to admit there were way more facets to his job than might appear at first. The tactical work, the rescues, the fighting criminal activity.

He packed an awful lot into his job and he did it all several feet beneath the water.

"If you need me to come into the precinct I can take a look at it."

"I'd like that. The captain wants you on this from now on. Anything we find, he said, is yours to handle. If you want the job."

"Sure I do. You know I'm always available to offer my services."

When he didn't even come back with a snappy retort about her highly paid services, she finally gave in and pressed him.

"Wyatt, what's really going on? You look like a cat who has jumped out of its skin after getting a bucket of water dumped on it. And while I appreciate the in-person service as well as the job offer, you didn't need to make a special visit for that. And—" She broke off before giving in to the upsetting thoughts that had kept her company for the better part of forty-eight hours. "And the way we left things the other morning had me thinking you didn't want to see me again."

"It's not that." He took the cap off his water and took another long sip, seeming to collect himself. "Really, it's not. And I owe you an apology for the other morning."

"You don't—"

Before she could get the rest of her dismissal out, he leaned forward across the counter, his gaze direct.

Unwavering.

"Yes, I do. I don't talk about my family but I usually have a better handle on how I respond to questions. The emotional check-out routine wasn't fair of me and I'm sorry." He hesitated for the briefest of moments before adding, "And even fumbling like a stupid jerk, I would like to see you again. Assuming I didn't ruin a chance for another morning run in the park or maybe even a date. You know, one with tablecloths and a menu that doesn't look like it's been chewed by a junkyard dog."

Once again, she was struck by how quick he was to not just apologize, but to come off like he actually meant it.

"I'd like that. Although, for the record, those pancakes were pretty great, scarred Formica table and chewed-up menu aside."

"They were pretty great but the company was better."

"Wyatt—"

His name hung there between them and Marlowe lost sight of what she wanted to say, that heavy-lidded gaze going a long way toward making her forget herself.

Even as the reality of both why he was there and why he'd shut down the other day hadn't gone away.

"I realize up until the past few days I've been a bit... prickly with you. But I do know what it is to have a challenging home life. I'm happy to listen if you need an ear. And, well, I'm a vault." She looked around her office with a rueful smile. "Chosen profession aside."

He seemed to consider her, a sort of sizing up that belied the usual interest she saw in his gaze.

But it was still a surprise when he began speaking.

"To your question the other morning, my father was a diver. One of the best."

She heard the past tense but opted to remain quiet, giving him the room to tell his story.

"He was one of the divers called out to the wreck of the Luxair jumbo jet that went down off the coast of Long Island almost twenty years ago."

Marlowe remembered that time. Although she was young, the news of the jet going down, mere miles from its take off at Kennedy Airport, had dominated the local news. "That was the one they thought might be a terror attack, right?"

"They'd thought that as well as any number of conspiracy theories, coming so soon after nine-eleven. But in the end, it was the sad reality of an overlooked fuel problem and a spark from a short circuit that set off a terrible chain of events."

Marlowe felt the involuntary shudder down her spine. She'd always loved travel, but it was never fully lost on her that she was willingly putting herself into a contained tube of metal that hurtled through the sky.

Morose? Yeah, a bit, she acknowledged.

But true? Still a very big yes.

"Your father dived the wreckage?"

"He did. He was one of the first ones called in, his skills widely known and respected. He'd dived the waters off Long Island his entire life. He knew the waters and he knew the terrain. And even he couldn't fully prepare himself for the work or the horror of diving a wreck at that scale."

She listened as he described the hellish conditions below the surface. The cold, horrible gray environment, with the jagged metal of the fuselage, the risk of pressurized airplane parts exploding if mishandled and, of course, the horrors of all the bodies trapped beneath the surface.

It took a special person to do that, Marlowe recognized. The same sort of person her grandfather was, spending his life working to right humanity's terrible wrongs.

And still, it was something to imagine the work Wyatt's father had faced at the bottom of the Atlantic Ocean.

"He took on the job, going down there day after day and doing his best to bring dignity to all those people who lost their lives."

"That's an amazing thing he did."

"He lost his life because of it. About three days before they were finally ready to pull one of the largest pieces of the wreckage up. He was working with the crew to attach the various cables and he cut himself. He got tangled in some of the wreckage and wasn't able to escape the sharp edges."

She watched as Wyatt fumbled with his now-empty bottle of water. With quiet movements, she cracked her own bottle and handed it over, giving him the space to gather his thoughts as he gulped down nearly half the bottle.

"The team tried to get to him, thinking they could at least share their air, but he was trapped in the tangled wreckage and they couldn't reach him."

"Oh, Wyatt."

He shook his head as he finished what was left in the bottle. "Even if they had gotten to him, they were much too far down and probably couldn't have gotten him to the surface in time."

He stared at something on the back wall of her office, somewhere over her shoulder.

Marlowe wanted to comfort him, but recognized there was more than the expanse of her worktable between them.

There were years and memories and something that felt unfinished hovering in the depths of his dark gaze.

"I am sorry, but I also know those words feel much too small and far too empty to really mean anything."

His gaze returned to hers, a little less lost, less haunted. "They're not meaningless, Marlowe."

Maybe they were and maybe they weren't, but in his retelling she realized there were so many things she wanted to know. Top of that list was how he lived with the reality of his father's death and still do the same work for his own living.

And a very close second was why he'd chosen to tell her.

To trust her with that emotional weight.

"Can I ask you something?"

"Sure."

"I'm not sorry you told me this. Any of this, so please take my question for what it is." When he only nodded, she pressed on. "Why tell me now? Did something happen on your dive? I can't imagine your father's death is something that leaves you, but I'd also imagine that after all this time it doesn't trigger quite this easily, either."

It was a risk asking. Emotional trauma had a way of sneaking up on a person, but that didn't mean they could accurately or meaningfully explain it when those fierce claws took you in their grip.

Hell, she'd learned that lesson long ago.

And yet…she was still curious. Was still full of enough questions to take the chance he might shut back down.

Forty-eight hours ago she was convinced any of the tentative steps toward attraction that had existed between them had effectively ended.

But now?

Now he was here, baring his soul all while requesting her work services.

What was the catalyst?

What did he find on that dive that had churned up emotions he clearly chose to keep buried?

Chapter Six

Wyatt couldn't stop the churning in his gut or the subtle trembling in his body that kept tripping through his nerve endings. It had been this way, off and on, since he'd gotten home yesterday after the dive.

After bringing the safe to the surface and handing it off to the bomb squad, he and Gavin had descended into the waters once more. They did two more dives after that and even with the extra focus they'd been unable to find a body. It was a reality he should have been grateful for, but all he could muster up was a mounting sense of unease.

One he couldn't run off in two loops around the park last evening.

One that was barely assuaged when the feedback finally came just after ten this morning from the bomb squad that the safe didn't hold any incendiary devices.

Even his complaining that it had taken them nearly eighteen hours to get the confirmation had fallen flat, a problem at a warehouse in Queens taking the full attention of the bomb squad and putting that as a priority above his safe.

Which had left him with that increasing unease and an odd, swirling need to see Marlowe.

To make things right for how he'd ended their date.

And, strangely enough, to share the story of his father's death.

He hadn't deliberately come to her shop with any intention beyond seeing her, asking for her help with the safe and apologizing for being so distant at breakfast.

Only the story of his father had come spilling out.

Now that it had, he had oddly settled, those strange trip wires under his skin finally calming.

Even with that leveling out, he couldn't deny her question. He'd already checked out on her once and he refused to do it again.

"No, my father's death isn't usually so raw for me. Or triggered so easily. He's been on my mind, this time of year always bringing back the memories of losing him. And—" He stilled, wanting to get this right. "And I hadn't realized just how close to the surface those memories were until we talked about my family the other morning."

"I'm sorry I asked."

"You don't need to be. It's on me. And, to be honest, it's given me a bit of perspective I didn't realize I'd lost."

That admission cost him, a sign that the happy facade he was always so determined to keep in place wasn't infallible. But in the admission Wyatt also saw another truth: the sky wasn't falling because he admitted to a moment of vulnerability.

He also discovered that he could talk about his father without it taking the strange, resentful overtones it normally took when the subject came up with his mother and brother.

Hadn't that been the difference between him and his brother? Where Charlie had enmeshed himself in anything that didn't have the trappings of dive work or a career that helped others, Wyatt had taken the opposite path. His brother was conquering boardrooms from one end of Manhattan to the other, with Paris, Dubai and Hong Kong on his regular list of travel destinations, all while Wyatt hadn't moved more than thirty miles from where they grew up.

Charlie, just like their mother, had taken the large settlement from Matt Trumball's life-ending dive and put it to use advancing themselves, both professionally and socially. Wyatt had bought a half-decent apartment and left the rest of his money to sit in savings, damned sure he wouldn't forget the memory of his father in the trappings of wealth.

"It's hard sometimes. How grief can lie in wait, leaving you to think you've got it handled before it whips out and reminds you it's still rather firmly in charge."

In Marlowe's words, Wyatt heard something that went beyond comfort. Beyond support.

He heard understanding.

And was once again reminded that while she might still have both parents living, that didn't mean there wasn't pain and that grief she spoke of in the relationship.

For all he and his mother didn't see eye to eye, Jessica Trumball Daniels had used a phrase for years.

Death isn't always the worst outcome.

He'd always thought it callous of her, but seeing the ghosts in Marlowe's eyes, he had to admit his mother had a point.

"I suppose that's truer than we want to admit."

His words lingered as silence once again hovered between them, but he also couldn't deny how nice it was to sit here with her. To sit with a woman he found attractive and not feel he needed to fill the air with lighthearted humor.

That he could be something more.

Sure, he could be a man who did find humor in the everyday but also a person with pockets of sadness in his life. One who could admit that and still be okay.

"I'm glad you shared that with me. That you trusted me with it. But I still get the sense that something else is bothering you."

"This dive. The safes." He shook his head. "I can't get a handle on why they frustrate me so much. Cases are rarely cut and dry and it takes a hell of a lot of work to get through them. And yet—"

He broke off, trying to find the right words for what he'd not been able to reconcile in his own mind. About this case and the emotions he was usually able to keep a tight grip on.

But Marlowe's gentle smile caught him up, stilling that frustration and softening it into something manageable.

"You were diving the waters around New York City looking for bombs, Wyatt. From where I'm standing your job is about a whole lot of bother."

"That's one way to look at it."

"I saw it for years with my grandfather and, in a different way, I even see it with my own work. Living and working in New York is different. The density of how we live. The mix of extreme wealth and extreme poverty and every imaginable level in-between. And those who prey in and among that, every day of every year. I'm not suggesting police work is ever easy, but it sure as hell is something extra here."

"My family doesn't understand why I do it."

"They don't have to understand. They just have to accept your choice."

"They don't do that, either."

She reached across the worktable, laying a hand over his. Her palm was warm, and he was surprised at how such a simple act of comfort made such a difference.

"Then that's their loss, Wyatt. In every way."

MARLOWE LAID HER tools out beside the recovered safe in the precinct conference room and considered the afternoon. Wyatt's arrival at her shop had been a surprise; his discussion of his family and his father's death even more so.

What sort of weight was that to carry through life? The loss of a parent was always heavy, but the tragic way his father had died? It had to leave endless questions. And a never-ending frustration that the outcome could have been different with a fraction of additional safety measures or a piece of metal that had shorn through and settled on the ocean floor a few inches farther away.

It would be maddening, running through those endless scenarios over and over. For anyone, Marlowe considered, but even worse for someone trained in the same profession.

If the only sadness was his father's death it might be something to work through, but there appeared to be a resonating grief on the other side of the accident with the rest of his family. And while Wyatt might not have overtly shared what had come after his father's death, she didn't need any special skill to read the mix of bone-deep anger and resentment at the mention of his family.

It did, however, make a bit more sense knowing how a cop could afford to buy a home in Park Slope with NYPD salaries being what they were.

If Marlowe had to guess, there had been a very large settlement from his father's death. One that had set his family up comfortably. One that had given his mother and brother a choice about their own lives and a path that was far removed from Wyatt's.

Resolved to think on it later, she took stock of her tools and gestured over to the young cop who'd sat at the end of the conference table keeping tabs on all she did. She might be a civilian consultant but the chain of evidence needed to be maintained at all times.

And now that she was set up and ready, it was time to call in Wyatt and the others who were all assigned to this case.

"I'm ready when the team is."

The young man stood at attention near the door, the wide-eyed gaze he'd given her throughout her prep growing even wider as Wyatt walked into the conference room, their captain on his heels.

"Marlowe." Captain Dwayne Reed crossed over to give her a hug.

"Captain Reed." She hugged him back, the man yet another friend of her grandfather and someone she'd grown up knowing.

"You don't have to stand on formality." His eyebrows narrowed over dark eyes, careworn lines creasing his deep brown skin.

"Nonsense. Inside these walls you're Captain Reed." Even if he was Uncle D whenever she saw him on more social terms.

Wyatt stood behind his captain, his hands clasped behind his back. That earlier sense of restlessness in her shop had vanished, replaced with the cool bearing that seemed to define him.

It was fascinating to see the change, but where she'd previously thought that even demeanor bordered on cocky, their conversation had suggested something else. And after she'd seen the pain in his eyes, she was more and more convinced the man she'd believed she knew was something of a facade. Not a lie, per se, but a cover up for the raw emotions and terrible life lessons that had shaped him.

Couldn't she relate?

She was prevented from considering that too deeply as

Dwayne shifted their conversation to more social matters. "How's Anderson?"

"Wily as ever," Marlowe said, shaking off the lingering memories of her own parents.

"Don't I know it. I've been meaning to get him out for a meal. I'll give him a call later to do just that."

While she appreciated the social connection, Marlowe was well aware of why they were standing in the conference room and she shifted her attention toward the table. "Your arrival is timely. I just let Officer Preston know that I'm ready to begin whenever your team is."

Dwayne nodded before turning to Wyatt. "This is your show, Detective. Consider me one more deeply curious observer on this case."

"Thank you, Captain." Wyatt moved closer to the table and addressed his fellow officers, who'd moved into the room and filled in the space around the conference table. "Detective Hayes and I were on bridge duty yesterday morning, reviewing the waters around the Brooklyn and Manhattan bridges. Detective Hayes discovered this safe nestled near the northeastern base of the Brooklyn Bridge."

Marlowe listened to him walk through the details of the discovery, how he and his partner handled the dive and their subsequent search for a body based on the similarity of the safe to the open cases currently under investigation. Although she'd heard it all earlier, the official, almost clinical, retelling didn't pack any less of a punch.

What was going on here?

She didn't need her grandfather's stories to know that in a city of eight million people the full spectrum of what humanity was capable of happened on a daily basis. The local news ensured she had a steady diet of the creepy, the odd and the downright criminal.

But the safes were a mystery.

They weren't large enough to hold much, yet they were tied to so many unknowns.

And death.

An involuntary shudder gripped her at that thought, even as she was silently grateful the safe she was about to open hadn't been strapped to a murder victim.

Wyatt turned from where he addressed the room. "You can begin whenever you're ready, Marlowe."

The evidence team had set up a video camera to record the opening of the safe—more chain of evidence needs— and she addressed the lens as she began to describe what she was doing. Just like the others, her standard masters she always tried first wouldn't unlock the safe. With that determined, she explained for the camera her next steps.

"I can drill into the unit, ultimately bypassing the locking mechanism."

She tapped the face of the safe once more, even though she was familiar with the model and brand. Yet even with that level of knowledge, it wouldn't do to damage whatever was inside. Satisfied she could proceed, she lifted her drill and bore a small diameter hole, still large enough to get her pinhole camera through. If the safe was more complex, she'd have hooked her camera to the room's video feed, but this would be open so quickly it would only waste time so she kept it to her own small screen.

The camera revealed what she'd expected—the inside had been tampered with just enough to negate her master. The pins still locked in but needed her manual work to fully open. With her tools she overrode the lock and felt the door of the safe give.

Stepping back, Marlowe gestured Wyatt forward. "It's all yours."

Light clapping erupted through the room but she kept her face still. Although she stood by her resolve not to look inside, the lingering questions she'd seen in Wyatt's eyes earlier kept her engaged in all that came next.

What was in there?

Drugs had appeared to be the primary motive in all that had come before. Was this another drug run gone bad? Or had someone been transporting the safe and dumped it after getting spooked at a late stage of the game?

Wyatt allowed the evidence team to photograph the interior of the safe as he pulled on a pair of thin gloves, but it was impossible to miss the confused look stamped across his face.

Especially when he finally reached inside and pulled out a thin manila envelope encased in a large plastic bag.

Was this a joke?

Wyatt could feel the small stack of papers inside the envelope and couldn't help but wonder why someone had gone to all the trouble.

"Is that all?" Captain Reed asked from where he stood across the room.

Wyatt gave a quick shake of his head. "I don't understand it, but that's all."

With careful movements, he pulled the papers from the plastic, then unhooked the small brads that kept the envelope closed. Each discarded piece was carefully laid on the conference table as evidence before he pulled out the papers. The stack was small, not more than four pages of printer paper, but what was on the notes seemed so strange.

Someone sank a small safe where they were sure it would be recovered, only to enclose a few photocopies inside?

He scanned each page, puzzling through three photocopies and a fourth page that had minimal writing scrawled across the center of the blank page in heavy black marker.

NIGHTWATCH 1995.

Wyatt flipped back to the photocopies. One was of a *New York Times* article on a jewel exhibit at the Museum of Natural History. The second was for a parking ticket issued in 1995, the numbers that made up the license plate detail smudged to the point it wasn't legible. And one diner receipt from a place in Brooklyn that, based on the address, wasn't there any longer.

What the hell was this?

He handed over the pages to the forensics team, their movements as gentle as Wyatt had been as they settled each piece down on the conference room table to photograph from every angle imaginable.

He glanced over at Marlowe but she'd stepped back, clearly ceding the space to the cops. Her attention was focused on him, not on the activity happening at the table.

But her raised eyebrows and mouthed, "That sure is a surprise," had him moving closer.

Marlowe gestured toward the table. "If I can just get back in there to retrieve my tools I can get going."

"You don't have to leave."

"Yeah, I probably do. It looks like you've got a bigger mystery on your hands than you expected." She shook her head, her gaze drifting to the table. "An envelope? That's really all there was?"

"With a few sheets of paper inside that make no sense and are dated from 1995."

Something flashed in her dark gaze at the date reference but it was gone so fast, Wyatt wasn't entirely sure he'd seen anything.

"Were the victims who were strapped to the safes even that old?"

It was an interesting angle and he was impressed she'd leaped there so quickly. "They were alive, but all would have been children nearly three decades ago. So it feels like a stretch to think there's an overt connection."

"Is it at all possible it's just a coincidence?"

He couldn't quite hold back the grin at that one. After the severe tension of the past few days, he was surprised to realize just how good it felt to smile. "I'm a cop. Do you think I actually believe in those?"

Her smile was swift and immediate, a little zing of understanding arcing between them. "Yeah. My grandfather has never been a big believer in them either."

And that acknowledgment reminded him yet again, Marlowe McCoy might be a civilian, but she had the genes of a cop.

"I'll help you gather up your tools but would you mind waiting for me?"

Once again, something flashed in her gaze he couldn't quite capture before it vanished. "Of course. I'll be in the lobby. Take your time."

He handed her the various items she'd used—the small hand drill, the long thin metal instrument with a hook on the end she'd used in the drill hole, and the small video screen for the pinhole camera that nestled into a padded pouch— and in moments she had slipped out of the room.

The forensics team continued to work with the evidence and Wyatt made his way over to his captain.

"Any theories?" Dwayne asked, his voice low.

"Not a damn one. And each clue we get is more confusing than the last. That's deliberate." Wyatt gestured in the direction of the safe. "A manila envelope with random photocopies inside?"

"Oh, it's definitely deliberate. And it's got a gamelike quality I don't appreciate." Dwayne crossed his arms. "The murders are frustrating enough but now a little game of Clue on top of it?" The man shook his head. "Damn infuriating if I'm honest."

A game was exactly what it felt like, Wyatt thought. He spent a considerable amount of his active training working on strategies to stop criminals. Some were simply dumb and thug-like in their approach to life, the same qualities that made them willing to commit crime making them somewhat more straightforward to catch, as well.

But he had worked cases in the past that never fit the open-and-shut profile. Ones that didn't have the same rhythm or flow of a run-of-the-mill thug on the loose. These cases had more layers to them, and oddly, more finesse. Those criminals not only thought they were above the law, but would like nothing more than to keep the cops running in circles while they did their criminal deeds.

This case had those marked overtones.

It was puzzling and strange and obviously dangerous, but with that taunting aspect underneath.

Seemingly unlinked victims who went down with the first three safes.

Questionable amounts of heroin discovered inside each safe. Nothing miniscule but not exactly a major drug bust, either.

And now this. A trail of unlinked clues he and his fellow officers would have to go on a goose chase to pursue.

News clippings and diner receipts?

A hell of a lot of nonsense they'd spend time on while missing out on taking the needed next steps to reach the endgame.

Their forensics lead set down her camera and gestured them both over. "We're going to take all of this, but as soon as I get to my computer I'll email you the images so you can start digging into this. The information's not clear on all pieces, which my gut tells me is deliberate."

Wyatt nodded. "I'll keep you posted but for the record, I don't think you're wrong there."

"We'll get the handwritten note into the lab and see if we can get any better sense of the pen used or the paper or even if someone slipped and included a fingerprint. We'll let you know."

"Thanks."

The woman rounded up her team and filed out, leaving Wyatt, Dwayne and Gavin in the room.

"It's a hell of a thing," Gavin started in once the room had cleared. "And what is Nightwatch?"

"Hell if I know," Dwayne said, a mix of disgust and puzzlement coloring his tone. "And I was on the squad in ninety-five. Nothing rings a bell."

"We'll check the files," Wyatt said. "See if we can find anything or any reference. I'm not sure if the date's a help or something to throw us off the scent but we'll start in the mid-90s and work our way forward and backward from there."

Dwayne was quick to provide his support. "Let me know how it goes and if you need more help on this. Seems like your dive skills are at a premium right now."

His captain looked Wyatt straight in the eyes before giving Gavin an equally serious once over. "Be careful down there."

"Yes, Captain," they said in unison.

"I'll leave you both to your evening, then." Dwayne left

the room, the weight of their work riding his shoulders as much—if not more, Wyatt thought—than his own.

"I'm going to get a head start on this Nightwatch stuff."

"Take a look but knock off at a decent time. We're down again tomorrow and the captain's right. We can't lose focus on our dives."

"You got it."

Wyatt watched him go and once again considered the weight on Dwayne's shoulders.

The load that bore down on all of them.

And wondered, yet again, what madness they were up against.

Chapter Seven

Marlowe waited on a small bench near the front of the precinct. It had been a surprise to realize just how much time they'd spent in the conference room and it was nearly seven when she'd finally taken a seat, settling her tools beside her.

Settling in to wait for Wyatt.

It was an oddly cozy moment and she fought to keep her head about her. She wasn't a woman made for cozy moments or domesticity. Her background had ensured as much. Yet the more time she spent in Wyatt's company the more she wondered if she could be made for that.

For the bond that kept two people in each other's orbit, day in and day out. Sharing space. Sharing a life.

The deep thought was far too intense for someone she'd had a pie date with that had also included her grandfather and a second date over a run and breakfast. Yet the thought remained all the same.

She was intrigued.

And with the intrigue came the addition of that flutter low in the belly that spoke of anticipation and need. Two things that left her vulnerable and wide open to hurt.

Worse, the vulnerability opened her to the potential for deception.

Did she ever want to be in that place again?

A dating relationship was hardly the same as parental family bonds, but she'd lived with the reality of betrayal. Of what it meant to put your hopes on someone who wasn't worthy of them.

And it hadn't just been her father. He might have done the work of a criminal but her mother's reaction to Michael McCoy's thievery and deception was to abort ship and emotionally abandon her child in the process.

It had only been her grandfather who had provided a safe harbor.

Anderson McCoy had done his very best, but none of it could fully make up for that betrayal.

Could anything, ever?

Even as she knew that for truth, she had to admit Wyatt hadn't had an easy time of things, either. It wasn't a competition—no one wanted to play "who had the worst childhood?"—but he had lived with pain, too.

And if she'd read between the lines, that pain had followed him into adulthood, just like her.

"Those look like some serious thoughts for a late summer evening."

She glanced up out of those serious thoughts that never felt too far from the surface to find Wyatt. He'd changed out of his slacks and dress shirt that had an NYPD logo in the corner to a pair of jeans and a gray T-shirt that had the word "Brooklyn" emblazoned across that always impressive chest. A few weeks before she'd have looked at him and disdainfully thought "frat boy" and mentally moved on.

After, of course, she admired that impressive chest.

But now that they'd spent time together, she recognized the flirty, nonserious behavior she'd always associated with him was a bit of diversion. Not the sleight of hand her father was best at, but something of a protective layer Wyatt wrapped around himself.

"There's lots of serious to think about," she finally said.

"Want to go out and find some of the less serious?"

"I'd like that."

He took her work bag without being asked and headed for the exit. Marlowe didn't even muster up an argument. The bag was heavy and it was nice to share the load.

But she did keep pace beside him as they both said goodnight to the guard on front desk duty before walking out into the pretty September evening. The sun was low in the sky, backlighting the street in front of the precinct in a reddish gold hue, the last rays of sun filtering through the three-and four-story buildings that made up the block.

"I love September in New York."

His agreement was immediate. "It's the best. Still warm but not oppressive. And some of the prettiest sunsets over the water you'll ever see."

"What's your favorite time of the year to dive?"

"As long as there isn't a hurricane coming in, right now's pretty nice. All summer, really. Even with the layered suits, the job is a lot less enjoyable in winter when it's stone-cold freezing."

"I'll bet."

They talked off and on about the intricacies of his work before coming to Baker's Pub. It was a newer entrant in Sunset Bay's young professional renaissance and she had only been here once with a group of friends.

"This work?" He nodded toward the bar and the lively sounds spilling out to the street.

"This is great. Though I am a bit surprised."

"Oh?" Wyatt pulled the door open for her, more of that happy, lively noise greeting them.

"I'd have thought you'd take me down to Yancy's."

"You want to go to a cop bar?"

She shrugged. "I figured that's where we were headed."

His grin was swift and once again, caught her hard at the knees.

"What's that smile for?"

Wyatt gestured her into the bar. "You've got the bug and you want to talk about the case. Maybe some hard-boiled detective talk over a few beers?"

"Don't you want to talk about it?"

He leaned in beside her, his voice nearly a purr in her ear. "I want to talk to you. If the case happens to come up in the course of conversation, so be it. I have zero interest, however, in hanging out with a bunch of cops."

They were heady words and her earlier thoughts of cozying up to Wyatt had a pedestrian sort of sweetness that had nothing to do with the shots of desire that speared down her spine before radiating out through her body like a sparkler. With his hand low on her back—sending out more of those sparks—she wove her way toward an empty booth on the far side of the room.

Wyatt gently deposited her work bag on his side of the booth before sitting.

"Thank you for that."

He glanced up as he reached for the menus stuffed against the side wall. "For what?"

"For not tossing my bag into the seat before you."

A small line creased the space between his eyebrows. "You have expensive equipment. And even if you had feathers in there, it's not my bag to toss around, gorilla style."

"Thanks all the same."

He let whatever he was about to say drop as a waiter came

up to them. After he'd departed with their drink and appetizer orders, Wyatt once again focused on her.

"Now it's my turn to thank you. For the help today. For waiting around." He quieted before continuing on. "For listening earlier at your shop. I appreciate it."

Although she avoided speaking of her parents with anyone other than her grandfather, Marlowe realized a small offering was more than fair. "It's so hard to lose a loved one. But what comes after? That's hard, too.

"And it's difficult to realize your parents aren't who you thought they are. Or maybe better said, who you hoped they were."

"Even if those are the hopes of a child?"

Wyatt's face drew up in serious lines and once again, Marlowe recognized something there in his relationship with his mother. Something that had struck an incredibly deep well of disappointment.

"Becoming an adult doesn't change our family bonds. I don't think we ever lose our need for our parents." She hesitated, before adding, "I never did."

He nodded at that but didn't say anything further. Yet despite the quiet, Marlowe got the distinct sense they'd gained another layer of understanding between them.

Even as she was grateful she didn't have to tread her own personal scorched earth and talk about her parents.

Maybe she'd be ready at some point, but not tonight.

"Thanks as well for taking on the safe work for this case. You're a pro, Ms. McCoy."

"They're puzzles and I love solving them. Locks. Combinations. Even where to drill. It's a perpetual challenge."

"You had a lot of safes in your office." His gaze narrowed. "And I was so busy talking I didn't even ask any questions earlier at your shop. You had a lot of tools laid out on your work table. Were you working on something when I interrupted?"

"You didn't interrupt. In fact, you provided a very welcome diversion from a puzzle that was not revealing any clues to me."

At his ready interest, she added, "I regularly test new offerings for various safe companies. I have running contracts with several of them to test their products, give suggestions and discuss weak points."

"You really are a badass safecracker."

"I prefer lock and vault technician." She aimed for a serious demeanor, but it rapidly dissolved into amusement. "But yeah, I'm a badass safecracker."

"How'd you get into it?"

"That love of puzzles again. And too much time on my hands one summer as a kid."

She considered telling him more—how that summer she'd played with every lock in the very large house by the ocean her parents had taken her to. It was one of the more idyllic summers of her childhood, even if it had been lonely. It was in the time before the world knew the depths of her father's crimes and, if her mother had known of them, had still looked the other way, pretending they didn't exist.

Pretending the glamorous life they were living was funded in some way other than through theft.

That summer had also provided endless challenges to a kid left alone for far too much of it.

"Sounds like a lot of kid ingenuity," he said.

If Wyatt sensed there was more to her story than a summer of modest mischief, he ignored it.

Biding his time? Or had she just gotten that good in breezing through her background that it was as commonplace to her as breathing?

The questions—and their vastly different answers—faded as Wyatt continued.

"Whatever way you developed the skill, the NYPD is certainly grateful for your talents. I'm grateful for your talents."

Marlowe reached across the table, the move as instinctual as it was natural, and laid a hand over his. "What you do, Wyatt. It's not easy. I never thought it was but seeing this case up close? It's reminded me that police work isn't just hard, it's all-consuming. There's no laying it down when the day is over and walking away."

Once a cop, always a cop. It got in the blood.

He'd said as much the evening he'd taken her home after talking with her grandfather, and in those words Marlowe recognized the truth.

"Maybe not," he said, turning his hand over beneath hers, "but there is something to be said for taking some enjoyment at the end of a hard day. Let's do that."

As she looked at him across the table she saw the weight of the case on his shoulders. But she also saw the willingness to set it aside for a bit.

How could she deny him that?

Why would she even want to?

WYATT TOOK THE LAST, satisfying bite of his burger, and marveled at the evening. He'd asked her to stick around after she'd completed her work in the precinct conference room because he wasn't ready to say goodbye. The off-kilter way he'd left her after their breakfast, followed by the unnerved retelling of his father's death in her shop had left questions in his mind and he'd wanted a bit of time alone with her to see if she'd already written him off.

To his delight, she not only hadn't written him off but was an engaged, enjoyable dinner companion.

Or maybe, dumbass, your instincts were right and she was one of the few people you could actually talk to about your father.

It wasn't a particularly enlightened thought, but it did have merit. Especially because he spent so much of his time trying to avoid the topic that not talking about it had grown a bit heavy in his mind.

He also recognized a kindred spirit in her acceptance of his life experiences. He hadn't told many women he'd dated the specifics about his father's death, but it did come up from time to time. Any relationship that progressed to something even moderately serious included discussion of family, parents at the top of that list.

He'd always received compassion when he'd spoken of his father's death, but he hadn't always sensed that deeper layer of understanding.

Because while she might not be living with the death of a parent, Marlowe lost her father as surely as he lost his. It was clear in her understanding and in all the things she didn't say.

Even her story of how she got interested in her work smacked of sadness and a sort of lonely existence he'd sensed.

And then somehow—miraculously—she managed that conversational magic that seemed to be her stock-in-trade and made him forget about his family and his maudlin thoughts entirely.

"Okay, so I told you the strangest thing I've ever pulled out of a safe. It's your turn. Weirdest thing you ever pulled up on a dive."

"Weird weird or gross weird?"

"Either." Her eyes lit up. "No, actually, how about both?"

"Okay, so gross weird is body parts."

Marlowe settled her burger down. "Do I really want to hear this?"

"You asked!"

"Fair." She smiled and picked up her burger. "Have at it."

"To be honest, you probably don't want full details. But I will say it's a more persistent aspect to the job than I'd ever expected."

"But you do body retrieval."

"Yes," Wyatt agreed, "which was what I expected. It's the body *part* retrieval I wasn't quite ready for. My first year on the team we pulled up four severed hands, quite a few fingers and a body part every man would prefer to have left on him, even in death."

"Oh." Her mouth formed a small O. "Oh, wow."

"Yeah. Fortunately that was a one-time thing." He laughed in spite of himself. "Rookies are already given a hard time. I was the butt of a lot of jokes for about six months after that one."

"Okay. Fascinated though I am, I would like to finish this really outstanding burger. So tell me about the weird weird."

"Doll heads."

"Well, yeah, they're part of the creepy hat trick for a reason."

"Creepy hat trick?"

"Doll heads, clowns and little twin girls with pigtails and matching dresses standing at the end of a long hallway. They're classics for a reason." Marlowe popped a fry into her mouth. "Where did you find these doll heads?"

"We had an evidence retrieval up in Spuyten Duyvil."

"And equally creepy place since it's Dutch for the Devil's Whirlpool."

"You're good."

"I love my New York history and there's no lack of it here.

But that's got to be pretty hard to dive. Those waters were named that for a reason. And—" She broke off, a pretty blush covering her cheeks. "I'll stop now since I'm talking like a walking encyclopedia."

Her knowledge of their home was a pleasure he'd never expected. "I was actually thinking what a lovely dinner companion you are."

That heightened color remained, even as she smiled. "Then I'll keep going with my questions. Because those are tough waters, aren't they?"

"Most of New York is with how the Hudson River meets the Atlantic Ocean."

"Is it hard to dive?"

He considered her question and the speed with which she zeroed in on an aspect of his work. "Diving's never easy. There's a lot of training involved for a reason and you can't forget where you are or what you're doing. But yes, working the waters around the city has additional challenges based on time of day, the tides and the overall mass of humanity and boat traffic in and around the waters."

"You always dive in teams, though?"

"We do."

A strange expression came over her face and he couldn't resist pressing her. "What is it?"

"Never mind." Marlowe shook her head. "It's dumb."

"You can't lead with that and not tell me."

"What about sharks?"

Now that was a question he got a lot. The whole team did and he knew the public fascination with sharks made for an easy way to talk about what he did—or divert from the less public aspects of the work.

"They're a part of the job and we do see them from time to time."

Marlowe's gaze narrowed. "How often is time to time? And how can you be so casual about it?"

"I'm not—" Wyatt broke off and reached for his beer. "Okay, so I am a little casual. But we work around them. They're more active at dawn and around dusk so we try to avoid those times for our routine work. Helping victims in an emergency will always take precedence, but for our standard surveillance work we avoid them."

"Okay, that's one way."

"We also dive in pairs so we can keep watch for each other and we avoid getting near any situation that looks like they're feeding."

"It still seems like a risk."

"What I do is a risk. But believe it or not, there's a lot more risk dealing with criminals than marine life. Sharks really just aren't that interested in what we're doing. And if you add on the Zodiac boat is following us and there's crew keeping watch there to alert us if we need to surface it's not a big source of difficulty."

"Color me unconvinced." Marlowe smiled as she reached for her glass of wine. "But then again, I watch *Jaws* religiously every year over Memorial Day weekend so maybe I'm a bit influenced by that."

"To your point about the dollheads, it's a classic for a reason."

She toyed with the stem of her wineglass. "What you're really saying, though, is that the sharks on land give you a lot more trouble than the ones in the water."

"I guess I am."

"And those notes today? In the safe?"

"We'll handle it. The forensics team will do their part and we'll start running down the information on each page."

"It seems like a lot of running around."

He eyed her over the rim of his beer. "You sure you don't want to try out for a job on the force? That was the exact conversation I had with Captain Reed after you left. It feels like a decoy of some sort and a deliberate waste of everyone's time."

"It's an awful elaborate trick."

He was already replaying his conversation with Dwayne and Gavin in his mind when Marlowe's comment stuck a hard landing. "Trick?"

"Well, yeah. First you have the murders and the fact the safes were strapped to someone. Any way you look at that it's a significant crime all by itself. Then you put a fourth safe in a place where it's sure to be discovered by a dive team?" She tapped a finger on the table. "You said the other morning that the regular dive checks aren't public knowledge. Not truly public or just something that's not publicized?"

"The latter. Our presence in the harbor isn't a secret. And the remit of my team isn't a secret, either."

"Which means someone went to a whole lot of trouble to put a standard-sized valuables safe at the base of the Brooklyn Bridge. Something that could have easily gotten them caught and in a heap of trouble."

"Yeah."

"What's the endgame? Because it's like they're doing it backward. Killing people only to then bury a safe with some photocopies in it? It's backward. Wouldn't you work up to killing people?"

"You'd give your grandfather a run for his money."

That smile was back, even brighter than before and without a trace of her earlier bashfulness. "That man lives, sleeps and breathes casework. I've heard him talk about his work my whole life. Clearly some of it sunk in by osmosis."

"But you are right. Murder is a sad outcome, but it is often an endgame. Not the place a criminal begins."

"Which leaves the bigger question. What's the real endgame here?"

DUTCH ANSWERED THE burner phone in his pocket and his contact on the other end wasted no time in sharing an update.

"The cops got it. You can consider the package received."

He debated how much he wanted to ask—paid-off marks were notoriously tricky—but he wanted an answer.

An answer would dictate the next step.

"Safe's in evidence?"

"Yep. Contents, too."

"McCoy do the work?"

"She's the only one they're using on these jobs."

It was an interesting development and one he hadn't been able to plan for. But Marlowe McCoy's reputation preceded her. Locksmiths might be a dime a dozen but one who could genuinely crack safes was another story.

When that safe cracking came with the McCoy pedigree, it was like catnip and comfort for the cops, all rolled into one.

And it made his work that much more satisfying.

"So the payment?" his contact asked, her voice shifting toward anxious for the first time.

"It'll be where we discussed."

"Now?"

He avoided sighing and instead pushed a smile into his tone. "In place and ready for you to pick it up."

She mumbled a quiet thank-you and ended the call and Dutch sat there for a long while, considering the mark. She'd been an ideal choice, her ex-husband's gambling problem ensuring there wasn't any money left over to pay for child support. She needed the cash, but he knew the work didn't sit well with her.

That light quaver in the voice always told the truth.

And payoffs to those who were desperate never worked quite as well as those in it just for the money.

He had a few more safes planned but would cut her loose as soon as the work wrapped.

And hoped like hell there didn't end up being a need to take her out.

Chapter Eight

Marlowe glanced around the elegant midtown restaurant and wondered why she was here.

Curiosity?

Personal amusement?

Or was it that persistent childhood need for her mother's approval, even when she'd never receive it?

Sadly, she knew it was the last.

It was always the last, no matter how badly she wished she were able to find some sort of smooth, cool detachment from the relationship.

Her mother's call and surprise announcement—that she was in town from Arizona and could they meet for lunch?— had come in while Marlowe was at dinner with Wyatt. The light, airy happiness that had followed her into her apartment after dinner had vanished when she'd listened to the message.

Her mother had traveled more than two thousand miles and hadn't bothered to mention it until she was already here?

Marlowe had lived with Patty McCoy's dreamlike disposition so long she shouldn't be surprised but, like it or not, she could still be flustered.

Damn it, no. She could still be mad and hurt and emotionally wrecked.

And wasn't this the problem with cozy?

With those flutters in the belly?

Something always waited in the wings to snatch it all out from underneath you.

Although she didn't know her mother's reason for visiting, there was some discussion her father's parole hearing would be moved up from the following spring to this October. And while her parents were long-since divorced, anything that involved Michael McCoy always involved his ex-wife.

If for no other reason than Patty loved the drama. Even the whole "finding herself in Arizona" smacked of a rather large sense of self-involvement and dramatic license on how to explain away the poor decisions of her life.

"Darling!" Her mother's greeting—part coo, part cry for attention—echoed from four tables away.

Marlowe waited for her mother's arrival and considered the woman she hadn't seen in three years.

The long, flowing blond hair was a bit more platinum than Marlowe remembered, but still worn in that long, straight bohemian style her mother favored. Her skirts were flowy and her bracelets jangled, but that clink was most definitely eighteen-carat gold.

No roadside crafts or hammered bronze for her mother.

She might have perfected the boho look, but it was tinged with the distinct signs of wealth.

Wealth that had come only from the riches of others, no matter how Patty had managed to spin that truth to herself.

Their embrace was surprisingly warm and her mother held on a bit tighter than Marlowe expected before pulling back. "Darling. How are you?"

"I'm good, Mom. What about you? And what a happy surprise you're here."

"I love New York in September and I realized I was well overdue for a visit."

"Where are you staying?"

One gold-wrapped wrist jangled in a casual brush off. "I got a hotel in the city. Thought I'd get a bit of sightseeing in while I was here."

Marlowe would be the first to call her relationship with her mother strained, but they were cordial to one another. And while it might have been years since their last visit, whenever Patty came east she always stayed with Marlowe in Brooklyn.

All this only added to the underlying questions about the impromptu visit.

Settling into their seats, Marlowe recognized the only way to understand what was going on was to let things play out, however Patty ultimately chose to work up to it. But by the time she walked out of the restaurant, all would be revealed.

They ordered lunch and fell into simple conversation over sparkling water and mixed green salads. Her mother's careful questions about Anderson and Marlowe's work carried a practiced air.

"You're still doing your lockwork?"

"Lock, safe, vault management. Yes, all of it."

"I still can't believe there's enough work in that to make a living."

Marlowe hesitated to tell her mother that her business had cleared more than a half million dollars the prior year. Or that she was currently contracted with three safe companies in addition to the private work and the consulting jobs she did. She was proud of her work, but it didn't matter to her mother.

Because Marlowe hadn't taken a traditional "female" job, nor had she found a husband to take care of her.

For all the suggestion of casual independence the bohemian look implied, her mother was shockingly traditional. Antiquated, even.

"There's plenty of work."

"Yes, well." Patty let that hang there before continuing on. "Have you spoken to your father?"

"I visited him back in July. That's the last I've seen or spoken to him." Marlowe took a sip of her sparkling water, her question casual when she finally spoke. "You?"

"Last week. Michael believes his parole hearing will be moved up and that he'll be out before Christmas. Wearing one of those horrid ankle bracelets if he gets out." Patty shuddered. "But away from that wretched place."

"He's serving his debt to society, Mom. Those in charge expect it to be paid in full, whether he's in or out of prison."

"As if he's some common criminal."

"He is a common criminal."

They were hard words but they'd gotten easier over the years. It had been a fantasy to think her father wasn't "like the other prisoners." That his code of ethics—sketchy though they might be—elevated him out of the garden-variety criminal category.

Only time and acceptance had helped Marlowe recognize the truth.

Her father had dedicated his life to stealing from others. Her mother could delude herself that his behavior somehow elevated him from murderers and rapists, but the law didn't.

And Marlowe had long since gotten past her anger about that.

Sadness, yes.

But anger or fury? That was nothing but wasted emotion when it came to her father.

"Well, it will still be good to know he's not rotting in a cell."

"Who knew you cared that much?" Marlowe chose her words carefully, but even she realized the small talk and the charade of ignorance had gone on long enough.

"I've always cared, Marlowe. You know that. It's because I cared so much I had to move away. Had to get away from the knowledge my husband was in that horrid place."

"Apologies if my violin isn't in easy reach."

"Don't you sit there casting judgment on me. Your father wasn't the only one who lost his freedom the day that sentence came down. I lost my life."

"Your life of lies."

It was old ground but her mother had never doubled down quite so hard, either.

Which was the first inkling something more was going on. Smoothing her napkin, Marlowe settled back in her chair. "What's really prompted this visit?"

"I've met someone."

"Oh. Oh, wow." Whatever she'd been expecting that wasn't it. Although she wasn't naïve enough to think her mother—a single, unattached divorcée—didn't date, Patty had always had a quality that had suggested she wasn't fully over Michael McCoy, either.

It was subtle—a sort of longing for an earlier time—but had always been somewhat distinct. And a clear roadblock to finding her own happiness.

"Well, that's great for you. Really, Mom. I'm happy for you."

At her acknowledgment, Patty smiled her first real smile since they'd sat down.

"His name's Brock and he retired to Arizona about three years ago from California."

Patty spent the rest of their salads and most of their entrées detailing the wonders of her new relationship. How she and Brock met, their active social life and the fact that she believed he was going to ask her to marry him.

"I'm glad you found each other."

"Yes, well—" Patty broke off. "It's your father I'm worried about."

"I hardly think Dad would stand in your way. He's only ever wanted your happiness."

"Maybe so, but, well… Brock doesn't know about your father. And he can't find out."

"You're lying to him?"

"It's an omission, which is hardly the same thing. And why would I risk running him off?"

It was as if a cold bucket of water had been dumped over the top of her head and all Marlowe could do was sputter. "You claim to love him."

"I do love him."

"So be honest with him."

"My ex-husband is a convict. That's not liable to go over well with a man who's done quite well for himself in life and currently serves on three boards in his retirement."

So there it was.

That distinct sense of self-preservation that had always lived beneath the dreamy, airy facade Patty showed the world.

That self-defense had allowed her to ignore the realities of her husband's life for more than twenty years of marriage.

The same self-delusion had allowed her to believe walking away from her child, leaving her to fend for herself, would all be okay in the end.

"If you want to enter the bond of marriage under that cloud, that's your call. What does any of this have to do with me?"

"Brock and I are in town. He had some business to conduct and suggested we could meet you for dinner. He'd like to know you."

"And this was the advance show to make sure I didn't spill the beans on dear old Dad."

"I'm asking you to behave with a bit of decorum, Marlowe. That's all."

Decorum?

That's what the kids were calling lying your ass off these days?

Marlowe wanted to say no. Way down deep inside she wanted to walk away and wash her hands of all of it.

But that same little girl who still missed her mother—who still craved her attention and affection—was the only one who managed to find her voice.

"Sure, Mom. I'll go. Just tell me where I need to be."

WYATT COMBED THE silt beneath his gloved hands and mentally counted off the minutes he had left before his ascent. They were in the Hudson, running an op to recover a weapon, but all he could do was count the minutes until his shift was over.

It was a new sensation. He loved being in the water, and he loved what he did. But even Wyatt recognized the current mystery they were dealing with was firmly on land.

What was it with those sheets of paper? And why would anyone go to all that trouble?

It'd been three days since Marlowe opened the safe they'd discovered under the Brooklyn Bridge and still not a single clue had been unearthed from the strange documentation discovered inside.

A *New York Times* article? While interesting, a review of that case had turned up nothing in the archives. There hadn't been any crimes reported in or around the museum and nothing about the exhibit featured in the article.

A diner receipt and a parking ticket? Nothing to find on either of those.

And what the hell was Nightwatch?

Endless questions, with no answers.

He continued with the diving exercise, returning his focus to the evidence they were trying to run down. A report had come in just as he'd gone on shift that there was a fight on one of the ferry crossings that morning. Said fight had ultimately resulted in a switchblade being pulled, and then subsequently tossed overboard when security came to break up the fight.

The fact that the switchblade had also damaged internal organs on the victim had put Wyatt and his dive partner on the hunt for evidence. He was diving with Kerrigan Doyle this morning and while they hadn't been partnered often, he was incredibly pleased to see her progress. She'd been with the team for about two and a half years and was a strong, focused diver.

The alert on his comms unit that she'd found the knife only added to his positive impressions of the young woman.

Damn, she was good.

And because she'd found the knife so fast and they were in a fairly shallow depth, they could ascend without any concerns.

Moving in close and tapping her on the foot to alert her to his presence, he signaled his intention to head up and got her thumbs-up in return. She'd already put the knife in an evidence container and begun her ascent, as well. They reached the Zodiac one after the other and they waited while Amos took the container and stowed it before helping Kerrigan and Wyatt into the boat.

Free of his breathing apparatus, Wyatt tilted his head towards the evidence. "Great job, Kerrigan. That was a fast find."

Kerrigan glanced up from where she settled her oxygen tank in the Zodiac. "I got lucky, but I'll take it. Of course, luck may not be the exact right word. I did manage to get a handful of dead rat first before landing on the knife."

She was unnecessarily modest, but with the rolled eyes and moue of disgust, Wyatt couldn't help but laugh. Unfortunately, the disgusting aspects of the job were something they could all relate to.

Unbidden, Wyatt remembered his conversation at the bar with Marlowe. Although she had teased him, he hadn't missed how fascinated she was by the things they often pulled up out of the water. "Funny enough, the subject of the less appealing things we pull up off the seafloor was dinner conversation for me the other night."

"Aren't you the sparkling conversationalist, Trumball," Kerrigan teased him.

"I heard it was more than dinner," Amos said with a smile, all too anxious to get in the conversation. "I heard you were out with Marlowe McCoy."

Wyatt was careful with his answer but he wasn't going to deny it. "She's helping with the safes we keep dragging off the harbor floor."

"Yeah, yeah, it was just a casual thank-you dinner. At Baker's no less." Amos waved a hand. "I realize the woman grew up around cops, but those are some pretty rank sweet nothings you're whispering at the great Anderson McCoy's granddaughter. If you're gonna romance her, where's your game, Wyatt?"

Marlowe McCoy's not a game.

The words were nearly out of his mouth when he snatched them back. Both because he had no interest in being the center of gossip and more because he felt the congenial facade that usually carried him through any manner of work conversations fading hard and fast from some harmless ribbing on Amos's part.

"It was a few drinks and burgers."

Amos shot Kerrigan a knowing eye but seemed to recognize it was time to shut up.

And with it, Wyatt tried to get out of his damn head. Date or not, he had been out with Anderson McCoy's granddaughter. The whole evening could have been perfectly innocent and they'd have been the center of gossip.

The fact he was interested...

He'd better figure out a way to handle it around the rest of the team because people were going to talk.

The call came in, alerting them to a new problem and forcing the worries about gossip to the back of his mind.

Amos picked up the radio, answering even as Wyatt and Kerrigan sat and waited for what would inevitably be new direction and a new set of orders.

"You got it," Amos said. "We're close enough to follow in the Zodiac and my officers have second tanks with them. Estimated arrival three minutes."

Wyatt and Kerrigan began checking equipment, reviewing the two fresh tanks they'd already stowed in the Zodiac in anticipation of a possible second dive on the knife retrieval. Amos signaled to the larger NYPD boat they worked with and followed as soon as the larger boat was in motion.

"We're headed to Chelsea Piers," Amos hollered over the sound of the engine. "Tourist in the water."

Wyatt muttered a curse before hollering back. "Alive?"

"Dispatch says yes."

"Then let's aim to keep it that way."

Kerrigan settled in beside Wyatt as Amos maneuvered them out of the harbor and up the Hudson River. She pointed to the evidence container still attached in the far corner of the Zodiac. "I guess I should consider it lucky I found the knife already."

"Damn fine work, Doyle."

Kerrigan shook her head in seriousness, but it was hard to miss the sarcasm in her voice, even over the high-pitched whine of the engine. "Could've been even quicker if it hadn't been for the damn rat."

Wyatt was grateful for the laugh as they helped each other with their tanks, getting set into position. The joke was also enough to diffuse the lingering tension from the good-natured ribbing over his date with Marlowe.

Because it had been a date.

In the days since their evening at Baker's, he'd tried to convince himself otherwise, but even he knew better.

The department might be talking about him and Marlowe, but gossip ran in the halls of the 86th like fresh-flowing water. And when he wasn't the subject of any of it, he rode those currents with as much pleasure as the next person.

So he had no right to get touchy about it now.

As Chelsea Piers came into view, activity abundantly clear up against the waterfront, Wyatt put it out of his mind.

Even if he did vow to call Marlowe tonight and ask her out again.

MARLOWE PRIDED HERSELF on being a levelheaded woman. She took responsibility for her actions and for her life. It was a simple detail she knew and understood about herself and it had absolutely no bearing—nor was it a help—on the wildly raging emotions she had experienced for the better part of seventy-two hours.

Had she and Wyatt gone on a date?

Were they going to go on another date?

And was she actually contemplating inviting him into the ridiculous charade with her mother?

Even if it did feel a bit like getting an ally on her side for what would inevitably be one of the most awkward evenings of her life.

"Get the hell out of your own head," she muttered as she logged into her email after being out on a job site all morning. "Find something productive to do. Even I'm sick of myself."

It wasn't like she and Wyatt hadn't spoken or that he'd pulled a jerk move and ghosted her. In fact, it was the opposite. He'd texted every day since she'd last seen him and he'd called one evening to see how she was doing. He'd asked her on another morning park run for the following week, his schedule of morning shifts this week interfering with his morning runs.

He was mature.

Honest.

Open and transparent.

And she was torn between asking him to commit social subterfuge or pulling a jackrabbit and walking away from the man like a quivering lump of fear.

What the ever-loving hell, McCoy?

Since she'd just opened ten emails and hadn't read any of them, she took a deep breath and tried a new tack.

She might have agreed to meet her mother's new boy-friend but she didn't have to go. There were a million excuses she could make up and likely a few that weren't even BS. What she needed was to think through what she really wanted to do.

Lie, which sat uncomfortably on her shoulders.

Chicken out of the evening, even if it only solved the problem for a short while.

Or decide if it was time to take the more nuclear option and cut her mother out of her life.

Since all options sucked she refocused on her computer, surprised to see an email from her father's lawyer as she continued to scroll through what had come in. The email held the details of her father's upcoming parole hearing—now moved up to late October—with information about the case under review included.

There'd been a time when she'd cared deeply about her father's case, but it had been years since she'd even bothered to do an online search. The details had consumed her when she was younger, but in time she'd come to realize that the endless combing through articles had no bearing on her life.

None of them were fully accurate portrayals of the man she knew.

Nor were they entirely inaccurate about how he spent his life and how he'd ended up caught for a crime he'd committed. One that had come after a long line of crimes he'd also committed yet escaped any consequence.

With the case number noted in the email she did log into a search program, curious to see how the facts matched her memory.

The case details were heavy on the legalese but she read through the specifics and knew they were as damning as she remembered. The heist of a downtown Manhattan loft, pur-

ported to hold art to rival a museum. Her father had set his
sights on a small sculpture and an exceedingly rare bronze
that had been worked in Florence during the Renaissance.

He'd nearly gotten away with it, too. But a recently installed video camera on the building across the street from
the loft, as well as a telling confession from a known as-
sociate who was looking to cut his own deal on a different
crime, had been enough to put her father away.

More curious than she wanted to admit, she pulled up
a fresh search bar and typed in the name of the known as-
sociate.

Harry Kisco.

The search returned several pages of info, but she clicked
on the images option first, curious to see if she recognized
the man who'd put her father away. Shots that had clearly
come from outside a courthouse showed a big man with
his arm up, hiding from the camera. A scroll farther down
the page finally turned up a mug shot some enterprising
reporter had included in a story.

Did she know him?

Had he been a part of her parents' social circle?

Her mind drifted back to the story she'd told Wyatt of
how she'd first gotten interested in locks. Was it possible
Harry Kisco was there, that summer in the Hamptons when
she'd spent hour after hour alone in the big rambling house
with the locks and the picks she'd found in a drawer and an
old library with a big safe in the wall?

They were old memories but she really didn't think she
recognized the man in the photos.

She'd nearly closed out of the search program, aware that
this was not only a pointless waste of time, but likely a dump-
ster diving exercise tied to the situation with her mother.

Way too many emotions churning up old memories.

"Put it away, McCoy. Get up. Clear your head." She'd nearly done just that when her gaze caught on an image at the bottom of the page.

The man she'd been looking at—Harry Kisco—stood with his arm around another man, photographed in front of a nightclub. The logo on his shirt caught her attention before she realized it was a match for the branding on the sign behind them.

Nightwatch.

She clicked on the image and quickly read the caption underneath.

Harry Kisco and partner, Mark Stone, launch new Brooklyn nightclub, Nightwatch, in Williamsburg.

Nightwatch?

Although she hadn't been privy to the information coming out of the safe in the precinct conference room, she had seen the oversize writing on one of the sheets of paper Wyatt pulled out of the business-sized envelope.

NIGHTWATCH 1995 it had said.

What was one of her father's known associates doing with information that matched evidence coming out of the safes from the harbor?

Her exchange with Wyatt as they'd left the 86th whipped back into her thoughts, a distinct echo of the questions now roiling in her mind at the image of the two men and their nightclub.

Is it at all possible it's just a coincidence?

I'm a cop. Do you think I actually believe in those?

Yeah. My grandfather has never been a big believer in them, either.

Coincidences.

Any way she played it, there wasn't a single scenario she could muster up where this was an accident of fate.

But what to do about it? She could ask her grandfather but she wanted to respect Wyatt's work. And if she hadn't been standing on the perimeter of the conference room she'd never have seen the scrawled note anyway.

But she had.

And now she had an odd, albeit tenuous, connection to her father?

The date of his parole hearing was coming up. Would this ruin his chances of getting consideration for early release?

A heavy knock echoed from the front of her shop and she crossed out of her office and into the reception area, ready to send whoever was there away.

And came face-to-face with Wyatt, standing on the other side of the glass door.

Chapter Nine

For the second time that week, Wyatt stood outside Marlowe's shop, the need to talk to her overriding his natural inclination to simply text.

It felt like a bit of overkill but he'd already intended to ask her out and the rescue at Chelsea Piers had ended up being more intense than he'd anticipated. What had started out as a standard water rescue had turned into a bigger issue when the husband of the woman who'd fallen overboard decided to go in after his wife. While a deeply moving gesture, the man hadn't anticipated the height of the pier or the shock of the water and Wyatt and Kerrigan had needed to split their efforts against two people along with the rest of the rescue crew.

And tough rescue or not, you just want to see her, Trumball.

Which made it that much more startling when he caught sight of her face, starkly serious, through the door of the shop.

He'd already come to understand she wasn't a woman of easy emotions. It fascinated him more than he'd have expected, but in moments like this he had to admit that depth could be jarring, as well.

Was she okay?

Marlowe opened the door and stepped back to let him in, but before he could lean closer to press a kiss to her cheek she stepped out of range.

Deliberately?

Wyatt recognized the broader truth—they didn't know each other that well, despite the obvious interest that sparked between them—and he opted to give her a bit of space and see if they'd come far enough that she'd trust him with whatever was bothering her.

And if she didn't?

Wyatt mentally shrugged it off. He'd worry about that later.

"I hope you don't mind I came straight over. I was going to text you but went on impulse once my shift wrapped up."

"Okay day?"

"It was challenging, but successful, so I'll take it." He watched as she played with a small card rack on the counter, straightening the rectangular shape so it was even with the counter edge. "I thought you might be up for another evening out, but it looks like I might have caught you at a bad time."

Her gaze shot up at that. "Why? I mean, why do you think that?"

"You seem distracted. Busy. I can take a raincheck."

"That's probably better. My mother made a surprise visit to town and she wants me to meet her and her new boyfriend for dinner. So another night would work."

Wyatt nearly left it at that but something in the way she described the impending dinner with her mother—or perhaps the subtle frown that wasn't typically part of her demeanor—clued him in.

"You don't want to go?"

"I—" She let out a small sigh. "I wish it were as easy as that."

"I have a few minutes. You did a damn fine job listening to my family drama the other day. If you want to talk about it, I can lend an ear."

It was hard to miss the struggle stamped across her face. And as someone who kept their family life exceedingly private, Wyatt understood her challenge to open up.

To share details that—when spoken to another—forced acknowledgement they even existed.

But her small smile that broke through the clouds ultimately made him glad he asked.

"Why don't you come back to my office? It seems to have the right ambiance for family confessions."

Once settled, funny enough in the same spots they'd sat the other day for his own retelling, Marlowe recounted the unexpected arrival of her mother into town.

"We don't have a great relationship but she does stay with me when she comes to town so that was my first clue something was off. But when she began telling me about Brock it sort of made sense. And then she dropped the bomb on me about lying about my father."

"What does she want you to say?"

"She wants me to omit any mention of him or the fact he's spent the better part of over ten years in prison upstate."

"Are you going to go?"

"Unless I can come up with a better excuse than rearranging my sock drawer, I'm not sure I can get out of it. And I hate being this weak."

Marlowe dropped her head into her hands before seeming to think better of it, her spine straightening until she looked about to shatter.

"I'm in charge of my life. I work hard, I own my own

business. Damn it, I'm not a pushover. But with her—" She broke off, misery stamped across her physical form like a brand. "With her it's like I'm twelve again and I crave her approval in the worst way."

"Without putting too fine a point on it, of course you do. It's your mom."

"It's ridiculous. She's ridiculous." Marlowe stopped, then stilled as those words hung between them. "That's unkind. But I keep circling around that description and can't seem to come up with a better one.

"She sat there all excited about this new man in her life and how she hopes to marry him. And in practically the next breath she's telling me how we're going to simply omit the truth of the past years of our lives. Hell, the reality of her marriage, whether she knew what my father was up to or not."

"Did she know?"

"I've asked myself that for years and the answer never changes. I just don't know. At the end, yeah, of course she did. But before then? Before he got himself in too deep?" Marlowe shook her head. "I think she found a way to delude herself so that she never looked too hard under that rock."

It was oddly cathartic to hear Marlowe recount those experiences and even more, humbling to realize he saw traces of his own relationship with his mother in the absurdity of Marlowe's retelling.

While he'd always believed his parents had a love match, his mother never made a secret of her fears for his father and what risks he took as a professional diver. And when he ultimately took on the Luxair job and lost his life because of it, his mother had been all-too-ready to take the very large legal settlement and move on.

Move on past their modest home and solidly middle-class existence and into the wealth his father's death had perversely bequeathed to them.

He'd spent a long time being angry about it, but now faced with Marlowe's experiences, he recognized the layers of anger were far more nuanced. Yes, they were threaded with grief, but they also held resentment, disappointment and that sense, even if rather subtle, of disgust at how easily Jessica Trumball had moved on.

From their family life.

From the memories of her marriage.

And, in less than two years, into a new marriage with someone who was most definitely not his father.

He'd spent a long time feeling guilty about that and maybe he needed to cut himself a break. Especially since he didn't hold Marlowe accountable for her mother's actions.

Or her poor decisions.

"You're not weak, Marlowe. You're the furthest from weak I can possibly imagine."

SHE WANTED TO believe him. Oh, how she desperately wanted to believe in the gentle kindness and subtle strength Wyatt offered.

But how?

She was seriously contemplating endorsing this ridiculous scheme of her mother's. And now she had this strange, coincidental clue about her father and the case Wyatt was working and she was keeping it to herself.

For all her inward self-aggrandizing that she was a woman of honor and conviction, it had taken a shockingly quick holiday at the point of having something to hide.

Or potentially hide.

Which only added to the confusion. Was it because she was reticent to tell him about that weird, tenuous connection to her father? Or did it just feel like a bigger deal than it really was because she was keeping it close to the vest?

And all in the face of him being so warm and considerate and, as she was fast coming to understand, just Wyatt.

"Thank you for saying that."

"You don't sound like you believe me."

"I'll work on that part."

Maybe she would after she got a handle on this whole business with her father's known associates. She hadn't even gotten a chance to look further into the two men who were in that photo. And she needed to call her father and follow up on his parole hearing.

Michael McCoy had never been forthcoming with her about his former life, but if she worked her way into the conversation with him she might be able to get some information.

Then she could tell Wyatt.

After she understood what they were possibly up against.

Because coincidence or not, what would a long-gone, nearly thirty-year-old nightclub have to do with dead bodies and safes in the harbor? And could she dare risk her father's parole hearing on something that might be nothing?

Wyatt slipped off the stool on the other side of her worktable and moved around the room. He stopped before a large biometric safe she'd been tinkering with over the past few days, an upgrade to the software part of a series of tests she was running for the manufacturer.

"Is this one of the safes you mentioned working on and trying to crack?" He tapped the large front door, currently bolted shut.

Reluctantly, she let the imagined conversation with her father go. She'd do a deeper dive into those two men and see what she could find as a search engine detective. Then she'd call her father. And then she could tell Wyatt what she knew, no matter how important or inconsequential.

"It is. That's a top-of-the-line biometric safe. They've made continuous upgrades since bringing it to market and wanted me to try to get through the new protocols."

"How'd you do?"

The laugh came quick and easy and, with it, the realization that she hadn't smiled so naturally since the last time she was in his presence. "Knocked it out in under a minute."

"Ouch." He winced. "Sounds like they need to do a bit more innovating on their side."

"Yes and no." She came around the table to stand beside him. "The basic construction of the safe is unchanged from last year's model so I had a leg up since I already knew how to get in."

"Why not change that up, too?"

"Much as the business is always trying to keep up with criminals there are some things that are just too hard to change. Reengineering an entirely new safe takes time and there's no way to make those sorts of structural changes to the entire line on offer every single year. So there are tweaks. Upgrades. And with the advent of the biometric product offerings, a lot of work software can further support the integrity of the safe."

"Such as?"

His question was simple, but the heady, intense way he looked at her as he asked had those damnably wonderful flutters kick in just below her breastbone.

"This safe for instance," she said, pointing to the electronics panel. "Once installed, this unit will connect into a security system, can record fingerprints for authenticity and there's even an upgrade option for iris recognition."

"So even if someone gets in, they've left a biometric record."

"You bet. It's a game changer. Where safecracking used to be tied to finding a way in, now it's also about risking what you're going to leave behind."

"But you still got into it in under a minute."

"That's my job."

The vivid blue of his eyes remained steady on her, lightly roaming over her face. She detected his scrutiny, but instead of feeling the need to run, she discovered it only fueled her own hunger to look her fill.

To somehow commit him—to commit this moment—to memory.

The hard lines of his face, chiseled over a solid jaw and a sharp, straight nose. The full lips, almost too much except for the wide, even smile beneath. And those eyes.

God, why did she never remember just how blue they were?

Or how intense it was to have the full interest of his gaze, holding her captive?

It was fanciful and borderline ridiculous, those thoughts, Marlowe acknowledged. Yet as he closed the space between them, his hand moving up to her shoulder as he used his body to press her back to the solid wall of the safe door, she could hardly argue with the overwhelming reality of Wyatt Trumball.

"I think you're entirely too modest about your skills." His voice was a whisper against her lips. "And under a minute is impressive in any field, anywhere."

Before she could muster up a response, his mouth closed

over hers, those firm, generous lips coaxing hers open beneath his.

Had she really thought them too full? Marlowe wondered as she opened her mouth beneath the gentle assault, nearly moaning when his tongue swept inside to expertly stroke hers.

The large hand on her shoulder slid down to grip her hip, his fingers gently cupping her flesh as he pressed more directly against her.

This wasn't the quick move in the park or the light kiss they'd shared the night he drove her home from her grandfather's. This was something different.

Hot.

Needy.

All-consuming.

And it had the distinct notes of the inevitable, laced beneath the all-consuming pleasure.

Was sex with Wyatt inevitable?

And had all their flirting and increasing time spent in each other's orbit been about driving to something more?

She wanted it, Marlowe admitted to herself as she ran a hand through the hair at his nape, using gentle pressure to pull him even closer to her. Allowing him to take the kiss even deeper, the carnal pull between them so electric, she was half surprised they didn't manage to set the tech panel on the safe to sparks.

With one last press of his lips, he lifted his head, staring down at her. That vivid blue was hazed with desire but she also saw a spot of mischief.

"Do you need someone to go with you to the dinner?"

"Dinner?"

She was so involved in the kiss the change in topic had her stumbling over the meaning of his question.

Those notes of mischief sparked a bit deeper in his gaze. "With your mother."

"You'd…want to do that?"

"I want to support you. If sitting through that dinner with you helps, then I'm happy to go."

She nodded, the taste of him still so fresh on her lips she couldn't imagine saying no to anything he asked. "I'd like that."

"When is it?"

"When is what?"

"Dinner."

"Tonight. Eight o'clock. In a restaurant in Manhattan. Midtown…" Her voice trailed off. "Steak."

"I'll come get you around seven?"

"Sure. Yes." She tried to focus on his question, even though the feel of his hand still on her hip and the heat of his body pressing fully against her chest had her imagining far more interesting ways they could spend the evening. "Seven sounds good."

Wyatt pressed one last, firm kiss to her lips before stepping back. "I'll pick you up then."

She remained where she was, her back pressed to the safe, slightly worried she didn't have the ability to stand fully on her own yet. So she stayed there, turning her head to watch him go.

It was long moments after he left, her gaze trailing around the room as she weighed the strength in her legs that Marlowe recalled what she'd been doing before he arrived.

Her attention landing on the open lid of her laptop, she remembered the search query still open on the screen. And the lingering questions of whether or not Wyatt's current case had any possible connection to her father.

On a hard sigh, Marlowe pushed off the safe and crossed to the laptop, snapping the lid into place.

And regretfully acknowledged she might have more in common with her mother than she thought.

WYATT PULLED INTO the parking garage at the end of the block where he and Marlowe were meeting her mother for dinner. It had been a quiet ride into the city and she hadn't said much.

Which had left Wyatt to replay their earlier kiss over and over in his mind. Not like it had been too far from his thoughts from the moment he'd left her in her shop.

But damn, the woman had gotten beneath his skin.

He was interested, sure. But this deeper need that continued to kick up? It had all the hallmarks of interest and a healthy dose of good old-fashioned lust, but there was something more there. He was a man who trusted his instincts in every way and something about this developing attraction between him and Marlowe was rapidly pushing him out of his comfort zone.

Did he mind?

He chose to ignore that sneaky question as it slipped and slid through his thoughts, crossing around the car to help Marlowe out. But the moment her hand gripped his, those beautiful legs swinging out of the car, he was right back to that place she always managed to send him. Outright fascination and tempting desire.

You're meeting her mother, Trumball.

Meeting.

Her.

Mother.

Tamping down on his hormones, he took the ticket from the valet and reached for her hand.

He didn't normally drive to Manhattan, usually opting for the convenience of a car service, but he didn't want to risk them being late because of a surge in driver demand. And knowing how important this evening was—whether she wanted to admit it or not—Wyatt didn't want to end up forced to take Marlowe into the city on the subway because they were rushed for time, either.

"There it is." Marlowe pointed toward the end of the block. "Marino's Steakhouse."

"It'll be a good meal."

"Sure. Right." She nodded as is psyching herself up. "It'll be great, lying to my potential new stepfather."

"Your mother's doing the lying."

Marlowe shot him a side-eye as they headed for the restaurant. "Wyatt. Whatever we're doing tonight, let's please not pretend I'm not aiding and abetting this whole charade."

"Fair enough." He squeezed her hand. "But before you judge yourself too harshly, why don't you let it ride and see how things play out? Your mother is likely viewing all of this from a point of embarrassment. Use this evening to get a feel for this guy she's seeing and maybe you can gently persuade her to come clean."

He saw the moment his words registered, a distinct softening in her mouth and a brightness filling her gaze. "I hadn't thought about it that way."

"I appreciate how you feel, but I meant what I said. You've been dragged into this, but it isn't your lie or your relationship. Give her a chance to do right."

It seemed to be the correct sort of pep talk because he saw the distinct relaxation in Marlowe's posture and disposition as they walked into the restaurant. A woman who was clearly her mother, both in build and similar coloring, was hanging on an older gentleman in the lobby of the restaurant and Wyatt did a quick assessment as the tableau played out before him.

The light tinkle of laughter from the woman who practically cooed his name as they were introduced.

The firm handshake of her partner, a man with a booming laugh and slightly self-deprecating air that still never let you forget he was large, rich and in charge.

And finally the gentle hug with barely there kisses against each of Marlowe's cheeks as her mother pulled her close.

Although he hadn't intended to invite himself into her evening with her mother—and up until thirty seconds ago had blamed his reason for being here on his unmitigated and raging hormones for the woman by his side—now that he was here he was glad for it.

More, he recognized it was exactly where he needed to be.

Especially because the older couple who preceded him and Marlowe to their table checked every box Wyatt had been expecting. Patty McCoy might be playing a role, but Brock Abernathy wasn't exactly a slouch.

This only added to his expectation that the guy Marlowe's mother was desperately hoping to make husband number two had already done a rather thorough search of his own on one Patricia McCoy and the background she'd rather forget.

"So Wyatt, Marlowe tells me you're a diver for the NYPD." Their waiter had barely cleared the table from taking their drink order when Patty started in.

"Yes, I am."

"That's fascinating." Brock quickly took over. "How did the two of you meet?"

Patty's face set into slightly pinched lines but Wyatt kept his smile broad and his answers breezy. "Marlowe is one of the NYPD's favored lock and vault technicians. You'd be surprised by how often we have to have a locked piece of evidence unlocked and no one's quicker or more efficient than Marlowe."

Wyatt sensed Patty's relief as the conversation of how they met bypassed Marlowe's connection to the 86th via her grandfather.

"And I guess since Marlowe's a civilian you can date on the job like that?" Brock asked.

Wyatt pumped in the charm, tossing a broad, unrepentant smile at Marlowe before turning back to Brock with a wink. "I didn't ask for permission."

"We've only been on a few dates but I thought it would be fun for us all to get together this evening." Marlowe kept the conversation smoothly moving forward. "And speaking of dates, how did the two of you meet?"

Patty's excited retelling got them through cocktails and appetizers and on into the start of their entrées.

"Wyatt, are you a native New Yorker?" Brock asked as he cut into a steak so rare Wyatt wondered how it wasn't still mooing.

"I am. Born and raised on Long Island before settling in Brooklyn once I joined the NYPD."

"I'm west coast born and bred myself." Brock shook his head. "Never got the appeal of living here."

Well, gee, let me put you in touch with the tourism commission, Wyatt thought. "The city's not for everyone, sir, that's for sure."

"All these people. And all this crime," the older man sputtered as he waved a fork. "The fact you have to have a damn scuba team, for Pete's sake, to keep the city safe. It's madness."

Wyatt didn't quite make the connection. Every denizen of the city could be angelically perfect in their behavior and the NYPD would still need a scuba team. New York City and water were inextricably linked.

"There's no place like New York," Marlowe chimed in. "And to Wyatt's point, the city might not be for everyone. But for those of us who choose to live here, we love it."

"What brought you to Arizona, darling?" Brock turned his attention to Patty, sensing the cold shoulder even if he couldn't quite pinpoint the increasing chill from Wyatt and Marlowe.

"Oh, that's a tale as old as time." Patty waved a hand, even as Wyatt wondered how that particular line of questioning never came up. "I wanted a change after my divorce."

"Right, right. And when was—"

Patty steamrolled through any additional questions with a sweet smile and an added, "Just like you, dear. Sometimes we're just done with a place and want to start over somewhere new."

Whatever else he was, Wyatt was a reader of people. And if these two made it to the altar, he pegged them for two years, tops, on the marriage.

It was one more facet that shed light on Marlowe's life.

Her mother was fine, all things considered. A bit ridiculous, especially with this absurd charade she was perpetrating, but relatively harmless overall.

But she was careless.

It didn't settle very well that he saw strains of his relationship with his own mother, especially since she'd also moved onto her second marriage and the new life that had come with it.

Was it like Marlowe had said earlier?

Were they always destined to seek a parent's approval,

regardless of whether or not the parent even deserved to give one?

Because as they sat here, it was evident that Marlowe had to live with the consequences of Patty's selfish streak. One that might be steeped in the woman's own sense of hurt at her ex-husband's actions but which had dire consequence on their child.

For someone who'd spent his adult life avoiding the emotional realities of losing his father as a teenager and all the difficulty that came after, it was jarring to realize how his time with Marlowe had upended it all.

And how quickly the veneer of breezy humor he'd built around himself had cracked, simply by spending time with someone who made him look more deeply inside himself.

Those thoughts kept him company throughout the rest of the meal, along with the tedium that had set in even before their dessert and coffees were delivered.

"Mom, Brock. It's been a lovely evening, but we should get going. I know Wyatt's got a day of diving tomorrow and I have to be on a job site by eight."

He looked over at Marlowe, only to find her looking right back. And in that moment, he realized they'd spent the entire dinner as partners.

Not the adversaries they'd been up until that evening at her grandfather's.

And not the interested unattached adults who'd been dancing around each other for the past few weeks, trying to figure out their next moves.

But real partners.

He'd come tonight to give her support and ended up humbled that she had his back as much as he had hers.

That feeling carried them out of the restaurant on more air kisses, hearty handshakes and the instruction to meet them the following weekend for a farewell dinner before Patty and Brock flew back to Arizona.

"Whew. That was a whole deal." Marlowe had already tucked her hand in the crook of his arm as they walked back to the parking garage.

"You handled it beautifully."

"Right back at you on that one. But seriously." Marlowe practically danced beside him down the sidewalk as she relayed her impressions of the evening. "What is my mother thinking? He's got the good old boy routine down well but there's ice in those veins. Does she honestly think she's going to keep her past from him?"

And once again, Marlowe proved that subtle sense of street smarts and a lifetime of training at a cop's knee as Wyatt handed over his ticket to the valet.

"He's already run her. I'll bet you a year of dinners he knows every last detail about your father, including what cellblock he's in."

The post-dinner excitement that had ridden Marlowe's tone dimmed as they waited for the car. "I've no doubt he does. Which doesn't exactly make me feel good about this. I walked in upset with her lack of ethics on this, but can't get over a creeping sense of distaste over his, too."

Wyatt had kept the stub off the ticket while they waited for the valet to bring his car up and handed it over as the man jumped out of the driver's side. The valet had stopped just shy of the sidewalk to allow them to get into the car and Wyatt pulled open the passenger side door.

And immediately shoved Marlowe down, head first into the seat, as the sound of gunshots rang out, echoing off the metal frame of the car in a loud series of pops.

Chapter Ten

Marlowe's cheek pressed against the leather of the passenger seat, the heavy sounds that had pierced the air and then into the frame of the car fading away. Wyatt's large body still covered hers from behind and she tried to catch her breath against the heavy, solid weight of him.

"Wyatt." His name came out on a strangled moan and she reached behind her to grab his hand. "Wyatt!" She squeezed, the move enough to have him shifting and giving her a chance to gulp in air.

"Are you okay?"

"I'm fine but you're heavy. I need to breathe."

"Don't move from where you are. The seat's low enough you're covered by the dash. Keep your head down and as low to the floor as you can. I want to check out what's going on."

Hard, unflinching cop lined each and every word that fell from his lips, including the fact that he'd given an order he had every expectation would be obeyed.

But what had happened?

Was this a random act? She lived in a large metropolitan area and knew it wasn't only possible, but it happened to people every day.

Yet even as she considered it, with the sounds of shouts

outside the car a steady accompaniment to where she still lay in wait for Wyatt's all clear, she couldn't help but wonder if that was delusional thinking designed to make herself feel better.

Wyatt was working on a major case.

Was it possible this shooting was tied into that and not really random at all?

And if it was, what had Wyatt actually uncovered on the bottom of the harbor?

Even with her grandfather's career on the police force and her father's criminal acts, she'd spent no part of her life with active exposure to violent crime. The idea that it was closer than ever settled into her bones with chilling clarity.

"Marlowe. Come on out." Wyatt's hands were gentle on her shoulders as he helped her up, pulling her from the vehicle. A wholly irrational shot of fear raced through her as she was suddenly free of the car, her body exposed to anyone who might be walking on the street or hiding with a gun pointed right at them.

"Are you sure?"

"It's okay. Cops are here and the area's under watch."

"Watching where? Those shots came out of nowhere."

"They actually came from a nearby office building, three floors up." He gestured with his head to the area behind them. "A team's already on it and running down all the clues they can find, but the window the shooter was in has been cleared."

It should have made her feel better, especially since they'd run down the origination of shots so quickly, but those lingering questions still filled her thoughts.

Was this deliberate?

And if it was, who was the target?

Who would even know she and Wyatt were headed into the city tonight? Or their exact location and where they parked.

"Is this about the safes?" The question was out before she could stop it, along with a shot of adrenaline that set her teeth chattering as her body processed the overload of fear and shock to the senses.

"The safes?" Wyatt's eyes narrowed as lines creased his forehead. "Why do you ask?"

"It doesn't feel random."

"No, it doesn't," he said before pulling her close against him. That same large form that had pressed against her in her office and then again in protection against the seat, now surrounded her offering comfort.

Protection.

And the promise that she had a safe place to land as her body worked off the rush of hormones that controlled her baser need to fight or flee.

Marlowe leaned into him, burrowing into that sense of safety and security, even as her thoughts continued to toss around like pinballs, scenario after scenario playing through her mind.

Random or deliberate?

A warning or an attempt on their lives?

Was she the target or was Wyatt?

When that adrenaline response flared once more at the idea the shots were directed at Wyatt, Marlowe knew her first real moments of bone-crushing fear.

This thing between them was new—so new they were still fumbling their way through text messages and dates and questing kisses.

Yet it was real.

More real, more quickly, than she could have ever imagined.

THE BACK OF a squad car was never very comfortable—and no one really liked knowing they had no way of opening a car door on their own—but Wyatt bit down on his own internal frustrations and kept his focus on Marlowe.

Arlo and another officer from the 86th had shown up about an hour after the gunshots. Wyatt had exhausted any and all leads with the midtown precinct that managed that part of the city and was just about to call for a car service when Arlo had shown up to escort him and Marlowe back to Brooklyn.

There'd been a brief discussion about whether or not to call Anderson but in the end, the fear her grandfather would hear it from someone other than her had Marlowe dialing him at close to midnight.

He hadn't needed any help to piece together Anderson's side of the conversation, the older man's voice ringing loud and clear through the squad car.

"What do you mean shot at?"

"Wyatt and I were in Manhattan, meeting Mom and her date for dinner."

"Your mother?"

"Yes, Pops. She's in town like I told you."

"Are you okay, Lowe?" A hard exhale came through the phone. "Were you hurt?"

"No, Pops. I'm fine. I'm in a squad car now being driven back to Brooklyn and I'm with Wyatt. I'm fine."

Arlo's attention had remained riveted on the conversation, but there was a distinct glance in Wyatt's direction when Marlowe had made mention of spending the evening together.

When all he got was a dark, pointed look from Wyatt he'd turned his attention back to the drive across the bridge into

Brooklyn, but Wyatt had no doubt the quelling look hadn't diminished Arlo's attention to the call.

Or his curiosity as to the status of Wyatt's relationship with Marlowe.

"Have the squad car bring you straight to my place."

"Pops, I swear I'm alright. The cops will see me to my door and I'm sure I can even get them to do a full sweep of my apartment. It was a long night and I want my own bed. But I'll come by first thing in the morning."

She'd made several more promises that she was fine and that she'd be by bright and early before disconnecting the call.

"He's worried," Marlowe finally said. "He usually gets a solid dig in at my mother when he's able and the fact he let it slide says he's worried."

"Of course he is. We can still swing by there. I'm sure he's awake."

"No, the morning will be fine. I need to get home and get my morning appointment canceled. I'll head to his place instead of going out first thing on a job."

The squad car maneuvered through Brooklyn, the late hour, on a weekday no less, made it a relatively quick trip back to Park Slope. And then Arlo got out of the squad car and opened the back door for both of them to get out.

"Thanks for the ride."

"We'll wait for you," Arlo said to Wyatt, gesturing toward the front of Marlowe's building.

"No need. I'm staying here."

"Wyatt, you don't—"

Marlowe's protests were already expected and gave Wyatt the time to cut her off. "I'll sleep on the couch, but I'm not leaving you here tonight alone."

She looked about to argue before obviously thinking better of it. But she did give Arlo a stern look. "Let the record show that I argued on this one. Especially when the grapevine at the 86th gets a hold of this."

"Nah, Marlowe, Trumball's right. We'll all feel better if someone's here tonight." He shot Wyatt a dark grin. "I'm happy to volunteer, though."

Arlo ducked out of range before Wyatt could say anything and headed back toward the squad car, a decided spring in his step.

"Sorry he's being an ass."

"I thought it was sweet." She glanced back at her building. "And you really don't have to do this."

"I will be a perfect gentleman and I promise you're not going to become an object of gossip, but I'm not leaving you. And I'll go with you to your grandfather's in the morning."

"Bossy aren't you?" she asked as they walked up to the door of her building.

"When I need to be yeah." He waited until they were inside before he turned to her, laying a hand on her arm. "But this isn't being bossy. This is helping a friend and ensuring you're safe. And since we don't have a firm idea of what happened tonight, I'm sticking close."

Fascinated, he watched as a host of emotions telegraphed from her expressions and physical demeanor. From a frustrated sort of bravado to an aching sadness, he saw it all.

But under it all rested an overwhelming sense of relief.

"Thank you."

He might have been staying, regardless of her agreement to the idea, but was pleased to see her acquiesce without argument. And it added to his own need to take what minimal control over this situation he could find.

They had no idea who shot at them or why. The two of them appeared to be the intended target. Or was it just Marlowe or him? Wyatt had no idea, nor was he even close to a working theory.

He kept circling back to the safes.

But why?

They'd been put into the waters around New York City in a way that would ensure they'd be found. So now they were found and suddenly a faceless problem is taking pot-shots at cops?

He and his fellow NYPD officers knew they lived with risk, both in the execution of their job, as well as by virtue of the fact they put on a uniform each day.

But this?

It kept going back to his captain's point when they'd un-covered the papers in the last safe.

It all felt like some sort of game.

Why?

Beyond the fact the press had covered the murders of the kayakers, the precinct had kept the information about the safes on lockdown. And since they'd been sitting on a frus-trating lack of leads, he or any of his fellow team members hadn't even done a lot of interviews with potential suspects or even witnesses on the matter.

The information simply wasn't widespread yet.

But if the shots were about the safes, what was some-one afraid of?

More of the frustrating, endless arguments that seemed to abound with this case.

"Can I get you anything? Coffee or a glass of water?" Marlowe asked.

Exhaustion rimmed her eyes, a sure sign the adrena-line rush had sparked itself out and left the need for sleep in its wake.

"I can help myself to some water. Why don't you go on to bed? I'll take the couch."

"I can get you some pillows."

He glanced across the small area that made up her living room and pointed to the large blanket on the back of the couch and the colorful throw pillows propped in each corner. "I've got all I need there. Seriously, go on to bed."

She turned into him, pressing her lips to his in a soft kiss. The temptation for more flared, quick and high, but he held back.

Just like that realization after dinner—that Marlowe had been his partner tonight, in every way—Wyatt understood the needs of this kiss were different than the heated passion that had nearly consumed them in her office. And while he wanted her—and increasingly knew that was the inevitable trajectory between them—he liked being with her, too.

Liked this wonderful variability between comfort and desire.

Even if all he was willing to give tonight was comfort.

Because when the flames of desire spiked enough for them to act, he'd be damned if it was after they were exhausted and vulnerable.

He wanted it to matter. And he wanted them wholly focused on what was between them instead of using sex as a consolation prize.

She meant too much for that.

So it was with a gentle kiss in return that he pulled back. "I'll see you in the morning."

MARLOWE BLINKED AT the bright sunlight filtering in through her bedroom window, the events of the previous night slamming back into her thoughts and clearing the dreamy haze of sleep.

Wyatt was here.

Images of the night before kept assaulting her, a driving counterpoint to the oddly dreamless sleep.

He'd ridden home with her in a police car, then insisted on staying. Only instead of putting the adrenaline rush of the prior night to good use, he'd chastely kissed her and sent her off to bed.

What the hell was that about?

Because a man who kissed like the very personification of temptation—and she could still feel the scorch marks of his chest from when he pressed her against the safe in her office—shouldn't be able to turn that off at will.

It was hell on a woman's ego and, well, damn…

The mental tirade ended as she sat up and looked down at her clothes. She'd been so tired last night she hadn't even made it into her pajamas. Instead, she'd fallen facedown into bed in the light wrap dress she'd worn to dinner.

Damn the man, how did he know just the right thing to say and do?

She considered it all while changing into casual clothes and brushing her teeth, vacillating between grateful to annoyed and back again.

Because she was grateful.

He'd come to that farce of a dinner with her and supported her. He'd protected her in the midst of gunshots. And then he'd stayed last night, ensuring her safety and, likely even more important, her peace of mind.

Lingering guilt still remained over her father's known associates and the call she needed to make to him in prison, but she had a plan. And she would tell Wyatt what was going on once she had all the details.

Much as she needed to snip that loose thread, she knew that wasn't what had her so out of sorts.

So why did it suddenly feel like she was losing it as a wholly irrational itch settled under her skin?

Wyatt's protective qualities were great and she appreciated his presence more than she could say, but damn it, why had he rebuffed her kiss last night? She'd been all ready to consider putting sex on the table and he'd sent her off to bed.

Alone.

Without sex on the table. Or at least the proverbial one, though now that she considered it, her table was solid oak and looked fairly sturdy...

Pulling herself back, she got irritated all over again. Damn his honorable tendencies and the whole protecting her and sending her off to bed.

The damn fool man.

Marlowe padded out of the bedroom and found him, already up and playing on his phone from his position on the couch. She also smelled fresh coffee, which meant he'd been up long enough to do that, too.

"Good morning." Wyatt looked up from his phone.

"Is it?"

"You tell me." He grinned, seemingly unfazed by her grumpy, grumbled response. "I'm the one with coffee in my hand."

She had a sense that he hit the day with his normal, rather cheerful demeanor, like she'd already witnessed on the morning they'd run the park. She'd thought it enticing a few days ago. Now she just felt a bit mean-spirited and more than a little gobsmacked.

Especially since he looked as good this morning as he did last night.

Better, if she were honest. The night's growth of beard over his jaw was doing funny things to her stomach and wildly enticing things to parts lower.

When he said nothing further and Marlowe couldn't be entirely sure she wasn't going to blurt out something stupid like why hadn't he come to bed with her the night before, she turned on a heel and headed for her kitchen.

And was so wrapped up in her own frustration and focus on pouring a cup of coffee that she missed the sound of his footsteps and only realized he was standing behind her when she felt the hot, enticing heat of his body against her back.

"Are you always so grumpy in the morning?"

Hardly sweet nothings or pillow talk, but the low purr of his voice against her ear—even though he hadn't touched her with his hands—was enough to have her coffee sloshing in the cup. Wyatt reached out around her and steadied the mug, his fingers covering the back of her hand. "Easy."

"I'm not grumpy."

"Excuse me." He deliberately ran a hand over her back as he stepped away. "I suppose the proper term is uncaffeinated, then."

"I don't think that's a word. And I just don't understand people who are excessively cheerful in the morning."

"I slept well, didn't you?"

"I slept fine." She took a sip of her coffee, willing the caffeine to kick in so that his eminently reasonable voice wouldn't scrape over her nerves. Because oh, my, did he look good. And all that glorious body heat pressed against her back as she'd poured her coffee had her imagining the way they'd kissed in her office.

Which, once again, only made her more frustrated he'd sent her off to bed last night like an overtired kid.

"Your couch is really comfortable. Those deep cushions were great and the sofa's plenty long that my legs weren't cramped."

"Well, good for you."

Even if it'd have been considerably more comfortable in my bed.

Only she didn't say that. Instead she turned and after another sip of her coffee tried valiantly to ignore her hormones and focus on the day ahead. "After I clean up I'm going over to my grandfather's. I know you said last night you wanted to go, but you don't have to. He just wants to know I'm alright."

"I am going. I'd like to stick close to you a bit longer so I'll see you over to his place and then on to your shop. I'd also like to ask him a few questions."

Although she didn't need a babysitter—and things felt a lot less dire with bright sunlight slipping through her small kitchen window—she also knew that Wyatt discussing the case with her grandfather would go a long way toward putting Pops at ease.

"He'll like that."

"I will, too. And we'll stop for bagels on the way and bring breakfast, too."

She shot him a gimlet eye. "You've got quite the plan going. How long have you been up?"

"Long enough to put on a pot of coffee and fold the blanket on the couch." He reached across the counter and grabbed the pot, refilling his mug, before refocusing on her. "I can't help but think you're mad at me this morning. Did I do something to upset you?"

"You're heavy-handed and bossy. And—" Marlowe stopped, aware the sexual frustration and tension that had ridden her since the night before was about to take on a whole new dimension. One that not-so-subtly suggested she was pining for him in some way.

"And what?"

"Nothing." She shook her head. "I need to go get ready for the day."

She set her mug on the counter and had turned away before his hand snaked out, grabbing hers. He pulled her close, his other arm wrapping around her. "You're not mad because we haven't kissed this morning?"

His chest was hard as it met hers—deliciously so—and warm through the material of her T-shirt. "Of course not."

Wyatt bent his head, his lips finding the edge of her jaw, just below her ear. "Because I could make it up to you. You know, if that was the problem."

Marlowe tilted her head slightly as his lips grazed the sensitive area below her ear, his breath warm against her skin while the vibrations of his voice sent shivers down her spine.

She fought to keep her annoyance in place, a ready defense against this aching need that seemed to sweep through her whenever he was around.

Because whatever this was, she didn't care for the slightly out-of-control sensation that hovered inside her, like moving a bit too quickly down a ski slope.

She didn't like to be out of control. In fact, she'd carefully ordered her life to avoid that state in every way. And yet, with Wyatt...

It all left a sort of breathless rush that was increasingly becoming addictive.

"That's not the problem."

"Okay."

The deep, husky quality of his tone vanished on that lone word as he stood up straight and backed away from her.

The change was so abrupt she scrambled for the counter, trying to catch her balance.

The mischief she saw sparking in those sky-blue eyes revealed just how well she'd been played. With a swift swat on his big, rounded shoulder, she stepped back. "You're an ass."

"And you're far too adorable in the morning."

Before she could even come up with any sort of reaction to that, he had her in his arms again, his mouth coming down to hers. Just before their lips met, he whispered, "I want you, too, Marlowe."

And then there were no words or emotions or anything other than sheer, liquid fire flooding her veins as his mouth consumed hers.

With bold strokes of his tongue against hers, Marlowe melted in Wyatt's arms, passion flaring between them like a flash fire. The restless frustration that had been a constant companion since she woke up faded at the knowledge he wasn't unaffected.

Not at all, she reminded herself as his obvious, insistent erection pressed seductively against her. That clear sign of his desire only pushed her own higher, her plans for the day fading away as this man quickly became the sole focus of her world.

Wyatt Trumball was all she wanted.

And, in a sudden rush of awareness she wasn't quite sure what to do with, she was fast coming to understand he might be all she needed, too.

Chapter Eleven

Wyatt hadn't been a teenager in nearly a decade and a half, yet sitting in Anderson McCoy's living room, spreading cream cheese on his still-warm bagel, he couldn't quite hide the flashes of embarrassed heat that kept rearing up each time he looked at Marlowe.

He was a grown man and he hadn't made excuses or snuck around with a woman since, well...what felt like forever.

But arriving at Anderson's with the man's granddaughter in tow had struck some sort of long-dormant, almost recalcitrant emotion inside him that smacked of fifteen-year-old reactions.

Especially since it had taken everything in him to pull away from Marlowe in her kitchen this morning and suggest she go get ready to set her grandfather's mind at ease and fill him on the details from the night before.

"And there weren't any drugs this time? And, thankfully, no body," Anderson added, almost as an afterthought.

"No, sir," Wyatt said, grateful for the older man's laser focus on the topic at hand. "This safe breaks pattern."

"Which means it's escalating in a new direction."

"Even without a murder, Pops?" Marlowe took a sip of

her coffee, her bagel still untouched on the table. "I thought escalation always resulted in something worse."

"It usually does, but this change in pattern could be gearing up for worse."

"Captain Reed called it a game."

"Oh, it is that," the wily old detective quickly agreed. "It's got every mark of taunting the cops. The random acts. The small cache of drugs with the bodies. And dropping a safe at the base of the bridge? That was no accident."

All of which had bothered Wyatt since he and Gav found the safe on the bridge check. The waters around New York's access points were heavily patrolled. Whoever was doing this was able to get down there to hide the safe with deliberate actions. Only a qualified diver could make the difficult trek under water and had to start that trek out of sight of the cops in the first place.

"That's it," Wyatt said, pissed it had taken him this long to realize it. "We need to look at divers. At who would possibly be qualified to do this."

"I realize your skills aren't common, but it's not impossible to find a diver, is it?"

Wyatt shook his head. "This isn't easy work in those waters. It's dark and murky and you have to have some real incentive to go down there. My money's on a disillusioned mercenary with some military training or a scuba teacher who found a way to make some cash on the side."

Anderson tapped the side of his own mug of coffee. "That's good, Wyatt. And it fits. You need talent to do that. And with talent usually comes a recognition of how to make some money off the skill."

Wyatt considered everything and realized it made sense. They'd been so focused up to now on the kayakers in the water that he'd clearly overlooked the scuba expertise needed on the last dive.

"Seems like I owe you once again, sir. I'd like to think I'd've come around to this eventually, but this is great insight."

"You would have come around to it and damn quick," Anderson said with a smile. "But it's fun for me to help. And sometimes it's just good to play theories off of someone else. Getting too deep in a case can often give tunnel vision."

Anderson shot Marlowe a pointed look.

"And it's a nice distraction from the fact my granddaughter dodged bullets last night."

"Come on, Pops. I called you."

"I know you did, Lowe. It doesn't change the fact that it happened."

She reached over and laid a hand on his. "No, I suppose it doesn't."

Anderson got a few more admonitions in as they all shifted their focus to breakfast, but his interest had clearly been piqued by all that was going on.

"You got any leads yet on the shooter?"

"I called into the responding precinct this morning. Spoke to the lieutenant who owns the case. Nothing's popped yet but we're working on the theory it is tied to the safes, while not shutting down any other avenues of inquiry."

"Details on the safes are that widely known?" Anderson asked.

"That's the problem," Wyatt said, once again battling the subtle embarrassment he needed help and the ready gratitude Anderson was willing to share his time. "Very few details have been released. The press picked up on the kayaker story quickly, but we managed to keep the aspects of the safe out of the details. It's always possible someone rather enterprising has continued to dig, but the press office would have given me a heads-up if they caught a hit on the story."

"I know we're tying it all together," Marlowe said, tapping the side of her mug, "but could it have been a lone shooter, coincidentally acting out of some misguided anger?"

"What do I always say about coincidences, Lowe?"

Marlowe smiled at her grandfather before giving Wyatt an even wider grin. "The same thing Wyatt says. They're highly unlikely in police work. It still doesn't mean it's impossible."

"Which is why the midtown precinct who answered the call last night is running down any disgruntled employees who could have had access to that floor or known the layout well enough to wait for an opening." Wyatt appreciated Marlowe's desire to keep an open mind but was firmly in the same camp as Anderson.

There just weren't coincidences in police work.

But why shoot at him?

Taking aim at a cop under any circumstance was a bad idea. But as a direct hit attempting to take one out? The motive didn't play for him. Those safes were all planted so they'd be discovered. Add on taking potshots at cops and you had a set of behavior that was calculated and slightly unstable.

"Are you able to share what you found in the safe, Wyatt?"

For most he'd have declined to answer, but Anderson's experience and connection to the precinct put him in a different category. Add on he and Captain Reed had remained close friends and Wyatt wasn't concerned with sharing what he knew.

"That's what's odd. The first three were all strapped to the dead kayakers and all held the kilos of heroin. This one was sunk in a place it was sure to be found and held four pieces of paper."

"That's it?"

"Three photocopies and a name scrawled with magic marker on the fourth."

Wyatt shared the specifics on the photocopied information before sharing the last piece.

"Nightwatch 1995."

Anderson's rheumy yet alert gaze went rock hard at that name before he seemed to think better of it. With a quick dart of his eyes to his granddaughter, he stood and crossed the room to pour himself another cup of coffee.

Wyatt wasn't sure what to make of the abrupt shift or the fact that he saw the man's hand tremble as he poured the coffee.

But he knew, without question, that the man's next words were a lie.

"Sounds like someone's giving you the runaround, Wyatt. Trying to get you off the real work to play a bunch of games."

MARLOWE SAW THE sudden change in her grandfather, her stomach nosediving in a freefall. Whatever concerns she'd held about her father's known associates and that old nightclub photo, she knew, with absolute certainty, that there was a connection to Wyatt's case.

A connection her grandfather was, unquestionably, well-aware of.

No coincidences.

There never were, she thought as an odd hopelessness filled her chest.

This was her grandfather, the most honest person she knew. Hell, she considered herself a pretty honest person, as well. Yet one small link to her father and she'd betrayed every single thing she believed about herself and the way she chose to live as an adult.

More, she'd hidden it from Wyatt. Whatever was between them was new, developing, but not sharing the grainy internet photo with him had been a clear act of self-preservation.

One that now seemed particularly stark in the cold light of morning and her grandfather's shift in behavior.

Behavior he clearly had a handle on when he turned back from the counter. "Dwayne really does have the right idea. Games to draw you off the scent is what this sounds like. Your time's better spent running down a diver with the right skills."

"I can juggle a few angles here. The whole team can."

That congenial, respectful tone never wavered, but Marlowe didn't miss the subtle wariness that filled Wyatt's gaze. Or the distinct hardness that glittered in his blue gaze.

"Sure, sure," her grandfather quickly agreed. "All reminds me of a case years ago. Went down in the heart of Sunset Bay and the catacombs."

"Catacombs, Pops?" Marlowe asked. The change in subject was a bit odd, but her grandfather's reference was one she'd never heard before.

"The smugglers' tunnels along the water. They've been abandoned for years, mostly just popular with graffiti artists who try to resurrect the space every decade or so until the problem gets to be too much and they get rousted out."

"I thought the city took care of those tunnels years ago," Wyatt asked. "Sealed them all up. We don't even do dive detail on them."

Anderson shrugged. "City does close them and then some enterprising folks figure out a way to open them up again."

Wyatt's narrowed gaze was thoughtful. "You say this situation with the safes is like a case down there?"

"A lot like it. That feeling it's all a big game pervaded that case, too."

The tenor of the conversation might have shifted, but Marlowe wasn't following why anyone would even take the time to play games. She wasn't an expert on the criminal mind, but she'd always sort of assumed those trying to stay off the radar didn't go out of their way to attract attention.

Wouldn't taunting the cops be the opposite of that?

"I'm not questioning your collective instincts, but it feels like a waste of time and a hell of a lot of risk. Why do that?"

"It's not a waste of time if you think it'll divert attention off the real crime," Wyatt said.

His point had her grandfather nodding. "It was back in the mid-eighties. A local gang figured out a way to use the tunnels. Made them home turf for quite a few months before someone got a tip more was going on in there than some artists or kids messing around to get high."

"How'd they get caught?"

"Got lazy. Thought they were fooling the cops by planting evidence around the city, always drawing attention away from the water."

"But the cops figured it out," Marlowe said. "And they did it before every storefront and intersection had a security camera."

"They did, Lowe. Criminals don't do the best job of keeping their mouths shut. And too many gangs are willing to talk when an avenue's shut down to them but wide open to others. A few other gangs caught wind of how convenient those tunnels would be to hide their own work. Then got seriously pissed when they couldn't get access."

"No honor among thieves," Marlowe murmured, thinking of her father's work. He'd made it a long time without getting caught. Although he rarely spoke to her about his work, it was a fact he'd let slip once. Claimed that working alone had been the secret to his success.

Oddly, it had been her own personal mantra in her line of work. Only instead of risking the encroachment of other thugs, she only had to worry about people getting too close.

Wasn't that what she'd done with Wyatt?

She kept people at a distance and she liked it that way.

Yet here she was, interested in Wyatt—way down deep interested—and already battling what she would and would not say to him.

It was an odd reinforcement of why she liked being alone.

The thought continued to linger as her grandfather went into a rambling story about how they eventually caught the gang and got the tunnels sealed up again, but Marlowe couldn't deny how the discussion had shifted.

What had started as a genuine sharing of information now felt stilted. And, oddly, she admitted, like dinner with her mother the night before. She'd spent the entire evening convinced all of them were speaking parts, but never really taking the conversation a level deeper.

Or saying what was fundamentally the truth.

Why did she feel like that now?

And why was she suddenly so convinced Pops was hiding something very, very big?

WYATT STARED DOWN at the waters of the Hudson River and allowed the morning to play through his mind. He and Gavin were working with the FDNY this afternoon to dive through a damaged boat that was at the core of an arson investigation and they were waiting on some details before they began.

They were on point for the evidence recovery and then after everything was cleared a salvage crew would bring up the small pleasure boat from where it had settled just south of the George Washington Bridge.

"Did you know there were smugglers tunnels in Sunset Bay?"

Gavin looked up from where he checked the gauges on his tank. "The ones along the shore, south of the shopping district?" When Wyatt only nodded, Gavin added, "They covered them in our training, but I thought they'd been closed so long they'd almost become like one of those city legends. More of a fun old story than anything with substance."

"Apparently they had quite a bit of substance for a while. Talked to Anderson McCoy this morning. He said they were the center of an investigation in the eighties. A particularly enterprising gang had used them for a solid six months, improving their business quite a bit with their little shoreline hidey holes."

"Why'd Anderson bring it up? You think there's still something going on in the tunnels? Now?"

Wyatt wasn't sure of anything, which was the reason he brought it up to Gavin at all. He trusted the man implicitly, but he also wanted someone to bounce it all off of.

"That's what doesn't play. Anderson mentioned it, relative to the recovery of the safes."

Interest clearly piqued, Gavin probed on that. "How so?"

Wyatt relayed the earlier discussion and that continued suggestion there was some sort of game afoot with whoever was masterminding the safes. How Anderson had used the gang crimes in the eighties as another example when the NYPD was run in circles by a group of thugs.

Wyatt did stop short of mentioning the odd signals he

got off of Anderson, though. He hadn't imagined the older man's response—Wyatt didn't doubt himself in the least on front—but he wasn't ready to put suspicions in anyone's mind about the well-respected, retired cop, either.

But he would get to the bottom of it.

"Why don't we run past there after shift?" Gavin suggested. "Take a look around a bit. Anderson McCoy's knowledge of Sunset Bay is some of the best and deepest there is. The man *is* the freaking 86th. Maybe he's making a connection even if he didn't mean it that way."

"You read my mind."

"Since that's my job definition above and below the water, let's do it. I'll text Arlo to meet us there, as well, see if it sparks anything for him, either."

Gavin gave him a hard look. "We're going to get to the bottom of this, Trumball."

Wyatt nodded, a big part of him seasoned enough to know there came a stage in every large investigation that felt empty. But even when the work was a grind, there were answers.

He needed to separate that feeling from breakfast this morning with Marlowe's grandfather. Anderson had been incredibly forthcoming in each conversation he'd ever had with the man. Yet the moment Wyatt had uttered the word "Nightwatch" Anderson's entire demeanor had changed.

There was an alertness there and a distinct shift in the tone of their conversation that still bothered him, no matter how he turned it over in his mind.

But maybe Gavin was right.

The grizzled old cop might deserve his respect, but the man was still in his eighties. Maybe Anderson had made the connection between the safes and the tunnels off some old synaptic connection, even if it wasn't readily obvious in the retelling.

Because chalking it up to a simple story about cocky criminals making life miserable for the cops? The idea of law enforcement might be a relatively modern construct, but that push-pull was a tale as old as the human experience. There likely wasn't a cop on the force who couldn't tell a similar story.

Activity kicked up on the FDNY boat, pulling their attention. Wyatt waved back to the team on the deck. "Looks like they're ready for us."

They exchanged a few more instructions over the radio comms while their team member navigating the Zodiac positioned Wyatt and Gavin over the dive site and Wyatt was grateful for the sudden flurry of activity.

He and Gavin had a plan after work and that had to be enough. Right now, he needed the quiet of the water and the focus on something else while his subconscious worked through the mysteries of the safes.

He'd learned early in his career that sometimes deliberately thinking about something else provided the only way to shake loose a fresh idea.

But damn, this one had him in its hooks.

The sense an answer existed, just out of reach, nagged at him. But like movement out of the corner of his eye, Wyatt couldn't seem to catch it.

Which meant it was time to focus on something else and hope he'd get a handle on what had him so upside down later.

Marlowe?

The case?

The random gunshots the night before?

All of the above, Wyatt suspected, as he fitted in his

breathing apparatus into his mouth and positioned himself at the edge of the Zodiac.

Time to stop thinking and start doing.

Falling back, the dark water encased him and silence immediately muted his world as he oriented himself in the Hudson. The water depth maxed out at about seventy feet in this part of the river and he and Gavin made the descent fairly quickly, the wreckage of the boat coming into focus where it had settled in the silty bottom.

As they neared the recreational pleasure boat they separated, each focused on their pre-agreed search areas. The starboard hull was burned out just as they'd been prepped, and he could make out the stern where it lay embedded in the river floor. He'd take care of removing whatever evidence he could get off the inboard engine while Gavin sought any gasoline or chemical residue up in the small cabin housing the steering wheel.

The working theory was the boat had been taken out and torched by an angry mistress who wasn't happy to be downgraded to an ex. The owner of the pleasure boat had reported it missing out of the 79th Street Boat Basin and cameras had caught a woman's cloaked figure approaching the marina the night before.

Although he didn't condone the crime, Wyatt had to give the woman props for an impressive revenge plot. Not only did it take a lot of anger to do this level of damage, but the working theory was she'd done it all on her own, which was both careless and shockingly determined.

Wyatt used various tools to pry open the panel that housed the engine, working carefully to keep as clean a sample as he could. Although the woman was a primary suspect and the damage was consistent with arson, they had to rule out innocence, as well. His retrieval of the engine—presumably one without any signs of distress or wear that would put this firmly in the realm of accident—was essential. He knew his job and worked carefully to preserve the sample.

He nearly had the engine loose, the murky water and angle of the boat where it had settled in the riverbed making the work slow-going, when Wyatt felt the distinct sense of movement behind him.

Animal?

Debris?

A shot of awareness spiked hard as he realized that sense had become a distinct form, suddenly locked on him, with the build and motion and strength of a human. Wyatt just made out the solid figure of another diver when a hard tug pulled on his tank. The thick form wrapped around him with shocking speed, pressing him tight against the side of the boat. The other diver used Wyatt's splayed position against the undamaged portion of the hull for the engine retrieval to his advantage, pinning him in place.

He tried to struggle, moving on pure instinct to strike back, but the other diver was like an octopus, his arms and legs moving in a strange synchronicity that ensured he'd had time to plan this assault.

Forcing a calm he didn't feel in order to control his breathing, Wyatt lifted his hand in an uppercut, aiming for the guy's breathing apparatus or mask—whatever he could get a clean shot at—when a distinct change filled his own mask.

But those octopus moves had been deliberate and Wyatt recognized it immediately as he saw his breathing apparatus separate, the low pressure tube that connected to his tank floating in the murky water where it had been cut clean through.

The abrupt release of pressure against his body jarred

Wyatt as panic, sudden and absolute, gripped him in tight fists. The other guy was already moving away as Wyatt reached for his bailout bottle, only to understand what that initial tug on his tanks was all about.

The bastard had his bailout bottle, too.

Which meant Wyatt was seventy feet below the surface with no way up.

He fought to keep that panic at bay, slamming a hand on the boat to get Gavin's attention. Banging on the hull wherever he could find an undamaged place to beat his fist, he moved steadily toward his partner, aware the need to share air was a more pressing concern than risking a trip to the surface.

Even as each second passed without any fresh air hitting his lungs.

The burned sections of the hull felt endless as Wyatt moved diligently toward Gavin. As he reached the portion of the boat that held the cabin he could see Gavin moving inside, oblivious to the distress. Banging on the walls, the hull, and then finally grabbing his partner's foot, Wyatt desperately aimed for a calm he didn't feel.

He needed his focus.

And he needed Gavin.

Gav turned immediately at Wyatt's firm hold on his foot, his eyes going wide behind his mask as Wyatt laid a hand over his throat and then pointed at his breathing apparatus.

Whatever else they'd been taught, to focus on your partner first was priority.

Always.

Gavin moved out of the cabin immediately, his attention on Wyatt. Without hesitation, he removed his breather and handed it over and Wyatt concentrated on taking a solid, measured breath instead of the gulp his panicked instincts demanded.

His partner watched him through it, his gaze never leaving Wyatt's as those deep, steady breaths filled his chest.

On a nod, Wyatt handed the breather over, sharing the air with his partner. He gave Gavin time to breathe several breaths of his own before he took the breather again. Once he handed it back, they moved out of the cabin and swam away from the boat, their gazes scanning the cloudy water around them.

Assured they didn't see anyone lying in wait, they continued their movements in unison, an unbreakable unit. And with steady, constant movements began the ascent to the surface.

Chapter Twelve

"What in the ever-loving hell was that?"

Gavin had repeated that phrase, along with several colorful curses Wyatt would have admired under better circumstances, over and over. His partner had moved from shock to seething anger and back to shock for the past twenty minutes.

And all Wyatt could do was stare at his hands and replay what had happened under the water.

Where had the bastard come from?

Even as he knew the real question—the far more important one—was why? Why had he come after a set of highly trained NYPD divers in the midst of a shift?

What was the endgame?

Whatever Wyatt had believed up to now—and he was already damn sure there was something big going on—the discovery of those safes had to be at the heart of everything.

And somehow, some way, he'd become the face of the case.

The real question was if he was some sort of collateral damage to a bigger prize, or if this was all directed at him.

Because he'd discovered the first safe?

Because he was a target from something he'd worked on earlier in his career?

Or again, Wyatt thought in disgust, just that collateral damage in service to some bigger outcome.

The dispatch team had sent another set of divers out to the site to finish the retrieval he and Gavin had started, with the express instruction neither he nor Gav could go down on another dive today.

He'd never been that spooked by his job—and he'd had instances in the past that had certainly tested the limits of his personal fortitude—but this was a whole other ball game. Add on the mandatory shot of antibiotics he and Gav had already been administered for their oral exposure to the waters of the Hudson, and he'd chalk it up to a grand sort of day.

Dispatch had also sent a team to patrol the waters for the diver to surface, but Wyatt already knew they wouldn't find anything.

That guy was long gone.

Because whatever else he was, he had experience, training and a damn fine set of skills beneath the water. A set of skills that Wyatt had revised in his mind to both mercenary and ex-military since there was no way to build a set of capabilities like that without serious training.

He had the scuba experience, the muscle and the ability to take out a trained enemy.

He was going to counsel Dwayne to bring in some federal assistance if possible to start looking into someone who fit that profile. This person might have a disgruntled reputation layered on top of a government-funded background in lethal combat and recognizance tactics.

And as Wyatt considered it all, he knew something dark was going on.

While miniscule in the realm of the broader drug trade, the kilos of heroin in the first three safes still had street value.

Hits on cops required a sizable cash payment.

And scuba skills like he'd just dealt with?

Just more proof that nothing about this whole operation was cheap or easy.

Captain Reed was waiting for him and Gav on the dock as they came back into Sunset Bay. Since his equipment needed to be moved into evidence, Wyatt had turned to do that first, unwilling to let his tools out of his sight.

But Dwayne anticipated the move and boarded the boat, coming into the wheelhouse.

"Trumball? How are you doing?"

Since he was still fighting a round of shivers that seemed determined to turn the afternoon into a total loss, Wyatt kept his hands at his side and shot Dwayne a smile he was pretty sure missed cocky by a mile. "I'll live."

"I suppose you will, but that wasn't my question." Dwayne's dark skin creased in tense lines before he sighed, gesturing Wyatt toward a small table they used to lay out maps and plan a dive. "Sit down with me a bit."

Wyatt took the seat as instructed.

"Walk me through it."

His captain might have been briefed already, but Dwayne Reed had that incredibly special ability to actually listen. He gave his full attention to the conversation, only asking a few clarifying questions until Wyatt got through it all.

"You had no sense the man was there?"

"Not a bit. Gavin and I were focused on the work, but one minute I'm trying to dig out the engine and preserve the evidence and the next the bastard was on me."

Wyatt had been over and over it in his mind and no matter how he considered it, he had no idea how he could have played it differently. He wanted to believe his instincts could have been sharper or his sense of someone approaching keener, but how the hell did you suss out a silent threat in the murky waters of the Hudson River?

Especially when there shouldn't have been a human threat in those waters in the first place.

Unbidden, his own memories of the dive had twisted up with how he imagined his father's last trip beneath the water.

Through the years his study of his father's last dive had consumed him. He'd been over and over it in his mind's eye, imagining it all. And no matter what his father had dealt with—no matter how terrible the panic at the end—that dive had still been a result of a horrible disaster.

A risk—freely taken—that had resulted in tragedy.

But this afternoon?

Wyatt had avoided an attempted murder, plain and simple.

"Sounds like we've been looking at this all wrong."

"How so, sir?"

"We've been thinking of those safes as a diversion or a game to distract us."

"You think it's something else?"

"I absolutely do." Dwayne's mouth set in a grim, hard line as his dark eyes darted to Wyatt's destroyed equipment, piled near the door to the wheelhouse. "I have no doubt in my mind, in fact."

"About what?"

"Those safes are bait, pure and simple."

MARLOWE RACED THROUGH the Brooklyn neighborhood she'd called home for the past decade and abstractly noticed the early evening air had a slight chill to it. Summer was giving way to fall and while she normally loved that feeling, all she could do was put one foot in front of the other as fast as possible.

Her sole focus was getting to Wyatt.

She ran along the western side of the park, weaving her way toward the apartment Arlo had told her was Wyatt's.

Marlowe had no idea when her favored nation status as Anderson McCoy's granddaughter had flipped over to full cred on her own, but she was wildly grateful that the detective had called her and given her a heads-up on what happened to Wyatt earlier that day.

As well as trusting her with Wyatt's address.

She turned the last block and raced up the steps of the stoop on the brownstone that Arlo had noted as Wyatt's, taking them two at a time. Worry churned her stomach and she shifted from foot to foot as she waited for him to answer his apartment bell.

Was he okay?

Arlo claimed he was but had remained tightlipped about the rest of what had happened. Only that Wyatt had been in a scary situation earlier that day and she should give him a call.

"Hello?"

Wyatt's voice came through the speaker, strong and true, and Marlowe felt the first notch of tension slip. "It's me, Marlowe."

The buzzer rang before she could say anything more and she pushed into the foyer of the brownstone, glancing at the row of stairs in front of her. Before she could start up, a door opened on the first floor, Wyatt in the entry.

Whatever fear had carried her this far pushed her forward, straight into his arms. "Are you okay?"

He pulled her close, his arms tight around her, his lips pressed to the side of her head. "I'm good."

She heard the quaver in his voice and felt the light tremors that shuddered through his body.

Was he okay?

Keeping her hold tight, she pulled back to look up at him. "Arlo called and—"

The words vanished as his mouth took hers, the fervor of his kiss something she met immediately, allowing the passion and need between them to simply consume her.

Something raw and wanting and more than a little desperate flared between them and she marveled at the thick drumbeat of desire that had a drugging sort of excitement flooding her veins.

What was this they shared?

Why had she fought it for so long?

And why—

Once again, her ability to string thoughts together vanished as her whole world shrank down to that moment with Wyatt.

His tongue melded with hers, an erotic welcome that held as much promise as need. That shudder she'd felt as her arms had wrapped around him faded a bit, replaced with a physical intensity that spoke as much of need as it did a yearning to hold on to something real.

Solid.

Alive.

Marlowe couldn't deny him any of it, even as she still wondered exactly what had happened. Arlo's details had remained deliberately vague—his insistence that it was Wyatt's story to tell—but she knew it was bad. Had gotten that clearly from what Arlo didn't say in addition to the dark undertone beneath his words.

And still, despite wanting answers, she couldn't stop touching him.

Long moments later she heard the slam of the front door of the brownstone and realized they still stood in the open entryway to Wyatt's apartment. She pulled back as he shot a wink at the woman who stood near the stairwell, two cloth bags of groceries hanging by her sides.

"Hi, Wyatt."

"Hey, Zoe."

"You putting on a show for the super?" She lifted a hand in the direction of the ceiling. "Those hallway cameras are catching an eyeful."

A heavy blush worked its way up her neck as Marlowe shifted in Wyatt's arms, trying to face his neighbor to introduce herself. Since Wyatt still had a firm hold on her it was hard to do that with any measure of dignity so Marlowe finally gave up and smiled over her shoulder. "Hey, there. I'm Marlowe."

"The lock lady." Zoe shot her a broad smile. "Nice to meet you. I'm Zoe."

Marlowe wasn't sure if she wanted to know how Zoe knew of her so she just gave a small wave back. "That's me."

"Yo, Wyatt. My grandmother said you had a hard day. You doing okay?"

"I'm good." Wyatt's gaze dropped to Marlowe's before winging back to his cute neighbor. "Better now."

"I'll just leave you to it, then. You two have a good night. I'm off to make some art. After, of course, I enjoy the strawberry ice cream that's currently melting in one of these bags."

Zoe was off up the main stairwell of the brownstone as fast as she'd arrived and it left Marlowe in that awkward hold where she and Wyatt sort of still clung to each other. "Um. She's nice."

"Z's great. She's lived here about a year. She's an artist and since she was raised in the neighborhood she somehow knows everyone."

"That's how she knows what happened to you?"

"The neighborhood takes care of their own."

A vague reminder that something big had happened. With that thought, Marlowe finally found a way to disengage herself from his hold, but not before pressing a quick kiss to his jaw. "Invite me in and tell me about what happened. Arlo was insistent I call you but vague on the details."

In the request, Marlowe saw the vulnerability. It was brief, flashing quickly before he tamped it down, but it was clearly there. And in that moment, she realized that the man who'd just demolished every last inhibition she possessed was struggling with a very large problem.

She'd always see Wyatt as a larger-than-life figure. Even when their interactions were more steeped in his teasing and her responding eye rolls, she'd known him for his solid strength and capable demeanor.

Yet here.

Now.

He was badly shaken.

Willing the stormy, fiery passion that always flared between them to the back burner, she reached for his hand and tugged him forward, closing the door with her other hand.

Once they were inside his apartment, all alone, she turned to Wyatt, her voice soft. "Tell me."

MARLOWE STILL STRUGGLED to process the whole story ten minutes later where she sat opposite Wyatt on the couch.

Attempted murder?

Under water and while doing his job?

"Are you sure you're okay?"

"I'm better now that you're here." He extended a hand and laid it over hers. "That's not a line, Marlowe. I'm glad you're here and I can honestly say I'm more settled than I have been since it happened. I just—"

He broke off, scrubbing a hand over the back of his head before standing to pace. "I just keep going over and over it. How the bastard got the jump on us. How he knew where we'd be. How—" Something bleak settled in that blue gaze, turning it to ice.

"How he possibly did this. We're not an amateur operation, despite what this looks like."

"Of course you're not. You're highly trained professionals and the NYPD is one of the most sophisticated police operations in the world."

Her support seemed to add to his fire, his voice rising as he kept pacing. "We have process and protocol. We have patrols. People don't just go swimming in the waters around New York, shooting kayakers, dropping safes against bridges and attacking NYPD officers. It's just surreal."

"He's a professional, Wyatt. A determined one at that."

"But what's his bigger goal? What the hell is this all about?"

Marlowe wished she knew, but she also knew that she owed him her honesty about her father.

About the known associates she'd discovered in that old photo online.

Wyatt nearly lost his life today and no matter the risk to her father's parole, he needed every detail he could get his hands on to understand what was going on. It wasn't just a matter of putting away a criminal. It had become a matter of life and death.

"I need to talk to you about something."

His gaze sharpened once more, that quick reminder that whatever else he was, Wyatt was a cop.

"What is it?"

"It's about my father."

If he was surprised by her shift in topic, he didn't show it, instead taking the seat next to her again. "I know that's a tough topic for you. I've avoided asking you about him but I know the back story there." He looked uncomfortable but pressed on. "Most everyone at the 86th does. They don't gossip about it out of respect for your grandfather, but people do know about your father's crimes."

Marlowe had suspected as much, but it was some comfort to know that underlying and everlasting respect for Pops kept the story of her father in perspective for others.

"Unlike my mother's approach of trying to lie it away, it's just an aspect of my life I avoid talking about. I've moved past it and made a life for myself. Wallowing in the reality of who he is hasn't ever done much for my mental health and I learned a long time ago to set it aside."

"That doesn't mean it doesn't affect you. He is your father, Marlowe."

"No, it doesn't. And it's a lesson I've come to realize, with stark clarity, this week."

When Wyatt didn't say anything in response, nor did he press her, Marlowe realized it was all on her.

And, she had to admit, it was time.

Time to tell him the truth. Her own and the underlying truth about the father she loved, even as she'd had to mentally cut him out of her life in order to have a life.

"There are very few doors, locked or otherwise, my father has ever had any trouble getting through."

"Because he's a thief?"

"Because he's a charming thief." She shook her head, thinking even now about the man who still had a solid amount of sparkle and shine, even clad head to toe in prison orange. "And it draws people to him, believing in him even when there's a sleight of hand taking place behind his back."

"Like your mother?"

"I think my mother is the best example, but it wasn't just her. Everyone in Michael McCoy's orbit spends far longer there than they should because they're enjoying themselves so damn much."

She considered her grandfather, the most upstanding and honest person she knew. "It killed my grandfather. Slowly, over time, but I truly believe if my father hadn't finally been caught for his crimes it would have been the death of my grandfather."

"How so?"

"The disappointment. It's so deep and so severe. His son chose a life in direct opposition to all he believes in."

"Has he talked to you about it?"

She smiled at that, the limited conversations she and Pops had spoken over the years consisting of minimally voiced statements, only when pressed by outside circumstances like a parole hearing or an outreach by Michael's lawyer that needed handling.

"Like me, my grandfather's a vault. So that's more what I've pieced together than anything he and I have really discussed."

"Is that healthy?"

"Maybe yes, maybe no. But it is a rhythm we've managed to find over the years. Because there's processing grief and then there's a day when you decide that it can't be the dominant force in your life any longer. Pops and I have both done that. Or I thought we had until this past week."

"Is this about your grandfather's weird response this morning to our conversation?"

"Yes, but it's about me, too."

"What's really going on, Marlowe?"

"I don't know if I'm right or not, but I think I might have found a connection to your case."

"To the safes?"

"To the weird papers inside the last safe. And that scrawled name. Nightwatch."

"What do you know?"

"I found a dated photo online. Some men standing in front of an old nightclub in Brooklyn called Nightwatch. One of the men was noted in files as one of my father's known associates."

Wyatt's face was like granite, his jaw set in a line so hard she was surprised he didn't crack teeth.

Rushing on, she tried her best to explain herself, even as she suspected there wasn't much she could say to sway him.

And still, she had to try.

"I didn't mention it because I wanted to look into it on my own. I wanted to talk to my father and give him a chance to explain. To tell me more."

"You wanted to talk to him? This man you claim you've cut out of your life? You wanted to talk to him instead of bringing it to me, in the midst of an active investigation."

"I needed to know more, Wyatt. That's all and then I was going to tell you."

"You've known this? For a while?"

"When you came to my office yesterday afternoon I'd just found it online." She knew how it looked, but she had every intention of telling him. After she'd had a better idea of what she'd seen. "I swear, I wasn't going to hold this back, I just—"

"You just what? Thought it was okay to hold back information in an active police investigation?"

"No, I—"

"I, I, I! This isn't about you, Marlowe!" Wyatt stood again, his features a mix of anger and a raw sort of disappointment that lasered straight to the center of her chest. "I let you in on this. I trusted you. I trusted that you know enough about how police work was managed that you could act responsibly with the information you were privy to."

"But I did! I saw one old photo online. That's all. My father has a right to answer a few questions before he's somehow implicated in what's going on. That's all I wanted. To ask a few questions before making connections that might mean nothing. I couldn't risk him losing his parole over something that might be a coincidence."

A hard laugh spilled from Wyatt's lips. "Right. Because we've only talked at length that there are no coincidences."

"But maybe it is. Maybe—"

She broke off as Wyatt's eyes went wide.

"What?" Marlowe asked, aware the man she'd kissed in the doorway and attempted to comfort had completely vanished.

In its place was a hard-edged cop without an ounce of concern for her father's future.

"That's what this morning was about."

"What do you mean? What about this morning?"

"Anderson." Wyatt shook his head. "He knows something, too."

"What could he possibly know? No one knows anything right now. That's why I need to talk to my father."

"No." Wyatt shook his head. But it was his low, murmured words that had Marlowe's heart breaking.

Not because she thought he was wrong.

But because she was deadly afraid he was right.

"Your grandfather knew something the moment I uttered the word Nightwatch."

Chapter Thirteen

Wyatt stared at his computer screen, his eyes blurring at the overload of blue light.

And exhaustion.

And such a bone-deep disappointment he wasn't sure what to do with it.

How could Marlowe keep that news from him? She'd discovered a clear connection to his case—one she'd pulled up for him on his home computer before he drove her home.

The drive had been awkward and in direct opposition to the greeting they'd shared when she'd arrived. Where their conversation up to now had flowed freely, the silence between had been stilted and staid. And even as a small, sneaking sense of guilt had settled into his gut over his actions, he couldn't change it.

And, damn it, he had a right to be pissed off.

For a man Marlowe claimed she'd cut from her life, her willingness to trust her father before him chaffed.

Hell, it rubbed him raw.

Sitting here at his desk, poring over old files at one in the morning, wasn't making it any better.

He'd given Arlo a heads-up and whatever he found he'd pass on so his fellow detective could pick up the ball the next morning. But now that he'd also found out he and Gav were sitting out dives for the next three days, there wasn't any reason he couldn't take care of the extra legwork for Arlo.

It would at least give him something productive and active to do.

Something that might take his mind off Marlowe.

"Trumball, what are you still doing here? Especially after the day you had."

Wyatt looked up to find Captain Reed standing on the other side of his desk.

"I could ask you the same. And I'm still here especially because of the day I had."

Their bullpen arrangement of the detectives' work area meant Wyatt only had a lone chair that sat beside his desk, but Dwayne sank into it easily. "Hell of a day all around."

"Why are you still here?" Wyatt asked. Dwayne was an incredibly hardworking captain, but also a committed family man and hours like this were usually tied to a very specific case.

"Homicide got a big one in late this afternoon. By the time he lawyered up and the team took a shot at him, successfully, I might add, it was just shy of midnight."

Wyatt had heard some word of what was going on when he'd arrived back at the precinct after dropping Marlowe off, but hadn't realized the interrogation had run that late. "And you're still here because?"

"Because I'm still keyed up and thought I'd work for a bit." Dwayne flashed a bright white smile. "I can't say I've been all that successful notching the adrenaline back down."

"Some days are like that."

"What are you working on?"

Wyatt wasn't going to hold a damn thing back from his captain, but he didn't want to implicate Marlowe negatively, either. And certainly not Anderson until he had a full sense of what they were dealing with.

So instead, he opted for as simple an answer as possible and hoped like hell he wasn't committing the same lie by omission Marlowe had.

"Marlowe McCoy's father is about to come up for his parole hearing. In the process of looking through some paperwork from her father's lawyer, she came across some details on his last case. She got curious and did some internet diving."

Dwayne was clearly interested, his dark eyes sharp. Focused. "She find something we couldn't?"

"She did, sir."

Without any further preamble, Wyatt turned his computer screen toward Dwayne, the image of Michael McCoy's known associates standing in front of the Nightwatch club filling the space.

"Son of a bitch." The exhale was hard and Dwayne added a few more curses for good measure. "I don't believe it."

"I didn't at first, either, but it's a clear connection."

"And what we've been searching for."

"It's a start but the rest is still as puzzling as ever."

Wyatt hadn't had any luck on the other photocopied sheets from the safe.

He'd done several searches on the jewel exhibit that had been featured in the photocopied *New York Times* article. All that had come up was that a display of jewels had been on loan for three months, with the centerpiece of the exhibit a legendary Burmese ruby. He'd exhausted the NYPD archives and found nothing of substance on the exhibit other than a handful of vice bookings that had happened on the streets around the museum and a few assault and batteries that had been filed during that time, as well.

The event went off, seemingly, without a hitch.

The photocopied parking ticket had been a lost cause from the start. Even if he had been able to lift a license plate number off the ticket, their entire system had been archived in the late nineties and they'd have had to go digging in the NYPD archives to find the details.

Wyatt would have done it, too—he hated the archives warehouse but he wasn't a stranger to it when he needed information—but the lack of plate numbers made the photocopy useless.

And then the last piece—a diner receipt in Brooklyn—was the most puzzling.

Whoever put the packet of papers together did it with some intent. But all he came back to each time was lingering feelings of being toyed with.

Taunted, really.

"None of it makes sense, Dwayne."

His captain tapped the edge of his desk with his index finger. "It's been a long day all the way around. Maybe it's time to give it a rest tonight."

"Yeah."

Dwayne nodded. "I know you and Gav are off the dive schedule for a few days, but let's do a briefing tomorrow afternoon. I want us to get a handle on every possible way that guy got underneath the water and to you."

"He's a professional. And the water's muddy enough if he knew how to stay low no one would have spotted him."

"More reason we need to get on top of this and get it figured out. I put a call into a buddy of mine at the Bureau. Skills like that suggest ex-military, like we've been saying."

Wyatt was surprised by the decision. "You know if you bring them in with something that specific they're going to get involved."

Dwayne's smile was broad. "Why do you think I did it? Someone with federal training doing mercenary jobs against my cops? I want it figured out and I want them throwing every resource they've got on it."

"Thank you, sir. That means a lot."

His captain just stood. "I'm heading home and I suggest you do the same."

"Just going to wrap up a note to Arlo. Then I'm heading out."

"See that you do."

Wyatt watched Dwayne walk away and, not for the first time, was grateful for the family he had at the 86th. Bringing in the Feds on something like his and Gav's dive would most certainly muddy the jurisdictional waters and the Feds would likely toss their weight around a bit. Yet Dwayne hadn't hesitated.

He did right by his cops and he took the politics on himself.

It was a gift to have leadership like that. One he didn't take lightly.

Which brought him right back around to Anderson McCoy. The retired chief of detectives had a stellar reputation, even after being off the force for nearly two decades.

Was that reputation misplaced?

Before this morning's discussion in the man's kitchen, Wyatt would never have even considered it a possibility.

But now?

He was deeply concerned the man held the key to a large secret he'd rather keep buried.

MARLOWE HIT THE main circuit around the park just as the sun rose up over the tops of the trees. A few other early morning joggers were out as well as several people walking dogs in the cool breeze.

She normally loved this time of year. The last days of summer were giving way to fall and the air had a breeziness that kept her run comfortable. The rhythm of the city changed, with kids back in school and the shorter days ultimately ceding to falling leaves and crisp nights.

But not yet, she reminded herself as she hit the mental marker for mile one.

For now she'd enjoy what was left of the last dying days of summer.

And she wouldn't think too hard on the decision she'd made the night before as she lay tossing and turning in bed.

Those moments with Wyatt, confessing to him what she'd discovered, had been some of the worst of her adult life. His gaze—all cop—had morphed from sharp and dangerous to deeply disappointed as she'd struggled to explain her hesitance to tell him.

She wanted to talk to her father.

That was all.

It was the only reason she'd held back on showing that internet photo to Wyatt. She wanted a half hour with her father, using the time to ask him about those men and understand his connection.

No matter what her father eventually told her, she was going to tell Wyatt. She'd never have kept it from him, regardless of the answer she got from her dad.

But damn it, she'd wanted the time to actually get an answer.

Was that too much to ask?

Her father had been in jail nearly her entire adult life. She'd accepted long ago that their visits would consist of discussions through glass in the winter and the hawk-like audience of prison guards in a small courtyard in summer. It was the reality of the life he'd chosen and she had come to a place in her own life where she accepted it.

But if he had a real shot at getting out after serving his debt to society, was it so wrong she wanted to ensure he had that shot?

The man was in prison, for Pete's sake. There was no way he was actually involved in Wyatt's case. All she'd wanted was a chance to get some information before creating questions about his innocence.

She knew what it was to have people look at you sideways, even if you hadn't done anything. Yes, she'd chosen to stay in Brooklyn, but for the people who knew her or of her through her family's history, she would always be Michael's daughter, potentially at risk for doing bad.

Her chosen profession likely didn't help, Marlowe acknowledged with a small smile as she rounded the curve for mile two, but it still wasn't fair.

Even if you did keep details from Wyatt.

That small voice taunted her from underneath the self-righteous conviction that she had a right to talk to her dad.

"Damn it." She let out the short curse, shocked when a voice echoed from beside her, pulling her out of her head.

"You're out here early."

She nearly fumbled her steps and only Wyatt's steadying hand on her elbow prevented her from losing her footing.

"Easy."

"What are you doing here?"

He dropped his hand from her arm and kept pace next to her. "Couldn't sleep."

"And you decided to come find me?"

"I decided to take a run and hoped I'd find you."

She side-eyed him as they kept a steady pace. "After last night, I didn't think you'd want to see me at all."

"After last night, that's the exact reason I want to see you."

Marlowe kept running, unsure what to say. His behavior the night before was frustrating and upsetting, but she couldn't exactly blame him for his anger, either. If the situation was reversed, she'd likely have done the same.

Hadn't that been the very problem she'd struggled with, tossing and turning all night?

She wanted to be mad at Wyatt but there was a solid streak of mad at herself.

And a rock and a hard place decision she wasn't sure she'd make differently, even if she were given the chance to go back and do it again.

"Look, can we talk?"

Wyatt slowed to telegraph his intentions and Marlowe followed suit, heading for a nearby bench. They stood and stretched for a few minutes before finally taking a seat.

"First, I'm sorry for my reaction last night. I was upset and—"

Whatever she was expecting, an immediate apology wasn't it and Marlowe stopped him mid-apology. "I'm sorry, too, even though there's a big part of me that feels like it's disingenuous of me to apologize."

"Why's that?"

The early morning sun fell through a break in the trees behind him, spearing shoots of light over Wyatt. She couldn't dismiss the deep sense of exhaustion that rode him or the dark circles under his eyes.

"I really wasn't trying to deceive you, Wyatt. I wanted to give my father a chance to explain, that's all. Whatever his answer, it wouldn't have stopped me from telling you what I found."

Whatever mental gymnastics she'd gone through over waiting to tell Wyatt about the photo, she was beyond certain of that fact.

And as he studied her in the morning light, his gaze was oddly understanding, that hard glitter of cop eyes nowhere in sight. "I think I understand."

"It's why I'm going to see him this afternoon. I want to get this over with and get my answers."

"You shouldn't pull him into this, Marlowe. It's an active investigation and he can't know the details. Prisons aren't nearly as locked down as you might think. He can't have information like this."

"I'm not going to tell him about the investigation. I want to ask him about the men who were already mentioned in relation to him. I want to know who they are and how they relate to his circumstances."

It was a tenuous thread. While he had no right to tell her not to go visit her father, he was running an active investigation. She suspected if he wanted to pull in the full weight of the NYPD he could find some way to manage it so that her father was unavailable today.

"You swear you're only asking him about known associates. Without any details on the safes?"

"Of course not."

"Then I guess it's a good thing I'm off duty for the next few days."

He must have seen the question in her eyes because he continued right on. "I'll drive you upstate to see him."

WYATT WAS GLAD he and Marlowe were back on more even ground, but he couldn't deny that he'd done damage the night before with his reaction. He stood by it—his job required his absolute focus and after the attempt on him in the Hudson he could hardly afford to lose sight of that now.

But he still regretted the stilted conversation his actions had left behind.

"I hate this part of the drive," Marlowe murmured as Wyatt glanced at the GPS directions he had transmitting on his phone.

She hadn't said much and her words now felt a bit like a confession.

"Why do you hate it?"

"No matter how many times I come up here, this part's the worst. The highway signs began advertising there's a prison nearby and not to pick up hitchhikers."

Wyatt had seen those same signs starting about ten miles back. He'd noticed them—every prison he'd ever been to did the same—but he'd glossed over it as a matter of course.

"It's designed to protect people passing through. The ones who don't know there's a prison around."

"I know. It's just—" She broke off on a heavy sigh. "It's a sobering reality, you know? And proof that the pretty, rolling land outside these windows hides the home of maximum security criminals."

Wyatt knew there wasn't any answer he could give that would make that reality better for her, so he went with what was in his heart instead.

"I'm sorry you've had to live with this. That you've had to spend your adult life dealing with trips to prison. Even the other night's dinner with your mother. It's like this constant reminder of your father's choices."

"Thank you." She let out a harsh laugh, but under it he heard the slightest quavers of vulnerability. "It's nicer than I can say to have someone acknowledge that."

They made the rest of the drive in silence, both wrapped in their own thoughts. The front desk wasn't that crowded and their IDs were processed in the visitor log quickly before they were escorted to the outside yard where Marlowe would meet with her father.

"I like it better in the warmer months. The outdoors." She gestured around to the prison yard after the guard who'd escorted them out had led them to a table. "The fresh air. It doesn't feel nearly as claustrophobic as in winter when you have to sit in those ugly little cubicles and talk on a phone."

As a cop he normally spent his prison visits with legal counsel inside rooms designed for the purposes of discussion and questioning. Now that he was out here, Wyatt could see how this sort of visit would be far easier on a prisoner's family than being stuck inside.

A light breeze whipped up, catching wisps of Marlowe's carefully styled and pinned-up hair. As he watched her smooth them back, he saw the slightest tremble in her hands; watched the way her eyes kept up a continual scan of the prison yard.

And saw that expressive gaze still when it landed on the tall, impressive-looking man in prison orange who crossed the yard toward them.

"Marlowe." Michael McCoy leaned in and pressed a kiss to his daughter's cheek. His hands were bound before him in cuffs but Marlowe reached up and wrapped her arms around his neck, pulling him close in a hug.

"Hi, Dad."

They stood there for another heartbeat before Marlowe pulled back, turning toward Wyatt. "I'd like to introduce you to a friend."

Wyatt ignored the handcuffs and extended a hand to Marlowe's father. "Mr. McCoy. I'm Wyatt."

He got the impression he'd done right by the handshake if the small note of satisfaction in the dark brown eyes, so like his daughter's, was any indication. And then the three of them settled themselves at a table with single seats around each side of the square, all bolted to the ground.

"I'm glad you're here, Lowe, but I was surprised to get the notice you were coming. I wasn't expecting you for a few more weeks."

"Your lawyer reached out with the details on your parole hearing. I wanted to talk to you about that and, well, a few other things."

Michael's gaze darted toward him and Wyatt got the distinct sense the man anticipated something personal. It was only when Marlowe continued on that Michael's curiosity shifted to a strange sort of resignation.

"I did some research into your case. I read a few transcripts and looked at some of the court notes."

"You did that years ago, Lowe. It's old news, baby."

"I read those notes as a teenager. Now I'm reading them as an adult. I was surprised to realize you had known associates. I thought you always worked alone."

Michael frowned at that. "I did work alone, most of my career."

If Marlowe was bothered by her father's reference to a life of theft as a "career" she didn't show it. Instead, she simply pressed on. "Why did you change to working with others?"

"When various parties catch word of your reputation, things begin to change all on their own. Those parties get interested in a man with my sort of skills. Speaking of parties—" Michael's gaze fell on Wyatt, a direct hit, before he continued. "Now I have some questions for you, Lowe. Including why you brought a cop with you today."

Marlowe left Michael's question hanging there, but Wyatt had to give her credit; she played it as cool as her father.

"Wyatt's working on something and he has questions. I do, too."

"And you weren't going to tell your dear old dad the real reason for your visit?"

"I'd say the fault is mine, sir." Wyatt stepped in. "I wasn't intending to deceive you. But I did want to get a sense of things before sharing my real reason for being here."

Once again, Wyatt got the distinct sense he was being measured up and meeting whatever standard Michael had, because the man nodded. "A sense of what things?"

"If I could trust you with my case."

"Something that involves me?" Michael glanced down at his cuffed hands before lifting his gaze, as well as his bound wrists. "I'm hardly in a position to make trouble."

"You're not the one I'm concerned with. But let's not pretend we both don't know word travels as fast in here as it does on the street." When Michael's gaze remained steady, Wyatt took it as agreement and continued on. "Marlowe was the one who made the connection. Between men you used to work with and some recently discovered elements in my case."

"You're working with the cops now, Lowe?" Michael did grin at that, a clear sense of amusement threading his words. "There's more of my father in you than I realized."

"I got pulled into this by circumstance. The NYPD uses my services."

"Ah, yes." Michael's tone turned grave, even as his smile remained firmly intact as he shifted his attention to Wyatt. "My daughter's fingers are as clever as mine. Shame she's been so determined to put them to less creative pursuits than I did."

Since Wyatt had seen the woman work, he wasn't sure Michael's assessment regarding her lack of creativity was accurate but he let it go. He was about to explain what they'd been looking at when Marlowe pressed on, a sudden urgency in her questions that hadn't been present since they'd sat down.

"Tell us about Harry Kisco and Mark Stone, Dad. What do you know about them?"

He'd already understood Marlowe wasn't unaffected by this visit, but that urgency spoke of as much of a desire to solve what was going on as Wyatt and the rest of his team. It was a reminder, once more, that her reasons for keeping Michael's known associates to herself might have been different than Wyatt's, but it wasn't because she wanted to hide anything.

She wanted answers, too.

"Dutch and Mark were some of those interested parties I mentioned."

"Dutch?" Marlowe probed.

"Harry's nickname." Michael waved a hand. "No idea where he got it, but that's what his friends called him. It's what he told me to call him."

"How interested were those guys?" Wyatt asked.

"Interested enough to drag me into a job or two, despite the independent nature of my work." Michael's gaze roamed over his daughter and in that look Wyatt saw all he needed to know.

Michael McCoy appeared invulnerable, but he was as human as the next person.

And Marlowe was likely the chink in his armor.

"They threatened to expose my work if I didn't help them on a job."

"And what about Nightwatch?" Wyatt pressed on.

"Their nightclub?" For the first time Michael looked surprised by the question. "They ran numbers out the back, but for all intents and purposes, it was a nightclub. One of their few legitimate businesses, actually. Well, aside from the illegal gambling, of course. But it was a hotspot for a few years before public sentiment had them closing and shifting their interests elsewhere."

"And that's all?"

Michael nodded. "That's all I remember."

Wyatt hadn't intended to lay all his cards on the table, but Michael's forthcoming responses—and no evidence of prevarication on the older man's part—had Wyatt pressing for more. "What does any of it have to do with an exhibit of jewels at the Natural History Museum."

"The one with the Burmese rubies?"

For a man who clearly knew how to keep his guard up, there was a surprising amount of amusement and openness in his features as they spoke. "That was a job. A calling, really. I worked on that one for months, trying to find the angles to get in and get my shot at those jewels."

"Dad!"

Michael shrugged at the admonition. "Tried is the operative word. I never got my shot at them. The night I'd determined to go in and make my move the back entrance I'd been assured would be left open wasn't. I'd paid good money for that access but when I got there I was still locked out. When the window of time passed, I had to bug out. I didn't know then what happened and I never found out, either. But that job never happened for me."

"And you didn't go after your money?"

Michael shook his head. "I got wind about two weeks later that the accommodating guard who handled that door had retired, but he was just the lackey. Whoever was responsible got spooked and about a week after that I found an envelope with my full payment refunded in the mail."

"Dad, you have to know what this sounds like?"

"A simpler time, really." Michael's grin—and that charm Marlowe had spoken of was in full force—was broad as he shrugged his shoulders. "My work was to challenge me. I had no interest in being a common criminal or thug."

"A gentleman thief, you mean?" Wyatt asked.

Yet again, he was rewarded by the appreciation in the other man's gaze. "Yes, exactly that. I wanted the thrill of the hunt and the challenge of it all. Killing people or harming others was never in my wheelhouse."

It was one of the odder conversations he'd had in his career, yet in Michael's words, Wyatt got a sense of the man. His innate pride in his work as well as his belief that he wasn't a common criminal, despite his current circumstances.

Or, perhaps, Wyatt wondered, in spite of them.

His circumstances in the world, including two decades in prison, could have tarnished that view. It likely would have for most. Yet Michael's conviction was evident.

Even more so when his focus landed on Wyatt, his gaze direct, his words earnest.

"I know I hurt my family, Wyatt. I live with that every day. But I never behaved in a way that would hurt others. Their pocketbooks, maybe, but not them. Not in the places that really matter. But those men you spoke of?" Michael finally turned to look at his daughter. "They are the worst sort of criminal. They're the ones who prey on the innocent. Who have built their lives on the destruction of others."

"What do you know, Dad?"

"On your case, I'm afraid I'm no help. The Nightwatch nightclub closed years ago. I can't even imagine why it would be relevant now other than to say that yes, it existed for a time. But Harry and Mark? If they're involved in whatever you're dealing with?"

Michael leaned in across the table, his tone urgent. "If they're involved in this, you'd better watch your—"

Whatever he was about to say was cut off abruptly, his eyes going wide as he jerked in his chair.

His physical response was matched to the distinct ring of gunshots.

And as the screams registered around him, Marlowe's loudest of all, Wyatt moved into action, leaping out of his chair and covering her to keep her safe.

Chapter Fourteen

Marlowe heard the screams, seemingly coming from outside of herself, before she realized they spilled from her throat.

More gunshots?

More chaos from a distance?

Directed at her father?

At that realization, she pressed against Wyatt, wanting to move. Needing to get to her father.

"Marlowe!"

Wyatt hollered through the commotion going on around them, several guards running through the courtyard while inmates who'd been in the yard ran back toward the main building.

"I need to get up. I need to see him."

The shots had stopped, the three that had rung out seemingly all that would come. Wyatt lifted himself off her and the moment she was free of his weight, she crawled around the table to her father.

Once more, that inhuman roar crawled up her throat but she managed to hold it back as she reached for him, a strange whimper falling from her lips as she dragged him into her lap.

"Daddy!" Blood spread outward on his prison uniform, the red dark and insidious against the bold orange of the jumpsuit.

"Marlowe, I have to go after—"

She glanced up to see Wyatt bouncing on the balls of his feet. "Go!"

"I'll get help!"

He raced off in the direction of the security station at the corner of the yard and she already heard the call over the intercom system for a medic.

Even as she feared it was a useless exercise.

"Dad. Stay with me. They're sending help."

Her father was still in her lap, his face contorted in pain as he wheezed shallow breaths.

"There's help coming, Daddy. Come on, you need to hang on."

"Lowe—" Her name came out on a gasp and she held him tight, wishing there was some way to comfort him. "I'm sorry, baby. Sorry I couldn't be—" He broke off on a hard exhale.

"Shh, don't try to talk."

"Need to...say...it."

She stilled as he laid a hand over hers where she tried to keep a palm over the bleeding that seemed to be everywhere. That endless, spreading dark over the front of his clothes.

"You deserved better. You always did. I'm sorry I couldn't give it to you. But I'm glad..." He let out a hard exhale. "I'm glad my dad could."

Marlowe kept up the pressure on his chest, but felt his breath slipping away all the same.

A team of medics arrived, gentle but firm as they tried to pull her away from her father.

"Ma'am. You need to let us work. You need—"

She let out a hard cry as she felt her father's body go limp in her arms.

"I don't think—"

One of the medics reached around her, obviously preparing to pull her father from her lap. She nearly held on, unwilling to let go, when she felt arms around her shoulders.

"Marlowe. Let them do their work."

The warmth of Wyatt's body struck her as he kept his arms around her. She let the medics take her father away and then allowed Wyatt to pull her close. It suddenly dawned on her how cold she was, the shivers gripping her with fierce claws.

"I'm sorry, Marlowe. I tried to catch him. I couldn't get out of the yard. I'm sorry, I—"

He stopped speaking as a hard sob escaped her lips and instead, just held her close, rocking her against his chest.

She cried and shivered as she watched them work on her father.

Even as she knew there was nothing now that could bring him back.

WYATT COORDINATED WITH the local cops as well as the prison security team, but four hours after Michael McCoy had been shot and killed they were no closer to getting answers.

The initial review of the crime scene had confirmed the shots came from a distance, outside the prison yard, in the hands of a long-range sniper. Beyond that, they had nothing.

He'd coordinated with Captain Reed and Arlo, the two of them working through some of the jurisdictional requirements needed to expand their case upstate. Because there was no question in anyone's mind McCoy's death was somehow related to the cases with the safes.

The issue was how anyone knew they were here.

He hadn't known Marlowe's intentions to visit the prison until seeing her that morning. And while he'd shared his credentials as part of his sign in at the prison, it wasn't like anyone had a heads-up he was accompanying her today.

Were they followed?

Was someone keeping tabs on McCoy's visitor logs? Marlowe had mentioned to her father when they were talking that she'd scheduled the trip, but that meant a hell of a lot of behind-the-scenes coordination by whoever was running this con.

One of the medics had taken care of Marlowe, giving her a place to get cleaned up and offering her an oversized T-shirt from a small stash of clean clothes they kept in reserve. When she came out to meet him the shirt hung to the middle of her thighs. Something about that look—the way the material dwarfed her—had a hard fist lodging in his chest.

It was time to get her home.

He wrapped up the last few conversations he needed to have, adding the promise that he and Arlo would be back up in the morning, and then walked over to Marlowe.

"Come on. I'll drive you home."

She allowed him to take her arm, leading her back out past the entry and on to the car. In minutes they were back on the road, the pretty land around the Hudson River an odd backdrop to all the horror they'd witnessed today.

"I still don't believe it." She murmured the words after they'd been in the car about twenty minutes. He'd cleared the town that held the prison and had driven by a few more towns so that those signs she'd mentioned earlier—not to pick up hitchhikers—had finally faded away.

"I'm sorry, Marlowe. I'm so sorry for your loss."

"He was so close to parole. I really thought he'd get it

this time, too, you know? Served his debt to society and all that." She shook her head, her gaze on the land that passed outside the passenger-side window. "No longer a threat to the public and able to serve the rest of his time under a supervised schedule."

Wyatt kept shifting his gaze from the road to her and back again. "Based on the man I met today he had a good shot at it."

"And my grandfather. I have to tell him. And—" She broke off on a hard sob. "He said he was sorry. There at the end, when he could barely speak, he told me he was sorry that he couldn't be what I needed him to be."

"You don't have to figure all this out now, Marlowe. You deserve the time to take it in."

He reached over and took her hand, pleased when she held on through the tears. It wasn't much but a sign that maybe they could get back to that place where they'd been. That place where she trusted him.

The afternoon traffic back into the city was heavy and Marlowe's sobs tapered off as they drove. But in their place was a quiet heaviness that permeated the air.

What did all of this have to do with her father?

And why now?

Until the connection last night when Marlowe showed Wyatt the internet photo of Harry and Mark in front of the Nightwatch club, Michael McCoy wasn't even on their radar as part of the problem. Now less than twenty-four hours later the man's dead?

Wyatt played the case through in his mind. The first three safes had kept them all focused on the murders but looking back on it now, maybe that was the whole point. The fact that the three men were entirely unrelated and had no connection to one another increasingly seemed like the point.

Marlowe had used the term escalation when she referred to the fourth safe, over breakfast with Anderson, and it was so strange to look at it now and realize that's exactly what that fourth safe had been.

Burying the safe at the base of the bridge was deliberate. It amped up the stakes and the entire case changed and shifted with that choice.

The contents inside.

The attack on him during the Hudson River dive.

And now Michael's murder.

"I keep going over it and over it in my mind," Marlowe said.

Her voice was husky from crying and he reached for her hand again, squeezing her fingers in his. "It's understandable. It's all new and you're trying to process it."

"How did they know we'd be there? And how'd they know we'd sit there?" she asked. "Right there? We could have been anywhere in that yard, yet we were somewhere in shooting distance?"

"Say that again."

"That we could have been anywhere?"

Wyatt had gone over the scene in his mind, too, something lingering that wasn't entirely clear. Her reference to where they sat clicked a few thoughts into place.

"When I walked the exterior of the prison yard with the local police there were only a few specific places the shooter could have used, even with a long-range scope on the rifle."

"What are you saying, Wyatt?"

Excitement built, a sense that something—finally something—might give them a clue. "The table. When the guard gestured us where to sit. Did he give us a specific seat?"

"He directed us to that table." The heavy weight that had lain over her shoulders faded in the face of his questions and she sat up straighter. "I didn't think of it at the time but he very clearly directed us to that seat when he showed us to the yard."

"That's my memory, too."

Wyatt cycled through it again. Their stop at the front desk to check in and give their IDs. The guard who escorted them outside. Even the way he'd gestured to the table. He'd been casual, but specific in his guidance and since they'd had no reason to question it, they'd taken the seats he suggested.

"I need to call this in."

Wyatt dug the number out of his breast pocket from the detective he'd met from the local precinct and quickly explained to her the remembered walk out to the yard. She asked him a few questions and Wyatt fact-checked his memories with Marlowe, but by the time he'd hung up, he had her very real promise to get back to the prison to ask questions of every guard who'd been on duty.

"That was really good thinking," Wyatt affirmed once he'd hung up. "Detective Adams confirmed there were minimal sight lines outside the prison yard."

"Meaning?"

"Meaning a sniper, no matter how good, didn't have a shot all over the prison yard. There were limited positions and we were placed in one of them."

"Wyatt," she exhaled, her voice quivering again with tears. "He's dead because I went up there today. If I'd only have told you what I thought you could have handled it. I should have left you to do your job. Why did I need to see him? Why did I do this?"

"You didn't do this, Marlowe. A criminal with a deadly purpose did this."

"But if I'd have left it alone. Why did I think it was okay

to do this? To go up there and ask him questions and play freaking detective!"

The tears she'd gotten under control rose up again, her sobs hard and heavy as she shed her grief. He wanted to comfort her, but he knew there wasn't a thing he could say to help her past this beyond giving her a safe place to get it out.

He didn't agree with her assessment—and when things weren't as fresh he'd make sure she knew—but Michael McCoy wasn't killed because his daughter went to visit him in prison. He was killed today so he couldn't help his daughter and her NYPD accompaniment figure out what was at the heart of the case that had more twists, turns and curves than the Hudson.

Worse, Michael was killed because he was a loose end.

Wyatt didn't know all the details yet, but he knew to the depths of his soul that he was right.

For now, it was his job to figure out why.

CARSON BOOTH DROVE out of the employee parking lot at the prison and headed for the small meeting place at a highway rest stop about four exits down. He'd been wary at first of meeting in the open, but the guys who hired him had been fair and decent so far. Besides, it was late afternoon, the sun was still high in the sky and he carried a gun in his glove box.

What could possibly happen?

He'd gotten the first payment, just for meeting, just as promised. The second had come when all he'd had to do was nose around the visitor log files and share some information. Today, he'd collect payment number three.

And only for suggesting to a few guests up visiting the prison where to sit in the yard.

He felt bad about the outcome, but how was he to know

the seats at that table were visible off the property? He'd been paid to do a job and the whys of it were none of his business. And one fewer inmate was good for the taxpayers, right?

Besides, if he played his cards right, he could get more of these jobs. Who gave a rat's butt about the prisoners inside anyway? They'd just as soon turn on him if he so much as eyed someone sideways. No reason he couldn't make some good money on the side for spending all day working in that hellhole.

He took the exit for the rest area, pulling off into the long parking lot with diagonally drawn spots. The place had a few cars and he went to the far end, taking a spot near the picnic tables that overlooked a view of the river. A small building housed the restrooms and vending machines, but Carson was careful to stay far away from the building and any of the cameras that set at the corners of the structure.

The picnic tables were empty and he crossed over to the last one, taking a seat like he'd been told. If this drop followed the same as the first two, he'd get a call after he'd sat down and would be given additional directions from there.

He'd barely sat, squinting his eyes from the glare reflecting off the water, when his phone rang.

"Booth here."

"Mr. Booth. Thank you for your service today."

"I did the job as asked."

"Yes, you did. Perfectly, as a matter of fact. If you lean down and feel under the picnic table, you'll find your payment."

Carson bent to the side, his hand stretching to probe the underside of the table. Just as his contact suggested, Carson felt a thick envelope taped around the midsection of the wooden planks. His fingers closed over it, the peeling of tape audible as he pulled off the thick package.

He'd been promised a thousand dollars for this job and had requested it in twenties. But as his hand closed on the envelope, it felt like a lot more in there.

An additional advance for future work?

He couldn't wait to open it up.

It was the last thought Carson Booth would ever have as one single shot rang out, the bullet embedding itself in the back of his skull.

As his hand reflexively closed over the envelope, left intentionally unsealed, a slew of paper money from a board game flew out of the envelope, picked up on the light breeze drifting over the Hudson.

MARLOWE COULDN'T BELIEVE her father was gone. The man who'd occupied such a complex and complicated place in her life was still her father.

Still someone she loved very much.

And now he was gone.

Wyatt hadn't indulged her line of thinking about asking questions, but she was at fault.

She'd made the trip today.

She'd asked the questions.

She'd requested the meeting that killed him.

The drive back into the city had seemed endless as they'd waded through late afternoon traffic and it was almost seven by the time they pulled up to her grandfather's street. She'd requested that the police leave the responsibility for telling Anderson McCoy that his son was dead to her.

And now that she was here, about to tell him, Marlowe couldn't deny the mounting sense of dread that filled her bloodstream and curdled her empty stomach.

If she had a complicated relationship with her father it was nothing compared to the one Anderson had for his son. The love of a father combined with the disappointment of a parent.

As she'd told Wyatt, she rarely spoke of her father with her grandfather. For as much as they could discuss, the subject of his son had always been oddly off-limits with Pops.

Only now, on this one thing, she had no choice.

You can do this.

The mental pep talk—one she'd given herself off and on during the two-hour drive—floated through her mind, even as she had a hard time believing those words.

Wyatt came around the car, reaching for her hand. "Come on. We'll do this together."

They headed up the short walkway to the front door and Marlowe suddenly realized what she was wearing. The medic who'd checked her out had kindly offered her the clean T-shirt as she discarded her own blood-covered one. Staring down now, at the shirt that came well past her waist, brought the sense memory back of seeing herself in the prison bathroom mirror, covered in blood.

An involuntary shiver raced down her back.

Would she ever not see it?

Wyatt's large hand still enveloped her own and she tried to focus on the warm strength there and not on the terrible images that had forced their way into her thoughts all afternoon.

Marlowe had debated letting herself in with her key but since she hadn't wanted to give him advance warning they were coming, she knocked on the door, giving him the courtesy of answering. His smile was broad as he opened the door, the welcome falling as he caught sight of them.

"What happened?"

"Pops, I—" She moved into his arms, pulling him close. "Pops, I'm sorry."

"Michael." His arms went around her. "It's Michael."

She nodded, laying her cheek against his shoulder. "It's Dad. He's gone."

They stood like that a long time, his questions coming out in short bursts and her answers a jumbled mix of memories and facts that, bit by bit, told him what had happened that afternoon.

Wyatt had eventually moved them into the living room to sit down before heading into the kitchen to make coffee.

"Lowe, this can't be true."

"I know." She held his hand, the skin of his fingertips worn smooth. "I keep thinking it's a bad dream."

"I didn't even know you were going up to the prison this week."

Another wave of guilt hit her. The continued idea that she'd brought this upon her father by virtue of her visit striking a hard note in her chest.

"I did this. My determination to get answers."

"What answers?"

"The case, Pops. Wyatt's case involves Dad somehow and I wanted to know more."

"You don't need to be messing around in police work, Lowe."

For the first time since she'd uttered the words that her father was gone, something filtered through the clear grief in Pops's eyes.

"I needed to know if he knew anything. If this related to him." She took a hard breath. "Now, with this outcome? How can it not?"

"You don't need to know anything. You need to leave the work to the cops."

"He's my father."

The mulish expression that had settled on her grandfather's face twisted into a mask of pain and anger. "You're not a cop. This doesn't involve you!"

"Pops! This does involve me. It involves all of us now."

Her grandfather's outburst was a surprise, but as more bitter, hard-edged words filled the space between them on the couch, she realized there was so much more going on that she never understood.

Worse, that she couldn't have imagined.

"No, it doesn't. It can't involve you. I kept Michael safe. I made sure of that."

"You made sure of what?"

Marlowe had known this would be a difficult conversation—how could it be anything else? But as she sat there, taking in the stooped lines of her grandfather's still-broad shoulders and the obstinate set to his mouth, she saw something else.

That disappointed parent she believed she knew—that she'd believed was the very definition of his relationship with Michael—had more facets than she could have ever imagined.

"What did you make sure of, Mr. McCoy?"

Wyatt settled two mugs down on the coffee table before taking a seat in the well-worn chair her grandfather used to watch TV.

"I handled it. I made sure he was safe."

"Pops, what are you talking about?"

"That was my job. I'm his father and he refused to see that his work, as he called it, was a dead end. It was a destructive streak I never understood. But I had to fix it."

Grief and anger swirled like a storm underneath his words. Her father had been in jail for more than a decade, yet as she listened to her grandfather it was as if it had happened mere days before, the pain still so fresh.

"Why don't you take us through it from the beginning?"

Wyatt's voice was gentle when he spoke, but he asked the question with the clear expectation of receiving answers.

"I fixed it. Years ago, I fixed it all. I deliberately looked the other way in exchange for them to leave Michael alone. They used my son against me but I made the choices I needed to so I could keep him safe." Pops turned his gaze on her, pleading. "So I could keep you safe."

"Safe from what?"

"They wanted to use him. They wanted his skills to run the neighborhood. They would have found you, too."

Although he'd only half answered Wyatt's question, Marlowe began to put the various elements together.

Her grandfather's strange reaction when Wyatt had told him the contents of the fourth safe.

That lingering guilt he seemed to carry when she did bring up the subject of her father, cloaked in terse answers and as minimal a response as possible, obviously designed to change the topic.

Her grandfather's reputation was sterling, a testament to his work ethic and deep sense of honor.

It was overwhelming to realize her father's crimes had somehow ruined both.

Chapter Fifteen

Wyatt gave them a moment to talk, heading back into the kitchen to retrieve his own cup of coffee. It was a simple task, but he sensed that Marlowe needed the moment of quiet to process yet one more crack in the foundation of her life.

Hell, he needed a minute to process it. A fact that became evident as coffee sloshed over the rim of his mug when he poured too much in distraction.

He cleaned up the small mess with a paper towel and considered what he knew.

What "protection" Anderson spoke of?

And what Anderson had done to keep Marlowe safe?

There was only one way to fully know and as he headed back into the living room, Wyatt recognized the best way to get the answers he needed was *through*. Through pain and grief and a history that refused to stay buried.

"When we spoke the other day, sir, you seemed distracted. Am I correct in thinking that you did know what Nightwatch was?"

Anderson's stare was direct, no hint of the prevarication or distraction he'd shown the other morning. "I do. It was a nightclub down along the water. Two guys who ran it fancied themselves as businessmen but they were using the club as a front."

Michael had told them as much earlier, but Wyatt let Anderson tell the story, curious to understand how many details matched.

"A front for what?"

"Gambling mostly. Vice had kept a close eye on it when it first opened but I smoothed the way, made sure those eyes turned elsewhere. I was the chief of detectives at the time. I could shift and direct their focus as needed."

"And in exchange?"

"In exchange, they kept Michael out of their plans. They'd marked him for a few local jobs they needed his skills on but I made sure they left him alone as part of our deal."

"But Dad worked alone," Marlowe pressed.

"He thought that, too. And he spent most of his life managing just fine on his own. But he was in the game too long. Sooner or later, Lowe, skills like your father's get attention."

Anderson shook his head. "I hated thinking of him that way, but he was skilled at what he did. There was an aptitude there and, much as I hated to acknowledge it, I also understood why he didn't manage to stay under the radar."

That description—of skills in demand—had Wyatt thinking about the faceless sniper who'd shot at him and Marlowe, as well as Michael. And the diver who'd tried to take him out.

Were they one and the same?

That belief they were dealing with highly skilled ex-military persisted, as did the idea that they were dealing with criminals who knew how to keep a variety of those skilled professionals on hand.

Tools to meet an end, Wyatt realized.

"What about the other details in the safe? The article from the *Times* and the diner receipt and the parking ticket?"

"Michael was aiming for that exhibit. He wanted a shot at those jewels and I was afraid he'd do it, too."

"We asked Dad earlier." Marlowe recounted the discussion for her grandfather. "He said that he wanted a shot at it, too, but the back door wasn't open. That was his way in, the one he'd planned for, and it was blocked."

"That was their payment to me. Proof they could cut a gentleman's agreement if I looked the other way on their crimes. The diner was where we made the deal and the parking ticket is a message, I think."

"A message about what?" Wyatt asked.

"It was the first thing I overlooked. One of the nightclub owner's cars was double-parked. The ticket was the first small test."

Wyatt couldn't help but be fascinated by the entire operation. He and the team had batted a lot of theories around, but that sense of a game had been present from the start. But as he considered Anderson's retelling, Wyatt had to admit that the layers and nuance were amazing, like a large chessboard with various pieces all in motion.

Pieces that had sat on that board for a hell of a long time.

He was about to say as much when his phone rang. The number matched the one for Detective Adams he'd put into his phone earlier and he excused himself to take the call in the kitchen.

"Trumball."

"Detective Trumball. It's Olivia Adams. I followed up on the prison guard we discussed."

"Did you find anything?"

"Yes, his body about an hour ago. It's not verified yet,

but I'd bet my badge the ballistics are going to come back a match for the gun used on Michael McCoy."

She walked him through the discovery of the body by a traumatized couple at a rest stop not far from the prison. But the method of death—another execution from a distance— once again spoke of a military exercise.

They discussed a few more details and he promised follow up from Captain Reed the next day before disconnecting the call.

As he walked back into the living room, Wyatt acknowledged the truth.

One more chess piece had moved on the board.

MARLOWE HADN'T WANTED to leave her grandfather, but exhaustion finally took over around ten. Pops promised he'd be fine and claimed he wanted a bit of quiet time of his own.

"I need some time to think, Lowe. Wyatt." He'd nodded. "I'll be calling Dwayne in the morning."

"He'll come here, sir. You don't have to go into the precinct."

Her grandfather looked like he'd aged a decade since she and Wyatt had arrived, but his head was held high when he finally spoke. "I'll go see Captain Reed myself. It's the least I can do."

It was all she'd have ever expected of him, too, Marlowe thought as Wyatt drove her home. Even as her heart broke for the news he had to share. His reputation and a lifetime of work would be destroyed with the news of what he'd done.

One more facet of the devastation that was her father's life.

It pained her to think like that, but even through the pain, she couldn't extinguish the steady flame of anger, either.

How many lives were affected by her father's crimes? Even the dead guard discovered earlier. Yes, he'd made his choices and had obviously paid for it with his life, but it was also one more life lost in this entire mess that spanned decades.

More death and destruction and waste.

She'd spent a lot of years battling different opinions. About her family and her work. From the quiet gossip about her father's crimes to the questioning eyebrow raises at her own chosen profession, people had always had opinions. They'd ranged from outright suspicion to subtle amusement to clear support and the "good path" she'd chosen to build her own business.

All of it, including that subtly embarrassing sense of being watched, was because of her father.

"What are you thinking about?" Wyatt asked as they pulled up under a streetlamp about a block from her building.

She turned to him, his features outlined in sharp relief by the bright glow of halogen. "Other people's perceptions."

"People have a lot of them."

She reached for the car handle before thinking better of it. "Whatever people think about my grandfather? That's all going to change."

"Some."

She saw the hesitation there but was oddly grateful he didn't try to breeze through it, even with a polite lie. "Sadly, a lot. I think he knows that."

"Cops are a tough lot, but they know the job. Don't underestimate people's ability to understand the impossible choice your grandfather was dealing with."

"You're kind, Wyatt. The fact you can still say that, even

with all we saw today, is a testament to your character. But it wasn't only my father who died today. My grandfather's reputation died along with it."

He looked about to argue with her before he tilted his head toward her front door. "Why don't we go inside? It's been a long day."

"You don't have to stay."

"I'm not leaving you alone. There's still a threat out there."

"I appreciate it but really, you don't need to stay. Whatever the threat, it's not directed at me."

He ignored that, getting out of the car and coming around to open her door. She swung a leg out when she realized he still loomed over the open door, staring down at her. "Did you forget what happened as we walked out of dinner the other night?"

"But it's not me they want."

"You don't know that, Marlowe. And I'm not taking the risk."

He gave her the space to get out and she considered arguing but she was so tired. And sad. And...

"My mom! God, how could I have forgotten to call her?"

The thought of calling her mother got her moving, pushing away the exhaustion and the brewing argument with Wyatt as she headed for the front door of her building.

Even if he did seem rather immovable on the subject of staying. And if the idea of having him close left her with a sense of safety and security that she hadn't fully come to on her own?

Well, she'd think about that later when she wasn't so upside down with her emotions and so needy for these feelings for him that had only grown as the day progressed.

They'd started out this morning with a huge chasm between them. One she'd fully expected would slow down or
completely shut off the tentative relationship building between them. But as they'd spent time together—as he protected her once again from forces outside of them—they'd
been more partners than adversaries.

It was something she wanted, she admitted to herself.
Even in the midst of all the upheaval in her life, she wanted
to see where this relationship went.

But those were thoughts for another time.

For now, she needed to be responsible to another relationship.

Marlowe had her phone out by the time she and Wyatt
got into her apartment and dialed her mother, suddenly at
a loss for words once Patty answered the call.

"Darling!" Her mother's happy voice echoed from the
phone and Marlowe had the overwhelming sense of what
she had to do.

Of the news she had to deliver.

"Um, hi, Mom."

"Sweetheart? What's wrong?"

"Well, I'm sorry but…well, something happened today."

"Marlowe?"

"Dad died."

That truth—so hard to say—was finally out.

"He what? How? Michael?"

The tears she'd managed to hold back most of the day
burst through the layers of numb she'd cloaked herself in.
Wyatt moved in immediately, grabbing the phone from her
hand and taking over the call to her mother.

"Patty. It's Wyatt."

Marlowe abstractly heard him walk her mother through
the details as she took a seat on the couch. He was straight-

forward in the retelling, but kind, as he went over and then repeated information a few times to her mother's obvious questions.

"Why don't I have her call you tomorrow, Patty, if that's alright?"

Her mother must have agreed because after a soft good-bye, Wyatt crossed the room and laid her phone on the coffee table.

"I'm sorry."

"Don't be. She's got the information now and will talk to you tomorrow."

"I don't know why I couldn't tell her." She glanced up at Wyatt from where she sat on the couch with a shrug. "Maybe more of that family dysfunction I've managed to show you in every way?"

"There's no shame in being sad. None at all."

"I'm not ashamed of the sad, Wyatt. It's all the rest that's the rub."

The idea settled in, picking up a serious head of steam as she began to list her reasons.

"Mother deceiving her new beau. My father shot in a prison yard. And my grandfather lying to a precinct of people who've revered him for decades. Just a regular old day in the McCoy household."

Her voice cracked on the last, more tears spilling out to mix with the seething anger she couldn't seem to burn out of her system.

She'd carried it, in some way, for the majority of her life. That steady, simmering fury that the people around her— the people tasked to protect her and care for her—were so unwilling to put her first.

But this news about her grandfather had taken that low-level simmer and seemingly exploded it.

Which made the strong arms that pulled her close such a revelation. As she laid her head on his chest, settling in against him, Marlowe felt the first, subtle loosening of those tight, furious fists around her spine.

And allowed herself to land in a soft, warm, welcome space.

WYATT HELD MARLOWE close and let the range of emotions spill from her, one after another. She cycled through tears more than a few times, but the subtle yet steady loosening of her body as the time passed assured him she was processing the wild mix of feelings that she'd spent the day bearing up under.

Hell, that she'd spent a lifetime hauling on her shoulders.

Whatever lingering anger of his own over the internet photos she'd discovered had faded away. Although he'd have preferred she came to him first, the afternoon had reinforced for him that she was in an untenable position.

And that her family held a greater hold over her than she perhaps wanted to acknowledge.

It was a situation he understood…deeply.

He carried the burden of his own father's death and the resentment that still filled him over his mother and brother's decisions. It was family dynamics—the good and the bad.

"I can't believe he's gone."

Marlowe had been quiet for a while and her crying spell had left her voice throaty and raw.

"It's shock and grief. Give yourself time to process it."

"I've always loved him, but I guess I'd always thought that losing him would be easy, somehow. Or easier, maybe, since he's not an active part of my life." She shifted against his chest, staring up at him. "Now I see how badly I'd deluded myself."

"It's not a delusion. You've had to protect yourself and find a way to reconcile the person you love with the person who's made very poor choices. That's not an easy middle ground to exist in."

"It's going to be the hardest on my grandfather."

Since he'd worried about the same, Wyatt tried to encourage as best he could. "He's tough and he's got you."

Wyatt could only hope there wouldn't be too much fall out from Anderson's decisions so many years ago. The statute of limitations on nearly any crimes that would have happened at the time Nightwatch was an active club had long run out. Even so, no matter how long ago it had happened, the news of a chief of detectives looking the other way would still cast aspersions on the NYPD, especially if spun correctly by ambitious politicians or legal teams.

It was a bridge they'd cross once Anderson talked to the captain. Until then, Wyatt needed to keep his full focus on Marlowe.

For all her bravado in the car, dismissing his protection, he wasn't fully comfortable that there wasn't an external threat to her still out there lurking. It was unlikely, her position so close to Michael in the prison yard making both of them easy targets to a trained sniper, but he didn't want to take chances.

"Thank you for staying again tonight."

"You're welcome."

She still stared up at him and Wyatt recognized the unique torture of protecting her.

He wanted this woman.

And despite all that had happened the past few days, his feelings had been building for quite some time.

She lifted a hand, her fingers tracing a path over his jaw.

"Thank you for today. For being there. I don't know what I would have done if I was up at the prison alone."

"You don't need to thank me for—"

She shifted her thumb to press against his lips. "Thank you."

He just nodded at that, pressing his lips in a kiss against the pad of her thumb.

They sat like that for several breaths, their gazes locked, and for a few moments the heartbreaking malevolence of the day drifted away. It didn't vanish, but they got some respite from it in that all-encompassing heat between them.

He got the sense Marlowe was going to say something when she seemingly thought better of it, tucking her head against his chest.

For as much as he wanted her, Wyatt realized, he wanted this, too. That sense of having a partner at the end of the day. Someone to share it all with, even overwhelming and difficult days.

She'd come to his home the night before when she'd heard the news of his attack in the Hudson. And while he'd sent her away over Nightwatch, before that revelation he'd been grateful she was there.

Her very presence had made his nerves after the attack better.

Now, tonight, he only hoped he could do the same for her.

And as her breathing deepened and evened out as she lay against his chest, Wyatt realized one more truth.

She was the person he wanted to share his days and nights with. Because in an incredibly short period of time, she'd come to mean everything to him.

MARLOWE CAME AWAKE on a heavy rush, the weight around her midsection stifling. She nearly flopped off the couch until she finally realized she was about to struggle against a person.

A very warm person in the form of Wyatt.

Had they slept here? All night?

Since the last she remembered was laying her head back against his chest and now it was morning, it seemed entirely true, but why hadn't either of them woken up?

Which brought the second wave of memory flooding over her like a dam let loose.

Her father.

And the heartbreaking grief that he wasn't simply gone, but that he'd been taken in such a violent show of revenge.

She'd managed to put it out of her mind for a few hours, but there was so much still to do. Including a follow-up call to her mother to talk to Patty herself and a check in on her grandfather before he headed into the precinct to talk to Dwayne.

Catching herself, Marlowe waited, allowing the physical safety she felt in Wyatt's arms battle against the roiling thoughts and the emotional turmoil that refused to fully settle. As her breathing calmed, she decided to take full advantage of the large, firm chest she still lay against and simply be present for a few minutes.

After all, it wasn't every morning a woman woke up in such capable, strong arms. She and Wyatt had both been running on fumes, her father's murder and Wyatt's attack in the harbor on his dive having left them with very few defenses and minimal rest. Probably why they'd both dropped into an exhausted sleep.

Would it be so bad to give in and just take the physical for a while?

As she once again allowed herself to feel—the physical strength of the body that lay pressed against hers, the deeply male scent that hinted at the sea and the light scratch of whiskers against her forehead where she'd brushed against his chin—Marlowe allowed herself the fantasy of what could be.

And came to a decision.

For all the turmoil and upheaval in her life, she wanted this.

She wanted what was between them.

"Do you always think this loudly in the morning?"

The husky rumble of his voice, the cadence of it where his chest pressed against hers, had Marlowe nearly scrambling out of his arms like a wet cat. Clever as ever, he seemed to sense her actions before she did, tightening his arms around her before she could move.

"Going somewhere?"

"I just—" She brushed her hair behind her ears, suddenly conscious of how she looked. "I'm probably getting heavy and I'm sorry I woke you up."

"I'm not."

The words were sexy—the warm welcome in his eyes even more so—but he released his hold and she scrambled up to a sitting position.

"I can make coffee."

He grabbed her hand before she could get up and off the couch. "I was only teasing you about thinking out loud. Take the time to wake up."

For all her bravado as she'd laid there in his arms, a sudden sweep of nerves raced through her. They were attracted to each other—that hadn't been a secret—but what was the protocol to initiate sex after several traumatic days of heavy danger and emotional pain?

Was it crass? Opportunistic?

Or did it just come off needy?

Vowing to figure it out after brushing her teeth and fixing coffee, she got off the couch. "I'm just going to freshen up."

When he said nothing else, his gaze unreadable, she headed off to do both.

And was still considering the balance of danger and neediness fifteen minutes later as the coffee maker gave out its final gurgle, signaling a full pot.

Her apartment kitchen was surprisingly large for a one-bedroom apartment in Brooklyn, the room big enough to hold a small drop-leaf table for two. But just like the other morning when he'd woken up in her home, the space suddenly felt small and much too close when Wyatt walked into the kitchen. The twin scents of soap and toothpaste followed him, and she could see he'd washed his face, the front of his hair still sticking up in wet spikes.

Goodness, the man was adorable. Large and sexy and powerful and still, there was something sweet about those wet spikes. A small nod to what she imagined he'd looked like as a little boy.

"I can run out and get us some breakfast," he said, picking up the mug she'd set out for him on the small table.

"You don't have to bother. I have eggs or toast and I always keep a few bagels in the freezer we can defrost."

"Spoken like a true New Yorker."

"They are carb-laden perfection."

She'd already fixed her own mug and had just turned away from the counter to go to the fridge when his hand reached for hers, stilling her movement. "Are you upset I'm here? I got the sense the other morning it was awkward and I can feel it again. You don't have to make me breakfast or pour me coffee. I don't have any expectations of you, Marlowe. I'm here to watch out for you."

Wasn't that the problem?

She glanced down where their hands linked and struggled with the best way to play this.

And realized, after all they'd been through, the only real answer was the truth.

Looking up from their joined hands into his eyes, she said the words that had lived in her mind for a while now. "I want you."

He kept their hands joined as he moved closer to her, stopping just shy of their bodies touching, yet close enough that she could feel all that glorious heat. His face was serious, those blue eyes drawing her in. "That's not why I stayed."

"I know."

"Good." He moved those last few inches so that their bodies were flush against each other, his other hand going around her back to pull her close. "Because I want you, too."

Their mouths met, those hints of coffee and toothpaste sweetly endearing and domestic before the kiss turned incendiary. Heat and need and raw electricity arced between them as Wyatt deepened the kiss. She met him, her arms tightening around him as she allowed him greater access, their tongues mating in a carnal preview of all to come.

Long, sensual moments spun out, an enticing mix of lazy exploration and driving need that dueled for dominance. It was only as Wyatt stilled their kiss, his lips curving into a smile against her mouth that Marlowe realized the scales had tipped toward driving need.

"I'm not at all suggesting an aversion to kitchen sex, but maybe we could move into the bedroom for our first time together?"

"I think we can do that." She moved back, her smile broad. "You sure you don't want me to fix you that bagel first?"

His face fell for the briefest moment before he caught

the joke, diving for her and taking her in another hard kiss before he began moving them determinedly toward the bedroom. Clothes fell to the floor as they moved from the kitchen, down the short hallway to her bedroom, so that by the time they got to her bed, they were naked.

He kissed her down onto the bed, following so that he covered her with his body. Marlowe reveled in the things he did to her, his lips moving over her flesh like a caress. From the sensitive area behind her ear to light kisses over her shoulder to the fiery moments he took her nipple between his lips, each step in his exploration was a gift.

And as sighs grew deeper, breathier, she went on an exploration of her own. Hard planes of muscle flexed under her fingers as she ran her hands down his back. She knew he was well-built—the demands of his job ensured it—but the body beneath her fingers was a work of art.

Long, firm muscles. Slim hips. Sculptured shoulders. Every bit of him was perfect.

Suddenly impatient for more, her hand slipped between them, reaching for the hard length of him. She knew the moment firm strokes gave her the upper hand and she used his hard intake of breath to shift their positions, rolling him onto his back so she could straddle him.

Those firm strokes grew longer, bolder, and Wyatt's breaths grew more shallow as she put his body through the most delicious paces. And just when she was convinced she'd won the round, he neatly turned the tables on her, slipping his hand between them to stroke the most intimate part of her.

"Wyatt—" His name exhaled on a soft moan as he worked her sensitive flesh, tension building with each moment.

In a beautiful explosion of need and the deepest arousal she'd ever experienced, her body shuddered around him.

Wyatt pulled her close as he rode her through her orgasm, whispering sexy words of appreciation before he kissed her.

Had she ever…?

How had he…?

Marlowe's thoughts drifted with the waves of pleasure and she reveled in his touch. As he gathered her close against him, his arms cradling her, she felt her body stirring once more, shocked she could be ready so quickly.

And yet, as she looked down at the firm lines of his sexy, stubbled jaw, she knew there was so much more to discover.

So much more to experience.

Together.

Pressing her lips to his ear, she whispered, "Why don't you reach into my end table over there."

He grinned down at her, even as his hand was already snaking over to the drawer.

"It's hard to argue with a prepared woman," Wyatt said as he pulled a condom from the drawer. "And right now I'd like to add extra heaps of praise since I arrived unprepared."

"Then it's sure to be a most excellent morning for both of us."

Snagging the condom from his hand, she made quick work of the package and unrolled it over the hard length of him, adding an additional stroke of her palm against the underside of his erection for good measure. Not to be outdone, he quickly flipped her onto her back, rising up over her to fit his body intimately to hers.

She'd known they'd fit, but it happened so easily. So perfectly.

And as he began to move, long, sure, smooth strokes in perfect rhythm, Marlowe gave herself up to the moment.

To Wyatt.

And to this beautiful connection between them.

Chapter Sixteen

Wyatt wondered if he had to open his eyes and decided a man who'd just seen the heavens explode was entitled to a few more minutes of reverent silence. Since keeping his eyes closed had the added benefit of giving him a few more moments to simply savor every last drop of what it had meant to make love with Marlowe, Wyatt figured he had the right of it.

God, she was amazing. And not just because they'd started the day with what had to be the best sex of his life, but because she was warm, generous and giving.

All he'd imagined—and he'd imagined quite a bit—and so much more.

She'd curled up next to him as they'd both drifted on the afterglow before kissing him gently on the cheek a short while ago and slipping from the bed. He thought to call her back when her voice drifted to the bedroom, the greeting to her mother clear enough.

He opted to give her the space to make the call, but did keep an ear to the conversation, ready to step in if she needed his help once more.

Unlike last night, her voice had the quiet, confident notes he associated with her.

And also unlike last night, she was able to get through the conversation with her mother, even if he heard the tell-tale notes of tears lacing her voice.

Wyatt wished he could do something for her to make this better, but he knew the only way to deal with the loss of a parent was, sadly, to deal with it. More bad days than good at first, along with waves of grief that swamped you at unexpected times.

He'd been a teenager when he'd experienced it, yet he could still conjure those feelings. Hell, he even felt them now from time to time, a reminder those waves could still pack a powerful punch.

But the violent way she lost her father would place an added dimension on that grief.

He'd be there for her and he'd help her through it. And as that mental assurance floated through his mind, Wyatt realized one more thing.

He wanted to be there, by her side. Now and in the future.

A large part of him—the one who'd never been all that successful at long-term relationships—wondered when a sense of panic was going to set in at the mere notion of sticking around past a few more weeks or months.

And the part of him that had reveled in spending time with Marlowe, from that very first night over pie at her grandfather's, realized he wanted to stay.

He rolled that over in his mind, pleased to realize just how well it fit.

Maybe it's because of how well he fit with Marlowe.

The idea took root, settling in, but before he could think too long on it, Marlowe walked back into the room.

"Are you okay? How'd it go with your mom?"

"It was fine. She's still in shock." Marlowe sighed as she crossed to stand beside the bed. "And I know I'm being a bad person. She did love him once. But somehow the call ended up being all about her. How devastated she is and how she never got to say goodbye."

"What about how much she cares for Brock?"

"Never came up."

Wyatt had a career built on the oddities of human behavior, more of it bad than good. He chalked up much of what he saw and experienced professionally to the worst impulses people were capable of.

Yet it stung in a different way when he saw how Patty's careless behavior affected Marlowe directly.

"I'm sorry she couldn't be more understanding."

"It's dumb of me. To keep wanting that." She glanced up from where she traced her index finger over the mattress. "For her to be different, you know."

"It's not dumb to want her support."

"Yeah, but after proving over and over she's not capable of giving it, it is dumb to keep getting disappointed over it."

She'd slipped into a robe before leaving the bedroom and he was able to lean forward to tug on the oversize sleeve, pulling her down on the bed. He used her forward momentum to gather her up in his arms, pulling her so her back lay flush against his chest, his lips pressed to her ear. "I'm sorry she can't be who you need her to be."

Marlowe twisted in his arms, turning so she could look up at him. "I'm glad you can be." She pressed a firm kiss to his lips before laying a hand against his cheek. "Thank you."

"You're welcome."

They stayed like that for a long time, wrapped up in each other. And when they finally got out of bed and got ready for what would undoubtedly be a long day ahead, it was with the mutual encouragement and support formed in that quiet together.

WYATT WALKED ARLO through the details he'd found on Nightwatch, now expanded with the information Michael and Anderson had shared about the two men who ran the club. Arlo made various notes, adding them to their case board as they talked through implications and the additional runs they'd make through the case files from that time.

Once they'd agreed on next steps, divvying up the work since Wyatt was still off the dive list, he focused on the day before. As he gave Arlo a full debrief on the visit to the prison, Michael's death and what information they had on the dead guard, Arlo outlined his theories.

"The guard's the inside man, putting you, Marlowe and Michael into position, but it's the hired muscle who made the hit."

"I'll bet you he's the same guy who attacked me on the Hudson River dive."

He still hadn't fully gotten over the fact that the jerk had gotten the jump on him under water, but he kept consoling himself with the knowledge that they were dealing with someone who was likely ex-military and trained with an exceptional set of skills.

"That's a sucker bet, Trumball. No way I'm taking that one." Arlo scratched a quick note in dry erase marker beneath the section of the board labeled 1995. "You run the Nightwatch crew? Any kids?"

Wyatt flipped through the file, reviewing the list of facts about the business partners who'd owned the club. "No male children. No obvious connections to the military, either."

"You think the killer's a merc?"

"Working theory only. Captain's put some feelers in with the Feds. Between the attack on my dive and the ambush at the prison if there's a line to tug there Dwayne will find it."

Arlo eyed the various photos of evidence they had up

on the case board in one of the small precinct conference rooms. "If the captain's willingly introducing federal support into this it means a heck of a lot."

"Especially since he managed to hold them off when the fourth safe was recovered. If there'd been a bomb in there they'd have taken this case over."

"Let 'em." Arlo tapped a beat on his thigh with his fingers, a tune only he could hear. "Besides, I never fully understand the territorial fights over jurisdiction, anyway. Isn't keeping the city safe the real point of it all?"

Since that's the same philosophy Dwayne led his department with, Wyatt could only agree.

"So that's what I've got." Wyatt stepped back from the board and sat on the edge of the conference table, crossing his arms. "It's more than we had even yesterday, but it feels empty, too. Way too many holes still to plug to get this handled."

Wyatt studied the board, one of those holes suddenly staring at him in glaring neon. "The dive. The bastard who attacked me. How'd he know where we'd be?"

"I hate to break it to you, buddy, but you get taken out on the water with a bit of fanfare, between the police boat and the Zodiac that drops your crazy ass over and into the water."

His willingness to go that far beneath the water had always been a point of humor in their friendship, especially since Arlo had said on several occasions there was no way he'd ever put on scuba gear and drop below the water like that, even in the gleaming waters of the Caribbean instead of the murky waters of New York Harbor.

"Exactly. But whoever attacked me needed to get in position out of sight of us, which meant he had to swim to us for a bit." Wyatt shook his head, pissed he hadn't realized it from the very start. "The bastard was already in position to do that because he knew where we'd be."

Any hint of jokes had vanished as Arlo spoke. "There's only one way he knew that in advance."

"We have a leak."

HE AND ARLO laid it out for Dwayne in the privacy of the conference room. They'd called him in under the guise of walking him through a quick update in the case, but their captain had sensed the obvious seriousness the moment he closed the door behind them.

"These are serious charges but the implications are obvious," Dwayne said. "And it reinforces the pattern of strategically positioned insiders who gather information. The prison guard fits that, too."

"Insiders. A likely mercenary for hire. Even the heroin in the first three safes. There's a ton of upfront investment here," Arlo pointed out. "This isn't about a nightclub that closed nearly thirty years ago. I don't think it's even about Anderson or Michael McCoy. Not at its heart."

Wyatt had filled Arlo in on Marlowe's grandfather's role in looking the other way and Dwayne had confirmed when he'd come into the conference room that he'd already met with Anderson and had begun proper procedures with Internal Affairs.

Once again, the heavy weight that sat on his captain's shoulders was borne with grace and a stoic belief in doing the job.

And remained the inspiration for Wyatt of what made up the very fabric of the 86th.

"Let me handle the review of the logs from the other day." Dwayne's dark gaze roamed over the board before turning back to Wyatt and Arlo. "It looks like I'm opening a second discussion with I.A."

MARLOWE WANTED TO call her grandfather, but she settled for a text message after she got into her office, checking in to see how he was. He'd texted quickly back that he'd call her later. Since she'd gotten a response at all she took that as a positive sign, but recognized an intentional vagueness there, too.

And also recognized she needed to give him some space.

There was a new software patch she'd been sent that she could test on one of the prototypes. She'd downloaded the details but had only half-heartedly played with the locking mechanism before giving up.

The work needed focus and hers was scattered and jumpy, bouncing from mental squirrel to squirrel.

Her father, grandfather and mother had taken top spots in her mind, yet each time those thoughts got too over- whelming, she was rewarded with the delicious memories of making love with Wyatt and the ire and frustration faded for a bit.

Those lovely memories kept her company as she shifted gears to doing mindless paperwork and she tried to stay in that happier space in her mind instead of the dour thoughts her parents seemed so adept at spinning up.

As she worked through her invoicing software, she did have an additional moment of happiness when she realized just how strong a summer she had. There were only a few days left in September but based on the last few invoices she was loading in, it appeared she'd beaten her third quar- ter projections by nearly 20 percent.

"Hot damn, girl. You've earned yourself a fresh cup of coffee."

She crossed to the single-cup brewer she kept in her office and started fixing a fresh mug when her gaze alighted on the map of Brooklyn she kept tacked over the wall. She'd always acknowledged her workspace had the appearance of a local entrepreneur's business and a villain's lair, with maps, safe designs and lock schematics intertwined with a print from the Brooklyn Botanic Gardens and a movie poster for *Moonstruck*.

The space was uniquely hers and she loved it, but it certainly was far from a cubicle in a high-rise or even the communal bullpen feel of the 86th.

But definitely hers.

Her gaze alighted on that movie poster once more and she envisioned some of the key scenes of the film, nearly all shot in Brooklyn Heights. Images of the water and the Manhattan skyline set the backdrop for several of those water shots and Marlowe could picture them clearly in her mind. In fact, she mused, she and Wyatt should change up their running routine and consider a run along the water, curving around Brooklyn before stopping for breakfast in Brooklyn Heights.

Maybe that weekend.

It felt good to make plans, she thought as she doctored her coffee.

Even better to think about making them with Wyatt.

As she took a sip of her coffee the real implications hit her.

Weekend plans. A slate of activities. All with Wyatt taking center stage.

Quite beyond her imaginings, Wyatt had become a part of her life. An active part, where she planned time with him and saw him in her life.

It had been a long time since she'd been in a relationship

that felt this settled so soon. In fact, the more she considered it, Marlowe had to admit, it had been a long time since she'd felt settled at all, in or out of a relationship.

Yet Wyatt Trumball had changed that. With his twinkling eyes and steady attitude and that enticing mix of serious and fun, he'd snuck beneath her defenses.

And she loved him.

The weight of that stilled her and she set her mug down with a hard thud on the counter.

Love?

Unbidden, her mother's wailing that morning over how much she'd loved Marlowe's father filled her mind. The overdramatic crescendo of how much he'd hurt her yet how devastated she was that he was gone. The lifetime of love they'd shared, even though they'd spent the past two decades apart.

Marlowe had refrained from mentioning that Patty could have made a visit of her own up to the prison whenever she'd wanted. And, as she'd told Wyatt, she'd also avoided bringing up Brock because whatever happiness new love had brought into her mother's life was no match for the tragic heroine she now saw herself as the ex-wife—ex-widow?— of a brutally murdered man.

God, could it be more complex? And a little sordid, too, she admitted to herself.

This is what she came from. This was the emotional maturity of half her DNA. Was she doomed for a lifetime of the same?

It had been a fear, albeit a subtle one, she'd carried for years. But now that she was here—now that she could look to Wyatt and see someone she wanted to share her life with—she recognized those fears were unfounded.

More settled then she could have imagined, she snagged

her mug and went back to her desk, determined to power through her paperwork before heading home and reveling in the success of beating her quarterly projections by 20 percent. She'd stop at the market and pick up some things for the dinner she was going to cook Wyatt. And she'd swing by to see her grandfather, determined to assure him that he would get through this time.

She'd make sure of it.

With her accounting software open, she flipped through the work she'd done over the past two weeks and began the process of inputting itemizations for invoicing. Her gaze alighted on the address on Water Street, and she remembered the job she'd done in downtown Sunset Bay last week. The large warehouse renovation that needed interior and exterior locks installed as the final piece of the renovation.

She hadn't realized it then, but that warehouse was close to the old location of Nightwatch.

Her gaze caught on the map once more and she crossed back to look at it, her mind sifting through the various buildings on that stretch of blocks. The waterfront area had been rejuvenated over the past five years, young money coming into the area giving so many places a real shot at business.

She and Wyatt had gone to Baker's Pub, one of the bars benefitting from that renaissance.

The client she was billing had renovated a warehouse into a funky mixed-use set of apartments and retail.

But a small string of warehouses remained that appeared abandoned yet maintained just to the point of not being eyesores.

Was someone just waiting on the area's value going up enough to sell them at an even higher profit? Or was it something more? Was it possible Harry Kisco and Mark Stone still owned the space?

She'd gone off half-cocked with the internet search and wouldn't do that again to Wyatt. But she couldn't deny she was curious.

Glancing down at her watch, she considered what she knew about the area. It was the middle of the day and all of those shops and restaurants did a brisk business at lunch.

What's the worst that could happen?

Someone noticed her?

If it was still Harry and Mark's domain then, surprise, surprise, they were already well aware of who she was.

And if it was owned by someone else, she'd say she was being nosy and move on.

Win-win.

Besides, if she went she could take a look around and didn't need a warrant to do it. Wyatt wouldn't have the same leeway.

A ridiculous notion, but the sense memory of holding her hand against her father's chest, trying to stop the bleeding, left an awfully big incentive to try.

Picking up her bag of tools, she dug in for a few items. She'd stow the bag in the car but she did pull out a few picks to tuck away in her pocket. Snagging her phone, she made the call to Wyatt, not surprised when she got his voice mail.

"Wyatt, it's Marlowe. I had an idea and I'm headed down to the waterfront to nose around some of those warehouses. Call me back and meet me at Baker's for lunch and I can fill you in on whether or not I see anything."

She disconnected and grimaced at the excessively cheerful tone, especially because she recognized he wasn't likely going to be happy with her decision.

But seriously, what was going to happen in the middle of the day?

With that in the forefront of her mind she headed out

and navigated through Sunset Bay down to the waterfront. She managed to snag street parking and even left her bag of tools stowed on the floor of the front seat as an incentive not to linger. Anything visible through the windows of the car was fair game and she didn't want to lose them.

The warehouses matched the mental map she'd drawn of the south end of Water Street and she had to admit as she walked up to the doors that the location would have been fantastic for a nightclub. The proximity to the water and the location at the end of the main shopping thoroughfare would have drawn crowds. Young happy crowds who wanted to drink and party and enjoy themselves.

The warehouse was dark and the windows had a grimy film on them that made it hard to see anything. She pulled out her phone and took a few pictures before shoving it into her back pocket. But as she moved down the length of the building she saw a small patch visible through the window and realized she'd hit a dead end.

A long row of what looked like industrial machines filled the space. Vaguely, she remembered these warehouses had also housed a variety of businesses through the years, from bottling for a brewery to a high-end paper factory to a small firm that made cocktail additions like jarred onions and cherries.

Whatever she thought she'd find, this obviously wasn't used by a group of thugs any longer. It didn't look like it had manufactured anything for a while and she cycled back through her earlier thought that the owner was likely holding on until real estate prices shot up even further.

On a resigned sigh she thought about her tools still sitting in the front seat and high-tailed it back to her car. She pulled out her phone, but still no message from Wyatt. With quick fingers, she tapped out a text and hit Send, just as she came up on her car.

Still up for lunch? Warehouse is a dead end. Going to do a bit of shopping on Water Street. If I don't hear from you by one, come over later for dinner.

She toyed with adding a heart emoji and stopped herself. In love or not, she wasn't quite ready to start adding emotional nuances to her texts.

Since she wasn't sure if she should be amused or irritated for giving emojis a single bit of headspace, she shoved the phone back into her pocket.

Don't overthink it, McCoy.

Unlocking the car, she pulled her tools from the front seat and popped the trunk, determined to stow her things before killing some time in the shops. If she didn't hear from him in a half hour, she'd keep to her original plan and visit her grandfather and then get the groceries for dinner.

Musing about love and emojis and what she was going to cook for dinner occupied her thoughts when she felt a large presence at her back, the distinct press of something sharp and painful against her lower back.

"Don't make a sound."

Adrenaline beat hard in her chest and, knife or not, she was city-bred and staying quiet on the orders of a criminal wasn't in her makeup. A hard stomp on his foot gave minimal satisfaction just as she felt a distinct prick at the back of her neck.

All before the world went black.

Chapter Seventeen

Wyatt blew out a hard breath as he walked back to his desk. The morning had been difficult, but Dwayne had lived up to his reputation as a fair lawman and an equal proponent of swift action.

Callie Dumbrowski, a low-level administrator, had been called into a conference room with Captain Reed and Internal Affairs and in a matter of minutes, had disintegrated into a pile of tears over her sick child and her louse of an ex-husband who kept missing his support payments and the large payoffs she'd received for sharing specific information to a nameless, faceless buyer.

Wyatt and Arlo had watched from the other side of the one-way mirror in the interrogation room and both had remained quiet, lost in their thoughts. Although he couldn't speak for his friend, his own thoughts had been mired in questions.

Was Callie all that different from Anderson? Their balance of power and influence in the NYPD was different, of course, but the underlying reasons for their actions were the same.

Humans backed into a corner, desperate to fix something they felt powerless against.

It was the real sadness of his job and one he had never fully reconciled in his mind. While they regularly put away hardened criminals who had made their choices for nothing but ill-gotten rewards, it was easy to forget just how often they also put away people who were simply desperate and misguided.

And who somehow thought making a bad decision would miraculously fix a bad problem.

It still haunted him as he pulled his phone out of his pocket and sat down at his desk. The face lit up at the movement and he remembered he'd had a text from Marlowe about lunch that he'd glanced at and put away to look at later.

He opened the phone, only to realize he'd had a call from her, as well. He read the text first, intending to tell her he'd meet her later when he saw there'd been more to the message than the portion about lunch that had shown up on the face of his phone.

Still up for lunch? Warehouse is a dead end. Going to do a bit of shopping on Water Street. If I don't hear from you by one, come over later for dinner.

Warehouse?

The time in the upper corner of the phone was just after one so he'd missed lunch, but what was this about a warehouse? He listened to her voice mail and all that seething frustration he'd walked back to his desk with exploded.

"Damn it!"

"Trumball?" Arlo glanced over from his desk.

"I don't believe it."

He updated his partner as he called Marlowe, frustrated when her phone went to voice mail.

"Marlowe, it's me. Call me as soon as you can. What are you doing nosing around where you don't belong?"

He hung up and added a text to call him back for good measure, especially if she hadn't heard her phone ring inside a store.

Arlo settled himself in the chair beside Wyatt's desk. "You need to let her know this isn't okay."

"Hell if I don't know that?" He ran a hand through his hair, tugging hard on the ends. "What in God's name was she thinking?"

"That she knows this neighborhood and this town and it's the middle of the afternoon."

Arlo might have a point, but her actions still stuck a hard landing. And while he was happy she hadn't found anything, what if she had? What if something had happened? He and Arlo had already run the ownership for warehouses along the water and nothing had turned up so he admitted there was little risk to her, but still.

The fact that she'd put on that bright, chirpy voice and let him know what she was doing, like it was freaking okay, pissed him off.

Hadn't they gotten anywhere since her internet dive into her father's known associates?

Or was she somehow dismissing the seriousness of what was going on and the still-real risks to her own safety?

That last thought sat uncomfortably on his shoulders. Especially since he hadn't gotten a text back.

"What's the matter?"

"She hasn't texted back."

"It's not telepathy, Wyatt. Give her a minute."

"No." He shook his head, suddenly not comfortable. "I'm going to run down there."

Arlo stood. "Then I'm going with you. And when she

texts before we're out of the parking lot you can keep on driving and buy me lunch instead."

MARLOWE CAME AWAKE on the raw, pounding headache centered in the middle of her forehead. For the briefest moment, intense pain was all she could feel, until her mind quickly cleared with the broader implications.

What had happened? Where was she?

She sat up with a start, realizing immediately she was chained to a chair bolted to the floor. She had full movement in her hands but a shackle was attached to her ankle.

Panic hit hard in her chest, cratering in her stomach as she looked around. The space was empty, even more, just sort of blank. Other than the chair she sat in, she could see a toilet in the corner and a small sink that stuck out of the wall beside it.

This was clearly a place to hold someone because there wasn't a thing present that could do damage. There was barely anything here at all.

She cycled through what she could remember—the drive to Water Street and her intention to check out the old warehouses.

But she'd done that and hadn't found anything.

Right?

Questions still swirled through her mind, layering over that pounding headache, as she reached down to examine the lock on the ankle restraint. It was standard, but solid, and she had little ability to do anything to it with nothing but her fingers.

Wait—

She reached behind herself and felt the lock picks she'd stowed in her back pocket. She nearly retrieved one when she heard something outside the door. Shoving the pick back down in her pocket, she sat up and waited.

And watched as three men filed into the room. Two older men who looked similar in age to her father and a thicker, younger man with an impressive physique.

"Miss McCoy."

She considered how to play this and quickly determined playing dumb was not going to work in her favor.

"Let me guess. Harry, Mark and the man who killed my father."

One of the older men smiled, clearly pleased with her remarks, while the other one looked distinctly uncomfortable. The killer remained stoic, his hands behind his back as he stood in military stance.

Wyatt zeroed in ex-military, she thought as she considered the younger man. The idea fit.

"I should congratulate you then. You guessed right."

"What is this about?" she pressed.

"And why would we tell you that?"

"You kidnapped me and tied me up. What do you have to lose?"

"Oh, sweet thing, it's not that easy," the older man—the talker—said. "I hate to disappoint you, but this isn't going to be some big reveal party."

"Then tell me one thing. Why did you kill my father?"

The talker shrugged. "Loose end."

Whatever she expected, something hit with swift and furious fists at the casual response. Nay, at the dismissive response.

"You bastard."

He looked unaffected by her words, the insult flying off him like bullets against a tank.

"I've made my life as one and I'm good at it. Remember that, girlie."

The three of them disappeared as quickly as they showed up, but not before the young guy tossed a deli bag at her feet. After they were gone, she dug in to find a bottled water, sandwich and chips in the bottom.

The thought of food turned her stomach, the headache still so intense she was slightly nauseous, but she needed the food, too. Although their menacing routine had seemed cold and clearly designed so that she didn't get any ideas, she wasn't sure what their plan was.

Were they going to kill her?

A hard shudder flowed through her at that thought, the first time it truly settled in that she wasn't just in danger but in a situation she wasn't getting out of.

But why feed her?

As she cracked the tube of water, she had a second thought.

These men had proven themselves capable of the darkest of deeds. What if she was just bait for something far worse?

"WHY THE HELL did you take her?" Mark whirled on Steve the moment they got into the office.

The ex-SEAL shrugged, clearly unconcerned by the outburst. "She was nosing around. You already said you wanted to figure out a way to use her. I figured out a way."

"She was nosing around a piece of property we don't even own anymore!" Mark exploded.

Dutch watched the exchange carefully, even as he projected a casual demeanor as he kept his gaze on his laptop.

Steve had gotten cocky, his success on the Hudson dive as well as the two kills yesterday clearly motivating him to act on impulse. Dutch had worried they had given him too much autonomy, especially as they took advantage of his varied skills. He'd done the dives independently, burying the last safe as well as trying to take out Wyatt Trumball, carrying out Dutch's plans for both. And then he'd managed the sniper kills with perfect execution.

They needed him, but it also meant they had to deal with his increasing interest in directing the work.

"She's a loose end." Steve ignored Mark's ire. "Don't worry, I'll handle her. You don't have to get your hands dirty."

"Handle her? How many people are you planning to handle before someone gets wise? The cops aren't going to rest until they figure out what happened yesterday."

"You said you wanted McCoy out of the picture. I did that."

Although Dutch appreciated the proactive nature of Steve's work, the reality was he wasn't empowered to direct anything. He was hired muscle, nothing more.

Without checking the impulse, Dutch dragged a gun out of his desk drawer. Mark's fury had provided inadvertent cover and Steve sensed the aim of the gun a fraction of a heartbeat too late. His hand had just reached his own gun, tucked in his waistband, when Dutch's shot landed true, dead center of his chest.

It was clean and fast and Dutch watched Mark take a few steps back, his throat working around swallow after swallow as he stared down at Steve's body.

"What the hell are we going to do with him?"

"Same thing we've done up to now. We'll pay to have it handled."

Because for all his ambition and all his understanding of the big scores that still awaited them, Dutch had also figured out something else as he headed toward seventy.

New York was his oyster. And with the proper cash incentive, you really could pay for anything.

WYATT SCANNED THE street as he drove down Water Street. The lunchtime crowd flowed in and out of restaurants and shops, a thriving, busy area.

Was he overreacting?

Would they find her in a shop or maybe having lunch by herself on a patio?

Marlowe had texted that she'd found nothing at the warehouse and was heading into the shops. And he'd be fine with that outcome.

Thrilled.

Even if he was still going to give her hell for thinking she needed to go check out anything.

But in the end, all he wanted was for her to be safe.

"There!" He pointed to the sedan at the end of the street. "That's her car."

He pulled up alongside and got out, scanning the car but assured by the fact that everything looked good. Confused, then, that she hadn't called him back, he dialed her again, trying to figure out where she was.

And heard the distinct notes of her cell phone peal from the inside of her trunk.

MARLOWE FELT THE last bit of the lock's resistance give way under the pressure of her pick, the shackle springing open on her ankle. Although it hadn't hurt where it fitted around her body, she breathed her first easy breath at the physical freedom.

Now to deal with the door.

Although she'd hated the shackle, the chain had given her full range of motion around the room and she'd been able to examine the door before settling in to pick open the thick cuff. From what she could see, her picks weren't going to work from the inside, so she'd considered a few different courses of action on the door. She could try to use the end of the pick to jiggle the lock from the split between the door and the frame, or she could lay in wait with and use the strength of the shackle chain as a garrote, catching whoever came in unawares.

She might have a chance against the two older men, but the younger guy would flick her off like a gnat.

Which meant she had to try working the door.

Although heavy, she kept the chain wrapped in her fist, wanting to have the weapon close at hand if someone entered. Satisfied she could, at minimum, swing out with it if cornered, she bent over and went to work on the door.

And heard the distinct pop of a gunshot echo from somewhere on the other side.

Arlo was already running another set of ownership files on all the surrounding buildings as Wyatt moved around the building that had been the historic location of Nightwatch. The warehouse was truly abandoned, the grimy windows and discarded machines from whatever had come there after it had been a nightclub a testament to the passage of time and disuse.

So where was she?

There was no way she'd left her phone in the trunk and it gave him the worst sense something was wrong, even as he couldn't understand where she could be.

Arlo came up beside him, also peering in the windows in curiosity. "Nothing's flagging on these buildings."

"And we already checked and Harry Kisco and Mark Stone are no longer the owners of this building."

"They haven't been for a long time, nor were they listed as owners on anything else around here."

Wyatt slammed a hand on the window, the motion rattling the old, worn glass.

Damn it, focus.

Stilling his racing thoughts, Wyatt tried to puzzle together what had happened.

She'd parked her car and walked over here, which was about a hundred and fifty yards. He had the time stamp from his text of when she'd walked away and the phone was now in the trunk, which meant something must have happened around the car.

The car.

"Arlo! She has to be close. If someone has her, they had to drag her somewhere close. You can't just drag a woman blocks and blocks in the middle of lunch."

In unison, the two of them worked the perimeter of the warehouse, coming around to the back side, which faced away from Water Street. The distinct sounds of the ocean lapping against the boat docks that dotted the perimeter of the shoreline echoed in the afternoon breeze but not much else.

It was only as he turned from facing the water and to the back of the warehouse that Wyatt saw it.

"There. Where does that old path go?"

He and Arlo headed toward the path and noticed it took a sharp curve, the ground following the natural ebbs and flows of the shoreline.

They came to a stop when they saw a small outbuilding, about fifty yards farther down the shoreline.

MARLOWE REFUSED TO waste any time. The lock wasn't easy but she knew enough about its internal mechanism to use the end of her pick as leverage, finally jiggling the door loose. Carefully, she pulled the door open, peaking to the outside as soon as she had a wedge of space to see through.

The outer room wasn't that large, but she didn't see the men, either. Without waiting another moment she took off, racing for the door visible on the far side of the space. She had no idea where she was but saw bright light shining through the windows along with that subtle scent of brine and dead fish that spoke of the shore.

She couldn't be that far from Sunset Bay. And all she needed was to get to someone who could help her and she could get to Wyatt.

The door was nearly in sight when she heard a heavy shout. Without turning around, she kept on toward her goal. Falling against it, she dragged on the doorknob, struggling to turn it in her hand, the metal knob slipping in her grip.

On a hard, anguished scream she doubled down, wrenching at the knob and getting it to turn, opening the heavy door.

Bright sunlight greeted her and she felt grasping fingers against the back of her shirt, but pushed on, racing outside.

More of that salty, slightly fetid air greeted her and she took great gulps as she raced toward the water. Gulls screamed in the air, a match for her shouts for help.

She came around a twist in the land and saw Wyatt and Arlo in the distance.

"Wyatt!"

She screamed his name just as shots rang out in the air behind her.

WYATT RACED TOWARD MARLOWE, yelling for her to get down as he saw the men in the distance behind her.

Reaching for his side arm, he and Arlo crouched in unison, warning the shooter to drop his weapon before they both let off shots.

Marlowe had already dropped to the ground, her hands over her ears, as he and Arlo went to work. Two men had been in pursuit, one of whom had immediately lifted his hands in the air.

The other got off one more shot before he was hit in the shoulder, dropping his weapon and falling down.

He and Arlo sprinted to the men as Arlo called in for backup. Wyatt's gaze tracked on Marlowe as they passed her on the way toward the men.

"I'll be right back."

"Go! I'm fine but there might be a third."

Arlo nodded that he'd also heard about a third and they reached the men, subduing them.

"Where's your buddy?" Wyatt screamed out the request as he pressed the uninjured man to the ground, his arms behind his back.

"He's dead."

The man's voice was dull, his eyes empty, and while Wyatt wouldn't believe anything until the scene was cleared, that lack of reaction helped calm his adrenaline slightly.

Because they weren't far from Water Street, two cops on patrol had already arrived, running down toward the water from the high street. Arlo hollered out the instruction to watch their back, relaying Marlowe's instructions, but the guy on the ground just kept repeating the same.

"He's dead. It's just the two of us."

It was only when further backup arrived, two officers handling the man in Wyatt's custody, that he moved inside to sweep the area.

And found a very large man, dead of a shot to the chest.

Wyatt knew they'd have answers soon, but as he stared

down at that large form, he couldn't shake the sense that this was the man who'd tried to kill him beneath the waters of the Hudson.

MARLOWE ALLOWED THE adrenaline coursing through her body to do its work. She'd faced enough of it over the past week to know the only thing to do was settle in and take deep breaths.

And thank her lucky stars that Wyatt and Arlo were safe and that she'd walked out alive.

A swarm of cops from the 86th had descended on the old outbuilding, processing the crime scene and asking her any number of questions. She answered them all, over and over, while waiting for Wyatt.

What had she done?

She'd blithely headed off to the warehouse, well aware it wasn't the best idea. But she'd gone anyway and she'd put Wyatt and Arlo in danger because of it.

That thought kept her steady company as she shivered under a police blanket, staring out over the water.

Captain Reed arrived in short order, immediately coming to her and taking her in his arms, holding her close. "I'd really like a day without any McCoys in it. Can you try to work on that?"

"I'd like that, Uncle D. More than I can say."

He chuckled and rubbed her back, keeping her in a tight hold as she shivered her way through tears.

"Have you seen Wyatt?" She finally got her tears under control enough to ask. "I'm sorry I put him in this position and I'd like to apologize."

"I think I'm going to have to get in line behind Trumball to kick your ass for going out on your own, but I can't argue with your results. You brought them down, Marlowe."

"Who down?" She lifted her head and found Wyatt standing just behind Dwayne.

His voice hinted at his pride in her when he finally spoke. "The masterminds behind the safes and your father's murder and, from what details we found inside, a large cache of heroin that the DEA's going out now to intercept. It's about two days south of here on a ship working its way up the Atlantic."

"That's what this was about?"

"Best we can tell," Wyatt affirmed.

"That's why he called my father a loose end."

Dwayne's eyes narrowed at that. "Which one?"

"The one who was shot. He called my father a loose end."

"We'll get to the bottom of it. The bastard is entitled to his medical treatment but the moment we're able, we're getting him in a box. In fact," Dwayne said, glancing between the two of them, "let me go see about that now."

"Wyatt, I'm so sorry."

Wyatt moved up and pulled her close, wrapping his arms around her, thick blanket and all. "I'll yell and carry on later. Right now I just want to hold you."

She wrapped her hands around his waist, holding on for all she was worth.

"Is it really over?"

"There's all that'll come next, but the danger? The safes? The threats to you and your family?" He pressed a kiss against her head. "Yes, it's over."

A long, shuddering breath fell from her lips and she hadn't realized just how hard she'd been holding it in.

Her future was in sight. A wonderful place that had been waiting for her.

Past the secrets that had lived in a warehouse in Brooklyn for nearly three decades.

Past her father's and grandfather's mistakes.

Past her own lonely past.

And Wyatt stood in that future.

"You know, I realized something earlier."

"What's that?" he whispered again against her temple.

She stared up at him. "I love you. It sort of caught me by surprise, but it's as real as I could have ever imagined."

"You know, that's funny."

"Funny?"

"Yeah, because somewhere between admiring your legs in Prospect Park and racing you through it, I fell in love with you, too."

She'd hoped.

All while she'd tried on her feelings and committed to the idea of diving in and really loving him, she'd wondered how he felt. If he cared for her and if maybe he'd catch up to her feelings at some point.

How wonderful to realize he felt them, too.

"I love you, Marlowe."

"I love you, too." She kissed him, all the promise of that glorious future rising up between them.

But when they pulled back, their gazes locked, and she knew something else. Whatever more they shared, a foundation of fun, flirty humor existed between them. With the danger pushed aside, it was time to find that sense of fun again.

The carefree ability to laugh.

"You know, you promised me something this morning and I don't want you to think I'd forgotten."

He tilted his head, clearly trying to remember what they'd discussed. "What's that?"

"Kitchen sex, Wyatt. It's poor form to tease a woman with an offer like that and not deliver."

His mouth turned down at the edges, his face set in grave lines. But the twinkle in his blue eyes didn't have her believing his act for a second.

"Well, then, I guess I'm honor bound to take you home and deliver on my promise."

She smiled up at him and knew all the love she felt shined in her eyes. "See that you do."

* * * * *

Author Note

I had so much fun writing this book. It's always amazing to me when a small news story can suddenly spark a very big idea. The book you just read was a result of a local news piece I watched on the NYPD's divers that expanded into a series in this writer's imagination.

While I've done quite a bit of research on this special branch of the NYPD, there are some aspects of the divers' work that are not widely available. I suspect this is for both their safety, as well as the city they're protecting. To that end, I've used my imagination in crafting a series around the core idea of heroes and heroines who protect the waters around New York as their life's work.

I hope you'll forgive any license I've taken in service to the story. Any errors in actual procedure are all mine.

COMING SOON!

We really hope you enjoyed reading this book. If you're looking for more romance be sure to head to the shops when new books are available on

Thursday 3rd August

To see which titles are coming soon, please visit

millsandboon.co.uk/nextmonth

MILLS & BOON

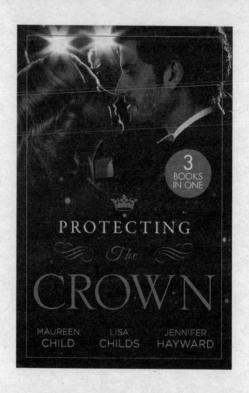